D1613243

Prefer Death

Prefer Death

A Matthew Paine Mystery

Lee Clark

Cypress River
Media, LLC

Burlington

Prefer Death

Cypress River Media, LLC
Burlington, NC 27215

First Edition: October 2021

Identifiers: ISBN 978-1-7368422-4-9 (paperback)

Dedication

Prefer Death is dedicated to all who deal with autism, anywhere on the spectrum, whether that's personally or with children and family members.

Acknowledgments

There's nothing like the tireless efforts of a couple of great editors, so my thanks to Genie Clark and Dorothy Whitley, each of whom poured many hours into editing this book. Bill Payne, my graphics guru, seems to be able to create anything I can dream up, so my most heartfelt thanks to him!

Contents

1. Hard good-byes

Matthew stood watching long after his ex-girlfriend had rounded the corner through the security area of the Raleigh Durham International Airport, beyond which he couldn't follow. Their long and confusing history had caused him internal battles for several years. He'd never doubted that he loved Cici, but their differing life goals had gotten in the way.

They'd broken up the year before and then reconnected when she was abducted the previous month. That event, Matthew figured, was a big part of the reason that she was flying into Heathrow. Even at her five-foot-nothing tiny stature, Cici was usually fearless and he knew that she had been shaken to her core by the incident. As a lawyer at a large firm in downtown Raleigh, Cici had agreed to spend the next year or so in London working with a high priority client. Matthew wasn't entirely sure how he felt about her leaving, except the word "heavy" came to mind.

Broad shoulders unusually slumped in his six-foot three-inch frame, he ran his hand through his soft, wavy brown hair as he finally turned and trudged out of the airport. The lights in the parking deck were brightening as the dusk of the May evening was gathering. Having paid the fee for parking, however briefly, he retrieved his car and circled down the tightly coiling exit ramp. Matthew was heading for his condo outside of Peak, the little suburb south of Raleigh. There, life that was much quieter than in the sprawling capital city of North Carolina suited him.

Maneuvering his black Corvette C7 through the waning evening traffic on I-40 as if on autopilot, Matthew was lost in thought. He and Cici had met at a small university south of Raleigh and they dated through the end of his osteopathic medical program and her final undergraduate year, law program, bar exam, and being hired into the most prestigious law firm in downtown Raleigh.

Cici hadn't been thrilled with his decision to become a General Practitioner at a family medical practice in the small town of Peak. She had wanted a glitzier lifestyle in the middle of the Raleigh social scene and Matthew, after his clinical rotations in Emergency Departments, had opted for a quieter one.

After seriously dating for over five years, they'd finally called it quits, deciding that their life goals were too different. Wanting a family, children, a house in the country, and a wonderful wife to share it all with, Matthew was dismayed that Cici had professed never to want children. Instead, her goal was to quickly climb the ladder to senior partner. She was off to a good start, he thought, having just made Junior Associate during the previous year when they were apart.

Only recently had Cici relented, and then only slightly, when she'd said maybe she didn't mean she "never" wanted children, but just no time soon. To Matthew's amazement, she'd admitted that the corporate ladder climb wasn't as meaningful without anyone on her rung to share it with when she got there. But did it mean anything, he wondered. Did it matter now?

So lost in thought was Matthew that he didn't realize he was driving below the posted speed limit in the right lane and that Christmas, still over seven months away, might arrive in the small town of Peak before he did, until his cell phone sounded. It took him a moment to realize what had disturbed his rumination. Clicking to activate the call through his car stereo system, he answered despondently and heard Danbury's brusque "Hey, Doc" on the other end.

Having met the month before when Danbury questioned Matthew about a murder investigation, which Matthew then helped to solve, they'd become friends. Detective Warren Danbury had recently accepted a new position as a Homicide Detective in Wake County and he'd convinced Matthew to sign on as a medical consultant.

"Can you consult?" Danbury said very seriously, entirely skipping any small talk, as usual. Matthew was used to Danbury's rapid-fire staccato questions and conversations.

"Medically or otherwise?" asked Matthew, less than enthusiastically.

"Both. But not personally."

"Sure, what's up?"

"We have one of your patients. I need his background. Anything you can tell me."

"You know I can't share his medical history, with the HIPAA governmental privacy regulations and our office's extension of that. I can't tell you much of anything without filling out the request form in the office and getting it approved. Which patient and what did he do?"

"Do? I don't know. He's dead."

"Dead? One of MY patients is dead? Who?"

"His name is Allan Lingle," answered Danbury. Matthew thought he detected a note of sorrow as Danbury added, "He lived near your office. Possibly murdered."

"Mr. Lingle is, or was, Dr. Garner's patient. He will hate this!"

Dr. Steven Garner, the senior partner in Matthew's practice at only 54, had been concerned about negative publicity the month before when a new patient that Matthew had seen exactly once was murdered. But he'd be upset for entirely different reasons if the murdered man was his patient, thought Matthew.

"Mr. Lingle lives, I mean lived," said Matthew, struggling with the past tense. "He lived on the dead end down past our office entrance in the big white house with the huge, very overgrown yard. The locals call it the 'Lingle Plantation,' I think. He and the house are a bit mysterious and I believe the neighborhood children are afraid of both. They swear that the house is haunted and they think he's some sort of apparition. He does keep to himself and move about quietly. I've seen him regularly up and down the sidewalks, but always alone. And he never speaks to anyone that I've ever seen. I tried, several times, to greet him and then gave up. And that's the entirety of what I can tell you about him."

"Yeah, kids are afraid of him. A couple of kids found him."

"Found him? You mean they found his body?" asked Matthew, alarmed. "Where? When? What happened and what do you need me to do?"

"Just down from your office. About 15 minutes ago. They spotted his feet. Sticking out of the bushes. You know, the overgrown hedge. Just as you enter his property. One of the boys is injured. But not seriously. Can you come take a look?"

Matthew sighed, "I just dropped Cici at the airport and I was headed home, but sure, I'll swing by. Have you contacted Dr. Garner? Or did you want me to?"

"We called your answering service. You're still on call. But I told them I'd call you. I'll ask them to call Dr. Garner. And get him to call us back."

"He's going to be upset. He takes his patient care very seriously. Could it have been an accident or?" Matthew swallowed the end of the unfinished sentence.

"Looks like a brutal attack. There's external bleeding. And lots of it. Around his head. Cuts and bruises all over his face. Most likely murder. The boys who found him are traumatized. They keep swearing they didn't do it. And not much else. At least, not yet."

"They didn't do what? Beat him up? Do you know what happened?"

"Blunt force trauma. But that's all I can tell. I don't know with what. Or why. I called for a Medical Examiner. So, there's an ME on the way."

"OK, I'll be there as soon as I can." Matthew gave a turn signal, looking quickly around him before he swung across the sporadic traffic to the left lane, and hit the gas pedal. He wished he'd known that he was going into Peak instead of home; he'd have opted for a more direct route from the airport.

*****

Passing the newly updated *Welcome to Peak, the Pinnacle of Good Living* sign as he drove into town, Matthew could see that the emergency vehicles were lighting the night sky above the buildings of Winston Avenue, the main street through the historic little downtown. He slowed to cross the railroad tracks on Center Street and passed the Chamber of Commerce building, which he admired because it reincarnated the old historic train depot, on his left.

Turning right onto Winston Avenue and then quickly left onto Chapel Street, the tiny street that ran one-way beside the cultural arts center and then looped between the back of it and the front of his office building, Matthew parked his car in his office parking lot. In front of his office building, Chapel Street paralleled Winston Avenue, leading to the Peak Police Department in one direction and in the other becoming a dead end into the Lingle Plantation property.

Sliding out and locking up, Matthew felt a strong gust of wind and saw the shadows from the fringe of trees along the parking lot dancing wildly on the pavement under the streetlights. He looked up to see high clouds scudding across a waxing quarter crescent moon, barely visible behind the clouds. Feeling a sudden shudder, he thought it was eerie seeing the moon through the fringe of trees with the wind whipping them around. Shaking off the momentary shiver, he walked briskly down the street and into the melee.

Police cars from Peak, an ambulance, and a fire truck were on the scene, as well as an unmarked black SUV that he knew to be Danbury's, and all with lights flashing. Voices scratched over a police radio and emanated from one of the Peak police cars that was straddling the road, doors open, ostensibly to keep onlookers at bay. It was far from effective.

Clumps of onlookers from the neighborhood behind Matthew's office were gathered, whispering, interspersed along the sidewalk and in the edge of the street. An occasional gust of wind whipped through the scene, tightening the knots of onlookers against it. As Matthew approached, he noticed three boys seated on a curb, with parents hovering behind, and an officer in a Peak uniform squatting in front of them, notepad in hand.

Surveying the scene, he noticed Danbury, who was a head taller than much of the crowd and looked a bit like a misplaced Viking, motioning him over. Seeing Danbury's signal, another uniformed Peak officer stepped aside as Matthew approached and allowed him to pass.

"Hey, Doc," greeted Danbury. "The ME just got here," he said, walking over to a white sheet covering what looked to be feet protruding from the overgrown hedge. "He's examining the body. The top half. Around the hedge. I don't need you to look. Unless you want to."

Matthew shook his head and asked, "Do you know what happened yet?"

"Not much. The boys over there," Danbury said, indicating the three boys who were seated on the curb. "They were walking down the sidewalk. They saw the feet. And started yelling. Folks over at the community center heard them. Abandoned their evening of *To Kill A Mocking Bird*. They came running. Called 911. And here we are."

"Why were they walking down here? There's nothing but the old Lingle Plantation down here, right?"

"You tell me. Then we'll both know," said Danbury with a smirk and a shrug. "They're not saying much. Pretty repetitive. 'We didn't do it! We didn't do it!' That's all I've gotten out of them."

"They were talking about the murder?"

"That's the obvious conclusion."

"Mind if I talk to them? I could check them for injuries or trauma with the parents' permission. I'm not in uniform, so I'd be less scary if there's something that they can tell us. The Peak officer could stand by, if you'd like?"

"One has a few scrapes. But yeah, while you're at it. See what you can learn. I'll have Officer Reeves hang back. Give you some space. To talk to the boys. Do what you do best."

"I'm scared to ask what you think that is," said Matthew over his shoulder as he strode across to the boys on the curb. He approached the parents, introduced himself, and asked quietly if the boys were OK and if he could have a moment to check them out. He was most concerned about the one on the right end who was shivering uncontrollably in the gusty, but otherwise still warm, May evening.

With the parents' permission, he checked the boys over. They had no injuries, except a couple of skinned knees and hands, and their pupils were the same size. He ruled out head injuries, so he asked a nearby EMT for Band-Aids and topical solution for the cuts and a blanket for the shivering boy. Shock could set in for myriad reasons and he was concerned that the traumatic discovery had affected this child in particular. He treated the cuts and asked them about how they'd discovered the body in the bushes.

"We were just walkin' down the sidewalk," said the boy on the left, who had apparently decided to be the spokesperson for the group. "And we saw…" he hesitated and gulped. "We saw feet stickin' out of the bushes. Umm…Marcus," he thumbed to indicated the boy beside him. "He kinda tripped over 'em."

That explained the skinned hands and knees, Matthew thought, "So then you started yelling for help?"

"Not at first."

"No? Why not?"

"At first, we thought it was a joke. 'Cause, ya' know, the old Lingle Plantation down there," he said pointing down the dead-end street. "It's haunted. So, we thought somebody stuck 'em there. Like a scarecrow, ya' know? To try to scare people."

"How did you figure out that they were real?"

"We peeked in the bushes and saw it was a person. A real dead person. And then we just, we just started yellin' and we were gonna run away but some people came from over there," he pointed toward the cultural arts center. "And then a man, all dressed up, he ran down there," he said, pointing, "around the bushes to see from the other side. And then he yelled to call 911, so the woman, she called."

"Are those people still here?"

"Yeah, they're right over there," he said, pointing again. "Talking to that policeman."

"Did you see anyone else? Was anyone else on the sidewalk or were any cars in the street down here before you found the feet?"

The spokesman and Marcus, in the middle, looked at each other, hesitating, and shook their heads in unison.

The smallest boy on the right just continued to shiver. "Tell you what," said Matthew to the mother who was hovered over the shivering child, as he checked his pupils and pulse again, "I'm going to ask if you can take him home now. I don't think he can help with the investigation, but if I give you a number to call, will you call if he tells you anything? Anything at all about tonight, whether it seems important or not?"

The mother nodded in thankful relieved agreement and Matthew said, "I'll be right back." He walked back to Danbury to explain the situation, make the request, and ask for a business card. Danbury agreed, handed him a card, and Matthew went back to the anxious boy and his mother. Giving her instructions for the night, Matthew told her to check her son's pupils every couple of hours to be sure they were the same size. He explained that she needed to monitor for a concussion in case the child had fallen and hit his head and he told her the symptoms to watch for.

Turning back to the spokesman of the group, he asked, “What’s your name?”

“M-m-m-Micah,” the boy stammered, tensing up noticeably.

“I think you’ll be able to go home soon, but will you tell me one more thing before I ask about releasing you?” asked Matthew, looking up at the woman hovering over the two remaining boys. She nodded her consent.

“I guess so,” said Micah.

“What were you boys doing down here tonight? This sidewalk doesn’t go anywhere but to the old Lingle house.”

“We weren’t doin’ nothing!” the boy shouted.

“Micah,” said the mom, leaning over. “Don’t be rude. Why did you choose to come this way?”

“We just did, that’s all,” said the boy, somewhat contritely.

“The boys were coming back to our house for a sleepover in our treehouse because tomorrow is a teacher’s workday and they don’t have school,” the mother explained. “Jacob Wheatly, the boy who just left, lives two blocks over, but one block back. He’s between Marcus and Micah’s ages and the boys play well together. But I don’t know why they came this way. It’s not exactly the most direct path between the Wheatly’s house and ours,” she grimaced.

“Thanks,” said Matthew, “I’ll be right back.”

Again, he walked over to Danbury and quickly summarized all that the boys had told him, which wasn’t much more than Danbury had already surmised.

“I think there’s something that they’re not telling me,” said Matthew. “But I don’t think we’re going to get it out of them tonight. Is it OK to send these boys home too? And maybe follow up with them tomorrow? They’re out of school for a teacher workday.”

Danbury nodded, handing Matthew another card. “Tell Libby to call me. If they think of anything else.”

Matthew hadn’t asked the mother’s name when he’d introduced himself initially and it surprised him that Danbury would know it. But then he remembered that Danbury had previously admitted to spending lots of time in the Peak Eats Soda Shoppe, a local combination diner and ice cream counter, as a teenager so it made sense that he might know people in the little town. Returning to the boys on the curb and finding a man also present, he introduced himself.

"Wayne Adams," said the man, who was of average build and height with golden brown hair that was receding slightly and greying at the temples. He could be considered handsome, perhaps, but his smile was enigmatic as he added, "Marcus and Micah's step-father," and offered a hand to shake Matthew's. He stood slightly taller than Matthew, but only because he was standing on the curb, Matthew noticed. He was maybe almost six feet tall, but he dwarfed his petite wife.

"You can take the boys home now," said Matthew and he gave their mother instructions for monitoring her sons to be sure there were no concussions or residual issues and he explained the symptoms to be concerned about if she noticed them.

"But you'll call Detective Danbury if the boys think of anything else, whether it seems important or not?" Matthew asked. Both parents nodded and agreed as he handed off another of Danbury's cards.

Matthew was called over to consult with the couple who had come running when the boys started yelling. He diagnosed a mildly sprained left ankle on the man who'd run around the hedge, Craig Hutchins, and told him to elevate and ice it. He got a blanket from a fireman for Craig's wife, Amy Hutchins, who, in a short thin-strapped dress, had reason to be shivering. The Hutchins were dismissed and Craig, having refused to have the ankle wrapped, hobbled back across the street leaning on his tiny wife more for balance than actual support.

Finally, the commotion started to die down after the scene had been thoroughly searched and photographed, and the body was properly processed, covered, and removed. After the big work lights were extinguished, retracted, and locked down to be hauled back to the Peak Police Station a couple of blocks away, the emergency vehicles began to depart, one by one. The road was corded off behind them at the end of the street, and the remaining police officers, including Danbury, were going down to the Lingle house to have a closer look around.

"You can go home, Doc. If you want. It'll be a long night. Up at the house."

Matthew knew he'd been tired before the drama of the evening, but his adrenalin had kept him alert. Yawning, he said, "Yeah, I want. I'll check in with you tomorrow and see how it's going."

"OK. G'night," muttered Danbury as he wandered off down the dead-end street toward the Lingle house.

2. Between the lines

A persistent and annoying noise woke Matthew from a deep sleep. Realizing that it was his alarm, he rolled over and turned it off. He felt a sense of heaviness as he fought to climb out of the fog of a deep sleep and then remembered that Cici had left and there'd been a murder the night before. No wonder he felt heavy and exhausted this Tuesday morning, he thought.

Picking up his cell phone, he saw that Cici had kept her word and texted to say that her flight was leaving JFK airport on time and she'd let him know when she had arrived safely at Heathrow. With over eleven hours in the air, he knew she would still be on the plane but he texted back thanking her for the update and telling her to call or FaceTime him later if she got the chance. He figured it would be evening, his time, before she had checked into her hotel and maybe managed to get a little sleep.

Max, the huge grey tabby cat that his older sister Monica had rescued as a tiny kitten and then foisted off on Matthew when she realized that her husband Stephano was allergic to him, wandered up from the bottom of the bed to have his head scratched. Rolling over, Matthew wanted to ignore Max and go back to sleep but he knew he couldn't. It was just Tuesday but he was exhausted from all of the happenings the day before.

He scratched the big cat behind the ears for a few minutes and then climbed out of bed to go start the coffee maker. Max followed, yowling loudly underfoot for his breakfast, so Matthew rinsed and refilled the water bowl and put a scoop of Max's favorite dry food in his food bowl before starting the coffee.

Debating between showering first or waiting for the coffee to brew, Matthew pulled out a mug, dumped in cream and a heap of sugar, and then wandered back down the hallway. Opting to at least lay out his clothes and start the water running for his shower before the coffee was ready, he felt behind this morning. Normally, laying out his clothes and setting the coffee to brew for the next morning the night before helped him to avoid making decisions in a foggy stupor. He was chagrined that he'd managed neither the night before. Matthew knew that he was not a morning person.

After a steaming hot shower, his one habitual frivolous indulgence in the mornings, he had a cup of steaming hot coffee, partially refilled twice, to accompany a breakfast of eggs and toast. Feeling somewhat revived, he picked up his new leather satchel from the end of the sofa. Cici had borrowed the previous satchel she'd given him as a gift and then it had been stolen, so she'd been adamant about getting him a new one. It was some designer brand that he'd never heard of and couldn't remember anyway, but she'd been very insistent. He'd learned, long ago, not to argue with Cici over something that she particularly cared about and about which he didn't.

Scratching Max on the head and under the chin one last time, Matthew pulled the key fob from the hook beside the door, set the alarm, stepped into the garage, and clicked to open the garage door. Beyond his end unit in the condo development the road came to a dead end and met with woods and the right of way for utilities, preventing the street from being extended to add any further development. For this he was thankful; he enjoyed the privacy and peacefulness of the setting in an area otherwise crowded with housing.

Sliding into his Corvette, he clicked to start it and backed out of the garage and down his short driveway. He put on his sunglasses and clicked to start his playlist. It was then that he noticed his busybody neighbor, Cordelia Drewer, out walking her cranky Pomeranian, Oscar.

Wishing she wouldn't see him and flag him down, but knowing there was very little chance of that happening, he took a deep breath and started slowly down the street. Soft-spoken Matthew wasn't purposefully rude to anyone, but with Cordelia Drewer it was more tempting to be so than with most other people.

Inevitably, she was flagging him down like she was hailing a cab, and he was sure she was calling out, "Yoo who!" though he couldn't hear her over his music. She scooped up Oscar as he pulled alongside, turned his music down, and lowered his window.

"Good morning, Ms. Drewer," he said, thinking that she looked more disgruntled than usual and Oscar growled at him menacingly from his spot tucked under her arm.

"Ants!" she all but shrieked at him. "Do you have those nasty little sugar ants invading your kitchen yet?" she asked.

"No," answered Matthew, both surprised and relieved, given the events of the previous evening, that this was her topic of conversation.

"They're all over mine and they're driving me crazy!" Matthew chided himself for thinking, "short trip," but he said nothing as she continued her tirade. "If I put something down on the counter, take two steps away and come back, there is already an ant crawling on it! I've cleaned myself in circles keeping the kitchen wiped down so there's nothing to attract them. I've called the association to get the outside sprayed, and I've called an exterminator for the inside but the receptionist there sounds like she must be 90, if she's a day, and she's slower than a three-toed sloth!"

Seizing the opportunity to derail her and make an escape, Matthew kindly interjected, "Ms. Drewer, do all sloths have three toes?"

Momentarily stupefied with the unusual question, she said, "Well, I don't, I mean, I never . . . ."

"I hope you get your ant problem solved. Have a nice day, Ms. Drewer!" Matthew said, smiling and waving as he drove off. He was rather pleased with himself for escaping what could easily have been another fifteen-minute diatribe against the ants and, interjected into that topic, any bits of recent gossip, embellished considerably.

As he turned left onto Highway 20 and passed the golf course, Matthew turned the stereo back up, deciding to enjoy the rest of his short drive to work. Unless he got caught by a train or some traffic horror, he could usually manage the morning trip in ten minutes or less.

Slowly crossing the railroad tracks a few minutes later, Matthew maneuvered the quick zig-zag, a right onto Winston Avenue, a quick left onto Chapel Street, and down Chapel into his office parking lot. As he parked and got out of his car, locking it behind him, he looked up to see

Gladys, one of the nurses in his practice, approaching from the spot where she usually parked her older Toyota. She waved, waddling her considerable girth quickly to catch up, and Matthew waited for her. Gladys exuded motherly protection, particularly where Matthew was concerned.

Gladys had earned her motherly protectiveness honestly with three children of her own, all daughters and all grown, who all married within a year of each other, in reverse age order, and started spitting out grandchildren in doublet. The youngest daughter produced the first set of twins, a daughter in the middle produced a second set, and then the youngest daughter accidentally got pregnant and produced yet another set. Twins did not, Gladys had sworn, run in the family. Her oldest daughter had, therefore, fearfully sworn off starting a family for a while and enjoyed that the parental pressure to do so had been alleviated by her younger sisters.

"Hey, Matthew, what in the world happened over here last night? I got a text message asking me to come in early this morning. Something about losing a patient?" she said between gasps as she caught her breath. He hadn't seen a text, so he raised an eyebrow in question.

She pulled out a cell phone, poked it a few times, and held it up for his inspection. The message was cryptic, indeed, but it had apparently gone out to the staff and asked them to come in early to discuss the loss of a patient. Deciding that there was nothing confidential about the situation because half the town had been on the scene the night before, Matthew pointed to the police tape across the end of Chapel Street where it adjoined the Lingle property, before dead ending there. It was just visible from the parking lot where they stood.

"Allan Lingle, Dr. Garner's patient, died last night."

At Gladys' sharp intake of breath, Matthew continued, "It gets worse. He was beaten. Likely on purpose. Probably murdered." He chided himself for sounding so much like Danbury, but then continued, "I'm sure it'll be in all the papers this morning, and I'm not sure what Dr. Garner wants to discuss about it, but that's what happened."

"Lord, help us all, if that sweet man didn't deserve better than that!" she exclaimed.

"You knew him, Gladys?"

"He's been a patient of Dr. Garner's for years. I've helped with his physicals and gotten his stats for probably twenty years now. At least that many. He's odd but there's not a mean bone in his body. I don't know why anybody would want to hurt him, much less kill him!"

Seeing that Gladys was genuinely upset by this news, Matthew reached down and put an arm around her shoulders, comfortingly, and they turned and walked into the building together. It was a little awkward walking that way and an odd sight, given his tall broad-shouldered frame and narrow waist and her short stocky build, but Matthew wouldn't have thought of that, nor would he have cared about it had anyone pointed it out.

A group of staff was gathered in the lobby and Trina, the eager young office manager, had brought in a selection of bagels and a box of coffee. Realizing only then that he hadn't remembered his usual travel mug of coffee, Matthew was happy to see it. He fixed a cup with cream and lots of sugar while they waited. "A little coffee with your sugar?" asked Gladys, who always seemed to be watching his diet for him. Matthew just raised an eyebrow but said nothing, as he took a sip appreciatively.

Dr. Garner entered the room from the main hallway and looked around, his dark forehead crinkled in dismay at having to share bad news, Matthew thought. He'd seen that expression before and it usually meant that Dr. Garner hated what he was about to have to say.

"Good, we're all here," he said. "I have some sad news to share this morning. One of our long-time patients, Allan Lingle, was killed last night, just over there," he said, motioning in the general direction of the Lingle property.

Hearing a couple of gasps and soft murmurs, Matthew realized that some of the staff hadn't yet heard the news.

"We will miss his presence in town, but we'll particularly miss his kind nature as our patient. We'll make ourselves available to the police for whatever they need. They have provided us with a warrant for information because this is being investigated as a homicide. Any time needed to pull Allan's records or provide interviews is already approved for all staff," continued Dr. Garner as he surveyed the room, glancing at each staff member in turn.

"We'll relax our usual standards, though. The police officers won't need to request patient information with forms and wait for approval.

We'll allow them to verbally request any patient information that they need, and we'll provide it immediately. Per the HIPAA laws, we can provide that information without getting consent because of the warrant. Remember, though, that the officers cannot remove from the premises any printed information that we provide. We will need to update the chart with notations that we provided it. As usual, please note in the patient chart to whom you provided it, when, and the extent of the information that you provided."

"I would also ask that you please not discuss any of this with our patients. If they should bring up the topic, kindly attempt to change the subject, but whatever you do, please do not contribute to the rumor mill gossip. And please do not provide any information or comments to the press. If you are asked, refer them to Trina." There was a moment of silence in which Dr. Garner took a deep breath, then added, "That's it. Please begin your morning routines."

He turned and walked slowly back through the doors, his broad frame filling them, then down the hallway and into the stairwell at the end. As the doors to the hallway swung slowly shut behind him, there was a definite pall in the lobby area and the staff members silently dispersed.

Matthew wordlessly slipped through the doors and headed to his own office to pull out his notebook computer and check his patient log for the morning. After putting on his lab coat, he began working his way through the exam rooms each in turn to see the patients waiting for him.

Trying to focus on his morning patients was a challenge because Matthew had so much else on his mind. Between Cici leaving and Allan Lingle's murder, Matthew barely heard his cell phone chirp as he was between examining rooms. Looking at the display on his phone as he pulled it from his pocket, he saw that it was his father, so he stepped into the alcove between the exam rooms to answer.

"Hey, Matt, just doing the mid-week check in. Everything OK down there?"

Refraining from pointing out that it was only Tuesday, Matthew replied, "Hi, Dad, yeah, everything is fine down here. Why do you ask?"

"We don't exactly live under a rock up here. We saw the newspaper this morning."

Matthew's parents still lived in North Raleigh, in the house he'd grown up in, which was a good half hour away from Peak, just in normal traffic.

"Oh," said Matthew.

"Was that you in the picture of the murder scene last night?"

"What picture?"

"It's on the front page of the local news section in the *News and Reporter*."

Amused, Matthew said, "Dad, you know I've never gotten the Raleigh paper."

"Well, you should. It was you, wasn't it?"

"It probably was. I just checked on three boys who found the body and treated a resident who had sprained his ankle running to the boys when they started yelling. But I didn't see any press there and I'm surprised there were pictures. It was pretty dark."

"It was just your back but your mom saw that there was a murder in Peak, took one look at that picture, and spotted you immediately."

"I guess there were bright lights over where the ME was examining the body and the police were searching for evidence and photographing the scene. But yeah, Danbury caught the case and he called me right after I'd dropped Cici at the airport."

"Was the victim a patient of yours?"

"Not directly, no. Of our practice, yes, but he was Dr. Garner's patient and apparently had been for many years. Dr. Garner looked shaken this morning."

"Sorry to hear that. And Cici's already left? Your mom was surprised to have her with us at church these past couple of weeks, and for Mother's Day yesterday. She'd never been very keen on the weekly family church and lunch routine before."

"Yeah, I know Mom doesn't think much of Cici," said Matthew a bit sadly.

"It's not that at all. She enjoyed having her there yesterday. And we were surprised because we knew Cici must still have lots of packing to do. It's just that your mom figured out a long time before you did that Cici wasn't entirely right for you."

"Well, that's a moot point at the moment. Cici's in London for the next year or so. Besides which, people do change and grow."

Joc Paine laughed and grudgingly agreed, "I suppose so. She could change a lot in London in a year."

Matthew just sighed, thinking that people could grow a lot after being abducted and drugged, as Cici had been a few short weeks before. "Thanks for checking in, Dad. I've got another patient waiting for me that I need to see before lunch, so I'll catch up with you later. Give Mom a hug for me and tell her not to worry."

His father laughed aloud at that, "As if that'll ever happen! But she's praying for you. Love you, Son."

"Love you too, Dad."

Matthew realized the truth of both statements. Jacqueline Paine, or Jackie to her closest friends and family, would pray at least as much as she'd worry. Checking his watch, Matthew realized that it was nearly lunch time and he hadn't called or heard from Danbury. The morning had flown by. He decided to check on the teenager in Exam Room Six, who was in for a follow-up visit after dislocating his finger playing basketball, and then to call Danbury.

"Good morning, Nick," he said, stepping into the exam room. "How's that finger looking?"

"When can I get back on the court, Dr. Paine?" asked Nick, immediately.

Matthew had to laugh at that, as he closed the door behind him.

*****

Finishing with his morning roster of patients, Matthew realized that he hadn't asked Trina to have his lunch delivered. It was a daily ritual that the young office manager had started, ordering out for lunch daily, and there was a rotating schedule of the restaurants they'd order from each day of the week. Tuesdays meant Mexican. Matthew went down the hall and into the office behind the front desk in the lobby to ask if it was too late to order lunch.

"Not if you don't mind tacos," said Trina. "After the morning announcement, I hadn't heard from everyone in time, so I just ordered some extra."

"That sounds great," said Matthew. "I'm going back to my office to update the charts for the morning patients. Just let me know when it's here, please?"

"Sure, Dr. Paine. I'm happy to."

Slipping into his office and shedding his lab coat, hanging it on the coat rack behind his office door, Matthew sat down at his desk and called Danbury.

"Hey, Doc. I was going to call. But I didn't know when was good."

"I'm getting ready to have some lunch in my office and do some chart updates, between morning and afternoon patients, but I wanted to check in and see if you learned anything else last night?"

"Plenty. But nothing fits."

"What do you mean?"

"There were footprints. At the murder scene. We have pictures. And casts of two prints. Likely the same shoe. Probably a man's shoe. About a size 11. Dress shoe. With a heel," added Danbury. "And somebody broke into the Lingle Plantation. Sort of. The side door was open. The back door was open. Malcolm is missing. Along with his Jeep. But nothing else is, that we can tell."

"Wow! What do you mean someone 'sort of' broke in? Were the doors busted open?"

"A pane of glass was broken. On a front window. But it was a bottom pane. Not near the latch. The window was still locked. And painted shut. No fresh fingerprints on the latch."

"Could it have been accidentally broken?" Matthew asked.

"There was rock in the room."

"Oh, I guess not then. But nobody could have come in through the window?"

"Not even close. You know it's an old house. Part of an old plantation. The windows have individual panes. The old wavy glass. And the panes are narrow."

"And who's Malcolm?"

"Malcolm is, or was, Allan's care giver."

"Oh, he had someone caring for him?"

"He did. Malcolm was there for five years. At least. Maybe more."

"Did he live there?"

"He did. On the first floor. In the newer wing. Off the kitchen. His room seems to be intact. Clothes still in the closet and drawers. Watch on the dresser. As if he just stepped out. Planning to come right back. But he isn't back. And nobody we've asked has seen him. Allan's bedroom upstairs was similar. Very neat and organized. Bed turned down. Pajamas laid out. Heavy drapes pulled. Like it was ready for the night."

"And no other family lives there? It was just Malcolm and Allan?"

"Right."

"And nothing is missing?"

"Nothing obvious. Everything appears neat. Undisturbed. Except a sitting room. That's a mess. But nothing seems to be missing. Electronics are in place. A safe in the study was unopened. The silver is still in the dining room sideboard. The attorney will inventory for us. Later today."

"The attorney?"

"He manages the Lingle estate. For Allan."

"Oh. There are no other Lingles? It was just Allan?"

"His parents are both deceased. He has an older sister, Penn. And a younger brother, Leo. The brother looks just like him. But nobody knows where he is. Not for several years. Not since their mom died. At least, nobody admits to it. Nobody we've asked anyway. The sister has been contacted. She lives in Colorado. She hasn't been home recently either. The Peak guys are still canvassing. Door to door in the neighborhood. Asking if anybody saw anything. Or heard anything odd last night."

"Who's their attorney?"

"You met him last night. Wayne Adams."

"Oh, Marcus and Micah's dad?"

"Step-dad, but yes. Tell me something. Why did you think the boys were hiding something? Not telling you everything?"

"I'm just kind of reading between the lines. Jacob Wheatly was too traumatized to say anything at all. I was worried about him. He's a patient of Dr. Rob's, and he couldn't stop shaking, so I asked Dr. Rob this morning if he had any issues that we should be concerned about, any reason other than the trauma of last night that would cause that reaction. He was much more affected by whatever happened than the other two boys."

Dr. Richard Roberts, lovingly called "Dr. Rob" by all, was the other member of the Peak Family Practice team of physicians. His specialty was pediatrics and he had joined Dr. Garner before Matthew had begun his medical program. Both of the senior physicians were older than Matthew, each a decade ahead of the next.

"And does he?" asked Danbury. "Have other conditions?"

Matthew pondered a moment on the confidentiality issue, deciding that the lack of a condition wasn't confidential, and then responded, "Nothing known."

"OK, so what else?"

"Marcus Adams said nothing and wouldn't even look at me when I was talking to them. He stared at the pavement, or at his brother Micah, like he was either feeling guilty about something or scared to tell me something."

"McVane."

"What?"

"Micah and Marcus aren't adopted. By Wayne Adams. Their name is McVane."

"Oh. Anyway, Marcus said nothing and Micah became the spokesperson. He told me what I told you about how they discovered the body. But when I asked why they were down the street there, when there's nothing down that way but the Lingle house, he got defensive. He yelled that they weren't doing anything down there."

"Ah. Which means they were. Doing something down there."

"Probably. Or that they saw something they wouldn't tell me about, for whatever reason. But they weren't telling me about something. By the way, I'd love to see the house sometime, the Lingle Plantation, whenever your people are finished with it. Maybe you could get me in to see it?"

"Why? You think we missed something?" asked Danbury, sounding slightly offended.

“No. I just like historic things and I’d love a look at it while it’s standing empty and before it gets sold off or who knows what happens to it. Call it the idle curiosity of a history buff. What’s its story, anyway? Do you know?”

“Yeah. The original building was early 1800 and something,” said Danbury. “It partially burned in the uncivil war. Or maybe before that. Why it didn’t burn to the ground, I don’t know. Old Eli Lingle was a determined rebel. Then the slaves were gone. The plantation wasn’t functional. His son sold the property around it. Most of it. All but the 5 or 6 acres the house is on. Where your office is, included. To finance rebuilding the house.”

“Wow!” said Matthew. “I’m sure land wasn’t worth much back in that day.”

“It was,” replied Danbury. “Think railroad money.”

“Ah!” he said, wondering how Danbury knew the history of the place off the top of his head. He didn’t strike Matthew as a history buff. “Still, I guess it’s a good thing there aren’t any Lingle statues by the train depot. That would be under heavy scrutiny now if there were slaves at that plantation.”

“True,” said Danbury. “I’m glad the town avoided that. The riots and hot debate. Like some of the other towns around. His slave ownership isn’t discussed. Nobody wants to admit it. A statue would force that issue.”

“Yeah, I’m glad Peak avoided that whole debacle.”

Just then Trina tapped on the door that Matthew had left cracked. He motioned her in and said to Danbury, “My lunch just arrived and I don’t have long before my first afternoon patient, so I need to go. Let me know what else you learn?”

“Yeah. Will do. Hey, can you grab dinner tonight? At the soda shop? I want to ask some questions. Allan Lingle ate there. Regularly.”

“Sure. What time?”

“About seven. They close at eight. On week nights.”

“OK, see you there at seven.” As he put his phone down, he added, “Thanks, Trina,” to her retreating back.

3. I prefer

History buff that he was, Matthew loved the historic little town of Peak that had been built on the railroad back in the 1800s and so named because it was the highest point along the railway for more than 15 miles in either direction. And he loved the historic buildings, including Peak Eats Soda Shoppe, originally an apothecary shop that had added a soda fountain and then kept the latter, nixed the former, and morphed into a combination diner and soda shop.

Hearing the bell jingle overhead as he entered Peak Eats, Matthew spotted Danbury in a back booth as soon as he walked through the doorway of the little diner. Sliding into the booth opposite, he was greeted with, "Hey, Doc."

"Hey, Danbury. How'd the afternoon go? Anything new?"

"Not much. Not since lunch," he said, trying and failing to stifle a yawn. "Sorry, late night."

"Tell me about it! But, I'm sure it was worse for you."

"I slept in this morning. A little later anyway," said Danbury. "Oh, yeah. The footprint we found. It belongs to Craig Hutchins. No help there," he shrugged.

"The man with the sprained ankle who ran over when the boys started yelling?"

"That's the one. Hey, Frank," called Danbury to the guy behind the soda counter who'd just walked out of the back, "Who's waitressing tonight?"

"Just Lucy. I'll get her for you."

"No hurry. OK if she sits down for a minute? I want to talk to her."

"Sure," and then toward the swinging kitchen door, "Hey, Lucy, take 15 and go talk to Warren Danbury, will you?"

After a moment, the doors to the kitchen swung open and an older waitress that Matthew had seen before but whose name he hadn't noticed came out. Tiny, she was slightly stooped at the shoulders. Her pink dress hung a bit loosely on her and was cinched at the waist with an apron. With dark hair in a pixie cut that had to be dyed, as consistently dark as it was, maybe she wasn't quite as old as she looked, Matthew thought. She sidled over, sliding an empty chair from a nearby table with her, and pulled it up to the end of their booth, sitting down as if greatly relieved to do so.

"Hi, Lucy. How're you?" asked Danbury.

"Tired. I worked a double shift today. I came in at six to open at seven and worked until eleven and came back at four and I'm working at least 'til closing."

"Wow, that sounds like a rough day," said Matthew, sympathetically.

"I don't do it often, but we had a couple of the waitresses out tonight at some concert at the amphitheater up in Raleigh. Anyway, what can I do for you?"

"I need to talk to you. About Allan Lingle," said Danbury. "One of your regular patrons. Or so I'm told."

"Oh yeah, I Prefer? He's in here twice a week, once for lunch and once for dinner. Like clockwork. He always sits in the same seat and always comes in early enough to get that same seat. He sits just like he walks, ramrod straight the entire time."

"'I Prefer?'" asked Danbury.

"That's what we called him, the wait staff, because he always said that, no matter what. He came in at eleven in the morning, exactly, on Thursdays and always ordered the same thing for lunch. You could set your watch by him. Every week, he'd come in and say the same thing, 'I prefer two fried baloney sandwiches, with the crust removed, cut diagonally, with a cup of tomato basil soup and a sweet iced tea, no lemon.' "

"Once, I made the mistake of not getting the sandwiches cut diagonally," she continued. "He waited for me to come back and check on him and said, 'I prefer two fried baloney sandwiches, with the crust removed, cut diagonally.'"

"It took me a minute to realize that the diagonal cut was the problem, but he hadn't touched his meal. So, I took it back to the kitchen and had the sandwiches remade, cut diagonally, and he ate every bite. Once, I asked him if he wanted 'the usual.' Guess what he said?"

"What?" asked Danbury and Matthew in unison.

"I prefer two fried baloney sandwiches, with the crust removed, cut diagonally, with a cup of tomato basil soup and a sweet iced tea, no lemon."

"I see," said Danbury, who seemed to be genuinely trying to understand. "What about the evenings? Was it always the same night?"

"It was always the same night, at exactly the same time, and the same order. He came in every Monday night, at five, sat in the same seat, and ordered exactly the same thing."

"Monday nights? Did you work last night? Was he here?"

"Oh yes. He came in exactly at five, as usual, and sat right over there," she pointed to a table for two along the wall. "He said, 'I prefer the chicken pot pie, a side salad with ranch dressing and no onions, and a glass of sweet iced tea, no lemon.'" She sniffed, looking nostalgic, "I guess I won't ever again hear that." After a moment, she added, "I didn't wait on him, Mallory did, but I heard him give the order."

"I'm guessing that's what he always said?" asked Matthew gently.

"It's exactly what he always said."

"When is Mallory working again? Do you know?" asked Danbury.

"Um, I'm pretty sure she's back in for the morning shift, breakfast and lunch, on Thursday. I can check, if you'd like."

"Sure, thanks. But first, back to last night. Was anything different this week?" asked Danbury. "Was he alone?"

"He was always alone. He didn't talk to anyone except whoever was serving him."

"And then what? When he was finished eating?"

"He always left a two-dollar tip, and he was here exactly an hour, lunch and dinner, even if he'd only taken fifteen minutes to eat."

"An hour? What did he do? When he'd finished eating? Just sit there?" prodded Danbury.

"No, he had a little notebook that he always carried with a pencil in his shirt pocket. He always wore a shirt with a pocket. I never saw him without one, or without the pad and pencil. He'd sit there jotting or scribbling or something. I never got a good look. But he 'preferred' that we leave his plate until he left, and then we could clear the table. He was an odd little fellow but never caused anybody any trouble, as long as it all went the same way every time."

"And if it didn't?"

"He'd just state whatever was wrong, always beginning with, 'I prefer' whatever it was. He'd get a little agitated if you didn't get it the first couple of times, but he kept trying."

"And nothing was out of the ordinary? Monday night?"

She thought for a moment, and then responded, "No, he came in at five, had the chicken pot pie and salad, scribbled for a bit in his notebook, sipped his tea, put twelve dollars under the empty tea glass and walked out the door precisely at six to go to the church."

"The church?" asked Danbury. "Which church?"

"The Methodist one around the corner the next block down. They do Bingo for senior citizens every Monday night. Not that he was a senior, by any means. He was what, twenty something?"

"Thirty-three," corrected Danbury. "He played Bingo?"

"That's what I hear. Bingo starts about six-thirty, I think, and goes until eight-thirty or nine this time of year. It's earlier in the winter, you know, to get the seniors home before dark."

"Anything unusual in here last night? New patrons? Anybody make a fuss? Anything?"

"Not that I can think of," she said, shaking her head slowly.

"Thank you, Lucy," said Danbury. "You've been very helpful. If you think of anything else, call me?" He handed her a card and added, "Particularly about Monday night. If there's anything else that you remember."

"Happy to," she said, taking the card from him and tucking it into her apron pocket. Then, returning the chair to the nearby table and pulling out her order pad and a pen, she asked, "Now, what can I get you for dinner?"

"I'd thought about the chicken pot pie," said Matthew wryly. "But I think I'll have the meatloaf instead. With mashed potatoes and a salad with blue cheese dressing. And water is fine to drink."

"Good choice," she said, chuckling.

"Make that two," said Danbury. "Two helpings of meatloaf, though. With extra mashed potatoes. And green goddess on the salad. And peach cobbler. And just a glass of water. But coffee with the cobbler. Please," he added.

Matthew seconded the dessert and coffee order, amazed that Danbury could eat that much as the helpings were always quite generous, and Lucy left to place their order.

"Did you find Allan's last little notebook? On his body, or elsewhere on the scene?" asked Matthew.

"I was just thinking that. I'm pretty sure we didn't. But I'll double check."

"Are we going to the church next?" asked Matthew, with an eyebrow raised and his knee bouncing as he tapped his foot under the table in concentration.

"Nope," said Danbury. "Nobody there on Tuesday evenings."

"Oh." said Matthew.

"But the rectory is right next door."

"Ah. We should take them some peach cobbler."

"Great idea," agreed Danbury. "People are happier to talk that way. When you bring food. Oh Luceeeee . . ." he called mischievously. Then to Matthew, he added with a chuckle, "I've always wanted to do that."

Matthew laughed, welcoming the levity but startled by the uncharacteristic joking from Danbury, who he'd only known to crack jokes twice, and then only very dry ones with a deadpan face. He was usually so serious, stoic, and stolid. Lucy poked her head out of the kitchen door, not nearly as amused, and Danbury placed the take-out order for extra peach cobbler.

"And yes, Mallory is back in on Thursday for the breakfast and lunch shift. She's staying with friends in Raleigh until then," called Lucy before disappearing back into the kitchen.

"You sure you want to tag along? This evening, I mean. Probably very mundane police work."

"Yeah, I'm procrastinating about going to the gym. I'm too tired anyway," said Matthew with a grin. "That's all I was planning to do this evening, work out, go home and shower, and then spend some time with my acoustic guitar or mandolin."

"Oh, yeah. I forgot. You have musical talent. I saw the collection, earlier. The instruments at your house."

"It's what I do to relax and unwind sometimes in the evenings," said Matthew. "It's a release that allows my mind to wander. If there's something I'm pondering and trying to work out, like a patient problem, I can get that 'eureka' effect when I'm playing and suddenly I have the answer."

When their dinner arrived, Matthew was amazed, as always, at both the quantity and the speed with which Danbury devoured his meals. When they were finished, Lucy brought their checks. They settled up, left a tip, and then stepped out onto the sidewalk as the sky was turning lovely colors and the sun rested atop the distant tree line down the street. Almost reverently, without speaking, they walked the path that Allan Lingle, also known as "I Prefer," would have walked the evening before, just a couple of hours earlier.

Arriving at Goldman Street, just past the big Methodist church on the corner, they stepped up onto a small porch of a single-story brick house and Danbury rang the bell. They were standing under some sort of vine that wound up the rails of a portico above and Matthew wondered if it was the source of the fragrant smell that he was catching faintly on each waft of evening breeze.

The door opened and a rather jolly-looking portly man with a red face and receded hairline was standing on the other side.

"Good evening, Reverend White. I hope we're not disturbing you. I'm Detective Warren Danbury. And this is Doctor Matthew Paine. We brought you some peach cobbler. From the soda shop. Could we have a few minutes of your time?"

How very formal of Danbury, thought Matthew, as the older man smiled broadly and said, "Of course, come in, come in. We just finished up with the dishes and were settling in for the evening, but please, do come in." He stepped aside for Matthew and Danbury to enter and they found themselves being directed to a very cozy sitting room on the right where Mrs. White was perched on an overstuffed sofa with knitting in her lap.

She half rose in greeting until Danbury said, "Keep your seat, please. We'll only be a minute, really."

"Come on in and have a seat," she invited. "Make yourselves comfortable. Can we offer you something? Iced tea or coffee?"

"No thanks. We just had dinner," replied Danbury. "But thank you."

"And they brought us some peach cobbler from the soda shop," interjected the pastor from the doorway. "Does anybody want any?" Matthew and Danbury uttered their polite refusals and the pastor said, "I'll just go put it in the kitchen then."

"Matthew sat on a boxy overstuffed chair beside the sofa, leaving the other end of the sofa for the pastor, and Danbury perched on a nearby rocker, looking like a bull in a China shop. There were knickknacks and doodads on every available surface in the room, and most of them looked breakable.

"I'm sorry to bother you," began Danbury.

"Oh nonsense," said Mrs. White. "We love visitors."

The pastor returned and took a seat on the other end of the sofa, "Now, what can we help you with?" he asked.

"I guess you heard about Allan Lingle?"

"We did. Such a tragedy," said Mrs. White. "It's all so very sad. He was such a sweet boy, a little odd, but very sweet. He'd never have hurt anyone. I can't imagine why anyone would want to hurt him."

"That's what we're trying to find out," said Danbury. "I understand he played Bingo. Every Monday night. At your church."

"I believe that's true," said the pastor. "I wasn't always there because Pastor Don works with the senior citizens' activities. He's excellent with that age group and all of the bereavement care that's unfortunately associated."

"It does take a special sort of person for that job, you know," added Mrs. White.

"I'm sure it does," said Danbury. "Were you there last night?" he asked the pastor.

"I stopped by for a little while, around 7:30 or so, I think."

"Was Allan Lingle there then?"

"He was. He was concentrating on his Bingo cards when I first walked in. He always had three or four going at once."

"Did anything seem out of the ordinary? About him? About the evening, in general? Any new people there? Anyone cause any problems? Any arguments? Anything?"

"Not that I know of. Allan was sitting up straight in his chair, like he always did, until I heard him call out, 'Bingo!' He rose and took the board to the front of the room where the caller checked his board and asked what prize he'd like."

"What did he choose?" asked Danbury.

"He said, 'I prefer a notebook.' "

"Notebook?"

"We provide little trinkets for prizes, and I always saw him choose either one of those or a mechanical pencil, so we tried to have both on hand for him."

"Ah," said Matthew, turning to Danbury. "The little notebooks that he wrote in after he ate in the diner."

"Pastor White, do you know what time the Bingo game ended last night? And if Allan Lingle was there the whole time?"

"I don't know exactly. It was winding down when I left about 8:30, I think. Some of the oldest folks had already left, wanting to get home well before dark. Allan was still there concentrating on his Bingo cards when I left."

"Did you happen to notice a notebook? Already in his shirt pocket?" asked Danbury. "Before the one he won?"

"Well, maybe now, let me think." Pondering the question and pulling at a non-existent goatee on his chin, the older pastor answered slowly, "He might just have. I think he added the notebook he'd won to one already there in his shirt pocket. But I can't be certain," he added. "I was trying to make the rounds and greet everyone, so I'm not positive about that."

That meant, thought Matthew, that he should have had at least one small notebook in his pocket, albeit a potentially empty one.

"Did you know him well?" asked Danbury.

"Not really. He didn't say much. He didn't say anything, really, except to yell 'Bingo!' and 'I prefer' either the pencils or the little notebooks. I do recall, though, there was one week when we had neither and he was upset. He kept repeating that he 'preferred' the notebook or pencils and wouldn't be convinced to take a package of handkerchiefs or nail clippers or socks."

"What happened?" asked Matthew, intrigued.

"I think Pastor Don went and found a couple of pencils from his office and brought them back for him."

"Other than that, did he ever have any altercations with anyone? Any disagreements or arguments?" asked Matthew.

"Not that I can recall," said Pastor White. "He really stayed to himself. Some of the senior citizens, particularly newer ones, would introduce themselves and he'd nod quickly up and down and say his name. If any of them tried to shake his hand, he'd simply say, 'I prefer not,' and they were always gracious about it. I do think they had a nickname for him, though, that they called him. Not that anyone addressed him by it, of course, but when they were talking about how he'd won or helped set up or clean up, like that."

"What was that?" asked Danbury.

"I prefer," said Matthew and Pastor White together.

"Yes, exactly," said the pastor's wife. "I've heard him called that too."

"Thank you for your time," said Danbury, rising to leave. "If you think of anything else, please call me," he said, handing them a card.

"Certainly, certainly," replied Paster White.

"We hope you can find whoever did this to that poor man," added Mrs. White, as Danbury and Matthew headed to the door to leave. They exchanged pleasantries and stepped out onto the vine-covered porch and headed down the walkway back to the street.

"We didn't exactly strike gold there," said Matthew, looking up at the Goldman Street sign on the corner. As Danbury looked askance at him, Matthew just said, "Sorry, that was the worst of bad puns. I guess I'm just tired and a little punchy with all of this."

"Can you meet at the soda shop on Thursday?" asked Danbury as they walked back in that direction. "To talk to Mallory. And get some answers. Or at least to try to."

"I think so, but I'll check my patient load. It's normally much lighter, this time of year. Cold and flu season is over, the barrage of sports physicals and school immunizations hasn't started, and it's mostly allergies, injuries, and annual physicals. I'll call you tomorrow and let you know."

"Great. Thanks."

"You realize that I'm way outside of my purview on this one, right?"

"Yeah, I owe you a beer. I'll talk to Pastor Don tomorrow. And Wayne Adams. About the Lingle estate. Without your help," he added, pointedly.

Laughing, Matthew just said, "Have a good night."

"Yeah, you too."

On that note, they parted company, Matthew walking back toward his office, and Danbury turning left and heading for the Peak police station.

*****

Contemplating the things they'd learned about Allan Lingle, Matthew drove home. The guy was repeatedly characterized as very odd, but not mean or violent, with no known enemies or any reason to have any. So why was he dead? Matthew pondered, but he couldn't come up with anything.

Driving slowly and as quietly as he could into his condo complex, he was still amazed that the average age of occupancy was well above his own age and most of his neighbors were already in bed and many were likely already asleep. He hoped Ms. Drewer was too. Busybody that she was, he didn't dislike the woman. He merely wanted to avoid a gossip session with her. And he certainly didn't want to provide her fodder for him becoming the center of her next gossip binge as he had inadvertently done in the past. She, however, perpetually asked personal questions and was rarely dissuaded by vague or non-committal answers. Too kind to state the obvious, that it was none of her business, he sometimes wished he were that frank.

Relieved to see the street deserted, Matthew parked in his garage, lowered the garage door, entered the house, and went through his usual routine. As he locked up, hung his key fob on the hook by the door, and reset the security system, Max immediately appeared, rubbing up against his legs and meowing softly.

"I guess you're hungry, huh, Big Guy?" Matthew asked.

Slipping through the kitchen, he tossed his leather satchel onto the end of the sofa and knelt to scratch the big cat behind his ears. Max moved his head around to shift the scratching down the sides of his face and under his chin.

"Let's get you some dinner," said Matthew, straightening up and going into the kitchen to retrieve the cat food, put a scoop into his food bowl, and rinse and refill the water bowl. While he was in the kitchen, he set the timer on the coffee maker to brew for the next morning.

Trudging down the hallway, Matthew realized how tired he was and opted to skip his music and prepare for the next morning. After his nightly ritual of washing his face and brushing his teeth, he pulled clothes from his closet and laid them out neatly on the dressing table in his bathroom. He picked up a book he'd been struggling to read, a historical biography that he had thought would be intriguing but had instead been very difficult to get into, and collapsed into the bed.

Max jumped up and started bathing on the foot of the bed, which was the last thing that Matthew remembered until he was startled awake by an annoying buzzing sound.

4. A good start

Stretching, Matthew felt a few new kinks because he'd fallen asleep half propped up in bed with his lamp on. His book had fallen to his chest, and he and the book had remained in that position all night. Realizing that the annoying buzzing noise wasn't his alarm, he picked up his phone and saw that Cici was FaceTiming him, so he clicked to connect.

"Hey, Sleepy Head," she said. "Aren't you up yet?"

"Not yet," he muttered, swiping the back of his hand across his face.

"Wish I could say the same," she said. "My days and nights are reversed and all mixed up." She was perched on the edge of an office chair and he could see windows behind her. It would be almost lunch time on this Wednesday in London, he reckoned. "I got in and settled safely, but I guess you saw my text."

Realizing that he hadn't seen her text, he opted instead to address the jet lag. "It's not unusual to have your hours a little off at first. It'll likely take a few days, maybe even a week or so for you to get straightened out. How was the flight?"

"I tried to sleep through it, but there was a screaming child two rows in front of me. Ear plugs only marginally dimmed the racket."

"Uh oh," said Matthew, knowing that didn't bode well. "Did that set you back – what, five, six years, at least – on having children?" he teased.

Laughing, Cici said, "At the time, I thought it was more like ten, or a total reset back to infinity. But then, when I was getting off the plane, the most amazing thing happened. The baby had been quietly asleep for a couple of hours and the parents kept their seats as I went by, probably exhausted, poor things. But then that little person looked up at me and smiled. A very toothless, but radiantly adorable little smile."

Never having heard anything like this from Cici before, that babies were anything but annoying or that parents who couldn't keep them quiet deserved any sympathy, Matthew thought he was beginning to hear her biological timeclock ticking over FaceTime and across an ocean. He refrained from saying so but instead said, "Did you meet with your important client when you got in?"

"I did," she said. "Right after I got checked into the hotel and cleaned up a bit. Though I felt like there was sandpaper on the inside of my eyelids and I was at least one beat behind where I should have been for the whole conversation."

"I'm sure you were brilliant," said Matthew, meaning it.

"I've got plenty of time to try to be brilliant," she said. "I just needed to quickly get a handle on exactly what they are trying to accomplish."

"And did you?"

"Mostly. They're an old company in the UK but they want to expand into the US and they need lots of help with some acquisitions, accommodations, and legal procedures to incorporate and organize in the States."

"That's layman's terms, just for me, right?"

"Pretty much," she chuckled. "It's U.S. business law they need help with. That's oversimplified, sure, but you get the gist."

"I do. And business law is your specialty so they're in great hands."

"Thanks. What's happening with you this week?"

"I don't even know where to start," he said, but he tried. He told her about the murder, the investigation, and his involvement in it. She was both intrigued and a little concerned for him, both of which he found endearing. When they'd wrapped up their conversation, Matthew crawled reluctantly out of bed and went through his usual morning routine.

Scooping up his satchel and grabbing his key ring off the hook by the door, he set the alarm, locked the door, and clicked to open the second garage door for his Honda Element. Having only recently bought the Corvette, he'd had the Element from high school through college and medical school. He still loved it and drove it a couple of times a week in nice weather, but he relied more on the little Element in nasty weather when he didn't want the Corvette out or when he needed to haul something or drive back roads.

Waving at a couple of his older neighbors who were out for a morning stroll, he was relieved not to see Ms. Drewer and Oscar as he drove out of his neighborhood and the mile or so down Chester Road to turn onto Highway 20 and head for Peak.

*****

Matthew was busily in the middle of his morning routine with a heavy patient load, which was a bit unusual for a Wednesday in the spring. Wednesdays during the winter months with cold and flu season, those were anybody's guess, as he'd said many times before.

Feeling his phone vibrate in his pocket as he was finishing up with a patient, Matthew ignored it. As he stepped out of the exam room and into the alcove between the exam rooms, he looked to see that he'd missed a call from Danbury and poked at his phone to quickly return the call.

"Hey, Doc. I need your help."

"I've heard that before and recently," said Matthew jovially. "What's up?"

"I need you to talk to Ms. Lingle."

"Ms. Lingle? You mean Allan's sister? Penn, right?"

"Yep. She flew in from Denver. And she's refusing to talk. At least to us. Or, at least to me."

"Why won't she talk to you?"

"She has nothing to say. That's what she told a Peak officer."

"Doesn't she want to know how her brother died? To help catch whoever did this to him? Unless –"

"Unless what?"

"Unless she's somehow responsible, however indirectly, if she really was in Denver when he died."

"She was. We already checked that. Before she refused to talk. Makes her look guilty, though. You're right. I thought the same."

"It does. So, how can I help?"

"Talk to her. Get her to talk to you. Maybe even to us."

"You want me to just call her up and strike up a conversation?"

"No. I want you to bump into her today. Accidentally. I'll tell you where she'll be."

"Accidentally?" Matthew repeated. "Today? And I just show up and strike up a conversation with her?"

"Something like that. People talk to you. You put them at ease. Work your magic. On Ms. Lingle."

Matthew sighed heavily, "OK, tell me where she'll be when and I'll do my best."

"The soda shop at noon today. Sharp."

"How do you know these things?"

"I have my sources."

Matthew chuckled, "All right then. What can you tell me about her? At least a general description."

"Not much. Mid-thirties. Medium height. Medium build. Dark hair, to her shoulders."

"She sounds very ordinary. How will I pick her out of the lunch crowd, other than as someone I don't know and haven't seen before?"

"She's athletic. A physical therapist. Has her own business. In Denver. Strength training. Rehabilitation after injury. Body building. And a spa, I think. Like that."

"And otherwise, she's medium-sized and perfectly ordinary looking?"

Danbury hesitated slightly before answering, distractedly, "Ordinary. Right."

"I didn't know when I signed on as a medical consultant that there'd be so much, non-medically, involved in that," said Matthew with a chuckle. "But I'll try to get over there as close to noon as I can."

"Thanks, Doc."

“Oh, and I checked my schedule for tomorrow,” Matthew added before Danbury could disconnect. “Around lunch is pretty full but I could slip out a little early for a coffee break to go talk to the waitress at Peak Eats. I have a break in patients around 10 in the morning.”

“OK, that’ll work. Thanks,” and he was gone.

Doesn’t he have a partner to handle these things? Matthew wondered and he made a mental note to ask.

*****

Managing to finish his morning patient roster before noon, Matthew slipped into his office, out of his lab coat, and quietly out the side door before anyone could intercept him with questions or other patient issues. He had politely declined the offer of Reuben sandwiches that Trina was having delivered for lunch as well as his nurse Gladys’ offer to eat them together at the café tables on the outside balcony off the upstairs breakroom.

His office building was Palladian-style and looked like the architect had attempted to mirror equally the cultural arts center that was in front of his building on Winston Avenue and something more Romanesque. Matthew wasn’t sure they’d succeeded, but his staff well knew that he did enjoy lunch out on the balcony off the break room on nice days. Out over in, that was his preference for lunch dining, weather permitting.

Turning the corner and making his way down the sidewalk on Winston Avenue toward the soda shop, Matthew thought about the many times he’d seen Allan Lingle walk this same route and he pondered why he was killed. Did he see something in his travels through the little town that someone didn’t want known? Did he walk up on a situation? But what could that have been down at the end of the street that went nowhere but his own house? A drug deal? Matthew almost laughed at himself. This is Peak, he thought, not downtown Raleigh. Even so, bad things apparently do happen even in the safest of small towns, he thought, shaking off a sudden chill on the warm May day.

5. Dual dining

Finding a spot in the rear corner of Peak Eats, he slid into the last available booth with his back to the wall to watch the door. He'd arrived early to be able to spot a woman meeting the description of Penn Lingle, albeit a vague one, who should be coming through it at noon. Realizing that the description Danbury had given him could be applied to half of the female population of North Carolina, Matthew's eyebrow rose in concentration and his knee was bouncing as his foot tapped out the rhythms that were always running through his head.

Music was a serious hobby for Matthew and if he could get his hands on an instrument, he could very likely play it. In his own personal collection, he had keyboards, several guitars, including a classic Les Paul, drums, a mandolin, and a ukulele that his parents had brought him back from an anniversary trip to Hawaii.

Pondering how to approach a strange woman and strike up a conversation, and coming up empty on ideas, he glanced up as the bell above the door jingled. The woman who entered fit the description but she was a few minutes earlier than he'd expected. He was spared the arduous chore of striking up a conversation with a complete stranger because she did it for him. Glancing around quickly and then locking eyes with Matthew, neither she nor he looked away as she strode purposefully to his table.

"Excuse me," said the woman as she stepped around Evie, the overzealous server who was bringing a glass of water to Matthew, and approached his table. “Is anyone else going to sit here?”

“No, just me.”

“I prefer booths to the old soda counter and that’s all that’s left,” she said, rather pointedly, “Mind if I join you?”

Matthew noted her choice of words in preferring a booth. Recovering from the pointed insinuation that he shouldn’t take up a whole booth alone, he swept his hand across, indicating the opposite side of the booth and said, “Please do.”

Momentarily transfixed by the bluest eyes he’d ever seen, which were in stark contrast to the dark hair falling about her shoulders, he noted the spandex pants, short-sleeved quick dry t-shirt and Nike trainers the woman wore as well as the somewhat muscular form in them. He entirely missed Evie rolling her eyes and turning back to the waitress station to get a second glass of water.

“Hi, I’m Matthew Paine,” he said as he offered his hand across the table.

“You’re the new doctor at Peak Family Practice, right?” Matthew nodded as she added, “Penn Lingle,” and firmly took his hand in hers. “I’ll refrain from the obvious jokes about your name.”

“Thank you, though I’ve probably heard them all before.”

“An unfortunate name for a doctor, surely, but it’s just too easy,” she smiled at him for the first time and he noted the straight white teeth that had either extensive orthodontic attention or amazing genes. “Have you ordered yet?”

“No, I’d only just sat down when you came in. And, as you saw,” he added, stating the obvious, “there were no other seats.” Without waiting for a response, he added, “I’d recommend the special today. Chicken salad on whole wheat. It’s excellent.”

“They still have chicken salad for lunch on Wednesdays here? Wow, some things really never do change.”

“Yes, but usually only during the warmer months.”

Evie reappeared with another glass of water and asked if they wanted anything else to drink.

“Today, I just might,” replied Matthew. “How about a glass of iced tea that's half sweet and half unsweet, with a lemon?"

"Sure. Anything else for you, Ma'am?" she asked, turning to Penn.

"Just some lemon for my water would be great. Wedges, if you have them, instead of slices."

"Umm. I'll see if we have those," said Evie as she left with the drink orders.

Penn picked up a menu and Matthew decided to dive into the topic he'd come to discuss, "You're Allan Lingle's older sister, right?"

"Only by two years, but yes."

"How long have you been away from Peak?"

"Since college. I went to school in Deacon Grove, then I got married and moved to Denver."

Matthew raised an eyebrow, a bit disdainfully, at the mention of Deacon Grove.

"What?" she asked.

"Oh, nothing much. Just that I'm a State fan."

North Carolina State University, sprawling across downtown Raleigh and including a second newer large campus nearby, had long been known for its technology and science programs as well as its sports rivalry with the other huge state-supported university located in Deacon Grove.

"At least you didn't say Duke," she teased. "And I thought the adverse reaction was to my marital status. I'm not, by the way. Married anymore, I mean."

"Oh," was all Matthew could think to say to that.

Evie reappeared by their table with Matthew's tea, which she set gently on a napkin in front of him, and a small bowl of sliced lemons, which she set, somewhat less gently, beside Penn's water glass. "The lemons were already all sliced, so I just brought you a bunch of the slices," she explained to Penn's annoyed expression. "Are you ready to order?" she asked.

"You go ahead," Penn said to Matthew. "I might be a minute."

"I'll have the special, the chicken salad on whole wheat."

"Chips or fresh fruit?" asked Evie.

"I'll have the fresh fruit."

"Good choice," approved Penn. "And I'll have the chef salad but leave off the croutons and the cheese. I'd like your light Italian dressing on the side. And do you have low fat ham?"

"Low fat … ham?" repeated Evie, looking truly baffled. "I don't know. I mean, it's just deli ham."

Penn's blue eyes flashed momentary annoyance and then she said, "Fine then, I'll have 'just deli ham.' "

"Anything else?" asked Evie, cheerfully.

Penn shook her head no and Matthew said kindly, "Not for me, thanks."

"I'll get that order right in for you," Evie flashed a sweet dimpled smile at Matthew before leaving the table.

"She has a thing for you," observed Penn.

"What?"

"She's so obviously flirting with you and really annoyed with me. Any history there?"

Matthew laughed at the question, his eyebrow shot up, and he was shaking his head as he responded, "Only as a server when I come in for lunch, which is usually maybe once a week or so. She's a little young, don't you think? What is she, maybe 19?"

"Maybe that old," nodded Penn sagely.

Pondering how to begin to get the answers about her brother he'd come for, Matthew tapped his foot under the table, in concentration.

"So, you moved to Colorado with your former husband?" he began. "You never considered moving back to North Carolina?"

"Not really."

"Do you have children?"

"Oh, no!" she responded emphatically. "I was only married for three years when I found out that Jeffrey did more than just lead seminars with his colleague and frequent travel companion. We divorced, I took my name back, and he married her a few months later."

"I see," said Matthew, trying to proceed carefully. "Peak wasn't much of a draw for you, huh? Even though you had family here?"

"Not much of a draw at all, honestly. I was in the middle of the divorce when my mother died suddenly. My Dad died when I was 10, so she was the only parent I had. Anyway, my brother Leo came home after Mom died, and then flew the coop for who knows where. Leo is short for Leonard. Like Penn is short for my horrible name," she leaned across the table and whispered, "Penelope." Then added, shaking her head, "I don't know what my parents were thinking. They were always so sensible about everything else. Anyway, Leo has always been a bit of a free spirit and he just disappeared one day and I had no idea where he went."

"Leo is your youngest brother?"

"Yep. My parents were busy. Allan was two years younger than me, and Leo is nearly four years my junior."

"Any idea where he is now? I think the police were trying to reach both of you and our office had you both listed as the next of kin, but his number wasn't in service."

"Nope. None. The last I heard, he was up in Jersey doing who knows what. He was only 6 when Dad died and Mom never could control him. He was constantly in trouble at school, the class clown and town prankster. Between that and all of Allan's issues, I swear my mom died to escape it all!" She leaned across the table conspiratorially, and added, "It was incredibly selfish of me, I know, but when I got away, I didn't plan to come back. I was young and I didn't want to be tied down with Allan's issues or Leo's either for that matter."

"Allan's issues," began Matthew. "I've seen his medical record, so I have some idea of what those were but what was that like, growing up?"

"Oh, that's right. Allan wasn't your patient, was he?"

"No, he was Dr. Garner's patient."

"So, you didn't deal with him?"

"I didn't. I'd seen him around town but he kept to himself. He never spoke to me, that I recall. I'd say, 'Good morning,' or 'Good afternoon,' if I passed him on the sidewalk, but he just kept walking as if he hadn't heard me."

"That sounds like Allan. Unless he needed to interact with someone, he preferred not to."

"Funny that you use that word to describe him. It was one he used a lot, wasn't it?"

"Which word?"

"Prefer."

"Oh, that. Yeah, some shrink that he worked with as a young teen taught him that phrase as a coping strategy. Allan would lose control as a child and have terrible tantrums when things didn't exactly follow the same predictable pattern. Allan needed a regimen with very little variation in his schedule, people, and events. When some little thing wasn't according to that predictable pattern, he'd lose it, just totally lose control."

"And the doctor helped him cope with change?"

"There were many doctors and therapists, over the years, along with therapy groups and special classes, but one of them taught him to identify the issue and verbalize it."

"An ability that most of us take for granted."

"Right. But Allan had to be taught. If someone changed something, he learned to calmly say, 'I prefer' and state the thing that had been changed. I think he generalized it to ask for whatever he wanted that way. He said, 'I prefer' to nearly everything. I'm aware that people here in town call him that."

Matthew just nodded.

"But I'm sure he really didn't prefer to die!" she said vehemently. "He wouldn't have preferred death, if given that choice!" Choking back the first bit of emotion Matthew had seen from her, she took a deep breath and added, "It seemed to help, though. Verbalizing what he wanted helped him to cope in controlled social interactions. At least he could function."

"I'm glad. Many people with autism, even the most highly functioning, struggle with change in their routines. It's just one of several neurodevelopmental disorders that can cause stress in dealing with an ever-changing environment."

"He did struggle with change. He had Asperger's and several other diagnoses, as I'm sure you know, which made interacting with other people very difficult for him. It wasn't about mental acuity. The guy was smart. He just really couldn't interact with other people, and his life had to be organized, regimented really, in a certain way. He had learned to cope as an adult, but it was rough when we were kids. I think Leo resented that Allan got special treatment and I was just embarrassed by his tantrums."

"That must have been hard," said Matthew, sympathetically.

Just then, Evie appeared with their plates and conversation ceased as Matthew nodded, prayed silently, and both dug into their lunches.

Evie appeared again as they were finishing, flashing her dimples at Matthew, and asked sweetly, "Can I get you anything else?"

"Just the check," and, "I'd like a cup of coffee, please," answered Penn and Matthew simultaneously, and then both of them laughed.

"I guess I could stick around while you have coffee," said Penn with a devilish grin at Evie, who silently disappeared.

When she was out of earshot in the noisy diner, Penn turned back to Matthew, "You asked what it was like growing up here with Allan, why don't you ask Warren? He was in Allan's class."

"Warren? You mean Detective Danbury?"

"Yes. I hear that you're friends, though only recently acquainted?"

"Wow, you've been back in town exactly how long and you already know that?"

"A day. I jumped a plane and flew in yesterday."

Momentarily taken aback, Matthew finally asked the obvious question, "So, if you knew Danbury growing up, why won't you talk to him? Do you have any idea why your brother was killed?"

"None. No idea at all. That's part of the reason I don't want to talk to the police. I haven't talked to either of my brothers in a couple of years. I tried to call Allan regularly after Mom died and the conversation was always one-sided, so eventually I just checked in with Malcolm, his caregiver, occasionally and stopped calling Allan at all."

"Malcolm is missing, I'm sure you know. When was the last time you talked to him?"

"Umm, only very briefly a couple of times since Christmas. The last real conversation we had was before Christmas. The family attorney, who oversees everything, called to say that Malcolm needed a few weeks off to visit family for the holidays but he had a replacement lined up, so I called to work out those details. That was about as involved as I ever get in any of it. Malcolm was pure gold, though. He kept everything stable and predictable for Allan."

"Do you know if he has family locally? Malcolm, I mean."

"Not that I ever heard about. He was flying out to see family, an aunt who helped raise him. I believe she lives somewhere in California. That's why he wanted a couple of weeks to be there. But I don't know him well. All we ever really talked about was my brother and how he was doing. He seemed deeply invested in my brother's well-being. Like I said, pure gold."

"What can you tell me about him? Anything?"

"I think he had a rough youth but he was trying to get past that and he was studying to be a nurse when he wasn't caring for Allan."

"Why do you say that his youth was rough?"

"I'm pretty sure the attorney mentioned that Malcolm had a sealed juvie record. It was likely some petty crime that wouldn't impact his ability to care for Allan. And it didn't. He was very devoted to Allan."

"But that's all you know about him?"

"It is. Look, if you want to know more about Malcolm, talk to Wayne Adams. He's responsible for managing all of that and I'm sure he ran a full background check on the guy."

Matthew cleared his throat and raised an eyebrow, trying to be delicate, but Penn seemed to read his thoughts.

"You're wondering why, if my brother needed a caregiver, I wasn't more involved in his care, aren't you?"

Feeling his face flush slightly at her bluntness, his foot tapped under the table to the rhythms in his head that were helping him to sort out how to ask the hard questions without making her mad enough to stop talking to him and walk out. "I was, yes," he admitted.

Penn seemed to struggle momentarily with formulating an answer and then asked gently, "You don't know, do you? I thought it was all over town."

Matthew waited quietly for her to continue. Just then Evie approached with a steaming cup of coffee and placed it, a tiny cream pitcher, and six packets of sugar in front of him. "I know how you love lots of sugar in your coffee, so I brought you some extra."

"Thanks," he said as she beamed at him, placing his check beside the coffee. Penn wrinkled her nose in disapproval but said nothing.

"And here's your check," she said plopping it down in front of Penn. "I'll take it up whenever you're ready." Then to Matthew, she added, "But no rush. Enjoy your coffee."

When she'd left their table, Matthew prodded, "So where were we? Oh yes. Something that I don't know. I'm sure there's a lot that I don't know," he added, trying to resume their conversation with some levity.

"About my family," said Penn. "And the settlement of the estate."

Again, Matthew waited for her to continue. She sipped the last of her water and seemed to arrive at a decision. "My parents left almost all of it in a trust to Allan, to be overseen by attorneys and financial planners," she said at last.

"Oh."

"So, you see, I've had no real say in my brother's care or involvement in any of that decision making. And it's not like I could have any real relationship with him anyway, particularly long distance. There's simply been no reason to get involved."

"That must have been difficult," said Matthew. "When did you find out about that arrangement?"

"After my mother died. Leo and I both came home and I was thinking I'd have to move back to care for Allan. When they read the will, it was preceded by a letter from our mother explaining how she knew Leonard and I were making our own lives and we were capable of doing so. She said that she was concerned for Allan, who couldn't begin to keep a job, even at the local supermarket, because the work was too variable. I paraphrased that last bit, but that was the gist of it."

"That must have been a shock."

"Exactly. But after the initial shock wore off, I realized that it was actually a wonderful gift. I wasn't tied down here with responsibility for Allan, and I could go back to my life in Denver, such as it was after the divorce."

"Ah. You made peace with it?"

"I did."

"And Leo?"

"Not so much. He was furious. And resentful of Allan, I think, though they had been best friends, growing up. The historic house and all of the antiques that it contains are the tip of the iceberg. My mother comes from money so the estate was considerable."

"So, what happens to it all now? After Allan's, uh . . . demise?"

"I don't honestly know. If that was part of the will originally read to us, I don't remember it. I was trying to find Leo before meeting with the attorney. I'm set to meet with him in the morning, since Leo's in the wind again. But you can see why this might not look good for either Leo or me, depending on what the provisions will be now."

"I do see. It sounds like a considerable motive."

"I suppose so. I really just want to get back to Denver and not be stuck here tending to the estate. I never wanted to move back here, inheritance or not."

"Is that the reason you didn't want to talk to Danbury or the police?"

"One of them."

"There are more?"

"Yeah. Warren."

"You don't want to talk to him?"

"Not particularly, no."

Matthew didn't prod, but sipped the last of his coffee and refrained from motioning for Evie to pay his bill.

Eventually, Penn responded, "Things were pretty awkward between us when I left for college. I know that was a long time ago," she said, holding up a hand as if to ward off his judgement. "But he moved away, I moved away, and I haven't seen him since."

"Awkward?" prodded Matthew.

Penn took a deep breath and launched into the story. "I told you that he was in Allan's class in school." Matthew nodded, and she continued, "He was also Allan's self-appointed protector, taking up for him when other kids bullied him. Back then, Warren was a tall, skinny, gangly, and uncoordinated kid."

"Danbury?" Matthew asked in amazement.

"Oh yeah."

"You haven't seen him at all since?"

"Only in the newspapers and from a distance since I got back. Let's just say that he's changed considerably." She laughed and then continued, "At some point, I began to suspect that there were ulterior motives behind his interest in protecting Allan. Little did he know that I was a shallow, self-absorbed cheerleader with her eye on the star quarterback."

Reaching for her water glass, she grimaced when she realized that it was empty, but then continued, "There was a dance here in town after my graduation and Warren finally got up the nerve to ask me to go. He caught me by surprise and it wasn't my finest hour. I admit that I wasn't exactly graceful in my refusal. He avoided me rather obviously after that. I really don't blame him. Ironically, he filled out after I left and I heard that he became the star quarterback his senior year, two years later. He had multiple scholarship offers to play football in college, from what I heard."

"Ah. It's personal then."

"You could say that."

"Just one more thing. Do you know what Allan wrote in the little notebooks that he kept and if there was one of them in his personal effects?"

Sighing deeply, Penn shrugged and said, "What he scrawled all over those notebooks never made any sense to me. There must be hundreds of them in his dresser drawer at home, but they're unintelligible."

"How so? Random scribbles?"

"No, they're not random. And, knowing Allan, they all meant something specific. There were letters, numbers, and diagrams and letter strings circled and underlined. But it's not in words, so who knows what it's all about. And yes, he had an empty notebook in his personal effects. That, a pencil, his wallet, and a pair of glasses were all that were found on him, I believe. Why?"

"Just trying to piece together his movements on Monday night, along with anything he might have been carrying that would have interested anyone, that's all. It doesn't sound like the notebooks would have been particularly interesting." Retrieving his wallet, Matthew flagged Evie down. They paid their bills, and Matthew pulled his phone out to check his messages as they rose from the table. "I enjoyed lunch, but I've got a full afternoon of patients to see, so I've got to get back."

"Hopefully, I'll see you again before I go back to Denver. I'd love to see more of you. Here," she said smiling suggestively up at him as she handed him a business card. "Call me. Or better yet," she added as she snatched his phone out of his hand before he could protest and typed in her number. "Now you have no excuse. You can't lose my number now, can you?"

"OK," said Matthew, who didn't know what else to say. "Got it."

"So, use it," she said over her shoulder to Matthew and nearly bumped into Danbury who'd rounded the corner and was on his way into the diner.

"Hello, Penny," he said calmly.

"Uh, hi Warren," she said and blanched noticeably as she added, "And nobody ever calls me that anymore."

Amused, Matthew excused himself and headed back to the office, resisting the urge to look back.

6. Time lines

As he walked back to his office after his lunch with Penn Lingle, Matthew was thinking about all that Penn had told him and he had an idea. Instead of the usual side entrance that the doctors mostly used, Matthew walked through the front door and up to the front desk.

Surprised, Maddie, the young receptionist, turned and said, "Can I help you with something, Dr. Paine?"

"You can," he replied, "Could you quickly check the patient records and see if we have a Malcolm as a patient?"

"Sure, what's his last name?" she asked, as she turned to the computer keyboard and typed the query.

"I have no idea. That's one of the things I'm trying to find out."

"Ah, here, there's only one. Malcolm Freeman, 27."

"That must be him. Is there a next of kin or emergency contact listed for him?"

"There's a sister listed on the scanned copy of his intake form, but the phone number has been marked through a couple of times and it was rescanned. Or else Mr. Freeman changed it repeatedly when he filled it out initially. That's odd."

"Whose patient is he? And could the correct number be somewhere else in his records?"

As she was about to respond, a patient approached the desk to check in and Matthew quickly changed the subject, "Thanks, Maddie, I can look it up from there. I appreciate your help." Turning to the patient, he recognized his 1:00 appointment, and said, "Hello, Mrs. McFarland. I'm going back to get ready to see you now."

She greeted him and he slipped through the double doors and down the hallway to his office. Taking a moment to pull up the patient record for Mrs. McFarland to remind himself why she was there, he then pulled up Malcolm Freeman's.

Malcolm Freeman, listed as a black male, five-foot eleven inches tall and slightly plump at two hundred forty pounds, was Dr. Rob's patient. It appeared that he had only been in twice, though, once for a raging sinus infection, and once for a cut on his elbow that was closed with Steri-Strips when he refused stitches. Interesting, thought Matthew. If the man was studying to become a nurse himself, why would a few stitches bother him? Maybe it was the trip to the Emergency Department that he'd been avoiding.

Amelia Freeman was listed as Malcolm's next of kin and she had a rural address in the form of a post office box number in a small town that Matthew was familiar with just over the North Carolina state line in Virginia, but there was no phone number listed for her. Jotting down the name and address on a note pad, Matthew shrugged, not knowing what good it would do.

He slipped into his lab coat and was about to step out into the hallway to begin his afternoon appointments, beginning with Mrs. McFarland, who would soon be waiting for him in Exam Room Six, when he thought he'd quickly call Danbury.

"Hey, Doc, what's up?"

"Just thought I'd quickly fill you in on what I learned from Penn, which probably isn't much more than you already know. Did you talk to her at all?"

"Nope. She came out. I went in. Just got my takeout order."

"Ah. Well, she told me about her brother's issues and how her mother had left the estate in trust to him with attorneys overseeing it. She didn't have much knowledge of what had happened with her brother's care after her mother died, but she did mention that the family's primary attorney, Wayne Adams, would know the details. It seems that the caregiver,

Malcolm Freeman, was rumored to have a sealed juvie record but was studying to be a nurse while providing care for Allan. She seems to think well of him, but she admits that she rarely talked to him. Has anyone seen or heard anything from him yet?"

"Nope. Nothing. Neither he nor his Jeep. Both are missing. He's a person of interest. We need to find his sister. She lives up in the edge of Virginia. Little town called Benefit. She's his next of kin."

"Yeah, I know where it is. It's up on Walters Lake, or Biggers Lake, if you're from Virginia. The huge reservoir lake straddles the state lines for miles. It spans three counties in both states, and it seems that they can't agree on the name of it. More of it is actually in Virginia, so Biggers Lake should probably be the name. I used to camp and fish up there a lot with my grandfather. Do you have contact information for her?"

"Just an address. A PO box. No phone number. No street address. None that Adams had anyway."

"We don't either, at least not in our computerized record. I checked. If he was a patient here, then you should maybe ask one of the other doctors here about him; he didn't share a doctor with Allan – all of which is telling you more than I should."

"Ah, Dr. Rob, then. OK, I'll talk to him."

"You probably won't learn much, with HIPPA and the patient information protection laws, but maybe you can get a hint at something that'll help. Oh, and one other thing," Matthew added. "Penn said what her brother scribbled in his notebooks was indecipherable to anyone other than Allan, though she was sure that it was methodical and made sense to him. Strings of letters, mostly, some numbers, and diagrams with strings of letters circled or underlined. Did you talk to Pastor Don?"

"Yeah, he completed the timeline. Allan left shortly after eight-thirty. Right after Pastor White. With at least two little notebooks. He'd have been walking home. Couldn't have gone anywhere else. There's not enough time. He must have just been killed. When the boys found him. The 911 call was logged at eight fifty-two."

"We need to talk to the boys again. I think they can tell us more than they were saying. I'm pretty sure of it."

"Yeah, I thought so too. I've contacted the parents already. Tried to set something up. I'll let you know. When they get back to me."

"OK."

"We've contacted the local guys. Up in Benefit. They're working on it. They're trying to locate the sister. To see if she knows where Malcolm is. Or if she's hiding him up there. They have a description of the missing Jeep. I'm really considering going up myself. I'd like to get a lay of the land. Maybe talk to her. If they can find her. Ask her a few questions. See what she can tell us. I might just drive up. Maybe on Saturday. If he hasn't turned up by then. Want to drive up to Benefit? Sounds like you already know something about the area. About the lay of the land, at least."

"Just the lake and a couple of camp grounds up there, really," answered Matthew. "And some history of the area," he added, wishing it were a fishing or camping trip he'd be driving up for. "I could probably manage that. I really need to wash the pollen off my cars. They're both putrid shades of green. But maybe I could get to that on Sunday and just spray them off for now. Let me know if you decide to go. I'm sorry I wasn't more help with Penn."

"Hey. You got more out of her than I could. And thanks, Doc. You do put people at ease. It's a good trait. Especially for a doctor."

"Bedside Manner 101," laughed Matthew. "Hey, did you talk to Wayne Adams yet?"

"Yeah, I followed up. After the Peak guys talked to him. He's supposed to be putting together an inventory for us. Of valuables in the house. He was cagey, though. About handing over financial information. Investments and details on the trust fund. He did say that Allan didn't get it all. Penn and Leo each got a little bit of the estate. The bulk went to Allan, though."

"Do you know what's in the new will, now that Allan is deceased?"

"I don't. He was cagey about that too. Said he'd talk to me after Penn. And Leo."

"Leo? Aren't his whereabouts still unknown?"

"Yeah. We have an APB out on him. On both him and Malcolm. Maybe they could tell us more. If we can turn up one or the other."

"Or maybe they'd tell you nothing, because one or both are guilty of murder."

"That's possible too."

"OK, I'm off to see my afternoon patients now. Keep me posted on your progress and the weekend plans."

"OK," said Danbury, and he was gone.

*****

Having managed a workout at the gym after work, Matthew was happily spending a quiet and relaxing evening at home with Max, a quick dinner grilled out on his patio, and his acoustic guitar when his phone went off loudly. As he reached for it, he caught a glimpse of text messages from his best friend from childhood, Justin, and an incoming call.

First clicking to answer the call, figuring that he'd answer the text message afterward, Matthew heard Cici's chipper voice, "Hi, Matthew."

"Hey, Cici," he said. "Isn't it the middle of the night over there?"

"Sort of," she replied. "But my sleep schedule is still all mixed up. And anyway, I have a lot on my mind. So, I thought I'd call because I know it's not quite your bedtime yet, or is it, old man?" she teased.

"Not quite," he said, remembering how she'd called him an "old soul" when they were dating. "What's up?"

"I was wondering if you could maybe slip by my house and airmail me a box with some of my things? I'll Venmo you whatever that costs, but I underestimated the dampness here."

"Yeah, I can go and maybe get it shipped out for you tomorrow or Friday. How's that?"

"I hate to ask it of you, but there's nobody else around that I trust like you and certainly nobody I'd give the security codes to my house to. And you already know them."

"OK, could you just text your list to me?"

"Sure. I'll create a checklist note and share it with you. Then I can describe locations as well as items and build the list as I think of things today. I've had to buy a few things here. I love that I can replace my Burberry trench coat with one directly from London."

Matthew remembered that her rain coat was one of the items that had been stolen when she was drugged and stuffed in the frunk, or front trunk, of her Porsche 911 the month before. Cecelia Patterson was tiny and stood about five-foot nothing tall but anyone looking into the front trunk of the Porsche had been amazed that she could ever fit in it. Maybe that was due to her personality, though, Matthew had decided she seemed larger than life.

Tiny as she was, Cici was a force to be reckoned with and Matthew had often said that he would never want to be on the other side of a witness stand from her as a witness for her opposing council. She had the reputation for being tougher than nails, and she'd earned it honestly.

"That's great," he said. "I'm glad there's some good coming out of all of this. And that you can see it that way."

"I guess it is all in the perspective, huh?" she said, then abruptly added, "Just one more thing. And it's important. I think I want to sell the Porsche. If I set it up so that you can sell it for me and I tell you where the title is, would you?"

"If you're sure you really want to sell it. I know how much you loved that car when you bought it."

"I did, but it's kind of tainted for me now. Maybe you could find me something else before I come home?" she added hopefully. "Something equally as fun and sporty. Maybe a convertible?"

Laughing, Matthew said, "Sure. Just let me know about the title and how we handle this long distance and I'll do my best to sell it for you."

"You are a prince among men, Matthew!"

"At your service, M'lady," he joked.

They chatted a few more minutes, catching up with each other, and as they were saying their goodbyes, Cici added, "And Matthew? Thank you! I really do appreciate your help."

"You're welcome," he said, and there was a moment's pause of awkwardness before they ended the call. He knew she had no family anywhere nearby, with her divorced parents still living in the Boston area where she'd grown up. Her college friends had scattered to the high winds, so he understood why he was her go-to person.

Checking his text messages, Matthew saw that the first one was from Justin to a group of friends, including James and Alex. Justin was coming quickly through town and he was asking if the guys were free for dinner

Friday night at Sonny's Place, a bar and grille in downtown Raleigh. It was their usual place to meet and it was owned by another friend, Derrick, who had grown up with them.

Nobody was sure exactly what Justin did for a living but Matthew, more seriously than ever after Justin had been instrumental in rescuing Cici from abductors the month before, thought that it was likely one of the federal alphabet soup agencies. His best guess, if anyone had pressed him for one, would have been the CIA because Justin traveled to unknown locations frequently and stopped in for a sporadic evening now and again. Justin had been in the military, so it was also possible that he was still working for some specialized unit. His friends knew better than to ask him too many questions that he wouldn't answer anyway.

In a second message sent just to Matthew, Justin was also asking if his guest room was free for the night. The "Paine Inn," he'd called it, referencing the name given to Matthew's parents' house where he'd grown up, the door of which always seemed to be open to anyone needing a place to stay for a while. He'd grown up with au pairs and exchange students from various locations around the world, troubled friends of both his and his sister Monica's, and various friends and relatives just stopping in on the way through, staying in the guest suite.

Answering the group chat first, affirmatively, Matthew then singly answered Justin, texting, "*You have to ask? You know the 'Paine Inn' is always open for you.*" Justin would come in for a night, usually, but never longer, and he'd be gone before Matthew got up in the morning, regardless of the time they went to bed or how early Matthew got up.

Happy to manage an early bedtime, Matthew went through his evening routine of locking up and laying out and preparing for the morning and then climbed into bed, opting to forgo the book and just welcome the sleepy feeling as it washed over him.

7. Just some facts

The alarm went off on Thursday morning and Matthew awoke feeling refreshed after a solid night of sleep. He spied a lovely May morning through the slats in his blinds. Feeling hopeful, he spent a few moments scratching Max under the chin before he hauled himself out of bed, opened the blinds to embrace the day, and trundled down the hallway to the kitchen to get his coffee and begin his morning routine.

After his long hot shower, Matthew cooked and ate his egg and toast breakfast, filled Max's food and water bowls, and remembered to fill a travel mug of coffee for himself. Heading out, he locked up behind him.

The drive into work and then getting settled into the office was uneventful enough that Matthew had already seen several patients when he saw an incoming call from Danbury.

"Hey, Doc," said Danbury as Matthew quickly answered his cell from the hallway between patients. "You still on for coffee at ten? To talk to the waitress. Mallory?"

"Yeah, I should be free in about forty-five minutes. I've got two more patients to see, one of whom was actually scheduled. But I'll see you around ten."

*****

Disappointed after grabbing a quick cup of coffee with Danbury and a chat with Mallory, who couldn't add any new information, Matthew had returned to the office and worked through a deluge of patients. Mallory had nothing new to add about Allan Lingle's visit Monday night, other than verifying the timeline again and flirting overtly with both men.

Nearing the end of a busier afternoon than he'd have thought possible in the spring, Matthew had wanted to finish up early to get caught up on patient charting. He was surprised to see a call from Danbury. Skipping the formalities as Danbury often did, Matthew answered with, "Let me guess. You have a favor to ask and it isn't medically related."

"How'd you know?" Danbury asked, guardedly, and sounding a bit dejected, as if that were possible, thought Matthew.

"Just a guess," Matthew laughed. "It's fine. I've got one more patient before I'll be finished for the day. Tell me what you need."

"I've got Marcus and Micah here. At the Peak Police Station. Libby thinks they're withholding something too. She'd been trying to coax it out of them. All week. She asked for a junior 'scared straight' program. To get them to talk. But it backfired. We've tried everything. Including a pretty female officer. But they clammed up. They talked to you Monday night. Think you could get them to do it again?"

Sighing heavily, Matthew answered, "I can try. Dr. Rob is the one who's so great with the kids in the office, but he's already gone for the day. My only real experience dealing with kids is with my four-year-old niece, Angel, and I don't do the funny cartoon voices or magic tricks like Dr. Rob." Checking his watch, Matthew added, "I should be done, at least with patients, in about 20 more minutes. I'll walk over then, if that's OK?"

"Thanks, Doc. I guess I owe you one."

"Or a few," Matthew joked. "Actually, I think I still owe you a few for your help with Cici's abduction last month. See you in a half hour or so."

Arriving at the Peak Police Station twenty-five minutes later, Matthew was ushered by a uniformed officer into an interrogation room where Libby and her boys were seated around a table. Libby rose to greet him and turned him out into the hall, pulling him aside conspiratorially. She looked worried.

"Thanks for coming, Dr. Paine. I'm pretty sure my boys are hiding something about Monday night that they won't tell me about," she said. "They're good boys, mostly, but Micah can be a mischievous ringleader sometimes. He instigates pranks and Marcus just follows his big brother. I think the scared straight tactic worked a little too well and they're not saying anything at all now."

She paused for a moment, but Matthew could tell she wasn't finished voicing her thoughts, so he waited her out until she continued, "I just have this feeling," she said, and hesitated. "I think they know something, or did something, or saw something," she said, haltingly. "I'm not sure. I know my kids and something's not adding up. If it were just the murder that was bothering them, I think they'd talk to me about that. But there's something else. And did you know that Jacob Wheatly hasn't spoken a word since Monday night? Sherri is worried sick. She had him in your office Tuesday."

"I did know that. Dr. Rob checked Jacob over pretty well, but he found nothing physically wrong with him."

"Maybe my boys can help. If you can get them to tell you what they know."

"And you think I can coax it out of them?"

"I'm not sure, but Warren thinks you can and Wayne won't even try. He's no help at all. He just says, 'boys will be boys.' He encourages some of their bad behavior sometimes," she added, woefully. "Like bullying. Micah has a tendency to bully and Wayne undermines my attempts to get through to him, to get him to stop. Anyway, if Warren thinks you can help, that's good enough for me."

"Well, all I can say is I'll give it a go," said Matthew, thinking that Danbury's confidence in him was high praise and very surprising. He seemed to be full of surprises this week. "Anything else I should know?"

"That's it."

"OK, it sounds like they've had the 'bad cop' treatment," said Matthew pondering his options and wondering what Dr. Rob would do. "What do you say to changing venues? Maybe we go to the soda shop and I talk to them there? It's not at all threatening, and maybe we offer a bit of a bribe instead of a threat? Do they like root beer floats?"

Libby nodded, and just then, Danbury rounded the corner, "Oh, good. You're here."

"Yeah, we were just talking about a change of scenery, taking them over to the soda shop, maybe bribing them with a treat to try to get something out of them," said Libby.

"And maybe if we separate them, I could talk to them one at a time. Maybe starting with Marcus." added Matthew.

"Yeah, that's fine," agreed Libby. "Whatever you think might work."

"Good," said Mathew. "I didn't manage to have lunch and it's already two-thirty. I'm hungry."

Libby laughed, opened the interrogation room door, and said, "Boys, Dr. Paine here wants to take you to the soda shop for root beer floats."

Their eyes opened wide. They looked at each other and back at Matthew, Micah at first suspiciously. Then both boys jumped out of their seats and followed their mother down the hall and out the front door.

"There's only one thing you have to do for your floats," she said, turning to the boys who were following close behind her. "You have to talk to Dr. Paine and answer his questions."

Marcus, the younger of the two, looked wonderingly up at Matthew and then back at his mother as his older brother Micah asked warily, "What kind of questions?"

Trying to establish a connection with the boys, as they walked toward the soda shop, Matthew said, "Maybe I want to know why the sky is blue."

Marcus grinned but Micah still looked wary. "Or maybe I want to hear about your favorite things to do when you're not in school."

"Fishin'," answered Marcus, immediately. "We like to go fishin' with our Paw Paw."

"My dad takes them out on the lake in his little john boat," explained Libby.

"And girls. Do you have a girlfriend?"

Micah screwed up his face in disgust but Marcus blushed furiously.

The bell jingled over the door as they stepped out of the afternoon heat and into the cool soda shop that was mostly deserted. The lunch crowd was long gone and the older residents hadn't yet arrived for dinner. Matthew motioned to a table and said, "Libby, Danbury, Micah, why don't you grab us a booth. Marcus, you can come help me place the order at the counter."

"OK!" piped Marcus.

They placed orders for root beer floats for Libby, Danbury, and the boys while Matthew ordered a cheeseburger with fresh fruit on the side to quiet the rumble in his stomach.

"It sounds like you had an interesting time at the police station today, huh?" he asked Marcus.

"Yeah," he gulped.

"Did it scare you?"

Marcus leaned in and whispered, "Do you know what a 'cessory is?"

Matthew stifled a laugh as he looked into the child's upturned face and huge scared eyes.

"You mean an accessory? I do, but you aren't one," said Matthew calmly.

"How do you know?" asked Marcus.

"Because I saw you Monday night, remember?"

"Yeah, after I tripped over the feet, you put Band-Aids on," he said, holding up his hands for inspection.

"That's right, and that looks much better already," said Matthew. "Your scrapes are healing nicely. But I'm wondering about the rest of you. You'll heal up just fine on the outside, but I think there's something bothering you on the inside."

Marcus just looked down and said nothing.

"If I guess what it is, will you tell me if I'm right?" he asked. The child nodded without looking up.

"You saw something that you know wasn't good but you're afraid to tell anyone."

Reluctantly, Marcus nodded.

"Did you do anything that you think could get you into trouble?"

Marcus fervently shook his head no.

"Did your brother Micah?" Marcus froze. Gently, Matthew reached down under the boy's chin, pulling his face up. "Marcus, if you saw something that somebody else did, normally you'd both get in trouble for it. You for not telling an adult about it and the person who did it for doing it. You understand that, right?"

"Yeah," he answered at last. "I'm a 'cessory."

"Not this time. I know you didn't hurt Allan Lingle. I know that Micah didn't hurt Allan Lingle either. But somebody did and you might have seen something that can help us catch a bad person. So, if I promise you that you're not in trouble for tattling and Micah's not in trouble for whatever prank that he pulled, will you tell me what it was? Would you tell me exactly what you did and what you saw?"

After a moment of hesitation, Marcus asked, "Promise? I'm not in trouble and Micah's not either?" He snuck a look over at his mother, and Matthew looked too, nodding to Libby across the empty room. She smiled, encouragingly, at the child.

"Yes, I promise."

Marcus took a deep breath and sighed, "OK." He paused and Matthew just waited him out. "We went to the Lingle Plantation."

"Monday night?"

Marcus nodded.

"Why?" asked Matthew gently.

"Because it's haunted."

"You went to the house because it's haunted?" Marcus nodded, and Matthew could see the internal struggle in his eyes.

Finally, Marcus looked up and said, "We were gonna tell ghost stories at our sleepover in the treehouse." After a bit more hesitation, he added, "Micah said we were scaredy-cats and sissies if we didn't go with him to the house. He double-dog dared us. We didn't wanna go."

"You and Jacob? You didn't want to go to the house?" asked Matthew thinking that scaredy-cats and sissies were terms he hadn't heard in a long while and didn't realize kids still used them.

Marcus shook his head, "No. It's haunted. It's really, really haunted! Do you think a ghost killed Mr. Lingle?"

Matthew stifled another chuckle and said, very seriously, "No. A person killed Allan Lingle. And we want very much to find that person and put them in jail so that they can't hurt anyone else." That seemed to register with Marcus, so Matthew continued, "When you went up to the house, did you see the feet there then?"

"I don't know if they were there. We didn't go on the sidewalk. We went through the woods from Jacob's house. The haunted woods. Micah said we had to. It was so scary. He said he'd tell us a ghost story about the woods later if we went through 'em."

"When you got to the house, you came in through the woods from the side?"

Marcus nodded.

"And then what did you do?"

"We went around the house and hid behind that big old scary tree in front."

"Did you see anyone when you were at the house?"

"No, but we knew the ghost was there. And maybe people."

"How did you know?"

" 'Cause we heard it."

"The ghost?"

"Yeah, it goes, clomp-clomp, clomp-clomp across the front porch. But you can see the porch. There's nobody there. It's a ghost! The house is haunted."

"And that's why you thought people might be there too?"

"No," said Marcus, earnestly trying to make Matthew understand. "That was the ghost!"

"OK. There weren't any people at the Lingle Plantation? Just the ghost?"

"No, there were people."

"How do you know?"

"The curtains moved in the window. There was a light on inside, so we could see when the curtains moved. We were sure it was a ghost, but then we heard somebody. And it wasn't moaning and rattling chains, either!"

"Tell me what happened. What did you hear?"

"Somebody yelled."

"Yelled? Or screamed?"

"Yelled."

"Was it a man, or a woman? Could you tell?"

"It was a man, or maybe more men."

"Do you know what they were yelling about?"

Marcus nodded.

"Could you hear what they said?"

Marcus nodded, "They said bad words. I'm not allowed to say them."

"Were they yelling at each other?"

"No," he hesitated. Four root beer floats appeared on the counter but Marcus didn't look up. Matthew looked across the soda shop and held up a hand to tell Libby and Danbury to wait a moment. Micah looked annoyed and slightly concerned.

"Do you know what they were yelling about?" asked Matthew.

Marcus nodded.

"Will you tell me?"

"They yelled at us."

"They saw you?"

Marcus shrugged, "I dunno."

"Then why do you think they were yelling at you?"

"Because Micah," he hesitated, then tried again, "Micah said that old house didn't scare him!"

"And then what happened?"

"Micah picked up a rock, a big rock . . . ."

"And threw it through the window?" Matthew asked.

Marcus turned soulful tearful eyes to Matthew and nodded.

"It's OK, it's OK, you didn't hurt Mr. Lingle. If you can help us catch whoever did, you'll be heroes, not the bad guys."

Marcus looked up hopefully, "Really?"

"Really. Did you see them?"

"No," said Marcus shaking his head. "We didn't know people were in there until the curtains moved and then they yelled."

"And you don't know if they saw you?"

"No. When we heard them yelling, we ran. We ran so fast! I heard the door open. I think it was the one on the side, but we just ran. Down the driveway, SO fast, and then down the sidewalk."

Just then Micah approached, looking very concerned.

"It's OK, Micah, you're not in trouble," soothed Matthew.

"We could be heroes," added Marcus.

Skipping the bit about the rock throwing and the window breaking, Matthew asked Micah, "After you heard the men yelling from the house, you all ran, right?"

"Yeah," said Micah. "We ran. We all ran. We ran like the Flash."

Matthew thought Micah might be taking this hero thing a little too seriously and covered a grin as he asked, "And Jacob ran with you?"

"Yeah," said Micah. "But I ran the fastest."

"You saw him? Jacob was with you the whole time?" asked Matthew, as he formulated a theory as to why the child wasn't talking.

Marcus screwed up his face and finally answered. "I guess not at first."

Micah looked at him, surprised, "What do you mean he wasn't with us?"

"I saw him running to catch up when I fell. When I tripped over the feet."

"He wasn't with you then?" asked Matthew, trying to get a complete timeline of events.

"He came running behind us," answered Marcus. "And he looked really scared, like he'd seen the biggest 'ole scariest ghost. He was shaking all over."

"And then what happened?"

"And then Micah looked in the bushes and said the feet were real and we started yelling."

"This is important so try your best to remember exactly what happened, OK?" Matthew asked as he was beginning to get an idea about why Jacob was more traumatized by the ordeal than the McVane brothers.

Both boys nodded, looking serious.

"You're sure that Jacob wasn't with you until after you fell? Was Jacob shaking BEFORE you saw that the feet were real?" asked Matthew.

"Yeah, I remember. He wasn't with us until after I fell," said Marcus. "And then when he caught up, he was shaking all over."

"That's good, boys, that's very helpful. You might help us to catch some very bad people. Is there anything else you can think of? Did you see anyone when you first got to the house?"

Both boys seemed to consider the question for a moment and then shook their heads no.

"It was scary dark," said Marcus. "And spooky."

"It was not! I wasn't scared," said Micah, unconvincingly.

"What about outside the house? Was there a car? Or a bike or anything that you noticed?" he asked, trying not to lead their recollections overly much.

"Yeah, there were cars," offered Marcus.

"Two of them," added Micah, helpfully. "But I think one wasn't a car."

"How do you mean?"

"I think the one closest to the woods behind the house was a Jeep, but the other one was in front of it, so I'm not sure."

"What did the other one look like? The one you saw in front of the Jeep?"

"It was just a car," answered Micah.

"It was green," added Marcus.

"It was not, it was blue!" contradicted his brother, seeming to want to reclaim his job as the primary spokesperson.

"A light green or blue car? Or dark green or blue?" prompted Matthew. "Did it look like any cars you've seen around town?"

"Dark," said Marcus.

"It looked like lots of cars around town," answered Micah. "Jacob's

Mom has one. My Mom has one kinda like it, too."

Now that the story was out, Matthew feared that it'd soon be embellished beyond recognition, so he handed each boy two root beer floats and said, "Here, help me take these to the table." He nodded to Danbury as he turned and picked up his cheeseburger and headed for the table.

Resisting the temptation to dig into the cheeseburger immediately, he summarized the conversation he'd had with the boys, emphasizing that he'd promised that they weren't in trouble, and telling the boys that Detective Danbury needed their help and would have more questions to ask them. He asked if they would answer the best they could. They nodded their consent and both had brightened, excited to be part of the hero squad.

Turning to Libby, Matthew asked, "What sort of car do you drive?"

Surprised by the question, she answered, "I have a Lexus ES, why?"

"It's a four-door sedan."

"Yes."

"What does Sherri Wheatly drive, do you know?"

"She has a Honda Accord that's a couple of years old. Why on earth does that matter?"

Turning to Danbury, Matthew answered, "The boys saw a dark-colored sedan behind the Lingle house Monday night in front of Malcolm's Jeep." Then to Libby he added, "The boys described it as looking like lots of cars in town. They said that your car and Jacob's mom's car were similar, so I'm assuming we're looking for a dark-colored sedan."

As Danbury took over the questioning, Matthew finally tore hungrily into his cheeseburger.

The boys verified their story and that they thought they remembered two vehicles parked behind the house when they came through the woods. One, "just a car," matched the description of a sedan when they were questioned more closely about it and the other, Malcolm's missing Jeep. The color of the sedan was a mystery, but they seemed to agree that it was a dark color. Neither recalled having seen the license plate.

Libby headed home with her boys, thanking Matthew for getting to the bottom of it and promising not to punish the boys any more than they already had been, given the scare they'd had, but that she would have a serious talk with Micah. As the group dispersed, Matthew pulled Danbury aside.

"Two things," said Matthew. "First, there were no vehicles at the house when your team checked it out, right?"

"Right."

"How did the vehicles get out from behind the house without anyone seeing them go by on the street? If Craig Hutchins came running immediately when the boys yelled, and none of them saw the cars come out, then where did they go?"

"There's a back entrance. It used to be a service entrance. It was a road to an old lumber mill, years before. It's overgrown. Not easy to traverse. We didn't find tire tracks. It's too dry, with too many pine needles. But growth has been pushed down. And broken along the path. We're pretty sure that's how they got out. And the second thing?" asked Danbury.

"I need to call Dr. Rob," said Matthew. "I think little Jacob saw or experienced something the McVane brothers didn't. If anyone can get that out of him, it'd be Dr. Rob, who has seen him since infancy. All children love him, even when their visits aren't otherwise pleasant ones."

"OK, great idea. Do you need me there?"

"It might hinder him talking to us if he thinks he's in trouble, like the McVane brothers."

"Yeah, OK. Let me know if you learn anything."

"Of course."

They went in opposite directions, Danbury back to the Peak Police Station and Matthew to his office. So much for getting off early to meet the guys at Sonny's Place, he thought, realizing that he still had records to complete online for the final few patients he'd seen, as he poked his cell phone to find and call Dr. Rob.

8. Pouring Out

Matthew had apologized no less than a half dozen times for disturbing Richard Roberts on his way to the coast and his sailboat. Dr. Rob had taken the day off Friday for a long weekend, but when Matthew shared what he'd learned from the McVane brothers, the elder doctor pulled over and prepared to turn around.

"Would you mind calling Sherri Wheatly and tell her what you just told me?" asked Dr. Rob. "See if she wants to bring Jacob in this evening. I can be back by about 5:30 if I turn around now. Or tomorrow morning if that doesn't work."

"Sure. I'll let you know as soon as I can reach her."

"Thanks, Matthew. I've been worried about Jacob for two days now, so I hope we can get him to open up."

Matthew called the number on file in their office and left a message. As he was wondering what to do next, Trina buzzed him and put Sherri through to him on the office line.

"Dr. Paine?" said an out-of-breath voice.

"Yes."

"I'm sorry I didn't pick up. The number was blocked."

"Entirely my fault. I should have called from the office line."

"You said you wanted to talk to me about Jacob?"

"I do," and he proceeded to tell her what he'd learned from the McVane brothers. "So, you see," he concluded. "I think we might be able to reach Jacob once we tell him that we know what happened up to that point, that he's not tattling, he's not in any trouble, and we need to know what he saw or experienced that the other two boys didn't. I think it'll help him to open up and deal with the trauma of it all, and he might be able to help find Allan Lingle's murderer."

"Oh! I hadn't thought of that!"

"Dr. Rob was very concerned about Jacob and he's coming back into the office if you can bring Jacob back to the office in a couple of hours. Say, about 5:30? If that doesn't work, then maybe first thing in the morning?"

"Yes. Absolutely. Thank you so much for wanting to help my son. I'll see you at 5:30."

"That's why we're here," said Matthew as they exchanged pleasantries and disconnected the call.

Having studied Osteopathic Medicine at a small university in North Carolina that was about an hour south of his parents' home in north Raleigh, he believed in treating the whole person, not just the symptoms. He'd explained this holistic approach to many patients but he was thankful never to have had to defend it to Dr. Rob. Richard Roberts had majored in Psychology as an undergraduate and then decided he wanted to go to medical school instead of pursuing a PhD. Specializing in Pediatrics, he well understood how the mental and physical are interconnected.

After calling to tell Dr. Rob that Jacob was coming in at 5:30, Matthew went back to his patient records and was nearly finished when he heard Dr. Rob's voice in the hallway.

"Where is everybody?" Dr. Rob called out. "It looks more like a Friday afternoon in here than a Thursday."

Matthew laughed and called back, "And not during cold and flu season! In my office. I'm just finishing up some patient records."

As he logged out of the EPIC medical record system, where all of their patient records were stored electronically online, and checked his watch to see that it was 5:10, Dr. Rob appeared in his doorway.

As Matthew opened his mouth, Dr. Rob held up a hand. "Don't," he said. "He's my patient, and I'd rather be here trying to help him than out sailing on the sound."

Matthew just grinned in response. He had been about to apologize, yet again, for dragging Dr. Rob back from his sailing trip.

"Tell me what you know," said Dr. Rob, pulling up a chair opposite Matthew. "Tell me exactly what the other two boys told you about Monday evening so that I have all of the background."

Matthew explained everything from the boys leaving Jacob's house for the sleepover at the McVane boys' house and the detour they took through the woods surrounding the house to their discovery of the body and Jacob running up afterward.

"I think you're onto something," said Dr. Rob. "Jacob must have seen or heard something that the other two didn't. I hope we can pull it out of him and get him talking again."

*****

By 5:45, Matthew and Dr. Rob were both out of ideas for getting Jacob to talk. Matthew was amazed to see the great Dr. Rob not getting through to a pediatric patient. He also saw the look of frustration and deep concern in Dr. Rob's eyes.

"You know what, Jacob?" Matthew said, trying one last time. "Your friends, Marcus and Micah talked to me this afternoon at the soda shop and we got root beer floats. Do you like root beer floats?"

Jacob turned huge soulful eyes up to Matthew and nodded, barely perceptibly. Dr. Rob was jubilant to have gotten that much out of him and responded excitedly, in one of his best cartoon voices, "Well, by golly, let's go get some root beer floats!"

"Is that OK with you?" Matthew asked Sherri, belatedly.

"Absolutely!" she said. "I've fixed some of his favorite foods this week but he hasn't eaten much. I don't think I can take another night with macaroni and cheese or mashed potatoes. C'mon, Sweetheart," she said to Jacob, taking his hand. "Let's go get a root beer float."

The bell over the door jingled as they trooped in to Peak Eats and Matthew pointed at stools at the soda counter, "How about up there?" he asked.

Jacob released his mother's hand and climbed onto a stool, spinning around a couple of times before facing the counter. Matthew ordered the root beer float and then pulled up a chair, giving the stools on either side of Jacob to Dr. Rob and Sherri.

"We were sitting right here this afternoon," he said to Jacob. "When Marcus and Micah told me about going to the old Lingle Plantation and running away when they heard voices yelling. Did you hear the voices too?"

Jacob had spun to face Matthew, looking terrified, but he nodded slightly.

Sherri leaned in, hopefully, and encouraged him, "I'm so sorry that they scared you," she said.

The fear in Jacob's face was palpable. He was clearly terrified of something. Sherri rubbed his back and Matthew continued, "Marcus said you weren't with them when they ran, that you ran up after he'd tripped and fallen on the sidewalk. Did you see or hear something that they didn't?"

Again there was just the trace of a head nod and the abject fear in the boy's face. Dr. Rob, watching this process, perceptibly hung back a bit and let Matthew take the lead.

"And whatever you saw or heard really scared you, didn't it?" asked Matthew.

Jacob's head bobbed, more noticeably, in agreement.

"Marcus said there were men yelling, and he thought they were yelling at you boys. Were they?"

Again, the head bobbed in response. Sherri seemed to be holding her breath as Matthew continued, "Could you hear and understand what they said?"

Jacob froze, initially, and then tears started down his cheeks as he nodded again.

"Was it what they said that scared you?"

Jacob vehemently shook his head no.

"Something else happened?"

Just then, at the counter behind them, Frank was pouring root beer over vanilla ice cream in a large glass at the counter and the hiss and fizz caught Jacob's attention momentarily. He turned to see the float and then began to cry, shaking violently, as Sherri held him to comfort him.

Frank muttered something under his breath about never having seen that reaction to a root beer float before and slipped discretely away from the counter to give them their privacy. It was very early for the Friday night teenagers to appear, but two tables across the room had senior citizens seated, awaiting their dinner. Otherwise, the little soda shop and diner was deserted.

"Jacob, can you tell us what scared you so badly?" asked Sherri, as her voice broke on a sob for her son.

"Tttttthhhey," he choked out hoarsely, and then began sobbing again.

Waiting him out for a few moments, Matthew then calmly leaned in and said, "They who? Marcus and Micah?"

Jacob shook his head no.

"The men who were yelling?"

Jacob vehemently nodded as the tears still poured down his reddened face and he choked on a sob. Dr. Rob reached behind him, retrieving a glass of water and put the straw under Jacob's chin, "Need a sip?" he asked.

Obediently, Jacob sipped, and seemed to recover slightly.

Matthew looked up at Sherri, who nodded her consent, and then back at Jacob, "The men who were yelling, did you see them?"

Jacob nodded again.

"How many men did you see?"

Jacob held up two fingers without looking up.

"There were two men at the Lingle house and you saw them?"

Jacob nodded his agreement.

"Did you know them? Have you ever seen them before?"

Jacob shook his head no.

"Would you know who they were if you saw them again?"

Jacob nodded, his face registering terror. The tears streamed as he buried his face in his mother's shoulder and she wrapped her arms around him.

Undeterred, Matthew decided to take a familiar approach. "You know, Jacob," he said, "Marcus and Micah were really excited to tell me what happened after they found out that they would be heroes if they helped us to catch some really bad people. If we can catch them, they could go to jail. If they have hurt anyone, it would be for a really long time. You'd be grown with a family of your own before they got out."

At this, Jacob looked up hopefully.

"Rrrrreally?" he managed to choke out.

"Really," said Matthew.

"Can you tell me what happened after Marcus and Micah ran away? Why didn't you run with them?"

"I wwwas scccared," said Jacob.

"Too scared to run?"

Jacob nodded.

"Can you tell me what you saw? Two men, right?"

Jacob nodded.

"Marcus thought they came out of the side door of the Lingle house. Did they?"

Again, Jacob nodded.

"And then what happened? Did they see you?"

Jacob nodded, turning a peculiar shade of white.

"I rrrran," said Jacob.

"When the two men came out of the house and saw you, you ran?"

"Yyyyyyes."

"And that was it? You caught up with Marcus and Micah then?"

"Nnnoooo," Jacob's whole body seemed to tense.

"Something else happened?"

Jacob nodded and, once again, Matthew waited until the child's breathing had slowed and he was regaining control.

"Can you tell me what else happened?"

Jacob looked up and it was as if a dam had burst. He started talking faster than Matthew was initially prepared to listen.

"I was running but my feet were off the ground and I was kicking and trying to scream but I couldn't because the big man picked me up and he was squeezing me really tight, and I kept kicking and trying to run and he squeezed tighter but then the other man yelled and said, 'Put him down. Let's go,' and the man holding and squeezing me said, all mean like, 'Don't tell nobody, or we'll be back,' and then I fell, but then I got up and ran as fast as I could. I ran to catch up with Marcus and Micah, and then there were feet, and a body, a dead body, and the Lingle Plantation is haunted! There are ghosts on the porch, you can hear 'em and see them moving things around."

Matthew could see Sherri hovering, as if she wanted to console her son but knew that he needed to talk and get it all out.

Trying to make sense of the jumble that had just come pouring out of the child, Matthew said gently, "It's going to be OK, Jacob. We'll protect you. Can you be a hero too and tell my friend Warren Danbury what you just told me?"

Jacob nodded, and kept repeating the same story over and over and over as if it were cleansing to finally get it all out, while Matthew asked Dr. Rob to record it on his phone and he called Danbury.

Danbury arrived quickly from the Peak Police Station and Jacob was much calmer as he went through the whole story again. While Danbury was busily getting the story and asking questions, Matthew pulled Sherri aside and quietly asked about their security system.

"We don't have one," she replied. "We don't even lock the doors half the time. The kids run in and out of each other's houses when they're out of school. I guess that's a bit naive of me, isn't it? To think that Peak hasn't changed since I was a girl and we don't need to lock our doors."

"It's not that," said Matthew. "It's more about making Jacob *feel* safe. Could you install a security system? Even if you turn it off and never use it again after this is all resolved?"

"Absolutely. It sounds like we need to install it and keep using it," she nodded sadly.

"Danbury can recommend someone, and I'm sure he'll have patrol cars cruising through regularly, particularly at times that Jacob can see them. I'm betting he'll want a sketch artist to work with Jacob to get an idea of what these goons look like, so a tour of the police station might also be a good idea. We can introduce Jacob to all of the nice police officers who are there to 'serve and protect' him."

"Great idea," she said. "I am a bit worried about our actual safety. I'm a single Mom, so it's just Jacob and me, but as you say, I'm really more concerned about Jacob's perception of it. I've been working from home this week and I can continue to do that for a while longer."

"We'll see what Danbury has to say but my guess is that these guys either found whatever they were looking for and they're long gone, or they didn't find it and figured it isn't here to be found. I just wish we knew what that was."

"I've wondered that too, because Allan Lingle? Come on. That guy wouldn't hurt anything more than a fly and that only if it got in the way of his routine."

"Yeah, that's my perception of him, too," answered Matthew. "And I've learned a lot about him the past couple of days."

Dr. Rob had joined their little huddle and said, "Nicely done, Matthew. You didn't need me at all. You've always complimented my patience with kids, but you've got at least as much as I have, maybe more. You'll make a fine dad someday." He clapped Matthew on the shoulder and then added, a bit sadly, "Kids have to grow up way too fast these days, when they should be able to run and play and just be kids. I'm afraid Jacob here has grown up 10 years this week," he trailed off. Then he added, "I'll update his medical record online, so don't worry about that."

"Thanks," said Matthew, warmly. "For the record update, but more so for the compliment. I hope I'll be a great dad someday." That was surely his intention.

Turning to Sherri, Dr. Rob said, "It would be very normal for him to get scared again, to relive the traumatic experience, particularly at night. He might have nightmares, but just keep reassuring him that he's safe and let me know if anything else develops, or if you need anything else?"

Sherri nodded, thanking Dr. Rob profusely for coming back to talk to Jacob. Dr. Rob told Matthew that he'd leave for the coast again in the morning but to contact him anytime by cell if he needed anything else.

Then he slipped out to go update the patient record.

Danbury turned to the two of them and asked Sherri if it was OK to make a trip over to the police station to talk some more and to get an artist to try to sketch the faces that only Jacob had seen, "It's a long shot," he said. "But he has an impression. And that's more than we have now. I'm afraid it'll take a while. We can get him some dinner, to go. Is a cheeseburger, OK?"

Sherri nodded.

Matthew said, "Sherri, is there any place you could go for the night? Do you have relatives in town or nearby? And Danbury, can you recommend a security company? Sherri doesn't have any on her house currently, and the most important thing right now is making Jacob feel safe."

Danbury nodded, and said, "Yeah. Let me make a call."

Sherri said, "My sister lives on the other side of Raleigh, up in Ridge Woods. I'm sure we can go stay with her for a couple of days while the security system is going in. That's a good idea, to give Jacob a change of scenery. She'll spoil him rotten anyway. She's always been career-minded, divorced, with no kids, but she adores him."

Just then, Frank came back to the counter and said, "Let me start over on this root beer float. This one has already drifted too far."

"Can we get it to go?" asked Danbury. "And a cheeseburger with fries?"

"Sure, no problem. Anything for our young heroes," answered Frank, winking at Jacob and having apparently heard more of the conversation than he appeared to have heard.

"Do you need me at the station?" asked Matthew.

"I have no idea," answered Danbury. "Are you OK to be on call? If we need you tonight? These kids really open up to you. I hope you're planning on some of your own."

Matthew nodded. "Hopefully so," he answered, addressing that issue for the second time that afternoon and suddenly having an overwhelming urge to hug his little niece, Angelina. Usually called Angel, she had adopted Matthew as "her person" after he had helped to care for her as a tiny premature infant when his sister Monica was recovering from a very early and difficult delivery.

He shook hands with Jacob, saying, “Thank you for helping the police to identify and find the bad guys. Do you think you can help a Police Officer sketch what they looked like?”

“Yeah,” said Jacob, nodding. “The big one had scary eyes.”

“Scary eyes?” asked Sherri.

“Yeah, scary eyes. Really angry scary eyes.”

“Nice job dealing with some really scary stuff,” said Matthew. “Maybe they’ll give you a badge as an honorary Sheriff’s deputy,” he said more loudly, so that Danbury could hear him and noted Danbury’s nod at the request.

Jacob stood on the rung of the stool he’d been sitting on in front of the counter and saluted Matthew. Amused and wondering where the kid had learned that, Matthew said his goodbyes and headed back to his office to pack up and head for home.

On the way, he called his sister Monica. “Hey, Sis. Does Angel have plans for Sunday afternoon after church?”

“No, nothing much going on here after lunch. Why?”

“Think she might want to come and hang out with Max and me for the afternoon?”

“I’m sure she’d love it. Do you want to take her with you after the family lunch?”

“That’d be great. Oh, and bring her a change of clothes, would you? I need to wash my cars, and I figure all kids like playing with water hoses on hot days, right?”

Monica laughed, “This one does, for sure. What time do you want me to come get her?”

“I can bring her back by dinner time, if that works for you. How’s that?”

“That sounds great. I can’t wait to tell her. She’ll be so excited. Would you like to stay for dinner?”

“Sounds good.”

“OK, see you then.”

"Thanks, Sis. See you Sunday."

Clicking to disconnect the call, Matthew knew that he'd just ensured that his Sunday afternoon would be anything but calm and peaceful but somehow he welcomed the chaos and definitely the company. He adored his little niece almost, he thought, like he would his own daughter. But then, that was the closest he had to a comparison.

He had considered going by Cici's house to get the things she'd listed on the checklist of the note she'd shared with him, but the list seemed to still be growing and he was pretty tired so he went straight home instead.

9. In your dreams

Sinking soundly to sleep easily enough after the busy day on Thursday, Matthew was awakened by a very vivid dream. Rolling over, he saw that it was 3:40 AM Friday morning. He was both relieved that he could go back to sleep for a couple of hours and troubled by the dream. It had seemed so real.

In the dream, he had been running from someone and, looking back over his shoulder, he realized that it was Cordelia Drewer, his nosy neighbor, who was chasing him. As he lay there remembering it, he knew that it was a call to action and he didn't like it at all. Trying and failing repeatedly to get away from Ms. Drewer in the dream, he was suddenly stopped cold in his tracks when he clearly heard a deep and powerful voice say, "Stop. She's lonely."

"What?" he'd asked the voice in the dream. "She's into everybody else's business continually. How could she possibly be lonely?"

"Because she's lonely," said the deep and haunting voice again. That's what had awakened Matthew. The voice, the understanding, and the feeling that he was supposed to do something about that. Trying to shake it all off and go back to sleep, he tossed and turned restlessly until his phone went off at six in the morning, a half hour before the alarm he'd set.

Answering it groggily and a bit grumpily, he heard Cici's chipper, "Good morning, Sleepyhead. Happy Friday," on the other end. "I woke you again, didn't I? Would it help if I said I was sorry?"

"Not much," he grumbled, thinking that it was something she hadn't said very often near the end of their relationship. Then he quickly added, "It's OK, Cees," reverting to the name he'd called her when they were dating. "I just didn't sleep well last night."

She was talking to him more regularly from across the Atlantic Ocean than she had when she was living just a few small towns over from him, he thought.

"Oh! I am sorry for waking you. And I understand," she commiserated. "I don't think I've slept well since I got here."

"I haven't been by your house yet to get the things you want, but I'm having dinner tonight with the guys in Raleigh so I thought I'd go by beforehand and pick it all up then."

"No rush. I've been adding to the list."

Chuckling, he responded, "I noticed, which is the other reason I haven't been yet. Are you finished with the list now?"

"I suppose so. I added the title to the car to the list this morning and told you where to find it and how to open my safe. You'll need that, though, so don't mail it. I've decided that I definitely want to sell it. I'll send instructions to my law firm so that they can handle the transaction allowing you to sign for me when you're ready to sell it."

"OK. If you're sure."

"I'm sure. And finding another one could actually be exciting, you know?"

Matthew just smiled at her excitement. She knew he was a bit of a motor head so he asked her some questions about what features were most important to her and made mental notes. He had a few ideas for her but he thought he'd look around a bit and check prices before he told her about them.

After they'd disconnected, he lay there a few moments scratching Max between the ears and under his chin and then said aloud, "Cordelia Drewer is lonely, huh? Well, so am I," he admitted, acknowledging the empty feeling in the pit of his stomach, that wasn't just hunger. He wasn't sure what their status had been when Cici left, but he didn't like missing her and he wished that he didn't. He had gotten on with his life once without her in it, when they'd broken up the year before, and he could do it again.

With that resolve, he said to Max, "OK, Bud, it'll be another 15 minutes before the coffee maker starts so I guess I could go start it myself. If only I could train you to make coffee." Luminous green eyes stared sagely back at him, as if the big cat understood exactly what Matthew was saying.

After starting the coffee maker, Matthew steamed up the bathroom with his hot shower and climbed thankfully into it, hoping that it'd help wake him up and soak out the cobwebs which felt like they were clogging his brain. If that didn't do it, there was a half a pot of coffee waiting in the kitchen when he was finished, he thought.

Taking his time with his usual morning routine, he pulled out his computer to see what was going on in the world. He checked the Raleigh paper to see if anything new was being reported on the murder and he quickly saw the article that his parents had seen but there wasn't any update. Curious, he realized that he'd done a lot of helping out over the week but hadn't gotten an actual update on the bigger picture, so he decided to call Danbury.

"Danbury here."

"Hey, it's Matthew."

"Hey, Doc. What's up?"

Matthew laughed, "At least you didn't say, 'What's up, Doc?'" He wasn't positive but he thought he heard a chuckle on the other end. "I was just reading about the investigation and wondering how things are really going. We did a lot of questioning yesterday but I was just wondering if you got anywhere with the sketch artist and Jacob's description, if Malcolm had been located yet, if you'd gotten anywhere with Wayne Adams or learned anything new from the Lingle Plantation?"

"Whoa, Doc, one at a time," chuckled Danbury. "I was gonna call you later. The sketch was completed. From Jacob's description. Both guys look dark. Like Latino or Italian. But maybe it was just dark out. So maybe not all that helpful. Wayne Adams hasn't been at all helpful either. He answers what I ask. Mostly. But he isn't volunteering anything. And still no line on Malcolm."

"He is a lawyer. That's how they work. Anyway, thanks for the update."

"Sure, Doc. I've gotta run. Lots of leads now to chase down."

“OK, later.”

After feeding Max and himself, Matthew headed out to the garage with his satchel and travel mug of coffee, locking up and setting the alarm behind himself. Noticing again that his black Corvette was an alarming shade of green with the North Carolina pollen season, he decided to quickly spray it off. He opened the garage door, started the corvette, and backed it out.

Pulling the hose around from the side of the house, he rinsed his car carefully, determining to wash it more thoroughly over the weekend. Rolling the hose back up, he turned the water off and crawled back in his car, looking around as he pulled out. Relieved not to see Ms. Drewer out for her morning walk with Oscar, Matthew happily drove as quietly as possible out of his neighborhood. Despite his disturbing dream, he had a feeling that the day wouldn’t be boring, and he didn’t care to discuss any of it with Ms. Drewer. She, however, would feel differently. Of that, he was certain.

*****

Matthew was nearly through his first patients for the morning, and he was busily writing an antibiotic prescription for an elderly man with a serious infection that had developed from an ingrown toenail. When his cell phone went off, he surreptitiously checked it from his pocket. Seeing that it was Danbury, he figured he’d call him back when he was finished with this patient.

Stepping into the alcove between patient rooms, he returned the call and Danbury said, “Hey, Doc. We have another body.”

“Another body?” asked Matthew. “Whose? Where?”

“A male. Down a dirt road. In McGill’s Crossroads. Over in Joseph County. Hastily covered. In leaves and brush. A farmer’s dog found it. In the edge of some woods. It’s fresh. The farmer didn’t see or hear anything. But he doesn’t live near that field.”

“It isn’t Malcolm, is it?”

“The description doesn’t match, so no. It might match one of the guys in the sketches, though. From Jacob’s descriptions. Dark hair, dark eyes, darker skin but not black. So not Malcolm. Big guy, maybe your height but heavier. Late twenties to mid-thirties. That’s all I know now. We’re running his prints. He’ll be brought in for an autopsy. After the scene is cleared. All of that makes finding Malcolm more important. More a person of interest. He has a sealed juvie record."

"Yeah, Penn mentioned that he might. It must have been hard to find a healthcare job with a record," said Matthew. "Maybe that's why he was taking online nursing classes but was happy enough caring for Allan, maybe to get patient hours. But I guess there's no way to know if the juvenile offense was violent."

"Couldn't have been too bad. Or he'd still be locked up. And this expedites our trip. To talk to Amelia. Malcolm's sister. She's been located. By the local guys in Virginia. She's isolated. Off a state road up there in Virginia. Down a dirt path that looks like it goes nowhere. But she's got a cabin. Almost on the water. You still game for an early trip? We could drive up in the morning."

"Sure," Matthew replied and hesitated. "Not that I'm not in, but don't you have a partner for this sort of thing?"

After a prolonged silence, Danbury responded, "Ordinarily, yes."

"So why not now?"

"Because this isn't my case."

"I thought you caught this case and you're investigating the murder."

"No. I was told to stand down. To let the local Peak guys handle it."

"But you aren't doing that?"

"No. I took vacation. I'm on my own time. But they appreciate my help. Here in Peak. They're helping me though to help them."

"Why would you do that?"

Danbury sighed loudly. "I thought Penn Lingle already told you. This is personal to me. I grew up with Allan. He was never going to be a rock star. But he was a good guy. A kind and decent person. And he deserved better than this. He also deserves to have his killer caught."

Thinking that he couldn't argue with that statement, Matthew agreed to meet Danbury at his office in the morning at 6:30 to drive up and try to catch Amelia at home, preferably by surprise. After they ended the call, Matthew stood in the alcove a few more moments pondering what he'd learned so far. He knew that they were still missing key pieces of information.

The boys, he figured, had given him all of the information that they knew, at least that they had actively observed. He wondered if they'd seen anything else that they hadn't thought to mention. Human cognition is a complicated process, he thought, particularly in children as they assimilate information, the new to the known, to understand the world around them. Could they have noticed subtle differences in ubiquitous items that they hadn't actively attended to, like darkly colored sedans, for example?

Penn Lingle, while she seemed to be quite forthcoming with him and told him her story readily enough, was hiding something. Of that, he was certain. What he didn't have, however, was a solid idea about where in her story the hidden or manipulated portions occurred. She had told him of her childhood and her life since leaving the small town of Peak, and he couldn't pinpoint anything that sounded incomplete or purposefully manipulated.

Stepping out of the alcove and down the hall to his next patient, Matthew still pondered what he knew and what he didn't. Danbury had said that Wayne Adams was cagey about providing details on the investment portfolio for the Lingle estate. Why? What was he hiding?

Shaking the thoughts aside, Matthew slipped into the examining room to see Diane, one of the office nurses, getting patient stats. A young mother was holding a feverish infant and Matthew fervently wished that Dr. Rob hadn't taken a vacation day. Dr. Rob usually handled the children in the practice, sick or well, and Matthew hated having to poke and prod young children to whom you couldn't explain what was happening. "This is to make you feel better," or, "this is to keep you from getting sick," is incomprehensible to a scared child, he thought.

*****

Because his staff usually didn't schedule appointments for Friday afternoons, Matthew was amazed to see that it was already 3:00 when he finished with his last patient. But then, they were one physician short with Dr. Rob on vacation for the day, so he should have been prepared for it, he thought.

He'd done most of his charting over a "Mac's Maximum" sub at lunch, which he now questioned the wisdom of because he was experiencing a little indigestion from it. Deciding that a cup of coffee would fix almost anything, he went up to the break room on the second floor and found

Gladys Gantry, his favorite nurse in the practice, though he'd never admit that out loud, fixing a cup herself. He always marveled at how she managed to get just the right amount of cream in her coffee to perfectly match her lovely dark skin.

"Hi Gladys, you're still here too."

"Yeah, I thought we'd be out of here a couple of hours ago, but we got busy this afternoon, huh?"

"We did. I picked up a couple of children with Dr. Rob gone," he responded as he dumped a heap of sugar and some cream into his cup before pouring in the coffee.

Gladys just shook her head. "You and that sugar," she said.

Changing the subject abruptly, Matthew asked, "How are your girls? And all of the twins?"

Gladys always warmed to that subject and she happily whipped out her phone and showed him recent pictures of all of the grandbabies. Matthew marveled at the pictures of her sitting on the floor, smiling broadly, right in the middle of what looked to him like total chaos.

"I'm done for the day. I was just going to get my things together and head off to see that second set of twins this afternoon. Are you done for the day?" she finally asked.

"Nearly. I have a couple of charts from this afternoon to update and then I'm heading out too. Enjoy those grandkids," he waved as he slipped out of the break room and down the back stairs to his office.

After making the updates and packing his computer in his leather satchel, Matthew quickly pulled up Cici's list of things to ship and where to find them all, deciding to print it because it seemed to have grown exponentially over the past two days. Hanging his lab coat neatly on the coat rack behind the door, Matthew picked up the printed list and his satchel, turned the lights off, and locked up behind him.

Out in the parking lot, Matthew checked his watch and wished that he'd left a good hour earlier. Late Friday afternoon traffic was going to be rough, he knew. He was going by Cici's first and then to meet his friends at Sonny's Place in Raleigh. Slipping into his Corvette, he turned on the air conditioning as the afternoon heat was baking both him and his car. Then, making his way carefully out of town, he headed for Cici's house in Quarry.

10. Raucous Caucus

After spending nearly an hour in Cici's house and finding everything on the list, including the car title in the safe, he packed all but the title carefully in a banker's box that he'd found in her garage and stood looking at her Porsche 911. He'd helped her pick it out and he could clearly remember the radiant smile on her face, so excited was she to be not only buying her first new car but a racy one at that. The three years that had passed in the interim seemed to fade as he reminisced and he felt a deep pang of longing for Cecelia Patterson.

Matthew went back through the house, set the alarms, and carried the box and a large envelope containing the car title out to his car, putting it all in the trunk. Wending his way out of her heavily populated neighborhood in Quarry, he headed for downtown Raleigh to meet his oldest friends.

The drive was less grueling than he'd thought it would be and he arrived at Sonny's Place, Derrick's bar and grill, ahead of his friends. As he settled into a tall chair at one of the high-top tables in the bar area where they usually met, Derrick appeared behind the bar and came out to greet him, "Hey, Matthew! How's it goin,' man?"

"Hey, Derrick," Matthew responded with somewhat less enthusiasm than usual. "It's been a long week, so tell me what local brews you've got on tap and catch me up with you."

Derrick listed the selection and Matthew chose one. "You do look tired," said Derrick. "After that crazy mess you got yourself into last month, I'd have thought you'd be all rested up by now."

"I was and then I wasn't," replied Matthew, telling Derrick about the murder in Peak that week.

"Oh, yeah, I read about that and saw it on the news. Was that guy a patient of yours?"

"Of my practice, yes, but not mine personally. I've been doing a lot more than medical advisement for this investigation though and I'm just tired, that's all. How's your crew?"

Derrick married his high school sweetheart, Rena, while Matthew was in medical school and she had quickly birthed two little girls, less than a year apart.

"We're all good. The girls are still a lot. Rena is thinking about going back to work next year when they're both in school. We'll see. Now tell me about this murder investigation you're working on. How did you get involved in it?"

James and Alex wandered in before he had a chance to answer. Matthew had grown up with them since kindergarten, playing together all through school, and they'd remained friends throughout the years. James, the notorious womanizer, was already scanning the room on the way in and Alex looked almost as tired as Matthew felt. Alex had married Cynthia, who was a friend of Matthew's first. Matthew suspected that at least half of their friend group from their undergraduate years in college had expected that he and Cynthia would pair up. When Cynthia and Alex met, it was obvious who should be with whom, but they'd remained good friends.

"Matthew was just telling me about the murder investigation in Peak," said Derrick after greetings were exchanged and drinks ordered. "That guy who got beaten Monday night. Matthew's helping with the investigation."

"I'm not personally involved in this one like I was before, thankfully," Matthew clarified. "Cici's in London and, as far as I know, nobody is threatening her over on that side of the puddle."

Matthew was relieved to have the questions about his status with Cici, that he knew would be forthcoming but which he didn't want to answer because he had none, interrupted by Justin's arrival. Derrick and Justin exchanged their usual quips, Derrick beginning with, "My man, the secret agent guy who drives a Prius."

To which Justin responded, as usual, "And my man, the guy who opens a bar and grille and names it after somebody else." But then he added, before Derrick could, "I know, I know, it's your Uncle Sonny and he's good people. And it never gets old. Except that it does. It's old man. We need a new routine,"

Laughing, the two men clasped hands and half embraced from the side, clapping each other on the back with their free hands. "How's it going?" asked Derrick.

"All things considered, not too badly," responded Justin. "And with you and all of yours?"

"We're all good, man, all good. What can I get you?"

Without knowing it, Justin ordered the same local beer that Matthew had and the teasing about their parallel lives began, as usual in earnest. "Twins, separated at birth," James declared. "Siamese twins, surgically separated after birth," added Alex and the good-natured teasing about the geeks that both Justin and Matthew had been growing up continued loudly with Alex and James trying to outdo each other.

Finally, Derrick broke up the revelry when he told them about his specials for the evening and sent his "best waiter" over to take their orders. Matthew highly suspected that the "best waiter" Derrick always claimed to be sending their way was really whoever was most available and closest at the time. It hardly mattered, thought Matthew, because Derrick was meticulous in hiring and training all of his staff.

Matthew considered ordering something other than what Justin had chosen, just to avoid more good-natured ribbing, but he decided he'd brave it because the roast beef au jus with garlic mashed potatoes and grilled asparagus sounded too mouth-wateringly wonderful to pass up.

Without missing a beat, James jumped in, "What? Did you call each other last night to plan what you were wearing today too?"

Matthew just shook his head in mock despair and sipped his beer. Alex, thankfully, had burned out on that subject, but Matthew soon wished he hadn't when Alex turned and asked the Cici question. "How's it going with Cici? Did you two kiss and make up? I hear she's in London. Is that true?"

"It's true," replied Matthew. "I think she needed a serious change of scenery after last month and she'll be there for a while, probably a year, maybe longer."

"Wow," said Alex and James in unison. "And now you're hard up, huh, man?" asked James.

Matthew just sipped his beer and chose not to answer that question.

"Are you on again or off again?" persisted Alex.

"We didn't get back together before she left," replied Matthew. "If that's what you're asking. Though I have talked to her pretty regularly since she's been gone. She Facetimes me at ungodly hours of the morning and equally ridiculous hours of the night for her time zone."

"She's keeping tabs on you, huh?" asked James, pointedly.

"Nothing like that," said Matthew. "Though she did ask a few favors and I just came from her place."

"Yeah?" said Alex, clearly interested in Matthew's personal life that he usually talked very little about. "Like what?"

"Well, she sent me a list of things she wanted me to find, box, and ship to her," he said. "Oh, and she wants me to sell her car for her and maybe buy her something else sporty and probably convertible before she comes back."

"She's selling the Porsche?" asked James, incredulous.

"Apparently, she is."

"How much does she want for it? That's one sweet car. She's kept it in pristine shape, hasn't she?"

"I don't know yet," responded Matthew. "I told her I'd research the value, based on the mileage, which I forgot to check while I was over there, and let her know what I thought we could list it for."

"I want dibs!" said James. "Seriously, man. It's in really good shape, isn't it?"

"It is. It's either been in her garage at home or the parking garage at work most of the time. She hasn't taken it on long trips but just that one to Boston to visit her family, so it's got low mileage and everything is still pretty spotless."

"Yeah, let me know what you're going to list it for. Promise to talk to me first, before you list it? Deal?"

"Deal," said Matthew. "She'd probably be happy for you to have it. She really loved that car, but with recent events, it's just a traumatic reminder now, I think."

"Yeah, man, I get it. OK, just let me know."

The conversation had turned suddenly and uncharacteristically serious and the guys didn't seem to know how to handle that for too long at a time, so the good-natured joking began again and continued through the dinner until Alex nervously stood up as the plates were being cleared.

"I have some news," he said quietly, which was also uncharacteristic.

"Tell us!" said James. "Let me guess. You're dying of toe cancer!"

"You'd feel about this big," said Alex, holding up his index finger and thumb to indicate a tiny measure, "if I actually was. But no, it's nothing like that. We found out last month and we aren't really talking about it yet, so you have to keep this under wraps for a while, OK? Cynthia's pregnant. We're expecting."

"Expecting what, man, a lizard?" teased James.

"Wow. How's she going to manage with her job?" asked Matthew. Cynthia had chosen a career in the Emergency Department, one that Matthew admired her for choosing, but he knew he'd never want to trade places with her. "She has the most demanding job of all of us. Well, except maybe for Justin," he teased, trying to lighten his comments.

"We don't have all of that worked out yet," said Alex. "Honestly, I'm still pretty freaked about it. We'd talked about it, but we'd only just started talking about it. I'm gonna be a dad. Can you picture me as a dad?!?!"

Even James refrained from teasing as they could all see the fear in Alex's eyes.

"You'll be a great dad," said Matthew after a moment. "You love Cynthia more than you ever thought possible and you'll love this child like that too."

"But how do you learn to do it?" asked Alex. "I mean, I don't have much of a role model. My dad is a workaholic. He wasn't around much when I was growing up."

Nobody had an answer to that question, so instead, Justin said, “Hey! We need to toast this one!”

“I’ll drink to that!” James called back and the revelry continued, though Matthew could still see the worried look on Alex’s face.

As the evening was winding down, Matthew pulled Alex aside, “Hey man, maybe you could talk to Derrick or Stephano, my sister Monica’s husband. He’s a great dad, but he had to have been scared before Angel was born. I was doing my residency, so I wasn’t around much, but I do remember him being concerned. I can set it up if you want to grab a beer with him sometime. Or sit down and talk to Derrick. He had to figure it out fast.”

“Yeah. I could talk to Stephano, I guess. I’m not sure I want to hear what Derrick would have to say with two so close together like that, but maybe Stephano. Would he talk to me, do you think?”

Matthew nodded, “He would.”

“Let me think about that and I’ll let you know when we’re ready to start telling people. Maybe then would be good. Thanks, Matthew,” said Alex, looking slightly less panicked.

Usually, Matthew and Justin left first, with Alex and James still nursing drinks and laughing at their own bad jokes. Alex, however, was ready to leave with them, so James shrugged in surrender and they all walked out together, having settled their tabs and thanked Derrick for the great food and service.

None of them bothered teasing Justin about his Prius and they were all a bit somber, as if one of them having a baby meant the end of an era. Matthew was amused by their mood and a peppy little song was forming in his head about it, but he said nothing as they parted company and Justin said he’d meet him at home. Matthew had outfitted his second bedroom as an office that doubled as a guest room, mainly for Justin when he passed through. It was rarely ever used as an office because Matthew preferred to work from the little desk in his living room instead.

Matthew checked his watch as he was leaving the parking lot and was slightly chagrinned that it was already 10:30 and they still had to drive back to Peak. He knew Justin would be up and out in the morning before he got up, even though he was meeting Danbury early for their trip to talk to Malcolm’s sister. Pleasantly surprised to realize that he’d gone all evening without thinking much about the murder investigation, Matthew pondered what the next day might bring in terms of potential revelations.

11. Reconnoitering

Saturday morning dawned hazy and warmer than usual for May in North Carolina. Matthew was up before the sun this morning, but Justin had gotten up, showered and gone even earlier without a cup of coffee. How the guy managed to function so incredibly well on so very little sleep and no coffee Matthew had truly never understood.

Rinsing and filling Max's bowls, Matthew then took his mug of coffee back down the hall to properly steam up his bathroom with a hot shower, then shave, and dress for a day of who-knew-what.

Trying to decide between a pair of jeans or shorts the night before, Matthew had opted to wear shorts, a t-shirt, and his leather boat shoes, packing a small gym bag with jeans, long sleeves, and a pair of sturdier shoes. Just in case they had to wander through tall weeds or if he got muddy down by the lake, he'd be prepared. He knew the shores were mostly red mud and he knew all too well that it was pretty easy to come away caked in that shoreline.

As Matthew locked up and slipped out into the garage, he chose to drive the Element, though he was sure Danbury would be driving them up to the lake and on the back roads of Virginia. The neighborhood was still quiet, as he drove sedately. The sun was just coming up over the trees. Matthew hoped that the haze would quickly burn off and the day would brighten.

Pulling into the parking lot of his office a few minutes later, Matthew noticed two other cars in the lot, other than Danbury's. One of them, he assumed, belonged to the cleaning crew and the other looked like Trina's. Danbury wasted no time in a greeting and got straight to the point as usual.

"Hey, Doc. We got an ID this morning. On that body. One Fernando Hernández, 32. Last known address in Miami. He had a record. He's wanted in multiple states. He's likely not the guy who grabbed Jacob Wheatly. Doesn't match the sketch. But it might be the other guy."

"Oh, I meant to ask if you'd seen the sketches from Jacob Wheatly's descriptions of the two guys."

"Yeah. I have copies. On the back seat. Behind the driver's seat. If you want to look. They're in a folder. Jacob got a good look at one of them. The guy who grabbed him. That sketch is pretty distinctive. Very detailed. The other sketch is too generic. Could be anybody. We have the face recognition software running. And the detailed picture circulating. All over Wake County. And Joseph County. And surrounding counties. If he's spotted, I'll get notified."

Matthew opened the back door of the big SUV and pulled the folder out. It contained a copy of a statement from Amelia Freeman. It was nothing more than a confirmation that Malcolm Freeman was her brother, that he was not there, and a less than polite request for the police officers to get off her property.

The next pages in the folder were copies of the sketches. Matthew stared at one of them, transfixed, as the artist's rendering was stark and powerful. Dark eyes and strong features stared back at Matthew from the more detailed sketch on the copied pages.

The guy had thick bushy eyebrows. "The angry eyes," said Matthew. "This must be the guy who grabbed Jacob, the one with the angry eyes. I can see why Jacob thought so. It's his eyebrows. His eyes do look menacing under them. In this rendering, he looks menacing just in general. And you're right, the guy in the other sketch is pretty generic. It could be anybody."

Matthew replaced the sketches in the folder and returned it to the back seat. He reached in his gym bag and pulled out a wad of plastic-coated maps, handing them to Danbury.

"What's that?" asked Danbury.

"More detailed maps of the lake," said Matthew. "It's in several pieces, so be careful when you open it. It's a huge lake, so it doesn't fit on a single sheet. I'm not sure where we need to go, but you can see some of the back roads around the lake there, as well as the lake map with depths and such. Have a look, if you want. I need to check in here a minute," he said motioning to his office building. "Be right back."

"Sure," said Danbury as he was already unfolding the cluster of maps onto the hood of his SUV.

Unlocking the side door to his office, Matthew wandered through with one eyebrow raised questioningly, and called out, "Hello? Who's here? Is everything OK?"

"Up here!" he heard a harried voice answer and he followed it to the front office where he saw Trina perched on a stool with her notebook computer on the counter as her fingers frantically flew over the keys.

"Is everything OK?" he asked again. "No more emergencies, I hope?"

"No clinical or town emergencies, that I know of," she said. "Just a personal one. My internet went out last night and it's not back up yet. I need to get this paper finished and uploaded before noon today for a school deadline, and I can't access my online account from home." Trina was finishing up an MBA from Duke and Matthew knew she usually had night classes and some online, but he hadn't ever seen her so frantic about an assignment.

"Hey, is the cleaning crew here too?" he asked.

"Yeah, they started upstairs about five minutes ago."

"OK, I thought so. Good luck, Trina, with finishing up the paper and getting it submitted on time."

"Thanks, Dr. Paine, I need it!" she said over her shoulder as she continued the desperate pounding on the keyboard. He wondered what else he'd missed on Saturday mornings around the office.

Rejoining Danbury outside, he said, "So where are we going, exactly? You said Virginia, but most of the lake is up there, so that covers a lot of territory."

"Yeah. I just have state road numbers. No actual street names."

"That's not uncommon for rural roads in Virginia," said Matthew. "Sometimes state road numbers are all that there are. Show me where we need to go?"

"Up here. Around the top of the lake," he said pointing. "Just downstream from where the two rivers come together. As they merge into the dammed lake."

"Oh yeah, I've stayed at a camp ground up there. It can be treacherous, sometimes, in a boat up there because whole trees and animals come washing down from those rivers pretty regularly after it rains. You have to know to avoid small underwater islands, too, particularly if the lake level is low."

"There are multiple streets. Here and here." Danbury said, poking at the map. "Maybe neighborhoods. Off the state road here," he added sliding his finger in between. "That is close to the lake. Right there. I don't see roads. Not on this map. Not on any I've looked at. But that's in the right area."

"OK, I know where that is, more or less."

"You ready then?"

"Yeah, let's go," said Matthew, refolding the maps and tossing his bag in the back. "Have you had breakfast yet?" he asked Danbury as he climbed in.

"Sort of."

"Meaning that you can always eat and you wouldn't be at all opposed to stopping at a drive-through for me to get some breakfast?"

"Something like that," Danbury chuckled. "Did you have somewhere in mind?"

"Maybe. We're going up 540 to pick up 147 and then up US 15, right?"

"Yeah, that's what I was planning."

"OK, then yes. There's a Biscuit Town chain that has the best biscuits, breakfast and lunch. They're primarily west of here in the North Carolina piedmont, but there's one north of Durham up the Durham Freeway, up 147 just before it joins I-85." And then Matthew added, jovially, "If you've already eaten then, we should be able to make it that far before stopping for food."

Matthew was pretty sure he saw Danbury roll his eyes, but the comment was still apropos, he thought. They had traveled together the previous month so they each understood the musical listening restrictions of the other; Danbury didn't like Matthew's older rock and Matthew didn't like Danbury's older mournful country. As they headed out of Peak, Danbury turned the stereo to a pop station, which was the favorite of neither, but neither did either of them hate it.

"You spent time at this lake recently?" asked Danbury.

"Yeah, but more as a kid, camping and fishing with my grandfather. I was up there a couple of years ago on the lake with some friends. It's a huge lake, something like 50,000 acres, maybe more, and over 800 miles of shoreline. It's owned by the Army Corp of Engineers so they control the shoreline up to a certain height, and the lake level, which they can control with the dam."

"It's a hydroelectric lake," Matthew continued. "So, controlling the water level is more about that than any recreational pursuits. A full pool, as they call it, is considered to be somewhere around 300 feet and a flood pool is some 20 feet above that. I don't think I've ever been on it when it was above 312 feet. I've heard of catfish the size of Volkswagens being pulled out down near the dam, but you know how fishermen exaggerate. I think there was a 100-pounder pulled out of there not too long ago, though."

"Wow!" said Danbury.

"I know, it's a massive lake, with huge freshwater fish."

"I meant you remembering all of that!"

"Oh. I vaguely remember all of that but it's the history of the area that I know more about."

"Do tell," said Danbury, as he settled in for the drive.

"You really want to know?"

"Yeah. I like history. And you're a history buff, right?"

"Good to know. And yeah, I'm a bit of a history buff."

"Wish I'd paid more attention in school. To history and geography. But I was too busy. Trying to be cool."

Not knowing exactly what to make of that insight, Matthew just chuckled and said, "I haven't been accused of that too much. My friends from childhood still tease me about being a geek. Anyway," he added, "I purposefully didn't bore you with it on the trip to Savanah last month."

"Why not? Hate that I missed that."

"Because I decided years ago to talk about the history of places only if I'm there, if it's in some other way relevant, or only with someone who really wants to know. Otherwise, you might have to pry your eyelids open with toothpicks. And you're driving," added Matthew.

"We have over an hour. Tell me about Walters Lake."

"OK," said Matthew, settling into his seat and taking a breath. "It's the history of the native American Indians that seems to interest people most about Walters Lake. There were multiple tribes in the area, but one of the most loved and celebrated was the Occoneechee because they were traders, not warriors. There's an underwater island about 4 miles long off of the main channel up near where we're going that was their territory. Before the area was dammed up and flooded back in the late 1940s and early 1950s, the island was between the two rivers that ran together there, in that north west corner, which now empty into the top of the lake. The Occoneechee, being centrally located between the rivers, were peaceful traders and their island was a center of commerce until the 1600s. Other tribes, some of them warring, would trade with them from multiple directions. They are reputed to have been peacemakers."

"What happened to them?"

"An Englishman by the name of Bacon invaded, attacked, and decimated them on some trumped-up charges. Some survivors and descendants are said to have moved west and south along a river in the piedmont of North Carolina."

Danbury was momentarily silent as that information sank in.

"Not that I don't enjoy entertaining you with sad Indian stories and other intriguing historical accounts, but don't we need to talk logistics? What were the local police able to tell you from their conversation with Amelia Freeman and how are we going to handle this interview?"

"The local guys weren't able to tell me much. Just what you saw in that report," he said, thumbing over his shoulder to the folder in the back seat. "That was it. She wouldn't talk to them. She claimed her brother wasn't there. She wouldn't answer any more questions. She asked them to get off her property. Technically, it sounds like she's squatting. In an old cabin up there. But they respectfully left. I think they've cruised by, pretty regularly, since then. On the state highway there. But they haven't seen any activity. No Malcolm."

"They were able to verify that the woman living there is Amelia Freeman?"

"I don't know if they IDed her. But she said so."

"How do you want to handle talking to her today?"

"I approach first. Malcolm could be dangerous. If he's there. I don't think so. But let's play it safe. After that, I was hoping you would help. Your Bedside Manner 101 again. I had thought good cop, bad cop. But I'm tired of being the bad cop. And I'm not sure that would work anyway. We need her trust. To help us help her brother. If he's really innocent, she'll want help for him."

"OK, so I hang back until you're sure it's safe, but then what? We have nothing to offer her to get her to trust us, do we?"

"Not much, no," Danbury conceded.

Just then, Danbury's phone went off and he leaned over, picking it up to answer it. After a few noncommittal interjections and several "uh huh" remarks, he thanked someone and put the phone back down.

"Malcolm's Jeep was found. Early this morning. By a farmer. It was in his barn. Near where the body was found. There was a Louisville Slugger. In the front seat. With traces of blood and hair on it. Two types of blood. From initial testing. It's been sent to the lab. For analysis and DNA testing."

"You think that's the murder weapon?"

"Seems likely. And a little notebook with sketches. Probably the one Allan had on him. The night he was murdered. It was tossed in the back. But no Malcolm. Nobody heard anything. But there are no houses nearby. It's isolated out there. Fields and farms, mostly."

"Wow! The bat and the notebook in the Jeep near the body, but no sign of Malcolm, huh? And no other car?"

"No Malcolm. There were tire tracks outside the barn. Lots of them. They weren't from a tractor. And the farmer said they're fresh. So probably another car. At least one more. A few footprints too. But a basic running shoe. Nothing unique."

"Well, maybe you can get something off the bat that'll be helpful.

Maybe definitive DNA or prints. Do you suspect that Malcolm killed Allan Lingle? And maybe the other guy, too?"

"I did somewhat. Before they found the Jeep."

"How does that change things?"

"It doesn't add up. Why would Malcolm Freeman hide his own Jeep? If he'd killed Allan? Leaving it near the second body? He'd have left in it. Gotten as far away as he could. Unless he had another car stashed. That would make it premeditated. It doesn't appear to be. Not in any other way. But then, why would he leave the bat? If it came from the Lingle Plantation. And if it's the murder weapon. Why leave it behind? And the notebook. If he were the killer. Why leave that behind? Why are there two types of blood on the bat? One will likely belong to Allan Lingle. And the other to the body. The one found in the woods yesterday."

"Why would the murderer leave the murder weapon at all? Malcolm or whoever?"

"Good question. Maybe the killer thought it'd be a while. Before it was found. Maybe it was a set up. Leaving it in the Jeep. Made it look like Malcolm is involved. Maybe he is. I just don't think so. From what everybody said about the guy. It doesn't fit. The techs will go over the Jeep. And see if anything was left behind. Prints or DNA."

12. Sister act

Shortly over an hour and a half after leaving Peak, they turned onto State Road 858 from Highway 15 and started scanning for a rusting mailbox barely clinging to a bowed wooden post at the end of a path that looked to go nowhere. Along with the short report from questioning Amelia Freeman, the local police had provided Danbury with a general description of how to find her so that he wouldn't be wandering completely aimlessly.

"There!" pointed Matthew at just such a mailbox that was clinging precariously to a 4-foot tree stump, long ago devoid of bark, and looking like it would come tumbling down at any moment.

Stopping up short, Danbury turned down the pathway. They bumped along for three quarters of a mile down an overgrown path that was overhung with low tree branches from either side and then came to a clearing. A group of indignant chickens scattered in all directions as they pulled up in front of a log cabin that looked to contain two rooms, or three at the most. The clearing continued behind the house and there was a garden, in neatly planted rows, with a makeshift scarecrow guarding his small ward of tiny crops. Matthew could see a glimpse of the lake shimmering through the trees and down the hill beyond.

Squinting in an attempt to figure out what it was, Matthew saw things hanging from the top of the door frame. Brightly colored objects were swaying from cords of differing lengths. Matthew raised an eyebrow in surprise as he said, "Are those painted chicken feet?"

“Yeah. Looks like it,” replied Danbury.

Danbury parked to the left in front of the cabin and got out, stretching his legs after the ride, and Matthew cracked his window to hear whatever was about to transpire. As Danbury approached the two steps up to a narrow porch, a woman parted the hanging charms slowly, with slender hands, and stood under them. She wore long robes of layered brightly colored fabric and had dreadlocks that hung over one shoulder and nearly to her waist, the top layer pulled back and tied in what appeared to be a brightly colored rag at the crown of her head. Her features were wide and symmetrical in a round face, her skin dark. Her Rastafarian appearance intrigued Matthew.

Danbury greeted her, identifying both himself and Matthew in the car behind him. As he flashed his badge, she bared white teeth in more of a menace than a smile.

“Why are you here?” she asked in a lilting dialect that sounded to Matthew to be from the Caribbean Islands. “And what do you want?”

“Are you Amelia Freeman?” asked Danbury.

She slowly nodded once in acknowledgement.

“I need to talk to you,” replied Danbury. “We need to find your brother, Malcolm.”

At this, she bared her teeth, her head lolled back, and her eyes rolled back in her head. Reaching out both hands and touching the crossed chicken feet charms that dangled around the doorway, she said, in a lilting voice with the lovely Island dialect, “Mistress of holy death and darkness, My Lady of the deep.”

“Ma’am,” said Danbury, undeterred. “We think your brother can help us. To find a killer. We really need his help. We just want to talk to him.”

Matthew watched as she spread her arms widely through the hanging chicken foot charms and continued her chant in the lilting voice and dialect, “Protect me as I come before you, My Lady. Center my focus on you. Cloak me from my enemies and all of their vehemence, traps, and snares.”

“Ma’am,” Danbury tried again. “We just need to talk to Malcolm. We’re not enemies. This isn’t a trap. We can help him. He can help us. Please tell me where he is.”

"Through the mist and darkness, see me here seeking you," she continued until she was abruptly interrupted by a chubby man limping around the corner of the house.

The man was shouting, "Me! Stop with the act! I want to talk to them. It's OK."

Turning, and taking in his earnest face, she nodded once. "It's not an act," she said quietly as she started back into the cabin.

Danbury turned and motioned to Matthew, who then joined him on the hard-packed dirt walk in front of the narrow porch.

"No, wait, Me, I want you to hear this too," said the man who met the description of Malcolm.

"Fine. But stop calling me that! It caused enough problems when we were children," she shot back, as the dialect, the tension, and the drama faded.

Intrigued, Matthew asked, "What caused you problems?" just as Danbury was simultaneously asking, "Are you Malcolm Freeman?"

The man nodded. "Yes, I'm Malcolm Freeman. And calling Amelia 'Me' caused problems, but only for my sister," he grinned up at her.

She rolled her eyes, this time in mock annoyance at Malcolm. "You got me in trouble calling me that," she replied in a soft, smooth measured southern drawl, the Jamaican lilt gone.

"When our Mama would ask who did something, I'd answer 'Me,'" said Malcolm, mischievously. "And Mama wasn't sure if I meant myself or Amelia. 'Who broke the latch on this cabinet?' 'Me.' I was telling the truth. I did it, whatever it was, but Mama couldn't tell the difference."

As Danbury shifted from one foot to the other, obviously wanting to get on with the questioning, Matthew stifled a laugh and just nodded, "I see."

"Malcolm, we need to talk to you. About Allan Lingle."

"Yeah, Allan," he said, looking down, "Is he OK?"

Matthew and Danbury looked at each other. "OK?" repeated Danbury, in surprise.

"Yeah, I shouldn't have left him alone like that with those goons after me."

"Mr. Freeman," said Danbury, recovering from the surprise. "We need to talk. Is here OK?" he asked, indicating the porch.

Malcolm nodded and he and Danbury perched on the edge of the porch as Matthew looked on. "Can you tell me what happened? In sequence. The night you left?" asked Danbury.

Malcolm nodded and said, "I was at the house and I'd just laid out everything for Allan, his favorite pajamas, folded at the foot of his bed, like always. I'd drawn the drapes and turned on his bedside lamp. I knew he'd be home from Bingo at church any minute and everything needed to be ready," he hesitated. "You know, everything has to be exactly the same for him to function. No variations, big or small."

"Yeah, we know," nodded Danbury. "What happened then?"

"I was about to go downstairs to fix some warm milk for him when I heard car doors slam and I went through the bathroom to look out the back. There was a car that I hadn't seen before and two guys were looking up at the house."

"Did you get a look at them? At the car?"

"Not really. It was getting dark out, so I couldn't see them very well."

"Had you seen them before? Either of them? Could you tell?"

"No. I just figured they'd finally found me."

"Found you? Who had found you?"

"Reggie's goons." Malcolm took a deep breath and added, "I'll get to that."

"OK, what happened next?"

"I started downstairs to see what they wanted and I heard an explosive noise. I realized that it was the side door and they'd either kicked it in or slammed it open into the wall."

"Then what happened?"

"Then I ran down the last couple of the back stairs, through the edge of the kitchen, and through the basement door. I left it cracked so I could see what was happening. They were starting to ransack the house. They were in the back sitting room and I was going to go hide down in the basement when I heard glass breaking and then they ran to the front of the house, shouting. While they were in the front room and making so much noise, I ran out the back door and I was going to leave but I realized I didn't have the keys to my Jeep. They were laying on the kitchen counter and I didn't want to go back in the house. I knew I couldn't let them see me."

"Why not?"

"I figured they'd finally found me."

"Who finally found you?"

"Reggie's guys. Friends of the guy I testified against. But they didn't look right."

"What do you mean?"

"Reggie never would have sent two Latino guys. They'd have been black. So that didn't make sense."

"Who's Reggie?"

Malcolm looked at the ground. "I was hanging with a bad crowd when I was a teenager and I got in trouble when I was fifteen. Our Mama sent me to live with her sister in California for a couple of years after I testified on tape against some of Reggie's guys and put them away. I didn't have to take the stand. They just made a voice recording and then I signed a statement that it was true. And they let me out of the Juvenile Hall I'd been assigned to."

"Got in trouble for what? Is that why you have a record? The sealed juvie record?"

Malcolm nodded. "I was driving the getaway car without a license, just for starters, after a shooting I didn't know was gonna happen. I heard the gun shot and it scared me. So I jumped out of the car and ran, but then I was caught running from the scene and I was charged as an accessory to a murder that I didn't know was going down. Those guys didn't tell me what they were doing in there. Just that I had to wait and be ready to drive out as soon as they came back. I thought maybe it was a drug deal or roughing up somebody who owed Reggie money. And it might have been, but it got ugly if that was what it was."

"You testified? In exchange for what?"

"I was allowed to walk away and the record was sealed. Three of the guys who worked for Reggie were put away for a while, but they couldn't get Reggie for anything because he wasn't there. He wasn't happy about any of it. I guess I knew he'd find me eventually and he'd want revenge.

Anyway, that's when our Mama sent me to California to try to get me away from all of that and through high school."

"Then you came back? To work for Allan Lingle?"

"Not at first. Amelia lived with Mama in Durham until she died. And I wasn't there, but I couldn't help thinking that I might have saved her if I'd been there and been trained. I came home right after that and decided I wanted to go into healthcare. I worked some junk jobs at hospitals and worked my way up. Then I finally started nursing school at night after I got the job working for Allan Lingle to get patient care experience. That's the best job I've ever had."

"OK," said Danbury. "I can appreciate hard work. Back to Monday night. You left out the back door?"

"Yeah, then I realized I didn't have my keys. And then I realized that their car was blocking me in anyway. I ran around it, trying to figure out if I could get my Jeep out, but the Jeep was between two trees on the sides and backed into the edge of the woods. There was no getting it out from around their car, even if I went back for the keys. So I just started running down the back path."

"You did get a look then. At the car?"

"Yeah, I saw that. Up close and personal because it was totally blocking my Jeep," he added miserably.

"Make and model?" asked Danbury, "And color?"

"Dark grey, Toyota Camry."

"Did you see the license plate?"

"Yeah, but I can just tell you that it was a rental from Florida. I don't remember the number."

"Did it say which rental company?"

"Yeah, that national chain, Afford-A-Car."

"Well, that's a start," said Danbury to Matthew. "It could have been rented anywhere. But hopefully the company can help."

"Yeah, it's no longer a ubiquitous dark-colored sedan. I wonder where it is now. I guess we know when it was rented out, at least," summarized Matthew.

Back to Malcolm, Danbury asked, “Did you hear them say anything? About Allan Lingle?”

Malcolm screwed up his face, “No. The only thing I did hear was just before the window broke and it didn’t make sense.”

“What was that?”

“I’m pretty sure I heard one of them say that Leo had been home.”

“Leo?”

“Yeah.”

“You’re sure?”

“Yeah, that’s what I heard.”

“Did you see Leo?”

“No. It took me a minute to get who they were talking about. I guess they were talking about Allan’s younger brother. Allan has talked about him a couple of times.”

Danbury nodded and exchanged a look with Matthew. “Malcolm,” said Danbury. “Have you ever met Leo? Ever seen him?”

“No, just in pictures around the house. But they’re all older pictures. He looked a lot like Allan in those pictures, only more,” he hesitated, looking for the right word. “More lively or animated somehow.”

“When did you last see Allan?”

“Ah, about 4:45, I think. Just before he went to the diner for dinner, like he always does on Monday nights. He’d picked up the envelope of cash I’d laid out for him on the library table near the front door, opened it, put the envelope in the trash, and the cash in his wallet. I lay out exact change in envelopes for his meals each week. Then he can just pick it up by the day and have the amount that he needs. It’s always the same so that he can know what to expect and be able to function. I’ve been worried about him. Has he been OK with me gone? I feel so bad. I know that he needs me and I left him.”

“You haven’t talked to anyone, have you? Since Monday. Anyone from Peak?” asked Danbury.

“No,” answered Malcolm.

“How’d you get up here, then?” asked Matthew, finally too curious to be quiet any longer.

"I had my wallet, with my debit and credit cards, so I stopped at a convenience store and got cash. I paid a trucker who was headed north to bring me up I-85. Then I hitched a ride in the back of a pick-up truck back down Highway 58 and walked part of the way down 15 until I walked up on a guy at a house with a moped. I paid him twenty bucks to bring me the rest of the way down 15 to 858 and I walked down here from there."

Matthew and Danbury exchanged a look and Malcolm began to look concerned.

"I got here early Tuesday morning," he said. "And I've been here ever since. Amelia can verify that. I didn't break the window and whatever the guys stole from the house, it wasn't me."

"That's not the issue," said Danbury.

Looking truly worried, Malcolm said, "What aren't you telling me?"

Matthew looked askance at Danbury, who nodded, and then Matthew sat down on the other side of Malcolm and said, as kindly as he could, "Malcolm, Allan doesn't need you now." Pausing, not sure how to continue, Matthew finally added, "He was killed Monday night."

"What?!?!" asked Malcolm, jumping up, and wincing in pain. "When? How? Did those two guys kill him? Why? Why would anybody hurt Allan?"

Matthew continued, "We don't know who killed him yet, but those two guys are looking more and more likely, which is why we came to find you, to get your help to find them. We think Allan was on his way home from Bingo when he was killed. His body was found in the shrubs just off of the sidewalk on the way to the Lingle Plantation."

Malcolm looked like he might be physically sick, like someone had sucker punched him in the gut, as he sank quietly back onto the edge of the narrow porch, with his face in his hands, elbows on knees. His shoulders were shaking slightly and then he brushed his cheeks as he finally raised his face, staring intently at something on the ground that nobody else could see.

"Why?" he finally asked, choking on the word. "Why would anyone kill Allan? He is a little odd, but that isn't his fault. And he isn't a danger to anybody. He wouldn't even know how to harm anybody. Not on purpose. He's completely harmless. And he is, or," Malcolm corrected himself, taking a breath to steady his voice. "He was the sweetest guy I think I've ever known."

"That's what we're trying to figure out," said Danbury. "Nobody seems to know why."

"Why are you limping?" asked Matthew, ever the curious doctor. "What happened?"

"I bashed my knee when I was running down the back driveway of the Lingle house. I was off the edge, so those guys couldn't see me from the house. I stepped in a hole, or the ditch, or something and tripped. I fell down, hard, and my knee slammed into a rock. The pain was awful, but I couldn't stop. I still thought they were after me, so I had to keep going."

"Can I have a look?" asked Matthew.

"Oh yeah, you're a doctor in Peak, aren't you? Yeah, sure," he said, as he tried to raise his pant leg up over his swollen knee.

Matthew gently prodded the inside and the outside of the knee and around the knee cap, asking about what hurt most as he went. "We need to get some ice on this and you need to keep it elevated."

"Yeah, I know I should have," said Malcolm, ruefully.

"We can keep it propped up," said Amelia, leaning over her brother in concern.

"I can't stay here, Me. I need to go with them and try to figure out what happened to Allan. I owe him that. It's the right thing to do. And I have my studies that I can't get behind in. I'm nearly finished with my nursing program." Then he looked up at her and asked, "You gonna be OK up here by yourself?"

Ignoring the childhood name this time, Amelia just grimaced, muttered something about him not owing anybody anything, and slumped down on the porch beside him to hug her brother. Lifting her chin with pride, she said, aloud, "I was just fine before you got here and I'll be just fine with you gone."

"We can get some ice on the way out and wrap it up," said Matthew helpfully. "Is it OK if he takes the back seat so that he can stretch his leg across it?" He asked Danbury.

Danbury nodded and Malcolm stood, hugged his sister tightly, and then followed them, hobbling, to the SUV. Danbury removed the packet of folders from the back seat and Malcolm climbed gingerly in. As he was getting situated, Danbury flipped one of the folders open to the artist's rendering of the man Jacob Wheatley had described in detail and asked Malcolm if he'd ever seen the guy before.

Taking the picture and studying it closely, Malcolm finally responded, "Yeah, that could have been one of the guys. The taller one. He was a big guy, and he looked mean and like he meant business. Not somebody you'd want to meet in a dark alley late at night."

13. Possibilities

Making their way out of the back roads, they stopped at a chain convenience mart before getting back on Highway 15. While Danbury filled up the SUV, Matthew went in and came back out with a box of quart-sized zip-closure bags, a towel with Biggs Lake and pictures on it, a small Styrofoam cooler, two Cokes, a bottle of water, three hot dogs, and three bags of M&Ms.

After distributing the food and drinks, Matthew pulled the small cooler over to a large ice bin where he removed a bag of ice, broke it up and loaded the cooler with it. Then he pushed Danbury's seat forward to gain access and went to work on Malcolm's knee. Malcolm had his back to the door behind Matthew's seat and his left leg was stretched across the back seat. Wrapping the center of the towel over Malcolm's knee, Matthew crossed it underneath and pulled both ends up. Then he put ice in two of the zip-closure bags and placed them strategically on either side of the knee, tying the ends of the towel over them to hold it all in place.

"There," he said. "That should get us back to Peak. Malcolm, we can see how this does over the next couple of days but if it doesn't improve, I'd recommend an MRI to ensure that you haven't torn anything." Then to Danbury, he asked, "Can he stay at the Lingle house for now? Or, do we need to come up with something else?"

"It's not the murder scene and it's been processed," said Danbury. "Penn is still in town, but she's not staying there so if that's OK with her, it's fine with me."

"Can you call her?" asked Matthew.

"No. But you can," answered Danbury quickly as he reset his seat and they climbed back in.

Lifting an eyebrow in question, Matthew agreed and they set off over the bridge for Peak. "There's still one thing bothering me," said Matthew.

"Only one?" asked Danbury.

"Malcolm, you said you saw the grey Camry pull up behind your Jeep, right?"

"Not really. I heard the doors close, so I guess it had just pulled up, why?"

"If it was behind the house, where your Jeep was, how'd they get it back there? Did they come up the back drive? How'd they know that back drive was even there? And if they did, they'd have had to go all the way around on the streets to get there if they'd just been on Chapel Street to kill Allan. There were people going into the community center that evening. How did nobody see a car over there?"

"Good questions," said Danbury, scratching the stubble on his chin. "Really good questions."

"And the bat," added Matthew. "We are assuming it came from the Lingle Plantation, right? If those guys were just arriving at the house for the first time when Malcolm heard them, and if the boys broke the window, which Malcolm heard right afterward, then how did they get the bat if it came from the house?"

"What bat? What boys?" asked Malcolm, and Matthew explained that a bat assumed to be the murder weapon had been found and that some young neighborhood boys had broken a window by throwing a rock at the house.

"Were you at the house all evening?" Matthew asked Malcolm.

"No, I'd just gotten back, maybe a half hour before. I went out after Allan left for the diner. I knew I had a couple of hours before he'd be home after Bingo."

"And you didn't see the Camry anywhere around the house?"

"No. I didn't come or go out of the front, but it wasn't behind the house where I parked when I came in."

"Is there enough room to drive a car around the house from the front?" persisted Matthew.

"Oh yeah. I do it all the time if I drive in from the front, because I always park in the back. Nobody else used the back driveway anyway, except me. It's really overgrown now, and I'd thought about clearing it better to be able to keep using it."

"Is it possible that they'd been at the house while you were gone and they came in from the front after they killed Allan and drove around behind the house to hide the car?"

"Yeah, sure. It's possible."

"And the bat. Was there a wooden Louisville Slugger bat in the house anywhere that you'd seen?"

"That's possible too. If there was one, it was probably in Leo's old room. I think he played baseball in school. There are pictures up in his room of him in a baseball uniform. I think there's a baseball mitt up on a shelf in there and maybe a baseball, too."

"Just one more question," said Matthew. "What was with the chicken feet and the act your sister put on back there?"

"It was only partly an act," replied Malcolm, chuckling. "Our father is Jamaican. He's back there now, somewhere in a rural area outside of Kingston last we heard. He's very much a Rasta and Amelia was always drawn to it. His mother, our grandmother, practices a sort of Voodoo that Jamaicans call Obeah. She swears it's used for protection and not for love potions or calling down curses, but you couldn't prove that by me. Amelia looks a lot like her and acts like her sometimes too. She can imitate her perfectly."

"Was your mother Jamaican too?" asked Matthew, intrigued with Malcolm's history.

"No, she was American Indian, thought to be a descendant of some Native Americans who lived on an island that was between the two rivers which is now underwater near the top of the lake. Up near where Me is living now. She loves her heritage," he said. And then he added, "All of it."

"The Occoneechee?" asked Danbury.

"That's right," said Malcolm, sounding both impressed and surprised.

He didn't ask, and Danbury didn't volunteer any information about how he knew that, though there were streets and a camp ground bearing the name in that area. Smiling to himself, Matthew thought Danbury might make a very astute history student after all. The SUV grew quiet as each man was lost in his own thoughts.

Matthew took the opportunity to call Penn Lingle, who, though she was initially surprised to hear from him, readily enough agreed to allow Malcolm to return to the Lingle Plantation, at least for the time being. She explained that she wasn't sure what would happen to the house because Wayne Adams was now insisting on waiting for Leo to be found before presenting their mother's wishes, as expressed in her will should she and Leo be predeceased by Allan.

"I think they're still suspicious that one or both of us had something to do with Allan's death," she confessed. "As if!" she'd added vehemently before she asked Matthew to have dinner Tuesday night and they ended the call.

"That sounded interesting," observed Danbury.

"Yeah, she said that Malcolm can stay for now. Their mother's will, stating what happens if she and Leo are predeceased by Allan, hasn't been read yet because the lawyers say they're waiting for Leo to be found. But she thinks it's more because she and Leo are suspects, and she asked me to dinner Tuesday night."

Nodding, Danbury looked amused by it all, particularly, Matthew thought, that last admission.

*****

When they arrived back in Peak, Danbury and Matthew dropped Malcolm off at the Lingle house. They told him that his Jeep had been moved and then found, but it was now impounded as evidence. He seemed upset, but he assured them that he was fine in his ground floor bedroom without his Jeep for a few days. Danbury then asked if Malcolm could walk or at least hobble them through his movements in the order they occurred on Monday evening.

"Sure. I parked my Jeep there, in the edge of the trees," Malcolm said, pointing out the back door that they'd just come through. "I came in the back door here, and put away a few things I'd picked up from the grocery store. I realized what time it was, so I got out Allan's nighttime medications, put them in a little paper cup, and poured a glass of cold water. Then I took those up the back stairs to lay his things out and prepare for his return."

They followed as he hobbled up the back staircase. Allan's room was the last, at the end of the hallway near the back stairs, on the left end of the house as viewed from the front. Malcolm confirmed, when Danbury asked about it, that it was the bedroom Allan had always occupied growing up, and he hadn't wanted to move out of it, even to the much larger master suite at the other end of the hallway.

"OK, so then what? What did you do next?" asked Danbury.

"I put the glass of water and his nighttime medications on the bedside table there, turned on the bedside table lamp, and drew the drapes, just like always."

"Did you look out the window? Out front?"

"I don't think I did, no," he answered slowly, pausing to consider. "I didn't really look. I just pulled the curtains closed and then I turned the sheets back and laid out Allan's favorite pajamas, thinking that he'd be happy to see them fresh from the wash."

"Anything else? Before you heard the noise? And went to investigate?"

Malcolm paused to ponder. "I don't think so. I think I was just finishing up in here when I heard the car doors and walked through to the bathroom over there to see out the back window."

They followed him across the hall as he pointed out the window.

"And that's when you saw them? The two guys? Looking up at the house?"

"Yeah and walking toward the house."

"Then you went back downstairs? To the basement?"

"I did. And fast. I wanted to hide down there until I could slip out and escape, because I thought Reggie had sent them and they were after me."

"OK. Show us what you did," said Danbury, and they followed Malcolm down the back stairs, through the corner of the kitchen, and down the basement steps. The basement smelled old and musty from disuse. A single bulb was mounted on the ceiling above the steps and Malcolm flipped a switch on the wall so that they could see into the dank dark basement below.

"I didn't do that Monday. I didn't want to let them know I was here. But these steps are steep, so be careful."

"You hid here. At the top of the stairs," prodded Danbury. "Could you see anything? Or hear anything? Through the crack in the door?"

"I did hear a noise from the basement down below me, or at least I thought it came from down here. I'd heard it before, though. There was no light anyway, so I didn't go down the stairs to check it out. It was right after that when I heard the crash and the two guys went running to the front of the house."

"OK, we'll look in a minute. You ran out. What did you see? Walk us through it."

Malcolm led them through the back door and said, "I bolted out of here and was half way to my Jeep before I realized that my keys were in the house on the kitchen counter. And then I saw that their car was completely blocking my Jeep anyway. My Jeep was pulled in here," he indicated two trees that were spaced far enough apart to park a vehicle between them and get it almost completely out of the yard and into the edge of the woods. "And their Camry was parked across directly behind it."

"Which way was it headed?"

"Out, like it was facing the back drive," he said, pointing.

"Let's go back to the basement," said Matthew, contributing to the conversation at last.

"OK," said Malcolm, taking a breath and hobbling back to the house.

They descended slowly down the steps and stood on a cement floor beneath another single bulb that was suspended from the center of the ceiling. It was dark, dank, and Matthew imagined spiders, mice, and other creepy crawly things on the brick walls and along the dusty floor, though he didn't see any.

Walking around the room, Matthew pulled his cell phone out and shone it around the walls, floor, and ceiling. As he looked around, he noticed a large furnace at the far end of the room that appeared to be ancient. Behind it was the only wall in the room that wasn't brick. It was a slatted wooden structure through which piping, wiring, and duct work disappeared. Something was niggling at the back corners of his mind, but he couldn't identify it. As he pondered it, Danbury interrupted his thoughts.

"This used to be the root cellar. About a quarter of this size though. Accessed from a storm cellar door. From outside. It was expanded into a basement. When they added the back extension. The kitchen, pantry, bathroom, laundry, and Malcolm's room and bathroom. The beginning of last century."

Malcolm nodded, "I've heard something like that, too, about additions to the back of the house."

"What was the sound you heard? Coming from down here?" asked Danbury.

"It was a loud screech, like metal scraping on metal. I'd heard it before."

"From down here?"

"Maybe. I'm not sure. It's one of lots of odd noises in this house. That's one of the reasons people swear the house is haunted," Malcolm added as he turned the light off and began hobbling back up the stairs. "There are random squeaks, creaks, and thumps pretty regularly. Doors are opened that I know I've closed, or closed that I know I've left open. Lights will be on that I know I've turned off, or vice versa, window drapes are pulled back, things rearranged. I asked Allan about it a couple of times, thinking that he'd opened doors or moved things around."

"What did he say?"

"It's just Leo, it's just Leo."

"Leo?"

"That's what he said when I asked him about it, and he wouldn't say anything more. It was odd. I asked Penn, in one of our phone conversations, why Allan would say Leo was making noises in the house. She said it was probably a reference back to their childhood when Leo was constantly pulling pranks."

"Do you think the house is haunted?" Matthew couldn't help but ask.

"Yeah," he said. "I think it's haunted."

"So, you do think that there are ghosts in this house?"

"I do, but they don't bother me. I mean, you met my sister," he said with a chuckle. "She says she talks to our mother regularly." He shrugged as he asked, "Who am I to say she doesn't?"

After a quick check to ensure that the doors were locked up tightly with the newly installed locks, Danbury and Matthew left Malcolm with his ghosts. Malcolm was sadly wandering through the downstairs, looking at pictures and picking up various items absent-mindedly, as Matthew admonished him to ice and elevate the knee.

Danbury offered to drop Matthew back at his office parking lot to get his car, but Matthew declined, opting instead to walk. He went out through the front door, locking it back behind himself, and paying attention as he went.

Why the neighborhood children thought that the house was haunted was certainly obvious to Matthew, whether or not, as Malcolm believed, it actually was. All of the boards creaked, inside and out on the porch, as he walked across them. He reached over and gently rocked one of the chairs on the front porch and chuckled to himself as he heard the loud clomp-clomp, clomp-clomp of the rocker rails across the old wooden boards of the porch.

Add the overgrown yard to all of that creaking and the fact that Allan Lingle had been a bit odd, and it was definitely the stuff that ghost stories could easily be made of. He pondered how he could convince the boys that the house wasn't really haunted, as he stepped off the porch and walked down the long driveway out to Chapel Street. Having seen bits of the house only perfunctorily to trace Malcolm's steps the evening that Allan was murdered, Matthew really wanted to linger and explore the rest of the historic house thoroughly but he figured he'd save that for another day.

Two things were still bothering him, he realized. The first was the issue of how and when the Toyota Camry came and went. How would anyone not connected with the house even know about the back entrance? Could they have followed Malcolm? And something about the basement was still bugging him, but he couldn't quite put his finger on it.

Shrugging it all off to ponder over his guitar later, he slid into his car and was thankful for an uneventful drive toward home after what seemed like a very long day. Matthew realized that it wasn't quite dinner time yet and he decided to make a quick side trip to the grocery store to stock up on supplies for the coming week as well as kid-friendly treats, like goldfish and juice boxes, for Angel's visit the next day.

After putting the groceries away and feeding Max, Matthew couldn't help wondering how Cici was faring on the other side of an ocean, as he carefully wrapped and packed the things that she'd asked him to send to her. He figured she'd be asleep by the time he stopped trying to convince himself not to contact her, so it was a moot point anyway.

Enjoying the peace and quiet of an evening at home, he prepared and ate a dinner of wild rice with shrimp and vegetables that he'd cooked on skewers on the grill, and then he spent some time with his acoustic guitar allowing his mind to wander over the events of the day. His foot tapped to the rhythms in his head that were pouring softly from his fingers on the guitar fret and strings.

The knowledge that he was missing something important was visceral, more than merely a thought. He could feel it. Even with his guitar, which could often provide the eureka effect that he was seeking, he couldn't identify it. It still eluded him. If he was expecting an epiphany of any kind, it didn't come this evening.

Eventually, he put the guitar down. Happily settling in for an early night after an earlier than usual morning, Matthew thought it had been a successful day. He drifted off to sleep wondering when and how they'd catch Allan's murderer and particularly if they'd ever figure out the motivation behind the seemingly senseless nature of it. Not that any murders were ever sensible, he thought as he drifted off, but this one was particularly mysterious.

14. What dreams are made of

Sunday morning was peaceful and quiet as Matthew awoke to find Max curled happily around his head. Moving the big cat over, he scratched under his chin, procrastinating just a bit about getting out of bed and ruining the peace and quiet of the morning. Picking up his phone, he saw that Cici had texted him. He texted back the good morning wish and then added that he had boxed her things but hadn't had a chance to drop them at a carrier yet.

After a few back-and-forth texts, his phone lit up with a FaceTime request from her.

"Hey Matthew," she said. "I was just thinking about last Sunday when I was with you and your family and I miss that."

Wow, thought Matthew, she'd never been much interested in being a part of his family, and particularly not his Sunday routine with them. But what he said was, "I miss you, too, Cees. My Mom enjoyed having you there for Mother's Day last week."

"She did? I thought your mom only tolerated me."

"It's not you. It really isn't. It's that Mama Bear thing. She saw how much I was hurting and how I struggled after we broke up last year and I think she's just feeling protective and doesn't want me to have to go through that again," he said, honestly.

"Wow, I wish my mom were that tuned in. She never has been though. She was having trouble with Dad and their marriage when I was young, and then the divorce, and then the dating, and finally the remarriage. She's always been too self-focused to see how I'm feeling about any of it."

What do you say to something like that, Matthew wondered. That was honest and transparent. He didn't recall Cici ever being so open about her family life before and he wasn't sure how to respond. After a moment, he simply said, "I am very thankful for my family. They're very supportive, no matter what."

After wrapping up the conversation with Cici, Matthew wandered down the hallway to find coffee and enjoyed smelling it even before tasting it. He decided to fix breakfast first this morning and refreshed the food and water bowls for Max, cooked and ate his egg and toast breakfast, creating an omelet from his shish-kabob leftovers, and then refilled his coffee to take with him to shower, shave, and dress.

On his way out, he set the alarm and picked up the keys for his Honda Element. He'd be bringing Angel back with him so he'd need it to get both her and her booster seat in and out. The clam shell doors made that relatively easy.

The church he attended with his family in north Raleigh was part old historic brick church sanctuary and part huge new worship center with an atrium, coffee shop, baked goods shop, and bookstore. The congregation mirrored that juxtaposition well. It was the church he'd grown up in that he and his family still attended together on Sundays, followed by a family lunch afterward, a tradition born of years of repetition and one that he enjoyed being able to depend on. When life got crazy, his family's Sunday routine was like an anchor in the storms of his life.

He found his family in the usual spot. It's not that they were proprietary about a particular seating arrangement, he thought, but just that they usually congregated in the same general area, which made it easy to find each other in the large worship center. Settling in with his family, he was ready for the final installment of Pastor Bill's teaching series, "God Speaks," about how God communicates with his people.

What Matthew wasn't prepared for was the impact that the teaching for this particular week would have on him. Transfixed, Matthew was hanging on every word about God speaking to his people, throughout both the old and new testaments, in dreams. God spoke, explained Pastor Bill, to prophets and ordinary people alike. The dream Matthew had just had Thursday night was telling in this context. And also very upsetting, he thought, because it meant that he needed to do something about it. Cordelia Drewer was lonely. He shook his head trying to understand how that could be possible.

After the church service, his mother Jackie looked questioningly at him because he was quieter than usual as he pondered what the dream meant, and what he was meant to do about it. He picked Angel up from children's church and they went through their usual routine of her hiding and him pretending not to be able to find her, but even she looked quizzically up at him because his enthusiasm was lacking.

Finally, over lunch, Jackie couldn't stand it any longer and asked what was wrong.

"Nothing's wrong," he said honestly. "That sermon this morning just got me thinking, that's all."

"Anything you care to discuss?" she asked.

"Not yet," he said. "I'm still mulling it over myself." As he said it, he felt a slight twinge of guilt because he knew his mother had a wealth of wisdom to share but he really wanted the chance to formulate his own understanding before leaning on hers.

As he was getting Angel's car seat and the bag Monica had packed for her into the car, he was rethinking their afternoon plans. The car washing would be first, he had thought, and then maybe a trip into Peak if there was anything interesting happening at the Cultural Arts Center. But those plans could wait, he decided, as he helped Angel climb into the car seat and said aloud, "How about we make some chocolate chip cookies this afternoon?"

"Oh, YUM!" she exclaimed. "You make the BEST chocolate chip cookies, Uncle Matt!"

"I'm glad you think so," said Matthew on a chuckle, deciding not to admit that his famous chocolate chip cookie recipe was the one on the side of the Nestle chocolate chip bag. That could be his secret, he thought. He'd been known for making them in college, and he had the recipe memorized anyway, so no need to confess as far as he was concerned.

"Cookies?" asked Monica. "What happened to car washing?"

"I had a dream . . ." began Matthew, with a chuckle. Then he added, "I have a neighbor who I think needs some cookies and a visit from an adorable four-year-old."

Jackie and Monica exchanged perplexed glances and Monica finally said, "Well, OK then. Enjoy your cookies," as she leaned in to give Angel a kiss. "And be sweet for Uncle Matt," she instructed.

"I will!" called Angel as Monica closed the doors, then waved as Matthew and Angel set out.

Angel's favorite travel game, at the moment, was I Spy, so they played on the way to Peak, just outside of which Matthew had decided to stop briefly at the grocery store to ensure that he had everything he needed to make cookies.

Angel was well behaved in the grocery store, Matthew thought, and made a mental note to tell his sister how refreshing it was not to have a child begging for everything she'd seen like so many he'd overheard in the stores lately. Monica and Matthew as children hadn't been spoiled in stores either. In fact, Jackie had usually let each of them pick out one thing that they most wanted and, if they whined about it or anything else, it'd go back on the shelf. Monica had most often chosen Oreo cookies and Matthew Lucky Charms cereal as their treat for the week, he remembered.

Angel refused her option to choose one treat, much to his surprise, and said she was saving room for the chocolate chip cookies instead. Sometimes, he thought, it felt as if he was talking to a miniature adult, one who had just been shrunken down a few feet but was at least thirty-five. After getting the needed supplies, he'd packed Angel and the groceries in the back seat and they'd played I Spy until they passed the new Peak sign.

As they drove into Peak, Angel exclaimed, "Hey, you got a new sign! And it says, 'Welcome to Peak!' Right?"

"It does," chuckled Matthew. "And then it says, 'The Pinnacle of Good Living.' "

"What's a pinnacle?" she asked. "Oh, is it one of those things that goes 'round and 'round when you blow on it?"

Hesitating momentarily before understanding dawned and he burst out laughing, Matthew answered, "No, that's a pinwheel. Pinnacle just means the top of something."

"Oh," she said, undeterred. "What are we on the top of?"

Deciding to sidestep the discussion of the dual meaning, both literal and figurative, with a four-year-old, he chose an idiomatic response instead. "I'm on the top of the world when I'm with you!" he exclaimed and starting singing his own version of the old song with lyrics that included Angel in them. He enjoyed the peals of laughter emanating from the back seat.

As they drove in, Matthew waved at a couple of his neighbors who were out for a Sunday afternoon stroll, but he didn't see Ms. Drewer. He hoped that she was home as he unpacked Angel and the groceries that Angel helped him carry in.

The usual excitement to find Max ensued as they entered the house and Angel petted the big cat sweetly as she cooed to him, "Who's a good boy? Max is the best boy!"

Matthew pulled a little folding step ladder that he used to get to the cabinets at the top of his nine-foot kitchen ceilings from behind the refrigerator, washed his hands, and started setting out supplies. After a few minutes with Max, Angel wandered over, climbed the stool, and washed her hands too. She asked if he had an apron and he managed to find a grilling apron that was given to him as a joke, which said, "Kiss the cook." Pulling up the straps and doubling the length across her chest, he managed to tie it all up neatly.

They mixed and stirred and only once did Angel lose her grip on the spoon and knock a dollop of cookie dough onto the floor. Max sauntered over and sniffed it before turning his nose up at it. Then he wandered over to jump up on a bar stool, the only surface above the floor in the kitchen that he was allowed on, where he could watch the proceedings with a disdain that only a cat could muster.

Four cookie sheets were filled, baked, and cooled. As Angel carefully placed the cookies into two plastic containers, she was humming happily to herself. Meanwhile, Matthew was throwing out the parchment paper and wiping down the counters, having already washed the bowls and mixing and measuring utensils while the last batch of cookies were baking.

"Good job," he said to Angel. "Do you want some milk with your cookies?"

She nodded as she stopped humming and answered, "Yes, please. I like to dunk my cookies in it."

That was a habit that Matthew had never developed, but he'd seen Monica dipping cookies in milk for as long as he could remember. They enjoyed two cookies and then, guiltily, Matthew allowed them each to have a third. He'd made them smaller than he usually did, so he figured it all evened out.

"Now are you ready to take a little walk and deliver this container?" he asked as he placed their plates and cups in the dishwasher.

"Where are we going?"

"I think one of my neighbors needs some cookies and a visit," he said.

"Sure!" she said, as she picked up the container of cookies and bounced out of the front door ahead of him.

Walking the short distance down to Cordelia Drewer's house, Matthew realized that he'd never been there before. He'd only ever seen Ms. Drewer out walking Oscar but he'd never actually been to her house. He allowed Angel to ring the bell and he stepped back to wait. He knew immediately that she was home because Oscar ran to the door barking. Ms. Drewer rarely went anywhere without the fussy little Pomeranian.

A look of surprise registered on her face momentarily as she opened the door and scooped up Oscar. Matthew scooped up Angel as the storm door opened and Ms. Drewer said, "Well, hello, who do we have here?"

"Hi, Ms. Drewer. This is my niece, Angel, my sister Monica's daughter," as if that last bit were entirely necessary. Matthew had only one sibling but he wasn't sure that Ms. Drewer knew that.

"It's nice to meet you," said Ms. Drewer, kindly, holding out her hand, "I've seen you down at your uncle's house a few times before."

"We brought you cookies, and they're homemade!" said Angel as she offered the container to the older woman.

"How sweet! Thank you. Homemade are my favorite kind," she added with a wink. "Would you like to come in?"

"Sure!" answered Angel, as she wiggled down, before Matthew got the chance to ask if they were intruding. Oscar also wiggled to get down and Angel reached out to pet him.

"Wait, Angel!" Matthew said, "I'm not sure he likes . . ." and then stopped up short as he saw Oscar licking her hand. She giggled.

"He loves children," said Cordelia Drewer as she motioned for them to follow her into the kitchen and she put the cookies on the counter. "He's not too fond of men, particularly big ones, but he loves children."

Right on cue, Oscar looked up and growled at Matthew. "Oh, stop it, Oscar," she said. "We already let him in. It's too late to protect me now." Then to Matthew, she said, "He is very protective of me and I'm thankful, since I live alone. Would you like to come in and have a seat?"

"If we're not intruding," answered Matthew, carefully.

"Not at all, not at all. I was just writing some notes and doing a little reading this afternoon," she said as she cleared the sofa of the detritus of those efforts and motioned for him to have a seat. "Can I get you anything?" she asked, still hovering. "Tea? Coffee? A glass of water?"

"No thanks. We just had milk and cookies ourselves."

As she sat on the other end of a long sectional sofa, Matthew noticed that her condo, on the other end of the attached unit from his, was a mirror image of his own, comfortably well furnished. The room was done in muted mauve and cream tones that were tasteful but decidedly feminine with ruffles along the edges of the drapes which were drawn back over plantation-style shutters.

Angel perched momentarily on an ottoman as Oscar jumped up beside Ms. Drewer and raised himself, in prairie dog fashion, onto his back legs for Angel to scratch his belly. He seemed to tire of that after a few moments and snuggled up beside Ms. Drewer. Angel then began to take in the room, standing up and wandering from an end table to a library table that held pictures in various sizes of gilt gold frames.

Matthew was watching her like the proverbial hawk, afraid that she would pick up or knock over something important. Angel stopped in front of a black and white picture, pointing, and said, "Who's this?"

"Angel," said Matthew, in a tone that he didn't recognize as quite parental. "Those are Ms. Drewer's personal pictures."

"Oh, it's all right. I don't mind. That's me with my husband, Mick. A long time ago. Bring it over."

Angel carefully picked up the picture, then sat beside the older woman, with Oscar in the middle. Handing the picture over, Angel said, "You have a husband here? I thought it was just Oscar."

"I had a husband. He was killed many years ago. We weren't married very long before he got sent off to war. See? He's in uniform here in the picture."

"Oh!" said Angel, looking more closely at the picture. "I'm sorry. You're really pretty in this picture," she added.

That was all news to Matthew. He'd always called her "Ms. Drewer" in deference to her age but never considered that it should be "Mrs. Drewer." He'd make a point of addressing her properly in the future, he thought.

"Do you have any children?" asked Angel.

"Angel," started Matthew, but Mrs. Drewer just waved his pending objection to his niece's curiosity away with a hand and she answered, "I had lots of children at the school where I worked, but I never had any of my own. I had meant to. I really did. But I never remarried after Mick died and, well, I wanted to have a Daddy to be a Mommy."

"Ohhh," said Angel, as she had returned the picture to its place on the table and sat by Mrs. Drewer, stroking Oscar, who seemed content to be nestled between the two of them. "I have lots of children in my school too. And the best teachers!" she added. "Are you a teacher?"

"I was a teacher and a librarian, but I'm retired, so not anymore," she added sadly. "I miss it. I miss the children, anyway." And then, turning to Matthew, she added, more typically of the neighbor he thought he knew, "Not the politics in the school system these days, though. I don't miss that at all!"

"You could come teach at my school!" said Angel excitedly. "Or you can come read to us! Lots of Mommies and some Daddies and even Granddaddies come to read to our class sometimes. I like the books the best," she added. "My favorite ones are about Madeline."

"Oh, I love Madeline, too!" said Mrs. Drewer. "I can do anything," she whispered, quoting conspiratorially as she leaned over toward Angel, smiling at her. "I have some of those books here. Would you like to read one?"

"Yes!" said Angel, excitedly, bouncing on the sofa.

Cordelia Drewer looked over Angel's head at Matthew, who nodded, and then she got up with Oscar in tow and said, "I'll be right back."

Angel continued to bounce on the seat excitedly and Matthew just smiled at his little niece, thinking that he might invest in a collection of Madeline books before her next visit. He was thankful that he'd brought her along because she could draw out an adult, particularly an older woman, in ways that he couldn't have begun to do. He marveled at the woman he thought he knew and how different she was in the presence of his niece.

When she returned with a stack of books, Matthew said, "Just pick one, Angel. We don't want to tie up Mrs. Drewer's entire afternoon. Besides, we'll need to get you home pretty soon. Aren't we having spaghetti for dinner? Your favorite?"

"OK, THIS one!" Angel said, choosing from the fan of 5 or 6 books that were being presented to her.

Holding the book out in front so that Angel could see, Cordelia Drewer began, in a musical tone, "In an old house in Paris that was covered in vines, lived twelve little girls in two straight lines. They left the house at half-past nine, in two straight lines, in rain or shine."

"And the smallest one was Madeline!" chimed in Angel.

"That's right," said Mrs. Drewer. "You'll be reading this book to me in no time!"

The book finished, Matthew was rising to go and saying his goodbyes to the neighbor he was beginning to like as he was getting to know her. He suddenly turned to her and said, "You know, Mrs. Drewer, you could read to Angel's class sometime. The children would love it and you know better than anyone, that the teachers would surely welcome the break."

"Yes!" enthused Angel. "Can she bring Oscar too?"

"We'll see," he chuckled. "Let's ask your mom to get in touch this evening, OK?" Angel nodded her approval enthusiastically.

Jotting her number on a piece of paper from a notepad that she'd cleared off the sofa earlier and handing it to Matthew, Ms. Drewer said, "Here. Tell your sister to call anytime. I'd love to go read to Angel's class. And if there are no objections, I'm sure Oscar would love to come too. He really does love children."

As they walked back down to Matthew's condo on the other end of the unit, he took Angel by the hand and said, "We're having spaghetti for dinner, huh? We should sing the meatball song."

"What meatball song?"

"You've never sung the meatball song?"

She shook her head so he began, "On top of spaghetti, all covered in cheese, I lost my poor meatball when somebody sneezed." She giggled and he continued, "It rolled off the table and onto the floor, and then my poor meatball, it rolled out the door. It rolled through the garden, and under a bush. And then my poor meatball was nothing but mush!"

Angel cackled with laughter throughout the song, clapping her hands in delight at the end and said, "Sing it again! Sing it again!" And he did.

Angel tried to learn the song all the way home. Thinking that Monica would never forgive him for introducing the silly ditty, he just grinned as Angel was joining in enthusiastically for most of it by the time they'd turned into his sister's driveway.

15. Dead ends or split ends

After an energetic dinner of "spasgetti" minus the meatball with his sister Monica, her husband Stephano, and Angel, Matthew had given Monica Mrs. Drewer's information and she had agreed to call. As he was driving home, he was thinking that the day had been a resounding success. He'd enjoyed his afternoon with Angel. She had shown him an entirely different side of Cordelia Drewer, who probably was truly lonely, that he would never have seen without the adorable four-year-old. He was incredulous that this side of Mrs. Drewer existed.

In that moment, he also realized that he hadn't thought about the murder investigation at all that afternoon. Now that he thought about it, he was curious to know what if anything had developed. He poked his phone, which was mounted in a cell holder on the air vent on his dash, to call Danbury. He put the conversation on speaker.

"Hey, Doc," answered Danbury.

"Hey, how's it going today? I had my niece this afternoon so I've been out of contact with the adult world."

"Not too bad. More dead ends."

"How so?"

"Well, not entirely, I guess. We got an ID on the body. The one found near the Jeep. Cuban guy. We think out of Miami. Last known address is old. Wanted for multiple counts of larceny. Arrested for assault and battery. Multiple times. In Dade County. Real nice guy," he added, sarcastically. “Likely the second guy. The one who said to let go of Jacob. The face vaguely matches the sketch.”

“That’s amazing that the kid did that well describing the guy. Wasn’t it nearly dark out when he saw him?”

“Yeah, pretty dark already. And under tree cover. Even darker.”

“Kids do amaze me. The things they can do that we don’t give them enough credit for,” he said, thinking about Angel connecting with Mrs. Drewer. “Where’s the dead end there? If you know who he is?”

“He’s an illegal, for starters. No current address. No known family. Associations are random. Mostly from previous arrests. Most still incarcerated. Or dead. And here’s the kicker. We have a line on the car. The grey Camry. It was a rental car. But it was stolen.”

“Stolen? Like off of a rental lot? I thought that would be pretty impossible to do, with the spikes in the exits and all.”

“No. Stolen from the renter.”

“Oh! Information about the renter doesn’t help much then. But you have a location? Where it was stolen from?”

“Sort of. The guy was squirrely. Told the rental agency one thing. Told us another.”

“Why would he do that?”

“It was stolen in Layettown. Not far from the military base. Just off of I-95, south of here. Behind a strip joint. NOT from a bookstore at the mall.”

“Yeah, one of the biggest military bases is down there, Fort Briggs. Was the squirrely renter military?”

“No. My guess? Probably, a married guy. Maybe an executive. Didn’t want it known. That he was at a strip joint. For whatever reason.”

“But the rental company can track the car, where it was and where it’s been, right?”

“They can. That’s how we got a straight answer. About where the car was. When it was stolen. And how we know it was at the Lingle Plantation. It’s the right car.”

“I’m sensing a ‘but’ coming.”

"Yeah. Good sense. But the car tracker stopped sending location data. After it left the Lingle Plantation. All locations are recorded. On the rental company's computer servers. Up to a point. Including the Lingle Plantation. But get this. The last known location? It was the farm. Where the Jeep and body were found. The barn, specifically. If the tracking data can be trusted."

"So, you can tie the two guys, the car theft, Allan's murder with the baseball bat, and the murder of one of the guys neatly together then."

"Well, circumstantially, yes."

"So maybe the guy who was killed was the tech guy, the one responsible for removing the tracker. And the other guy found out he hadn't done it and offed him," said Matthew, jokingly. Then, seriously, he asked, "How was the Cuban guy killed? The baseball bat again?"

"He had been beaten, yes. But the official cause of death, that was the bullet hole. Right between his eyes. At close range."

"Beaten by the other guy and then executed? That sounds like a lot of helpful information. Where's the dead end?"

"Where's the car now? We have no idea. What direction did it go? We don't know. Who's the guy still alive? No idea."

"Oh. I see."

"Hey, you free for lunch tomorrow? We can compare notes. Hash out what we know. Maybe not at Peak Eats, though."

"How about the balcony off the breakroom on the second floor at my office? We can get take out. The café tables out there aren't huge, but we can close the French doors into the break room and we'll be left alone. Sometimes one of my nurses and I eat out there, but I don't know that anyone else does all that much."

"Sounds good. I'll bring in lunch. What do you want?"

"Monday at Peak Eats," pondered Matthew. "Roast beef on rye with a pickle and fresh fruit on the side."

"Does 12:30 work?"

"I'll check my schedule as soon as I get home and text you if it doesn't. See you tomorrow."

"Bye, Doc."

*****

Arriving home, Matthew spotted no neighbors. As he saw the dead end of the road he lived on, he was mulling over what Danbury had said about hitting a bunch of dead ends. They didn't sound like dead ends to him, only more leads to pursue that ran off in potentially different directions. More like a woven rope that had come apart at one end, the split ends each providing new paths to follow. More like split ends than dead ones, he thought.

Still pondering the analogy, Matthew entered his house and, without consciously attending to any of it, went through his evening routine of locking up, setting alarms, turning lights off, scratching Max behind the ears, and rinsing and refilling his bowls. His mind was otherwise very much occupied.

Checking his schedule for the next day from his computer, Matthew texted Danbury to ask if noon would work because he had a patient scheduled for one. After setting up the coffee maker, changing into a soft t-shirt and his favorite sleep pants, and laying out his clothes for the next day, he saw a confirmation text back from Danbury that just said, "*Sure, Doc.*"

Pondering the facts, the people, and the circumstances that were so far known, he kept asking himself what he knew versus what was missing. Everyone, he thought, withheld or purposefully manipulated their statements because everyone in his experience had something to hide, something they didn't want known. In the small town of Peak, it was harder to hide information but even in the comparatively thriving metropolis of Raleigh, smaller communities formed and it was difficult to keep secrets in those as well.

He was no detective, but he wanted to visually evaluate what he knew so far, to see what people had said versus what he thought they might be hiding. He found a legal pad and pen in the desk drawer in the spare bedroom, and sat down on a bar stool at the island in his kitchen. Writing each person's name on the top of a fresh page of paper pulled from the legal pad, he laid those out in front of him. Then he started making notes on what each person had said about themselves and what they said they'd seen or heard.

Penn Lingle, who seemed to be forthcoming, was hiding something. Not that he was any expert on women, but he had a keen sense that she was withholding some key piece of information. Of course, she hadn't been completely forthcoming with him, a complete stranger, he thought. But maybe he could change that. Maybe dinner this week would be the key to getting her to trust him and confide in him fully. He wrote that down as an objective.

And what about Wayne Adams? Matthew hadn't talked to him except for the night of the murder, but Danbury had described him, in one of his typically Danbury ways, as cagey or squirrely, or something like that. The guy wasn't forthcoming with help and information apparently. He had lots of control over the Lingle assets, thought Matthew, and seemingly little accountability. He jotted those thoughts down too.

If Malcolm, Jacob Wheatly, or the McVane boys knew anything of any importance or relevance that they hadn't already shared, Matthew didn't think that they realized it. As he thought about it though, he didn't think they'd asked Malcolm about Allan's notebooks. Would he have any idea what the letters and graphics meant? Was it important? Would he have anything to contribute that they didn't already know about those? He jotted the questions on Malcolm's page.

Somebody, somewhere in the small town of Peak, had to have seen or heard something relevant. They held the pieces to the puzzle that would clear it all up, thought Matthew. The timeline for the evening worked, all except for the two guys at the Lingle Plantation, unless, he considered, they'd been there twice. Maybe they went once through the house, removing the bat and killing Allan, then back again, but for what purpose? He wanted another look through that house. He wrote that down as his next objective.

As intriguing as the exercise was, Matthew eventually realized that it was getting late and he wanted a closer look at his patient schedule for the morning so he neatly stacked the pages on top of the legal pad and pushed it aside. Logging into his computer, he clicked to authenticate with the firewall that protected the patient data and get into the EPIC system where he could not only see the patient schedule, but also the reason for each patient's visit.

It was too early for the onslaught of summer colds and fevers, but apparently the viruses in North Carolina had another agenda, he thought, though he wondered if what he'd diagnose would be more allergies and fewer actual viruses. After researching a couple of patient issues, he logged off the EPIC program and out of the connection through the firewall. He decided to print a label to mail Cici's box so that he could take that to a shipping store and ask about the best shipping method.

He'd sealed the box, attached the label, and had just gotten back into the house from putting it in his Corvette in the garage when he heard his cell phone going off from the kitchen counter. Snatching it up and answering it, he heard an excited Danbury who sounded a bit out of breath and, as usual, skipped the formalities, "We're going to have to reschedule. The lunch tomorrow. I just got a call. From a Sherriff in South Carolina. We had an APB out. On the Toyota Camry. I think they've found it. It's been burned. And it was under water. They're pulling it out of a canal. I'm on my way down now. To be there when it comes up."

"OK, no worries. I have other things that I can do at lunch tomorrow anyway," said Matthew with a shrug that Danbury couldn't see. "Keep me posted, though, on what you find out about it?"

"Will do. It could really help. Even if there's no physical evidence after being burned. It still gives us direction. Our guy was headed south. If it's the car."

"Ah, a split end to follow."

"Come again?"

"It's not a dead end. It's like a rope or cord that's split into multiple strands. You're following one of them."

Danbury just laughed. "The way your mind works," he said. "I don't understand it. Not sure I want to! Good night, Doc," he added, and then he was gone.

Before calling it a night himself, Matthew had one last thing to do. He wasn't sure what the best method would be to get the box across an ocean and safely into Cici's hands as quickly as possible. Back at the computer, he pulled up a search window to locate shipping stores near him. There was a store that he thought he'd seen in Peak, which handled multiple shipping companies. He vaguely remembered seeing it somewhere on the other side of Highway 64 and near the tiny Peak Lake.

Finding a listing for it and the website for the store, All Posts, he also found that it had moved and expanded. It was now closer to downtown Peak and that suited him nicely. Just off Winston Avenue north of the downtown area now, the store apparently offered all things postal, including shipping supplies, information about all carriers, post office boxes to rent, and even an internet café. They had thought of everything, apparently, so he noted the location and the hours of operation and shut his computer down for the night.

Checking the locks and making his final rounds through the house, Matthew wandered down the hallway and climbed into bed, thinking that sleep should come easily after the busy day he'd had. He was mistaken. While he was tired, he couldn't seem to make his mind stop racing down the cords of his rope, first one and then another. He tossed and turned, finally falling into a fitful sleep after midnight.

*****

Matthew had gotten through his usual morning routine at home, and he had just stashed his notebook computer and the legal pad with the torn off pages in his satchel, when his cell phone went off. The incoming call was from Danbury, so Matthew threw his satchel over his shoulder, clicked to answer the call with one hand, and locked up the house with the other.

"Hey Doc," he said, sounding tired. "I'm on my way back from South Carolina. I'm going to sleep for a few hours. After I'm back. Then maybe we can compare notes. For dinner. Instead of lunch. Does that work?"

"Yeah, sure, that works for me. Just call or text when you wake up and let me know what time. I don't have dinner plans this evening."

"Not until tomorrow night, right?" teased Danbury.

"Yeah, I need to call her. It was a nebulous plan, so I need to make it more concrete with a location and time."

Managing to open the garage door, toss his satchel onto the passenger seat, and push the button to start the car with one hand, he ended the call with Danbury. Maneuvering down the short driveway, he backed out easily into the street. As he looked down the street, he saw Mrs. Drewer and Oscar out for their morning walk. His initial reflex was to cringe, but then he thought about his visit with Angel the day before and hoped that version of the woman was the one he'd encounter momentarily.

He crept slowly down the street and eased the window down as he approached her, deciding to proactively greet her first and set the tone for the discussion, "Good morning, Mrs. Drewer," he said brightly. "It's a beautiful morning for a walk."

"Good morning. So it is," she agreed, looking slightly surprised at Matthew's sincere and joyful greeting. She'd scooped up Oscar and he, for the first time Matthew could remember, leaned over curiously to sniff but didn't growl. Matthew held out a hand for him to sniff but didn't try to pet him just yet. One step at a time, he thought, with both woman and beast, lest he get bitten by either.

Maybe, thought Matthew noting her reaction, she had known that he was annoyed with her most of the time. Maybe he wasn't as slick in avoiding her tactfully as he thought he'd been, he chided himself.

"I enjoyed our visit with you yesterday and so did Angel, particularly the Madeline reading. I'm going to get a set of those books to have here when she visits, since I now know how much she loves them."

"Don't wait too long," she advised. "Children seem to change their minds about their favorite things pretty regularly as they grow up, though Madeline should stick around for a couple of years." And then she asked, cocking her head to one side as if the thought had only just occurred to her, "Do you like barbecued chicken?"

"I do. I love it, in fact."

"I was thinking I'd marinate some overnight to grill out for dinner Wednesday evening. But I always have more than enough for myself and usually have leftovers for several more nights. Would you like to join me?"

"Mrs. Drewer, that sounds wonderful. I'd love to. What time?" he asked. Then, remembering his southern manners and upbringing, he added, "And what can I bring?"

"How about six? And you don't need to bring anything but yourself, unless," she added, slyly. "Unless you'd like to stop by the bakery and pick up something decadent that will totally blow my diet?"

Matthew laughed and agreed to do just that. "Have a wonderful day, Mrs. Drewer," he said as he was putting up his window.

"You too, Matthew."

Wow, he thought, in surprise. That was a cordial Cordelia, with no complaining and no nosy questions. He liked this version of his neighbor much better. That happy feeling carried him into Peak, into his office, and he began to see his morning patients with a spring in his step. He'd remembered to put his daily lunch order in with Trina since he wouldn't be meeting Danbury and decided that maybe he should eat quickly at his desk, and then make a house call to check on Malcolm.

He worked alongside Gladys most of the morning and they amicably caught up on each other's lives between patients. She'd had the two sets of twins for the weekend while her youngest daughter and her husband got a break, so she admitted to starting the week off exhausted. "I do know why only young people should have kids," she confessed. "And I don't know how my daughter does it. Have you heard anything from the redhead across the ocean?" she asked conspiratorially.

"She's a strawberry blonde," he corrected as Cici would have done had she been there. "And I have heard from her, yes."

"Didn't you tell me she went to church with your family before she left?"

"She did, and she said she missed that this week. I'm not sure how it can only have been a week. A week today since she left. A week since Allan Lingle was murdered. It seems more like a month!"

"I bet that made your Mama happy, but Mmm mmm mmm, I don't know what I think of that girl decidin' she likes church and then leavin' town like that. And that Allan Lingle murder. Have they found out who did that to him yet?"

Matthew shook his head, "Not yet."

"Are they close?"

"Gladys, what makes you think I know?"

"Oh, I know you know. You just aren't gonna share what you know, are you?" she asked, cocking her head sideways at him.

"I would if I could, Gladys, you know I'd tell you if I could."

16. Following a cord

As they finished their morning roster of patients and the lunches arrived, Matthew agreed to have his with Gladys on the second-floor balcony off the break room but explained that he had a house call to make and he'd have to eat quickly.

The Lingle Plantation was more than just a patient house call to Matthew though. There was some part of the cord he was following there. He was sure of it. Enough so that he wanted to have an unobstructed walk through more than just the historical aspects of it, which would ordinarily have had their own appeal and been more than enough to hold his interest for hours.

After his hasty lunch, he hung his lab coat on the coat rack behind his door and slipped out the side entrance. It was indeed a nice day for a walk, he thought, and he whistled to himself as he enjoyed the lovely spring weather down the dead end of Chapel Street and to the Lingle Plantation. He looked up in appreciation of the old house as he stepped up onto the porch and knocked loudly.

He hated to make Malcolm come to the door, with the knee injury and all, and he made a mental note to get a phone number for him to check on him more easily in the future. After a few minutes, the door was cracked and then opened wide when Malcolm saw Matthew standing there and smiled warmly at him.

"Hi, Doctor Paine," he said. "Are you making house calls now?"

"I am," said Matthew. "I thought I'd check the knee and see how it's doing. Then maybe if it's OK with you, I could see the rest of the house? I'm a bit of a history buff and I'm very curious about it. If you don't mind me wandering through by myself. You really don't need to be climbing stairs yet any more than you have to."

Nodding, Malcolm said, "Sure, come on in."

Getting Malcolm situated back on a sofa where he'd obviously had his leg propped and knee iced, Matthew moved the ice pack over and pulled up an adjacent chair as Malcolm rolled up his pant leg. Matthew switched on the lamp beside him and gently prodded Malcolm's dark skin around the knee cap. Even with the darker pigment of the skin, Matthew could see substantial bruising, but he noted that the swelling was down. He was also happy that Malcolm seemed less bothered by some of the areas which had been immensely tender the day before.

"It's looking worse, but seems to be better," reported Matthew. "But that's often the case with injuries like this. Blood is pooling and causing increased bruising but the swelling is down, so the elevation and ice are doing the trick. How does it feel, overall?"

"Oh, it's better. Not as sore. But I've been staying off of it. Just like you said. I knew that's what I was supposed to do from my studies. I just couldn't do it so well at Amelia's place."

"Do you need anything? Groceries or supplies?"

"Nah, but thanks. I've got a couple of weeks' worth of leftovers in the freezer out in the pantry. I appreciate the offer, though," he added.

"This is the room the intruders ransacked?" asked Matthew, looking around dubiously with an eyebrow raised.

"Yeah, I know I shouldn't have cleaned it up on this knee, but I couldn't stand to see it that way. It doesn't look like they made it into much of the rest of the house."

"I think they were spooked by the boys and left shortly after you did." Looking around, Matthew asked, "The front part of the house was built back in the 1800s, right?"

"Yeah, it was built sometime back in the 1800s. I'm not exactly sure when. It was an old plantation house, so before the civil war. I don't know a lot more about it though."

"That's OK. If I really get curious, I'm sure there's lots about it at the library." With that, Matthew got up and began exploring the ground floor. The interior of the house was much more lavish than the outside, he noted. The porch had obviously been rebuilt and he wondered if it too had been more grand before its reincarnation. In its current state, it was notably plain as compared to the interior. Perhaps that was purposeful, he thought. An old farm house in the 1860s might be left alone, whereas a prosperous plantation house would more likely be burned to the ground. Maybe the renovation was much older than he'd initially thought.

In addition to the comfy room with the overstuffed furniture where Malcolm was convalescing, there was also an elegant and stiffly furnished parlor, a library with walls of shelves filled with leather bound books of all sizes, and a study with dark paneling that smelled of lemon furniture polish and contained a massive oak desk. There was also a large dining room with a long table that looked to seat at least 18, and probably more, above which hung an ornate chandelier, and under which was a lovely but well-worn oriental rug. Sunlight filtering through the tree branches outside cast shadows that danced around the rooms. Some of the rooms, particularly the study, faded into dark corners that looked like they might harbor spider webs, except that the house was immaculate. The floors were all of wide hardwood boards that creaked and groaned in protest as Matthew walked across them.

Wainscoting covered the bottoms of the walls and it was painted in muted trim colors that matched the wide elaborate crown molding at the top of the walls of each room throughout the front of the house downstairs. He wandered, room by room, noting the elegant antique furnishings and thinking that the house must have once hosted some very elaborate parties. He wondered who the house could claim had "slept here" over the years if it could talk. If only it *could* talk, he thought.

There were painted portraits of long-dead family members, he presumed, along the main hallway walls, down a side hallway that led to the side entry door and in the study which was along the side hallway. He felt a momentary, but distinct, chill as he wandered down the main hallway past two of the older family portraits that had eyes which seemed to follow him as he moved along. If was as if they were telling him to get out of their domain and not to return.

Among the collection of portraits in the study, he'd noticed a more recent painting of three children dressed in white coordinating outfits in front of a fountain. He assumed they were Penn, Allan, and Leo when they were young. He'd heard that Allan and Leo looked a lot alike, but as he studied the portrait, he certainly hoped that their mother could tell which boy was which. Surely by their personalities she could, if nothing else. Though Leo was two years younger, according to Penn, he was about the same size as Allan in the portrait, and they could easily have been twins.

The back, more recently added, part of the house, dated to the turn of the twentieth century, which was still historic, but it was far less grand. Behind the original structure, the added kitchen, pantry, laundry room, powder room, and Malcolm's room and private bath, were accessed from the central hallway. A swinging wooden door separated that area from the front of the house. Surprisingly, it didn't squeak in protest as Matthew swung it closed behind him as he returned to the front hallway. He had explored all of the downstairs except for Malcolm's room off the kitchen, which felt intrusive, so he skipped that one.

As he wandered up the front stairway to the second floor, Matthew had noted the symmetry in the house. The wide winding stairway was central, a focal point that opened out onto a wide landing above, which overlooked the entry foyer below. He could well imagine women clad in long, flowing elaborately and intricately decorated gowns descending those steps.

There were four bedrooms on this floor in addition to the master suite, which encompassed the entire right end of the house. It had a sitting room off it and two closets and a bath had been added to modernize it. Matthew felt as if he were intruding because the rooms were untouched, as if their occupants had merely left for a few moments and would return at any time. A dressing table, by a rear window in a corner that seemed to have been created by the bathroom addition, still held an elaborately decorated brush and comb as well as a powder puff and several other toiletry items that were unidentifiable to his male eye.

The bathroom, that had been added, butted clumsily, Matthew thought, up against a window, barely leaving room for the window casing. The addition seemed too large for the bathroom which, by modern standards, was small. Closets still held clothing and shoes, undisturbed by all but a few dust motes floating in the sunlight that was streaming in the windows.

Turning, Matthew explored the other four bedrooms, two of which would have once been wider until bathrooms were added. The expansion on the back of the house provided large alcove sitting areas to the bedrooms across the back of the house. One of these looked to have belonged to Penn. Another bedroom between Penn's and the master suite on the back of the house was generically furnished, as a guest room he presumed. Two more bedrooms, the boys' rooms, shared the far end of the hallway to the left, on the front of the house on the other side of the balcony at the top of the stairs. As he wandered the upstairs hall, the floor boards here too creaked and groaned loudly under his weight.

He'd seen Allan's room the day before, so Matthew wandered into the room that he assumed to have been Leo's. Unlike the other bedrooms, this one seemed to be disturbed but not overtly so. The disturbances were subtle. The bed was just slightly rumpled, the door of the added closet was ajar, and the shoes in the bottom of it were slightly jumbled not neatly lined like the shoes in the other closets.

A drawer left slightly open at the far corner caught Matthew's attention and he walked over to investigate. A piece of woven wool was caught in the drawer, so Matthew opened it to find it full of sweaters and shirts, neatly folded on the right side. The left stack, from which the fabric sticking out had originated, looked to have been rifled through. Before closing the drawer, he snapped some pictures of the room with his cell phone and then moved on to Allan's room, where he looked more closely at everything.

The police had been over the entire house he knew so he wasn't sure what he hoped to find, but he looked it over carefully anyway. It was more sparsely furnished than his siblings' rooms in terms of knickknacks and childhood memorabilia. It had none of the trophies or sports pictures with which Leo's room overflowed. Opening one dresser drawer, Matthew sucked in a deep breath as he saw that it was full of small notebooks in varying colors, but all the same size, neatly stacked in rows. Reaching in, he picked up first one and then another, but the contents were as indistinguishable as they had been reported to be. It was as if Allan had his own code of letters, numbers, lines, circles, and arrows – pictograms that only he could decipher.

The entrance to the back stairwell was in a back corner and it looked to have been added with the back wing addition. From a small landing, Matthew saw sets of steps, one ascending to a top floor and another set descending to the main one. Climbing up the wide and creaking steps,

Matthew tried to walk on the outer edges of the steps to make them squeak less, but that proved to be a vain effort. Upstairs he found four tiny bedrooms along the back left of the house. The front had a steeply sloping ceiling with two large dormer windows adding light to the walkway down the length of the attic.

The walkway wasn't exactly a hallway, thought Matthew, and it was offset back from the center because the front pitch was much steeper than the back. The front roofline sloped from the floor to the point of the roof, interrupted only by the dormer windows. There was a wall that rose about waist high before butting into the roof line across the back. Above all but the bedrooms, the ceiling was unfinished beams and rafters under a tin roof.

No bathrooms or closets had been added on this floor, he noted, and it smelled dank and dusty from disuse. Small low windows allowed filtered sunlight into each of the bedrooms and the ceilings under the eaves were finished in these rooms. The rooms themselves were sparsely furnished and painted what Matthew assumed had once been a utilitarian white, but had since turned grey and drab with time, unlike most of the rest of the house. Servants' quarters, thought Matthew, which nobody has bothered to maintain or update.

Light filtering through the trees and the dormer windows cast shadows that flitted across the walls and looked like dancing spectres, apparitions that would raise the hair on your arms if you were of a mind to believe in ghosts. He did ponder momentarily what he thought about ghosts but he wasn't sure. That spiritual beings existed which were beyond human ability to experience with the five senses, he didn't doubt at all. But that the spirits of departed people who might have a grievance with the house or any of its occupants could still inhabit it, that he wasn't sure about.

An unfinished attic area occupied a smaller space across the right end of the top floor of the house, the opposite end from the stairwell. Here, the cobwebs, heavy and dark with dust, hung from the rafters. Half expecting a bat or two to descend on him, he kept looking over his shoulders at the shifting shadows. As he wandered by old steamer trunks and amongst the detritus of past generations, he saw wash stands and wash basins, chests of drawers, two old wardrobes, and a bookcase. Curious, he flipped open an unlocked steamer trunk and then coughed violently as dust and the pungent smell of moth balls from the neatly packed clothing assaulted his nose and mouth. He closed it quickly.

Noting that only the back stairwell went to the top floor attic space, he wondered how it was accessed before the back addition. He checked his watch and knew that he was running out of time to get back for his patient at one. As he was just about to descend the staircase to the first floor, he heard a thump, bump, and then a loud whump sound behind him. Startled, he turned and looked around but he saw nothing out of place and nothing that could have just fallen to make that noise.

Trying to shake off the feeling that he was being watched, he went down the back staircase to the first floor, rounded a corner, and opened the door to the basement. Something about that basement still bothered him, so he flipped the switches and turned on the light on his phone for one last perusal. It was as he'd remembered it – three brick walls, thick beams overhead, concrete flooring throughout, and the huge furnace against the wooden-slatted wall at the right end of the house.

It was that wall which bothered him, but he didn't know why. It seemed to merely hide the ductwork, electrical cords, and what appeared to be plumbing pipes that disappeared into it. Curious, he tapped around on the wall a bit. Not surprisingly, it all sounded hollow. Nothing moved though, no trap doors, no moving pieces. That didn't make sense to him either. How would a repair person access the utility lines if they needed to be repaired or replaced?

Back upstairs, he stuck his head in the sitting room to ask Malcolm about that and about Allan's notebooks. Malcolm didn't have an answer to either question, though he said that he'd never had to call a repair person for anything. If something broke, he'd just called Wayne Adams. "Like when the pilot light wouldn't stay lit on the furnace a couple of winters ago. I just left a message with Wayne's office and it was fixed pretty fast," he said.

"And the little notebooks, he carried them everywhere and he'd sneak glances at them sometimes when he thought nobody was looking. He didn't want me to see what was in them, so I respected his privacy. He left one on the kitchen counter once, and I did have a look at it before I put it up in his room. It was figures, letters, and numbers with arrows connecting things, like he was making a pattern. Of what, I have no idea. There's a whole collection in his dresser drawer upstairs. Help yourself if you think you can make sense of them."

"Just one more question. You don't clean the house, usually, do you?"

"Not clean, clean, no. I straightened up behind Allan and I did laundry, cleaned up the kitchen after we ate. Things like that. There's a cleaning service that comes once a week and they do the serious cleaning, vacuuming, dusting, polishing silver, scrubbing floors, all of that."

"When do they come?"

"On Tuesdays, usually, why?"

"The bedrooms upstairs are pristine. It looks like the family just stepped out and they'll be right back any minute. Nothing was left out of place. All except for Leo's room."

"Leo's room?" asked Malcolm, surprised. "It isn't clean?"

"Well, clean, yes. I mean, I didn't do a military white-glove inspection or anything." Matthew added. "But things were just slightly out of place. So I was wondering if it had been cleaned lately or why it might not be as perfect as the others."

"I don't know if they came last week or not. You could check with Wayne Adams. His associate handles all of the maintenance, cleaning, paying us all. If anybody would know, his folks would."

"He handles all of the household budget?"

"He does. I got allotments each month for groceries, clothes, and miscellaneous expenses. It was always enough to cover everything. The power, gas, and utility bills were paid directly. I never even saw those."

"Thanks, Malcolm, I really appreciate it. Hey, could you maybe not mention to Penn or Wayne Adams that I was here? I mean, if they outright ask you, I'm not at all asking you to lie. And I was checking on a patient," he said with a grin. "Just don't volunteer the information about me checking out the house too?"

"Sure. No problem. You were never here," he said, shrugging. "Just another ghost."

Reaching in his pocket, Matthew handed Malcolm a business card that he'd jotted his cell number on, "Here. Give me a call if your knee worsens and also if you hear, see, or remember anything that might help with finding Allan's killer?"

"Sure. Happy to. And thanks for checking in. I'll let you know if the knee gets worse."

"Or doesn't continue to get better."

"Yeah, OK, that either."

"I guess you have a number on file at the office. Is it OK to check in on you and the knee?"

"Oh, yeah, here, I'll text it to you," said Malcolm as he flipped over the card Matthew had given him and sent a text message to the cell number on the back.

"Ah, good. Got it," Matthew said, as he heard the phone ding and saw a new message come in. "I'll lock up behind myself, so don't get up. Thanks again," Matthew waved and then slipped out, locking the door behind him, and walked briskly back to his office where he knew that his patient would already be having vitals taken by Gladys or Diane, his dependable nursing staff.

*****

In the midst of Matthew's afternoon patients and his cup of afternoon coffee, Danbury called. Checking his watch, Matthew saw that it was already four and he knew that he still had one patient left to see so he quickly picked up.

"Hey, Doc," said Danbury.

"Are you back among the living?" asked Matthew, hearing the still tired voice and knowing that Danbury had only managed a few hours of sleep after being up all night and driving back from somewhere in coastal South Carolina.

"Mostly. How's dinner at the diner sound? Around six?"

"Yeah, that works. I'll be finished with patients in another half hour or less, but I'll have some charting to do and I need to go mail a package afterward."

"OK, see you then."

After treating a badly sprained ankle and prescribing rest, icing, and elevating, yet again, he was finished seeing patients for the day. Matthew quickly reviewed the charts that Gladys and Diane had prepared online, made a couple of updates to each, and packed up to leave for the day. It was only five, he noticed, so he had plenty of time to get to All Posts before they closed at six and then to meet Danbury afterward.

The Corvette was steamy as he climbed in, started it up, and turned on the air conditioning. May in North Carolina could go either way, he mused. It could be scotching hot as it currently was or chilly, breezy, and rainy. It was anybody's guess as to which way it would go. Like a moody child was the weather in North Carolina.

Reaching the All Posts store quickly, despite having to circle around to turn left on Winston Avenue because Chapel Street was one way coming in, Matthew realized that he could almost have walked faster. Up three blocks and over three blocks, just past the town hall and community center, to the corner of Old Chapel and Sandy Branch Roads wasn't a bad walk, he thought.

As he entered the store, he was impressed. There were boxes advertising various carriers stacked to the left of the door in front of the plate glass window and a tiny internet café with tables and chairs in front of the window beyond that. As he entered the store, Matthew was in an area enclosed by glass walls with a second glass door in front of him and to his right row upon row of postal boxes in varying sizes, the larger ones on the bottom. To the left and at the back of the store behind shelves of greeting cards, labels, tape, and other packing supplies, he spotted a counter and carried his box through the second door and over to it.

A woman had just stepped up to the counter in front of him and, hearing the ensuing conversation, he sighed to himself as he realized that it might be a while before he could get his box mailed. He had a rhythm running through his head that he was tapping with one foot while he listened to the woman plying the guy behind the counter with questions.

"I have a startup business," she explained. "And I don't want mail coming to my house. But neither do I want a PO Box number. I need a physical street address. One of my co-founders said you have those and you can hold all large packages for us?"

"That's right," said the guy behind the counter. "The addresses here are our street address on the top line and then your suite number beneath it. If you went with a larger box," he said, obviously going for the big sale right off the bat, "your address would be 1300 Sandy Branch Road, Suite 2000, for example. Getting the larger box would mean that you could get larger packages after hours if you needed to, without waiting for us to open the next morning."

"Getting mail after hours?" asked the woman. "How does that work?"

"We have state-of-the-art security here," he replied. "You'd have a key card and a clicker that together will open the outside door allowing you access to your mailbox at any time, twenty-four seven. If a package is still too big to fit in those larger boxes, we do hold those for you back here and you just come to the counter, present your key card, which will have your picture and name on it, and we hand you your package. It's as simple as that."

"What if one of us loses our ID card?" she asked.

"Your ID card has a QR code on it that's unique to your mailbox. We have an app so that you can access the QR code on your phone. If you don't have your card and clicker to access the building after hours, you can request a pin from the app. It'll get emailed to the email account we have on file for you, and you can just enter that on the keypad after you scan the QR code from your phone. Double authentication is required for access, one way or another, so your mail is always secure."

"So, what do I need to do to rent a box?"

"Just fill out all of the information on this card and indicate whether you want to be billed monthly, quarterly, or annually."

Matthew was relieved, at that moment, to see a second employee step up to the counter and ask if she could help him.

"Yes. I need to mail this package to London in the fastest and most reliable way possible."

"Certainly, Sir," the young woman said politely, and then proceeded to explain the shipping options and the forms to be completed for international shipping and customs requirements.

Catching a whiff of Cici's perfume as he handed the box over, Matthew felt the old gnawing longing for her. Fighting it off, he finished the transaction and noticed the woman who'd been in front of him in line was now off at a side counter dutifully filling out the required form. He shook his head in amusement at a business that was so technically savvy with their entrance security but used a paper card form for their customer intake. It was one of the many ironies that Matthew had encountered in the past week. His life seemed full of them lately.

17. Comparing notes

With the package successfully on its way to England, Matthew thought it too late to call, so he texted Cici to tell her to be on the lookout for it. One thing he realized he hadn't done for her was to check pricing for the sale of her car. He made a note to do that when he got home as he slid into his car.

Driving back into downtown Peak, Matthew parked and carried his satchel into Peak Eats. The bell jingled over his head as he entered, a full twenty minutes early. He had taken just a few steps in when he saw both Mallory and Evie head his way, pads poised mid-air. As they saw each other, they stopped to bicker and he side-stepped them, heading for the empty booth in the back corner that he was rapidly claiming as his own.

He hadn't thought that Penn Lingle was right about the waitresses, but what did he really know about the female mind? His experience, at least for the past six years, was a bit limited and he'd never been a ladies' man, like his childhood friend James. As he sat down with his back to the wall, age and seniority must have won out because Mallory quickly approached. She was blonde and curvaceous, and Matthew had heard from Mrs. Drewer that she had been very popular as a teenager, the head cheerleader in high school. Mrs. Drewer had also earlier reported that Mallory was terrified that she'd peaked early and that was it. A successful husband, Mallory thought, would fix that and get her back on track for where she thought she should be in life by twenty-three. He wondered if Mrs. Drewer's information might be accurate.

"Can I get you something to drink, Dr. Paine?" she drawled sweetly, flashing her toothy dimpled smile down at him.

"Just a glass of water with lemon for now," he responded, returning the smile and then decided to have a little fun. "Detective Danbury will be joining me in a few minutes, so I'll wait for him to order."

He wasn't disappointed. Mallory immediately dimpled, smiling broadly. With the big toothy grin, showing nearly perfect pearly whites, she said, "No problem. I'll be right back with your drink."

Chuckling to himself, he wondered what else he'd missed that seemed so obvious to women. Figuring that was too much of a loaded question to contemplate, he reached into his satchel and pulled out the papers he'd been working on the night before, with the legal pad, and spread them out before him. He sat contemplating them until Mallory returned with his water glass. He then he pulled them in briefly as he decided to add a page from his legal pad.

Writing *Warren Danbury* across the top of the page, he figured the guy knew a lot about the family, the house, and the neighborhood and he might have knowledge that even he took for granted as being irrelevant. Anything was possible, Matthew reasoned. Having just jotted down the protective relationship with Allan growing up and the unrequited crush on Penn, Matthew looked up as the bell over the door jingled and Danbury walked in.

Mallory wasn't far behind. With Matthew's drink and her pad and pen poised, she set the drink down and flashed her best smile at Danbury and asked what he'd like to drink. Apparently oblivious to her charms, Danbury ordered an iced tea without the lemon and greeted Matthew as he sat down. Neither of the men was looking as she wiggled her hips invitingly and walked away.

"What's all this?" asked Danbury, indicating Matthew's stack of notes.

"These are just my notes on what each person has told us so far. I'm pretty certain of two things."

"Which are?"

"Almost everybody we've talked to so far is either withholding something purposefully or there's something that they haven't told us because they don't think it's relevant. Yourself, included."

"Why me?"

"Because you knew Allan Lingle growing up. You knew Penn and Leo too. You might know more than you think you do about them. These notebooks that Allan was always scribbling in, for example. There's a drawer full of them in Allan's bedroom. The scrawling is alpha-numeric-graphic. That's the best way I know to describe it. It's as if he has his own coded language and nobody else seems to know how to read it. I wonder if you could."

"Doubtful, but I'll have a look. What's the second thing?"

"The Lingle Plantation, haunted or not, and I'd bet not, is at the center of this somehow. I just have this feeling, but it's more than that. It's visceral, like I just know in the depths of my being that the house holds the key. Or at least it holds a key. I'm not sure what it is yet, but it's niggling around the corners of my mind. It's like it's just right there but I can't quite grasp it."

"We'd call that going with your gut. Down at the precinct. You have a strong feeling. Maybe that somebody's guilty. Or maybe that they're not. Either way, it's just something you know. You don't know how you know it. You just do."

"Exactly! Now if I can just figure out what it is that I know about that house. It's driving me nuts."

"Huh," was all Danbury had a chance to say before Mallory reappeared with Danbury's drink and asked to take their orders. Looking up at the menu board across the room on the wall, Matthew asked, "What day is it? Oh yeah, it's Monday. I guess I don't want chicken pot pie."

Mallory looked confused as Danbury chuckled. They placed their orders, Mallory sparkled her toothy smile at them and disappeared behind the counter, unobserved wiggling all the way.

As they resumed their conversation about the murder investigation, Matthew told Danbury about his tour of the house that afternoon, everything he'd seen and observed, including how Leo's room was just slightly less perfectly neat than the others.

"I noticed when I walked through today that most of the house looks like a museum. It's like the occupants stepped out for a few minutes, leaving everything pristinely perfectly organized, and they'll be coming back any second. All but Leo's room."

"What about it?"

"It was clean but slightly off. Rumpled or something."

"How so?"

"The closet door was ajar and the shoes weren't neatly lined up. A dresser drawer was cracked open with a sweater slightly exposed from one side. On the inside one stack of shirts was pristinely neat and the other, the one where the sweater was closed in the drawer, looked like it'd been rifled through. Here, I'll show you," he said, pulling out his phone and pulling up the pictures he'd taken.

"See? It's subtle, but the bed is slightly rumpled. The others in the house look like you could bounce a quarter off them."

"Yeah, I wouldn't have noticed."

"If the rest of the house weren't so pristine, I wouldn't have either. Malcolm said it's cleaned every Tuesday but I bet it wasn't last week. Are there any pictures of this room from the police search after the murder?"

"What are you getting at?"

"Just wondering if it was messed up before the murder or after. And if it was cleaned last week, then it was well after."

"I'll check. There are likely pictures. Of Leo's room too. And Wayne Adams would know. If it was cleaned last week."

"Speaking of Wayne Adams, you said he hadn't been completely helpful with providing information about the Lingle Plantation and financial affairs. What did he tell you? And what do you think he isn't telling you?"

"It's in a trust for Allan's use. We knew that. Managed by Wayne's company. Which we also knew. He's just not forthcoming. On details with specifics. He's refusing to show us the records. We'll likely have to get a search warrant. Or court order. To get him to turn over those files. I think that's being worked on. By the Peak guys. I have an expert in Raleigh. Data forensics. Guy by the name of Ed Watson. He can take a look. And tell us if it's all legit."

"Good. From what Malcolm said, it sounds like everything is managed through Adams' law office. From the services on the house to the payment of all expenses, including Malcolm's salary and a monthly household stipend."

"Yeah, I knew that. Wayne told me that much. It's the investments.

That's where he got squirrely. He gave noncommittal answers. And then refused to answer when I tried to pin him down. Money in the trust is invested. Somehow. That's what he won't share."

"OK, that's a waiting game for now then?"

"Yup. We wait for the search warrant. And then the forensics. And then we get answers. Hopefully."

"Now tell me about the car they found in the swamp in South Carolina."

"It was a canal. Man-made. Narrow but deep. The car had been burned. Set on fire. Then pushed into the canal."

"Is it the one? The same grey Toyota Camry that we were looking for?"

"It is. The VIN was still intact. On the metal strip. In the corner of the windshield. The rental company confirmed it. It's the car. It's being examined now. In a lab in South Carolina. Probably pulled apart as we speak. They'll let me know. If they find any evidence. Fingerprints or DNA. Anything like that."

"Wow, sounds like a lot of work. I hope they find something that can help figure out who the second guy is and then if he murdered Allan."

"They also found a gun. Not in the car. In the canal. Divers found it. When they submerged to look for a body. No body. But the gun was about 20 feet away. It's being tested too. Ballistics will tell the story. If it's been used in a crime."

"As in if it shot the guy found out in Joseph County?"

"Yeah. We have the bullet. So ballistics should match. If that was the gun."

"And now you have a direction."

"Huh?"

"The guy headed south from here, at least."

"Ah. Yeah. Probably stole another car. Maybe headed to Florida. Where the other guy was from. Possibly."

Their discussion and conjecture were interrupted by Mallory bringing their plates. Both of them had ordered the Salisbury steak special. "Can I get you anything else? Any condiments or anything?"

Looking at their plates, Matthew declined but Danbury asked for some steak sauce. Matthew quickly blessed his meal silently and both men dived in without waiting for the steak sauce.

All was quiet at the back corner table as the plates were cleaned and as usual Danbury's had been heaped higher. Matthew ordered a cup of decaffeinated coffee when Mallory cleared the plates. They were getting ready to pay their bills when Matthew suddenly leaned over and said, "He should have been here, you know? It's Monday night. Allan Lingle should have been sitting right over there when we came in," and he pointed at the table by the wall. "I didn't know him at all, but I feel the wrong in this whole situation."

"Yeah, Doc, me too."

They were quiet for a moment as Mallory set the coffee down and picked up the checks and payment. As she walked away, Matthew said, "One other thing. When did you decide to trust Malcolm? It occurred to me to wonder at some point on Saturday how we went up there thinking we might be chasing a murderer and came back helping the guy."

"I thought we could early. I figured he wasn't the murderer. But when he was worried about Allan, I knew we could trust him. He really didn't know Allan had been killed. And then his reaction when we told him. That sealed it for me. I've seen insincere reactions lots of times. But that wasn't one of them. He really didn't know. That Allan was dead. He thought he was the one they were after."

"You trust him now?"

"As much as I trust anybody. In a murder investigation."

Matthew just nodded, taking it all in. "So now what? Where do we go from here?"

"We're waiting on information. Mostly. About the car. From Wayne Adams. One way or another. And for your revelation about the house. And maybe if you can pump Penn some more. Over your dinner tomorrow. She might have more to say."

"You think this will all eventually make sense?"

"Yeah Doc. I sure hope so."

"Me too."

Mallory brought their change back, smiling sweetly at each of them in turn and said, "Ya'll have a nice night now. Come back and see me."

She didn't, Matthew now noted, say "come back and see us," but instead she'd very specifically said "me." He smiled at her and responded that he'd see her soon. Then he and Danbury stepped out onto the sidewalk. The evening was cooling off as the sun was sinking and the heat from the day was radiating up from the sidewalk. It would have been a great night for a walk, thought Matthew, except that he'd driven over and was parked just around the corner.

As he drove home, Matthew's mind was racing with thoughts about the investigation and the recent events in his life. He pondered what they knew and what they needed so badly to find out about the murder, why the Lingle Plantation was haunting his mind, if the changes he'd seen in Cici over the past month meant anything. He was thinking about his dinner with Cordelia Drewer on Wednesday, and there was also the dinner tomorrow night with Penn. He still needed to talk to her to solidify their plans, but then what? Was it officially a date? He wasn't sure. And he wasn't sure how he felt about it if it was.

He drove quietly into the neighborhood, slipping in slowly so that his otherwise noisy Corvette didn't disturb his elderly neighbors. As he entered the house and locked up, Matthew immediately felt the soft brush of soft fur against the back of his leg and reached down to scratch Max between the ears and under his chin.

After depositing his satchel on the end of the sofa, he returned to the kitchen to feed Max and rinse and refill his water bowl. As the big grey tabby cat munched happily on his favorite dry food, Matthew picked up his cell to call Penn.

"Hi Matt," she answered. "I'm sorry, does anyone call you that? Or should I just stick with Dr. Paine and all of the associated jokes?"

"Most people call me Matthew," he said, "And thanks for skipping the jokes again. Unless you have some truly new and creative material."

"Doubtful. With that name, I'm sure you've heard it all."

"Probably. Listen, I was just calling about tomorrow night. We made tentative dinner plans, so I thought we should probably firm them up with a time and location. Do you have a favorite restaurant in Peak? Or would you rather go into Raleigh?"

"Going out is such a hassle. I'd say you can come over to my place and I'd cook for you but I don't really have much of a place here, do I?"

"Yeah, with Malcolm at Lingle Plantation, I guess you don't. You're welcome to come over here if you don't want to go out," he offered and then immediately regretted it. He wasn't sure what the dating dynamic should be, if this was indeed a date, because he hadn't had a first date in so long. He was pretty sure though that he didn't want a romantic candlelight dinner nor did he want any awkwardness about how long she stayed.

Jumping quickly on the invitation, Penn said, "I'd love that! I can still cook for you, if you'd like. I'm kind of picky about what I eat, which is one of the reasons I don't eat out a lot."

"That's fine, we can cook here," he said amenably and gave her his address and a general idea of how to find his place. "What should I be sure to have in the way of groceries?"

"Why don't you focus on a bottle of wine and putting together an organic salad? With low fat or fat-free dressing. I'll do the rest. Deal?"

"Sure. I can do that. What time?"

"Oh, say, seven?"

"That works. I'll have the salad underway and the wine chilled by seven."

"Great. See you then."

As they said their goodnights and ended the call, Matthew wondered what he'd just done. He hadn't dated in the year since he and Cici had split up, not really, though he'd had well-meaning friends try repeatedly to set him up with women. Somehow that required a leap of faith or something that he just hadn't managed to commit to, he thought. Could he now, he wondered. Convincing himself that it was a moot point because it wasn't really a date, he went through his usual evening routine laying out his clothing, setting the coffee maker for the next morning, and then decided to climb in bed with the book he'd been trying to read instead of playing his guitar.

*****

More tired than he'd realized, the next thing he knew, he was startled awake by the alarm. He rolled over and turned it off, picking up his cell phone in the process, to see two things. It was Tuesday, May the 20th, he noted, wondering how it could possibly have been over a week since Cici had left. Cici had texted, thanking him for sending her box. He decided to FaceTime her instead of waiting for her to contact him.

She picked up quickly, though sounding out of breath and hurried as she was clearly in motion and the background blurred behind her. Matthew heard, "Mind the gap," in the background and knew immediately that she was near a subway train.

"Hey, sorry I caught you at a bad time," he said.

"It's OK," she said. "It's always wonderful to hear from you. It's just that I'm going to lose you as soon as I step on this train. I'm surprised that I was able to pick up down here and have a connection. I'm not on wi-fi though."

"OK, there wasn't anything really important. I was just checking in."

"Maybe we can chat later today? Or tomorrow? Text me some open slots once you get to work, and I'll try to connect with you later."

"Sounds good. Take care, Cici." Even as he said it, he thought it sounded lame, but he really didn't know what else to say, so they disconnected and Matthew crawled out of bed to get on with his morning routine. Though usually a positive person whose glass was more than half full, Matthew felt sluggish and heavy, as if something difficult was just on the next horizon. It wasn't like him to be moody, so he tried to brush off the feeling as he set off for work.

18. Bluesday confessions

Somehow, Matthew managed to get through the day, but he was very aware that he was dragging through it and he wasn't sure why. He'd gotten a full night's sleep, so he had no real excuse for feeling uninspired, no excuse that he'd admit to himself anyway.

Partially admitting the source of his slump, Matthew checked his phone again to confirm that the last, and in fact the only, response he'd gotten from Cici was just a thumbs up on the times he'd sent her that he was available to talk. She hadn't taken advantage of any of them, including lunch, which he'd eaten alone at his desk.

Leaving the office a little early for a Tuesday, Matthew swung by the local market on the way home and picked up two bottles of wine, one red and one white, because he'd failed to ask Penn what she was planning to cook. Finding an organic spring salad mix in a container and then some tomatoes, baby carrots and red and yellow peppers, he figured that would make a nice colorful salad. Like the wine, the salad dressing was a bit difficult to pick for someone he didn't know at all, but he decided on a raspberry vinaigrette and a fancy lite Italian, both of which he figured he'd eat eventually if she didn't.

As he was driving into his neighborhood, he saw Mrs. Drewer and stopped to say hello. "I had meant to ask if you'd solved your ant problem," he said, conversationally.

"Why, are you worried that I might feed you ants for dinner tomorrow night?" she smirked at him.

Chuckling, he said, “That honestly hadn’t occurred to me.”

Oscar, whom she’d scooped up as Matthew pulled alongside her, stuck his nose over to investigate and Matthew put his hand out to be sniffed. Deciding that Matthew must be OK, Oscar allowed his head to be petted a couple of times before drawing himself back up under Mrs. Drewer’s arm.

“The ants are mostly gone now. Oh, and your sister called me yesterday,” she said. “I’m going to go read, Madeline books, of course, to Angel’s class next week. I’m looking forward to it. As much as I hated the politics that had taken over the school system when I retired, I do love the children and I miss them.”

“Angel’s a handful, but she will sit still to read books. I’m not sure about the rest of her classmates, but you’ll at least have one attentive listener to a Madeline book. I’m headed home to finish my charting for the day and clean up the house a bit before a dinner guest comes over this evening, but I’m looking forward to your barbequed chicken tomorrow night! Enjoy your walk, Mrs. Drewer,” he said, waving and putting his window up before she could ask about his guest.

He wasn’t sure how he felt about his guest himself, but he knew Mrs. Drewer would notice the rental car in his driveway so he figured he’d broach the subject and then run away in case she was feeling inquisitive today. As if there were any day when she wasn’t, he thought. The subject would surely come up the next night, so he’d have to work on his explanation in the meantime, he thought, wincing.

*****

When Penelope Lingle arrived, promptly at seven, Matthew helped her carry in three bags of groceries and a large Dutch oven. He wondered if she’d gotten the large pot from the Lingle Planation and if she was planning to feed his entire neighborhood but he asked her neither question. Helping her unpack, he spotted an array of ingredients, some of them in foreign-looking packaging, like some mushrooms that he’d never heard of and a small bottle of extra virgin olive oil, as well as familiar items like onion, garlic cloves, and fresh thyme.

“I didn’t think to ask what you were preparing,” he said a bit sheepishly. “So, I got a bottle of red wine and a bottle of white, just to be prepared.” The salad he’d already put together was in a bowl in the refrigerator and he moved it aside to pull out the bottle of white wine.

"Either one will do, really, though I think most people prefer red." she said. "This dish has burgundy wine and cognac in it. I brought both of those. Ever cooked coq au vin?"

"Cooked, no. Enjoyed eating, yes."

She laughed at his honesty as he helped her unpack the bags and set the ingredients out on his kitchen island. "I will need a few common ingredients that I didn't bring, but I assumed that you'd have."

"Name them," he said helpfully.

"Flour, salt, pepper, and butter."

"No problem," he said, getting the items from the pantry, the Lazy Susan by the stove, and the refrigerator.

"And a cutting board and sharp knife."

"OK," he said, retrieving and handing her those items as well. "Now, how can I help?"

"How are you with chopping?"

"Ah, I'm the sous chef this evening?"

"Could you dice the garlic and chop the thyme and mushrooms? I won't be ready for those immediately, but if you can just set them aside in bowls, that'd be great. And I'll need a plate or large bowl," she said as she pulled some sort of organic, free-range chicken out of the packaging and started washing it.

Matthew put a platter beside her and started working on his ingredients. They worked amicably side-by-side making small talk, mostly about Peak and how it had grown and changed since Penn had lived there.

After a bit of sauteing and mixing, Penn put the large covered pot containing the chicken in the oven and announced that they had a break while it cooked, so Matthew poured them each a glass of wine.

"We could have the salad as a first course out on my patio, if you'd like," he offered.

"Sure, why not?"

They served their bowls, she chose the fat-free raspberry vinaigrette, and they stepped out onto the patio to enjoy the cooling evening.

"That coq au vin looks like it's going to be really great," said Matthew. "Do you always cook so elaborately?"

She smiled, setting her glass of wine down. "I like to eat elaborately, and I prefer cleaner ingredients so I cook quite a bit myself. I can prep meals like this one on the weekend and many of them are actually better after having been in the refrigerator for a few days so I can eat them throughout the week."

"That's smart."

"It takes a bit of planning ahead, though, which I admit I'm not always that great at. I'm working on it. Food prep and planning are part of my new book that's coming out next month."

"You wrote a book?"

"I did. Co-authored actually with a friend of mine who's a nutritionist. It's called *Mindful Dining*. The majority of my contribution is about how to slow down and savor your food so that you don't over eat and you feel satisfied actually eating less. Lots of people, me included, love to eat delicious food, right?"

Matthew nodded his agreement, as his mouth was full of salad.

"For lots of people, it's not about what they eat as much as it is about portion control. It's just so good you just keep eating and eating and eat your way into weight gain. It takes intention to slow down and savor every bite. But, when you do that, you eat less and feel more satisfied after meals and snacks."

"That makes sense," said Matthew, thinking he was equally guilty of overeating and his mind wandered to Danbury who ate twice as much as he did but in half the time. He suppressed a small smile as he thought of Danbury and Penn together. They'd either kill each other over basic philosophies or fall entirely for each other as attracting opposites.

With their salad plates and wine glasses empty, they wandered back in and Penn pulled the huge Dutch oven out and finished off the meal preparation. They opted to eat inside. "Could you perhaps refill the wine glasses and light some candles for your little table there?" asked Penn, indicating the small table in Matthew's breakfast nook in the bay window. Barely larger than the café table on his back porch, it would be very intimate, he thought, and he wasn't sure candles would fit. He dutifully refilled the glasses and found a pair of white candles in brass candlesticks, put them in the middle of the little table, and lit them.

Enjoying the meal immensely, Matthew was trying to practice the "mindful dining" that she'd spoken of earlier and enjoy each bite thoroughly. As they finished and were cleaning up, he complimented her cooking and the eating strategy. She left the remains for him in containers in the refrigerator, slipped the clean pot in a bag, and then took her third glass of wine around the little corner to his sitting area.

She plopped down on one end of the sofa. As he sat down on the other end, she said, as if they'd been discussing the murder investigation all night, "You're going to seize all of the management records from the estate, aren't you?"

"I'm not," said Matthew, sidestepping the insider information she was clearly asking for. "I can't really speak to what Danbury and the Peak Police will do, but I'd say it's a pretty safe bet."

"You know what I mean. Anything to do with the finances from the estate will come out," she said, taking a large sip of wine as if for liquid courage. "It'll all come out, won't it? The good and any bad and ugly too."

Choosing his words carefully, Matthew responded, "Penn, I'm sure Danbury will do whatever it takes to get to the bottom of the murders, primarily Allan's. If that, in some way, involves the financial aspects of the estate, then yes, that information will probably come out eventually."

Leaning back into the sofa and forward in Matthew's direction, she said, conspiratorially, "I also have a confession to make. It's something that I'm sure will come out in the investigation into my brother's murder, and I'd like to get ahead of it. You're the only one I feel comfortable telling, but I trust you to share it with Danbury gracefully."

Matthew couldn't imagine what was coming next, but he just nodded his consent and said, "I'll do my best."

She took another large sip of her wine before continuing, "When I was home last, nearly ten years ago when my mother died, I was in the middle of a messy divorce. I had a small business, a gym, and I wasn't sure what was going to happen with it, you know, with the divorce proceedings and all. I'd thought that money from the estate would help me get by until I could get my business on solid ground and I had plans, which I had to put on hold with the divorce, to expand it to include a spa."

She looked down at her wine glass, swirling the liquid and sipping aggressively, as if the ability to continue could be found in it.

"I know I told you that I was relieved not to be stuck here taking care of Allan or dealing with Leo's antics, and that's true. Eventually, it was true anyway. First though I was dealing with disappointment over the will settlement because it wasn't split among the three of us. And then there was the guilt for wanting just the money and not the responsibility for my brothers or the house and grounds. Eventually, I decided that freedom was better than a huge cash infusion, regardless of how badly I could use a nice one right about then. And a large inheritance also didn't get tangled up in the divorce settlement, which was also good. But none of that was clear in my mind at first. At first like Leo I was very upset."

"But that wasn't enough reason for either of us to desert Allan like we did. He was such a sweet soul. He was really more bonded to Leo than to me, so I think I could assuage my own guilt in leaving him that way, by blaming Leo for leaving him. Leo could read and understand Allan better than anyone in our family. I was struggling with everything – my divorce, my financial situation, the guilt over wanting to run from Allan's needs."

She searched his face as if looking for a reaction, which he hoped he wasn't giving her, before she continued. "Wayne Adams had recently moved here from Ohio and he had taken over the estate administration, which then became the trust fund for Allan. I thought that he was escaping the shards of a life destroyed by a messy divorce out there and he was starting over. He'd started dating Libby by then. Pretty seriously, apparently, but I didn't know that at the time."

She stopped and Matthew waited her out. When she said nothing further, he offered, "Whatever it is, it's OK. You can tell me."

Looking up, sorrowfully, she said, "We had one night together, Wayne and I. I was lonely, I had been betrayed and I was vulnerable. I guess I just figured he was in the same boat and we just kind of clicked, you know?" She drained her glass and set it down, noisily, "Oops. Sorry."

"No problem."

"Anyway, afterward, he begged me not to tell anyone. He didn't want Libby to find out. I'll admit I was angry with him, furious even, and retrospectively I can see that I was taking out a lot of my anger for Jeffrey, my ex-husband, on him. I told him that if he wanted me to keep it quiet he'd better figure out how to carve off a little bit of that estate and send it my way. Otherwise, I threatened to tell Libby myself."

After a moment's hesitation, Matthew asked, "And how did he respond?"

"His face turned about five shades of red, then purple, and he said, through gritted teeth, that I'd have a seventy-five thousand dollar check in my hands by close of business the next day. He told me to stop by and see his assistant at five the next day and he'd have it ready for me. Then he escorted me out of his office with the general understanding that I was never to grace the doorstep to it ever again."

"Wow! But you had to deal with him later though with Allan's care, right?"

"Not really. And that's the other reason I wasn't telling you about earlier. The reason I left here, checked out on my brothers, and had no plans ever to come back. I was embarrassed. I was angry. And hell, I'd just swindled seventy-five grand."

"Is that an amount you'd asked for?"

"No, it was an amount I'd mentioned needing earlier, to ensure that my business was secure. I'd taken out a loan to augment outfitting my gym facility and I wanted to pay that back and then renovate some space in the back of my building as a spa. I knew that was a tiny drop in a huge bucket of what was in that estate."

"So, you blackmailed him," said Matthew. It wasn't a question, just a statement of fact that he hoped didn't sound too judgmental because he had no intention that it should.

"Yeah, I did," she said, sadly. "And I ran from my brothers when they both needed me. I had no use for complications in my life and I was a horrible sister. Then, I couldn't get away from them fast enough. Now, I just wish I had more time with them, with Allan. I wish I could go back and do all of that over again. I loved my brother but I didn't show it well. I hope he knew it!" she said, on a sobbing breath, as she brushed tears from her check.

Sliding over to her, Matthew put an arm around her, comfortingly.

"You're so easy to talk to," she said, leaning in closer to him and putting her hand on his thigh.

Matthew wasn't sure if he was more surprised by her confession or her reaction afterward. As he was pondering how to respond, he found her quickly leaning in and kissing him, slowly at first, and then with a hunger that he matched at least at first. Something down deep within him felt guilty, as if this was a betrayal of Cici in some way.

She must have sensed his unease and hesitation because she pulled back, looking at him longingly, and said, "What's wrong? You're not into older women?"

"Older? You're not that much older," he managed to splutter.

"Five years. You're thirty, right?"

"How did you know that?"

"I read your bio on the web site for your practice. Matthew Landon Paine, 30, a doctor of Osteopathic Medicine joined Peak Family Practice in 2017," she quoted.

"Oh."

"Is that a problem?"

"No. That's not a problem." After a moment's pause, he added, "And you're not the problem."

"Oh, here it comes. 'It's not you, it's me,'" she said with finger quotes in the air.

Completely frustrated, he tried to explain what he himself was struggling to understand. "You're a beautiful woman, Penn. And I am attracted to you, believe me, I am."

He caught her glancing down to verify that as he added, "So, it's not that. It's just . . . ."

As he struggled, she supplied, "It's just that there's someone else."

"Yes. I mean, no. I mean, wow. I'm not good at this dating thing at all, am I? I guess I'm really rusty." Leaning back into the soft buttercream leather sofa cushions, he took her hand in his, "There had been somebody else for over five years. We were pretty serious and talking about marriage. We broke up about a year ago because we realized that we wanted very different things in life. If I'd met you two months ago though, this would have gone very differently."

"You realize that makes no sense, right?"

Taking a deep cleansing breath, he continued, "We were brought back together last month through extenuating circumstances, not that either of us was trying to reconcile, and it just got complicated. Many of the reasons I had known we weren't compatible long term seemed to be resolving. She was changing, growing, and I admit that I'm not sure where we stand right now."

"Well, I don't see her here," Penn offered, huskily. "But I am here. And you are here," she reached out and touched his face.

"She's in London working with a client there, but I miss her and I wish I didn't," he said, honestly, turning to her as she ran her fingers through his soft, thick wavy brown hair. It felt really nice.

Studying him for a long moment, she must have seen the anguish in his eyes and she slid back, giving him room, and said quietly, "I'm sorry I pushed. When I see something or someone I want, I tend to go after it."

"It's OK," said Matthew, relieved and amused because that sounded very much like something Cici herself would have said. He wasn't sure what would have happened if Penn hadn't pulled back from him when she did because he had been fighting an internal battle. He'd never been able to juggle multiple women at the same time like some of his friends, like James, he thought. It just wasn't in his nature and, until he was certain where things stood with Cici, he wasn't ready for Penn or anyone else. But that didn't mean that he hadn't been sorely tempted and he knew it.

As they both relaxed, still facing each other and leaning back into the sofa, Penn said, shakily, "I'm really not a lush, I promise, and I never drink three glasses of wine." She hiccupped loudly before adding, "I don't usually drink more than one glass. I think I'm a bit tipsy."

"Hang on," said Matthew, getting up to get her a glass of water. "Here, sip on this," he said, handing it to her. "You're welcome to stay here, if you'd like. I have a spare bedroom. I don't want you driving even a little tipsy."

"You're sure it has to be in the spare bedroom?" she asked lasciviously but jokingly, wiggling her eyebrows at him.

"Yeah, I would never take advantage of a lady who'd had a few too many," he said, chuckling. "But, you can stay as long as you need to."

The admission, the wine, and the joking had broken the tension between them and they talked for over an hour, as if they'd been the best of friends for years. Penn told Matthew all about her brother Allan and some of the scrapes he'd unwittingly gotten himself into growing up. She told him about some of Leo's escapades and antics.

"They had this tree house out in the back yard," she said. "Leo was usually the ring leader because, despite Allan being older, it was Leo who had the vivid imagination. They'd hide out up there and cook up who knows what sort of schemes. They had their own secret handshake, secret code, and girls were forbidden entry."

Matthew felt a jolt of recognition, but he couldn't identify the connection. What was it, he wondered, but he didn't have time to ponder it as she continued, "I could have cared less because I was loathe to spend any more time than I had to with my younger brothers back then."

"Allan didn't get that but he was always sweet about it," she said with a faraway look in her eye like she was reliving her childhood with her brother. "If they were given some sort of treat for the treehouse or a party up there, Allan would always come find me and offer me some of whatever it was. Sometimes it was a sheath of Oreo cookies. Sometimes it was brownies that Mom had made for them or chocolate chip cookies. Allan loved those best but even so he'd always come and offer me one. I guess he didn't want me to feel left out and didn't understand that I didn't feel that way at all."

"Those are my favorite too." And then Matthew added, "I make some mean chocolate chip cookies. I made friends in undergrad by smelling up the hallway in my apartment complex with the aroma of baking cookies. It drew people in. What a way to win friends and influence people, huh?"

Laughing, Penn agreed, "Hey, whatever works. I could do with some homemade chocolate chip cookies. But not tonight."

"Tell me more about growing up here," Matthew said, intrigued, so she did.

The sweet and poignant way that she spoke about Allan suddenly made him real to Matthew, who realized that he'd been chasing a murderer for the sake of solving a murder case. It hadn't been as much because there was a real person who deserved the justice of having the killer found and held accountable. But Allan wasn't just a shadow of a person wandering, uncommunicatively all over town. He was a person with a life and feelings and a family, at least one member of which had regrets.

That motivation changed in those moments talking with Penn. Matthew's fire to find the killer was rekindled. As was true of several memorial services he'd attended to support the living whom he knew, he found himself wishing he'd known the deceased, whom he hadn't really known at all.

"Are you planning a service for him, Penn? If you are, I'll help with that in any way I can."

"That's so sweet," she said, sounding more herself without the slightly slurred speech, "I am. Just as soon as his body can be released to me. I'm not sure what just yet, but I do want to honor him. He was a sweet soul, so gentle and kind to the people he loved. He was capable of loving. Leo, me, our parents. We all knew that he loved us, even if he was aloof so much of the time. It was never his fault that he couldn't relate well and he had trouble expressing his feelings. He just had such a hard time. It was neurological, his inability to connect peripherally. But he connected deeply to his family. He and Leo were especially close."

"Just let me know how I can help. I am trying to help Danbury figure out who did this, but I'm happy to help you plan something nice for Allan." He knew as he said it that memorial services were more for the living than the dead, but he also wanted to honor a sweet, misunderstood soul whose life had been violently ended far too soon.

"Warren Danbury," she said, rolling her eyes. "Tell me about him. Can you?"

"I don't know him well. I only met him last month, though honestly it does seem like much longer. What do you want to know?"

They talked on for another half an hour until Penn was feeling better and Matthew was sure that she was OK to drive. After excusing herself to find his power room, she picked up a small purse she'd brought with her and the bag with the Dutch oven. Matthew walked her out to her rental car.

"Thanks for cooking that wonderful meal," he said. "And for leaving me the leftovers!"

She chuckled an appealing noise deep in her throat and said, "Too bad I'm leaving now. But I get it. I really do." She reached up and hugged him, then slipped into the car, backed out of his short driveway, and was gone.

Matthew wondered if he'd lost any common sense that he'd ever had to let her go like that, but he knew he was being true to himself, no matter how tempting it had been to do otherwise. As he wandered back into the house, Max immediately appeared, rubbing against his legs.

"And where have you been all night, Big Guy?" he asked, knowing full well that the big cat had been hiding, probably in the back of his closet, because there was a strange person in the house. He gave Max his nightly ration of food, rinsing and refilling the water bowl, and went through the rest of his evening on autopilot, setting up and laying out everything for the next day, locking up the house, and turning off lights as he got ready for bed.

He knew he'd have to tell Danbury about the money Penn had finagled from the estate, but he wasn't looking forward to that conversation. As he crawled between the cool sheets, he was thinking about the investigation and about how he'd deliver the news to Danbury. Thinking those thoughts allowed him not to think about the things that he didn't want to admit to himself, like missing Cici so much or wondering why she hadn't contacted him like she'd said that she would.

19. Conversations

Opening one sleepy eye to see what woke him, Matthew realized that he'd been dreaming frustrating dreams about trying to find someone in crowded places. Some of the places he thought were familiar, but in others he wasn't at all sure where he was. Getting pulled away from his search by one thing and then another that seemed important at the time, he realized later that they had nothing to do with finding the person he was searching for. Figuring he would deal with sorting that out later, he realized that it was his phone and not his alarm which woke him.

Reaching for the phone, he found the person he had most likely been searching for in the dream on the other end of a FaceTime call.

"Hey, Sleepyhead. Happy hump day. Nice hair," Cici said cheerfully.

As he reached up to run his fingers through his hair, he saw Max, still on his pillow, stretching, and knew why his hair was looking so rough. Hair by Max, again, he thought. The big cat loved to sleep curled around his head and Matthew had been too deep in sleep to notice or object.

"I waited until 6:15 your time to call. That should give us about fifteen minutes to chat before your actual alarm goes off," she added.

"How considerate," he mumbled, trying to push himself up in to an upright sitting position in bed. "How're things over there?"

"Crazy busy. I'm sorry I didn't get a chance to connect with you yesterday, but my client had meetings scheduled, and all of them ran over, overlapping each other instead of having breaks in between."

"Are you enjoying what you're doing, at least?"

"Well, I'm enjoying the new experience. Hey, thanks so much for sending the box and the tracking information. I really appreciate it."

"Sure, Cees, no problem. I have the car title but I've been pretty busy too and I haven't looked up the value online yet. I will though. I just need to go back over to your place and check the mileage first to get an accurate number. Did I tell you that James is interested in buying it? How would you feel about selling to him?"

She was quiet a moment, considering, and then said, "That would be fine. I'd still get to see it maybe from time to time. And I think he'd take good care of it."

"He would," Matthew agreed, waking up as he started talking about one of his favorite topics, cars. "We can talk about it more when you're ready to come home, but I really liked that little Mercedes SLK convertible that I drove last month. I think either it or the BMW equivalent, the Z4, would be great cars for you. Just something to think about. If you get really adventurous, you could always catch a flight over to Munich and order your own Z4 and ship it home. You know I'd love to see the BMW towers, the headquarters, in Munich. It's been declared an historic site, though it's only been in operation since the early seventies."

After the rest of a nice chat with Cici, Matthew felt energized somehow to get out of bed and get started with his day. He went through his usual morning routine and, as he was leaving the neighborhood, he waved as he saw Mrs. Drewer and Oscar just leaving the house for their morning walk.

Arriving at work twelve minutes later, in traffic that was inexplicably much heavier than normal, Matthew slipped through the side entrance and into his office to get organized for the day. After checking the records to see the morning lineup of patients and putting in his lunch order with Trina, he quickly called Danbury to give him the information that Penn had asked him to share. Not relishing the chore, he'd be happy to get that sticky bit over with.

"Danbury here."

"Hi, it's Matthew."

"Hey Doc. I didn't check the caller ID. Before I picked up," he said, sounding distracted.

"Did I catch you at a bad time? I have some information for you. Oh, and did you get the search warrant to seize the financial records for the Lingle estate?"

"No. In fact, it was denied. Insufficient evidence. To tie it to the murder investigation. Why do you ask?"

"I had dinner with Penn last night."

"Oh yeah," said Danbury, perking up with interest. "How'd that go?"

"It was a very nice dinner. She cooked and we talked, which is why I need to talk to you now. She told me something that she asked me to share with you. It might help you to get that warrant."

"Oh?"

"Yeah, it goes like this. When her mother died, she came home but was in the middle of a divorce back in Denver. She was hurting and connected with Wayne Adams. What do you know about the guy?"

"Not much. He came from Ohio, I think. To join the Higgins Law firm here. Over ten years ago. Probably closer to eleven. Maybe twelve. Came in as a partner. Must have had some experience."

"Ah. Well, here's where it gets dicey. When I say she connected with Adams, I mean they connected. They hooked up one night. She didn't know that he was already seeing Libby seriously and when he told her, after the fact, and asked her not to say anything about it, she got angry and blackmailed him. She was worried about hanging onto her business after her divorce and figured a bit of cash from the estate could help keep her afloat. She told him she'd go straight to Libby if he didn't hand over some funds, which he did, seventy-five grand worth of funding."

"Wow," said Danbury, whistling through his teeth. "You're right. That changes things. Would she sign something? An affidavit?"

"I don't know, but I can ask if you'd like."

"Yeah. I'd like. We'll need that information officially. To try again on the search warrant. That gives us precedent. Corruption handling the Lingle estate. Something to hide there. I'll set it up. Whenever she's ready. But it needs to be soon."

"I'll see what I can do," said Matthew, wondering how he managed to get himself so easily in the middle of that situation. He still remembered the renewed determination he'd felt the evening before, though, as Allan became a real person to him, someone he wished he'd known.

"And Doc," said Danbury as Matthew was just about to disconnect the call.

"Yeah?"

"Ask Penn if she will keep that quiet. Completely. I don't want Wayne getting wind of it. We can't spook him. He thinks he's off the hook. The search warrant didn't come through. He thinks he's golden. Let's not tell him otherwise. Not yet."

"That shouldn't be a problem," said Matthew. "Convincing her to agree to sign the affidavit will be the bigger problem. She's really embarrassed about the whole thing, starting with the affair and ending with the blackmail. But I'll try. Maybe we could draw up and have her sign the papers elsewhere? I mean, not at the Peak Police Station. I think I can sell that more easily."

"OK, good plan. Tell me when and where. I'll set it up."

Matthew had a few ideas about that location but he hurriedly donned his lab coat from the coat rack behind the door and headed down the hallway to see his first patient in Exam Room Six.

*****

After a morning full of back-to-back patients that he and his nurses, Diane and Gladys, could barely keep up with, he was heading for his office when he passed Dr. Rob in the hallway and they stopped to chat.

"You're helping with this murder investigation, aren't you?" Dr. Rob asked.

"I am, as best I can. I don't have the vested interest in this one that I did when Ellen was murdered and Cici was abducted, but I think Allan Lingle was a good guy and I'd like to see his killer caught."

"Yeah, Allan was a good guy. He was mostly Steven's patient but I saw him a few times over the years. It was difficult to get answers out of him, but if you were patient with that patient, you could get what you needed to know eventually," he said lightly. "We'll miss him. Do whatever you need to do to help find his killer and let me know if I can help in any way," said Dr. Rob as he was heading out to lunch. Turning, he added, "Hey, do you want to come get some lunch with us? I have some sales reps who've been hounding me to talk to them. I finally caved for a quick lunch."

"As appealing as that sounds," laughed Matthew, "I think I'll pass. I ordered from the lunch train that Trina organized."

"OK, some other time then," said Dr. Rob as he slipped out of the side entrance.

Matthew had ordered lunch from Trina that morning intending to have a quiet lunch at his desk, wade through the patient records from the morning, and leave early to get to his favorite bakery and back in time for dinner with Mrs. Drewer. What he hadn't counted on was having to make one more difficult phone call.

Taking a deep breath, he picked up the phone to call Penn and ask if she'd sign an affidavit about the blackmail against Wayne Adams. Putting it back down again, he realized that he'd need his cell so that she would know it was him and pick up. Just as he'd clicked Penn's number, Trina tapped on the cracked door and peeked in, holding up his lunch. Motioning her in, Matthew quickly said, "Thank you," just as Penn was picking up the phone.

"Ah, you're welcome?" Penn answered. "But I have no idea for what."

Matthew laughed as he said, "Sorry, Penn. I was thanking our office manager, Trina, for bringing my lunch in. She orders out for it from a different restaurant each day and has it brought in for anybody who places an order in time."

"That's a smart perk," she said smoothly.

"It's all Trina, so I can take no credit for that. But it is a nice option to dragging my lunch in every day, going out after it myself, or planning ahead enough to order it delivered myself. She keeps track of it all. How are you feeling today?" he asked, changing the subject, "No lasting impact from the wine last night, I hope?"

"Not the way you pumped water into me, no. I thought I was going to float out of there last night. But thank you. It helped. And I enjoyed it, at least most of it." And then she added, pointedly, "I'd have preferred to have enjoyed it more."

He couldn't help laughing at her blunt honesty but decided to plunge ahead with what he needed to talk to her about. "Yeah, me too, I'm sure. But Penn, I was calling to talk to you about the other chat we had last night. I called Danbury this morning and very carefully relayed your story."

"And? Was he shocked? Did he think me awful?"

"I don't think so. He was excited though and he wants your help."

"Of course, he does. I'm not making offers to just anyone these days," she joked. "Just you." Then, taking a deep breath and sighing heavily, she added, "What does he want?"

"He wants to get your statement and have you sign an affidavit."

"No!" she said immediately.

"Penn, he didn't get the search warrant to seize the records for your family's estate. Your statement would prove mishandling of funds and give some weight to a second request for it."

"I don't want this getting out. I only asked you to tell Danbury because I thought it was coming out anyway, with the search warrant. And I wanted the chance to tell my side of that story before Wayne Adams did. That's all. That's the only reason I told you."

"I don't know if this search warrant will turn up anything to help determine who killed your brother, but what if it does? Don't you want to catch his killer?"

"Of course, I do! But at what cost?" she all but yelled at him. "I don't want this to get out. Surely, you can understand why."

"I do. But have you met Danbury? If he doesn't get the search warrant this way, he'll find another way. This will make it faster probably, but he won't let go of trying to find a motive and he'll keep looking until he does. You can still be ahead of this story because Danbury has already heard your version of it, albeit through me, and I certainly didn't villainize you."

"Thank you," she said quietly.

"And Penn, I can make you some promises about this, OK? We can pick a location that isn't public. You don't have to do this at the police station. I've already gotten Danbury to agree to that. We can meet at my house, if you like. Danbury will have to bring a scribe and witness, but maybe they can be the same person. I can surely ask. We can swear that person to secrecy. You tell your story, and then sign your statement. From there it only gets submitted as evidence for requesting the search warrant. On a need-to-know basis only. How does that sound?"

"Like one of a couple of my most embarrassing moments coming out and in front of one of the people who already personally witnessed one of the others."

"Hey, he's a big guy. He can handle it," chuckled Matthew.

"Yeah, I guess so."

"OK, so you agree to those terms, if I can get Danbury to agree to them?"

"Yeah, I guess. We go to your house for the location, a single person is both the witness and scribe, and sworn to secrecy. You should have been a lawyer. You build a very compelling argument."

Laughing, Matthew thought that he'd almost been through law school merely by being in a relationship with Cici when she went through, but he'd never say that aloud to Penn. Instead, he just said, "Well, that was my other career choice if med school didn't work out for me. I'll get Danbury to agree to those terms and let you know when we can meet. I have plans with a neighbor this evening so maybe tomorrow? How does your afternoon look tomorrow?"

"Sure, that works."

"OK, I know you've been through a lot and it was brave of you to come forward with this information, so we'll hope that it helps get to the bottom of the murder," he said, trying to reassure her.

"Here's hoping. Talk soon," she said as she blew him an audible kiss and disconnected.

Truly thankful for his lunch that he didn't have to go pick up or drag in, he dug in and figured he'd try to catch up with Danbury after he finished it. But he need not have worried about reaching Danbury because his phone rang before he'd finished eating. He had to quickly swallow a bite of his Reuben sandwich to answer it. So much for mindful dining, he thought, as he spluttered a greeting and heard, "Doc!"

"Just finishing up lunch. Or trying to," Matthew said as he gulped and tried to rinse the bite of sandwich down with a swig of water.

"Have you talked to Penn?"

"Yeah, I just did. She's in agreement, IF," he said stressing the conditional nature of her agreement. "If you can use the same person to be the scribe for her statement to witness it. If you will agree to bring only that person to my house to get her statement. If that person is sworn to secrecy. And, if you agree to walk it through the process yourself so that nobody but the judge issuing the search warrant knows about it. Then she will agree to give you a statement."

"Wow. That's a lot of ifs," said Danbury. "OK, give me the afternoon. To find a qualified scribe. Can we print at your place?"

"Sure. Whatever you need. I'm out this evening anyway, so I suggested we meet tomorrow afternoon. Would that work?"

"Another hot date tonight, Doc?" teased Danbury.

Laughing, Matthew responded, "Oh, you have no idea." But he chose not to enlighten him.

"Yeah, let's aim for tomorrow afternoon. I'll find a notary public. Or a commissioner of oaths. I might have to be the scribe. But I'll work it out. Thanks, Doc. I do appreciate it. Everything."

"Hey, you helped me when Cici was threatened and I figure I owe you one. Besides, I want Allan's killer caught too. I don't want that person wandering around freely when Allan can't anymore. There's something very wrong about that. Let me know what you work out and I'll tell Penn. Unless you want to?"

"Nah. I'll have to deal with her soon enough. Later, Doc."

Danbury hadn't told him why he didn't want to deal with Penn, thought Matthew, but Penn had told him. Why, then did he have the feeling that Danbury knew that he knew? Odd, he thought, as he downed the rest of his sandwich unmindfully, tossed the wrappers into the trash, and put on his lab coat to get to his afternoon patients.

20. Sweets and nothing

After a full day of back-to-back patients and updating the charts in the half hour since seeing his final patient, Matthew was relieved to be leaving the office at 4:30. He was heading out of the building to his favorite bakery on the other side of Peak to get pastries to take to Mrs. Drewer. While he was at it, he figured he'd stop by the corner farmer's market and pick up a bouquet of flowers too. That still left him plenty of time to get by his own house and take care of Max first.

Arriving on Mrs. Drewer's doorstep with pastries and flowers promptly at six, Matthew was greeted first with Oscar's barking and then by Cordelia Drewer. Draped in a full-length apron that her small frame seemed lost in, Mrs. Drewer welcomed him in with a wooden spoon in one hand with the other cupped protectively underneath to prevent the red sauce on the spoon from dripping onto her beige Berber carpeting.

"Hush now," she said to Oscar, and then to Matthew, "Come on in. I'm just pulling the chicken out of the marinade simmer. It's my secret recipe and I slow cook it for just a bit before moving it to the grill," she said over her shoulder as she led the way into her kitchen.

"I brought you some flowers," said Matthew.

"Oh, I love daisies! I'll get a vase for them in just a moment when I get my hands clean again. Or there's one you can get from the other room, if you don't mind," she added. "It's the white one on the library table with the pictures."

"Sure, I'll get that. And I brought dessert," he said, placing the bag with the pastries beside the daisies on the island in her kitchen before going in search of the vase.

He noticed again the picture of the young Cordelia Drewer on the arm of her husband Mick, who was in what appeared to be dress blues, though the photograph was in black and white. That would be the service dress uniform that was adopted sometime around 1969, he thought. If he was right about the uniform, then this picture would have been taken sometime between 1969 and the fall of Saigon in the early spring of 1975.

Returning to the kitchen with the vase, he filled it, asked for scissors, clipped the daisy stems, and put them in the vase. He set it back on the counter and asked what else he could do to help.

"How're you with charcoal fires?" she asked.

"I think I can manage that. I have a gas grill on my patio though."

"I usually just simmer these until the chicken is ready to fall off the bone, but I thought grilling might be nice for a change, so I'll pull these out now if you can get the fire ready."

"Sure. Where are your supplies?"

She handed him a lighter and pointed to the patio, "The charcoal and lighter fluid are out by the grill."

Pondering when the last time was that he had lit a charcoal fire in a grill, Matthew decided it must have been on a camping trip a couple of years back. He managed to get the fire going and when the coals were ready, Mrs. Drewer brought out a platter heaped with chicken breasts, which he dutifully grilled until he was satisfied that they were well cooked. She had meanwhile pulled up the drop leaf on a little antique table in her bay window eating nook, set the table, and placed potato salad, coleslaw, and some fluffy white biscuits on it. She was just filling water glasses when Matthew brought the chicken in. "Did you want something other than water to drink? I have iced tea and lemonade, too."

"No thanks. Water is fine. This looks great, Mrs. Drewer," he said appreciatively as he heard his stomach growl in response to the array of food. As they took their seats, Matthew asked if he could say a blessing over the meal.

An odd look came across the older woman's face and she said, "A blessing? You may if that's what you usually do, but don't do it on my account. I haven't talked to God in over forty years. But you go right ahead. You do you, as they say."

This admission startled Matthew. He raised an eyebrow in question, but bowed his head and blessed the food and the cook anyway. After their plates were served he complimented the meal, all of which she'd prepared herself that afternoon he learned. Cordelia Drewer seemed to regress as they dug in.

"Did you know that Frank down at the diner has been running around with that woman from the Tarnished Weathervane, the new shop on the corner of Winston Avenue and Holt Street? Word is, they're an item already and she hasn't even been in town six months yet."

"No," said Matthew, shaking his head in concern, "I hadn't heard that." Not that he was concerned for Frank or whoever the woman was, but he was concerned that his new found friendship with his neighbor was reverting back to the way it was before he and Angel had visited with the cookies.

"And Libby and Wayne Adams," she added. "They were seen having a knock-down-drag-out argument outside his office yesterday evening. Until he pulled her back inside."

Annoyed as he usually was by the gossip, this time she'd hit on something he might actually want to know. He wasn't sure how to respond because he didn't want her to think that he was interested in gossip in general. Neither did he want her to see that he was interested in this particular topic. He need not have worried because she continued on her own.

"Libby was yelling about how he had his own life and wouldn't let her in, and Wayne was yelling about how he'd taken both her and the boys in when they needed him. You know, that's sort of a lie though because Libby didn't really need him. At least she didn't need his financial support. And he moved in with her. She already had that nice house. You've seen it, I'm sure?"

Matthew decided that nodding but saying nothing was his best course of action to allow her to continue with this story but without encouraging the gossip. Again his silence was rewarded.

"She inherited her Texan grandmother's oil money, so she didn't need his money. Maybe just a man around the house and a father for her boys since their dad was gone, but she didn't need him financially. You'd never know it though. She never lets on that she's an oil heiress. Do you know Libby?"

Choosing his words carefully so as not to get on the topic of the murder, Matthew responded, "I've spoken to her a couple of times. I've seen her and the boys around town a lot."

"What those boys went through the other night! Poor kids. And this little town doesn't feel safe anymore," she said, on the topic that he didn't want her to bring up because he didn't want her asking him questions about it. "It was so quiet and peacefully happy when I moved here, but that awful murder changed all of that. Everyone is afraid to go out after dark now. We're all living in fear that we'll be next."

She took a quick breath and then continued, "There wasn't any reason to kill that poor man, odd and quiet as he was. Allan Lingle was a sweet guy. He was just misunderstood, but he never gave anyone any trouble that I ever heard. Do you think it was those two guys the boys saw who killed Allan? Who do you think they are? Do you think they're still around? Why would they be here in Peak to begin with? And why Allan, of all people? I surely hope the police can figure out the motive and find the murderer before they kill anyone else," she said, without taking a breath between the questions. For that, Matthew was thankful because he didn't have answers and he didn't want her to think that he might.

"Me too, Mrs. Drewer. I'm sure they're working on it," was all that Matthew said in response, not volunteering any information and hoping that she'd ask for none.

Then the conversation shifted and she was onto other people and happenings around town which Matthew neither cared about nor wanted to hear about, so he changed the subject.

"That was a wonderful dinner, Mrs. Drewer. May I help clean up?"

"Let's just rinse the dishes and put them in the dishwasher," she said. "Then we could have coffee and dessert in the other room, if you'd like?"

"That sounds great."

"It's decaf. I hope that's OK," she said as she carried her dishes to the sink and he followed with his.

"That's fine. I'm OK, either way. Caffeine doesn't seem to keep me up at night. Or, at least it didn't when I was in med school. I could drink half a pot trying to stay awake to study and then go straight to bed and right to sleep."

"Whew, not me," she said as they rinsed the dishes and loaded the dishwasher. "That stuff will keep me up half the night. But I do OK with the decaf." After starting the coffee, she arranged the pastries on a plate and put that, with two cups, a sugar dish and creamer, and some napkins on a tray. She wiped down the counters while waiting for the coffee to brew and slipped Oscar, who had been at her feet the entire evening, a tiny piece of chicken that she'd set aside. "His doesn't have the barbeque sauce on it," she explained. "He'd keep me up half the night if I gave him that."

"Max doesn't get anything spicy either. On a rare occasion, I'll give him a tiny scrap like you just did."

"Max?" she asked, very curiously.

"Max is my cat," said Matthew. "He's an indoor cat so you won't have seen him out anywhere."

"Oh, you're a cat person," she said, quizzically, as if she was trying to make that new information fit the man somehow.

"I don't know that I'm a cat person, specifically. I'm just a big sucker." He grinned as he proceeded to tell her about how his sister Monica had rescued Max as a kitten and then found out that he, and two other cats she'd had at the time, were the source of her husband Stephano's allergies. So, she'd convinced Matthew to take the tiny kitten.

Mrs. Drewer filled the cups with coffee and carried the tray into the other room, placing it gently on the coffee table in front of the sofa. She motioned for Matthew to have a seat.

"What do you take in your coffee?" she asked, poised to pour cream into the cups.

"A little coffee with my cream and sugar," he replied, and laughed. "I'll fix it."

Nodding, she added a little cream to her cup and then leaned back into the sofa to allow him to doctor his. After he'd gotten his coffee the way he wanted it and set it on a coaster on the table beside him, she took a napkin and a pastry from the tray. "These look really good."

Following suit, Matthew said, before taking a bite, "I got them from my favorite bakery on the other side of Peak. They have the best."

They munched and sipped in companionable silence for a moment until she saw that he was staring at the old picture on the table across from them. "That's the only wedding picture I have out," she said, following his gaze. "That was taken the day we were married in the spring of 1972."

"Ah, I knew it had to be between 1969 and 1975," he said.

"Why would you say that?" she asked, sounding confused.

"I'm a history buff and I was really interested in war history in high school. I thought that looked like the Air Force dress blues, the version that came out in 1969. Your husband was in the Air Force?"

"Yes, I suppose that would be 'history' to you, wouldn't it?" Matthew nodded as she continued, "And yes, he was. We were married in the spring of 1972. I was twenty and Mick was three years older. We were living up in Chicago when that was taken," she said, indicating the picture. "He'd already graduated from college but he wanted to fly. I was still in college, studying to be a teacher and grateful that the Air Force would help with my tuition, but I wasn't thrilled about his air training."

"He insisted though that he'd do another two years in the Air Force, learn to fly, log some hours in the air, and then get out and fly commercially, which is what he really wanted to do. I'd begged him not to go to flight school because I thought that ensured that he'd be sent to that God-forsaken jungle. He said he wanted to get the flight hours in because it was the best way to become a commercial pilot after his time was up. He said he wouldn't reenlist after he flew for a year or two. We had this whole life planned out together and I was terrified that they'd send him as reinforcement to Saigon if he was a fly boy. It was a war we couldn't win and nobody our age then wanted to go. It wasn't like the first and second world wars at all. This one was different."

As she leaned back into the sofa, she sighed softly and seemed to drift farther into the past as she told him the story.

"I wanted him to crunch numbers at a nice safe desk here or break codes, anything that wouldn't get him sent over there. He was adamant that it was the only way to log the hours he needed to be able to fly commercially, and there was no talking him out of it."

"He was sent away to a flight school in southern California in the heat of that summer while we were still newlyweds. We had an apartment in the suburbs of Chicago, so I didn't go with him. We wrote almost daily. I saved all of those letters. He'd call once a week but long-distance phone service was expensive back then, so that's the only time I could hear his voice."

"He wasn't home but two months after he completed his training before he was sent off to a second school to be certified to fly helicopters, and I knew what they were setting him up for. He was home very briefly afterward and my worst fears were realized when he was shipped overseas to Vietnam. I cried and prayed continually for his safety. I heard from him sporadically. Conditions over there kept deteriorating and there seemed to be nothing that anyone on the home front could do but cry and pray."

"I had finished college and started teaching at an elementary school in Chicago. I'd settled in, as best I could, without him. Then, one day, there was a knock on the door and I knew before I got up to go answer it that it wasn't good news. I just knew it. As I got up and went by the window, through the sheers I caught a glimpse of two men in their dress blues and it took everything I had to go answer the door. I didn't want to open it. Everything within me was screaming not to open that door."

"They were so proud to tell me that he was a hero. He died during a rescue mission, trying to fly some of our boys out of a nasty situation in a remote area. I never learned what that was exactly but it hardly mattered. Neither did it surprise me to learn that he'd volunteered for the rescue mission. He was given a purple heart and silver star posthumously for rescuing so many before his chopper was shot down. There was a military service for him, though his remains were never found and brought home. That was hard to deal with. I kept expecting him to walk through the door."

"That was in the late winter of 1975, just before the fall of Saigon in late April. The cold outside in Chicago couldn't begin to compare to the coldness in my heart, in my soul, that swept through me. I was barely functioning through that whole next year. I felt nothing. Nothing. Just emptiness."

"They said I should be proud that Mick died a hero. I wasn't proud. I was just angry and confused. I guess I should have taken some solace that he died doing what he loved. He was flying his chopper trying to rescue his men, a fraternal connection that I have never understood. He wasn't holed up in a foxhole or in a dark cubby behind some enemy wall. Or somewhere in the tangle of the jungle being shot at by an unknown opponent. He hadn't been wounded and bleeding after hours and days of fending off some adversary that he couldn't even see. But I'd far rather that he were decoding messages state-side than having been there at all!"

Something she'd said struck a chord in the back of Matthew's consciousness and he sat bolt upright. Mrs. Drewer had said, "in a dark cubby behind a wall." She had also mentioned something about decoding messages, he repeated to himself, as the thing that had been bothering him finally came to the forefront of his mind. The right neuron fired in his brain and the connections were forming. Cubby hole. Decoding messages. Something Penn had said, something about secret codes flipped the switch in Matthew's brain that he'd been trying to access, that thing that he couldn't bring to the forefront of his mind. And then that other thing. There it was! Plain as day! Both eyebrows shot up and Mrs. Drewer looked startled by his expression, "Matthew?"

As understanding dawned, he was able to turn his attention back to her and he saw tears sliding down her cheeks. He knew he needed to focus his attention on her now and call Danbury later, so he tried his best. "I'm so sorry, Mrs. Drewer. That must have been so painful."

"The worst pain I've ever experienced," she said. "Worse than my parents dying or my sister. We had been high school sweethearts and we had a life planned together. I was so hurt and angry. And then I was just numb. I just felt nothing. Absolutely nothing. I had been teaching for a little while, but I quit my job and just wallowed in the pain and nothingness for almost a year. I saw other husbands and fathers and sons come home, all of them haunted by what they'd experienced. They weren't given a hero's welcome when they got here, and I felt for them and their families to some extent. But I was still angry that Mick wasn't among them. So very angry. I screamed at God, at the world, hating it all for a while."

"That's when you stopped talking to God," Matthew said, quietly understanding.

She nodded, "It was. I screamed at him and shook my fists at him, but I had no use for a God who allowed that war to happen in the first place and so many good men, including Mick, die so horribly there. How could a good God allow such horrible things to happen? I didn't understand it then and I never shall."

"How did you get to North Carolina?" he asked, feeling like he needed to guide her to more solid ground at least momentarily.

"That happened shortly afterward in 1976. The country was so excited about the bicentennial and I think the government hyped that, trying to make us all forget about the war. Forget about the people we'd loved and lost in an endless war that we should never have tried to fight. And instead bring unity and pride in being an American again. There was a 'freedom train' that hyped the greatness of our country and celebrated its 200-year anniversary. When I heard about that, I was on the phone with my sister, who had married and moved to Raleigh, and I was still angry. So very angry," she said vehemently. "I think I scared her. She begged me to move down here and get back in the classroom."

"I finally did. I packed up everything I wanted, gave away the rest to a veteran's group, and drove down here. I settled in with my sister and her husband until I could find my own apartment. I started back in the classroom in January 1977 and taught elementary school or ran school libraries in the Wake County school system for the next thirty-eight years. When the politics of the school system seemed to mirror those of the country, I had enough and I retired and moved in here," she spread her hands as if it were all just that simple.

"Mrs. Drewer, I really don't have words for all of that. I don't. I'm sorry."

"Oh Matthew, I shouldn't have unloaded all of that on you," she said, looking truly remorseful.

"It's OK, I asked and I'm interested. I admit I was interested in the picture for the historic value initially, but thank you for sharing your story with me. I consider that an honor."

She reached over and patted his hand, "That's the kindest thing anyone has said to me in a while."

Trying to shift focus to encourage her, Matthew said, "You mentioned that you're going to read to Angel's class next week. That's wonderful. I'm sure she'll look forward to it."

"Your sister was very sweet when she called and made it sound like such a favor that I'm doing for her and your niece."

"I'm sure she feels that way. Angel really loved reading the Madeline book with you."

"You have a close family, don't you?"

"I do," admitted Matthew, having a sudden rush of a half-formed idea that he'd need a moment to process. "We spend Sundays together, first in church, and then at a restaurant that we debate over ad nauseum. We discuss which restaurant we should go to into the ground and then go back to one of our favorites," he chuckled. "But I wouldn't trade my family. I know I'm very lucky to have them."

She just smiled a sad smile at him and said, "I'm glad that you do."

"Mrs. Drewer," he said, with the thought fully formed. "Would you like to join us this Sunday?"

"Join you? You mean intrude in your family time? I'm not sure I could do that."

"You will have to trust me when I tell you that my family would never consider it an intrusion. They're the most welcoming people I know. When I was growing up, I knew I could bring a friend home on a moment's notice." What he didn't say was that he could bring home any friend who was hurting and needed encouragement on a moment's notice and his parents welcomed them in and treated them like family. He didn't say it because this situation felt a little bit like that, only in the adult realm.

"To church? And then out to lunch?"

"Yes, Ma'am."

"To church? I haven't set foot inside a church in over forty years. I'm not sure I can do it now, or that God would ever want to see or hear from me again." She cocked her head sideways at him for a moment and then added, "Let me think about it, Mathew. I appreciate the invitation. I truly do. But that's a big step for someone like me. Just let me think about it, OK?"

"That's fine. Take all the time you need. If you don't want to join us this Sunday, it's an open invitation. Whenever you're ready."

As he shifted forward on his seat, he added, "Thank you so much for this wonderful dinner, Mrs. Drewer. Let me help you clean this up and then I need to get back to my house. We've been busier in the office lately than we usually are this time of year, and I admit that I'm tired."

He stood, placed his cup on the tray, and carried it into the kitchen.

Mrs. Drewer followed, insisting that he take some of the leftovers to have later in the week. Matthew accepted the offer with profuse thanks, as she put the small containers into a bag for him, wondering how he'd gotten so lucky with leftovers from home cooked meals this week.

Putting the bag with the leftover containers on the table in her sitting room, he carried the rest of the dishes back to the kitchen. When he returned, Mrs. Drewer was standing by the table in the front window holding the gold-framed picture of the happy smiling couple on their wedding day.

"Thanks, Matthew," she finally said. "If you're really interested in war history, would you like to see Mick's medals sometime?"

"I'd love to!" he answered enthusiastically.

"I haven't pulled them out in many years, but I'll find them for you," she said as he opened the door and stepped outside.

"Thanks for everything, Mrs. Drewer," he said.

"No, thank you, Matthew. Have a good night."

"You too," he said as she scooped up Oscar, who was standing on his back feet pawing her legs with his front feet.

As he walked the few steps home, Matthew's head was whirring with thoughts of Mrs. Drewer's story and the revelation and understanding of things resulting from it that had been bugging him for days. He needed to more fully formulate the thoughts that had popped into his mind this evening and then, he knew, he needed to call Danbury. Maybe he could explain it to Danbury or maybe he'd just set the process in motion and they would figure it out as they went.

21. Behind dark walls

Arriving home from Mrs. Drewer's condo on the other end of his unit, Matthew pulled out his phone and was ringing Danbury's number as he let himself in his house and locked up behind himself.

"Danbury here. Oh, hi Doc."

"Hey, Danbury. I finally figured out what's been bugging me about the Lingle Plantation. It's too dark and late to see anything now, but could you meet me there first thing in the morning? I have patients starting at 8:30, so maybe about 7:30?"

"Yeah, I can do that. Want to explain? Whatever it is that you've figured out?"

"Not yet," he said. "It's really just a theory and it sounds pretty far-fetched even to me right now. Oh, and one other thing. I have no idea if it's important or not, but there's something I just heard from my neighbor, who is always well informed about town happenings," Matthew began, thinking that put Mrs. Drewer in a much nicer light than calling her the busybody that until lately he'd truly thought she was. "She mentioned that Libby and Wayne Adams were seen having a yelling match outside of his office earlier this week before he dragged her inside and out of the public eye. I know the guy hasn't been very cooperative, but maybe you can get to him through his wife?"

"Yeah, maybe so. I hadn't heard about that. I have contacted a detective in Ohio. In Lima. Where Wayne came from. The police there remembered an incident. More than ten years ago. Which was about when he moved here. They couldn't tell me much. But they remembered a Private Investigator out there. One Wayne's ex-wife had hired. He was looking into some issues. Sounds like Adams left town with a black cloud over him. He was never arrested. But he was suspected. Of some sort of foul play. I haven't heard back yet. From the PI. Maybe he can tell us more about Adams."

"Ah, Adams is a person of interest too? He's been very evasive, hasn't he?"

"He is and he has. He's been so squirrely with information. He won't talk to me. Maybe it's easily explained. Maybe there's nothing there. Nothing to do with Allan anyway. But he's hiding something. And working hard at it too."

"Do you know Libby well enough to talk to her about him? Would she open up, do you think? Or would she try to protect him?"

"I have no idea. You know Wayne's her second husband. She had a rough time with the first one. So I don't know. But I can try. Maybe tomorrow."

Tired from the long conversation with Mrs. Drewer and not wanting to launch into any other lengthy discussions, Matthew said, "Good plan. Guess I'll see you in the morning. Oh, and can you take the collection of notebooks from Allan's drawer? I don't think anyone else will want them."

"Yeah, I'll request those."

"Thanks."

"OK. I'll see you there."

As he went through his usual evening routine, his mind was racing with possibilities on what they'd find at the Lingle house the next morning. He was pretty sure there was a faux wall along the right back end of the house, probably from the more newly added basement on the back. Maybe it was separate spaces off of each floor, Matthew thought.

Feeling like an old man for being tired at 8:45, he had put on his flannel sleep pants with a comfy t-shirt and settled in to play his guitar for a bit. Max settled on the back of the leather sofa behind his head as Matthew's mind wandered to Cici. He wondered when he'd be able to get back by her place to get the reading off the odometer. Maybe tomorrow afternoon, he thought. Maybe.

Playing a song all the way through was not something that he ever did during these times when he was just enjoying playing for himself, so his fingers wandered from a few riffs of one song to the chorus of another and back again. Then he started making up a morose song about love and war and decided it was time to quit.

A little over an hour later, he felt like an old man as he wandered back to his bedroom and climbed into bed with the book he'd been trying to read. It was a war history book about the brave men who flew fighter jets in World War II. It was closely linked to Mick Drewer's story in some ways and in others not at all. These men of valor, he thought, were at least recognized for their bravery and achievements when they came home. If they came home. Happy to have finally made a good start on it this time, at 10:30, he realized that his eyes were heavy so he put the book down and slid down under the sheets, allowing the breeze from his ceiling fan to lull him to sleep.

*****

When Matthew awoke Thursday morning, he promptly removed Max from around his head and the big cat snuggled by his side, enjoying the head scratching and obviously not ready to get up yet. Picking up his phone to turn off the alarm, he noticed that his cell phone was otherwise quiet this morning. No texts and no missed calls. Nothing from Cici, he thought, and felt a stab of disappointment that he hated to admit to himself.

"OK, Big Guy, I need coffee, and I have a busy morning ahead," he said after a few minutes and then slid out of bed and headed for the kitchen. Max immediately brushed up against the back of his legs, meowing for breakfast, so Matthew took care of his cat before his own morning routine.

Taking a cup of coffee with him back down the hallway, he quickly showered and dressed for the day, then nibbled on cereal squares while he cooked his breakfast. He ate hurriedly and cleaned it all up. Ready to leave for the day, he grabbed his satchel from the end of the sofa and headed out to meet Danbury at the Lingle Plantation.

It would be a scorcher of a day, Matthew thought, as he felt the humidity already heavy in the air and saw the mist rising from the fields as he drove down Chester Road and out onto Highway 20. Arriving in downtown Peak, he parked in his usual space in his office parking lot, deciding to walk the short distance to the dead end of Chapel Street and onto the Lingle property. He had just approached the front of the house when Danbury pulled up.

"Hey Doc. What are we looking for?"

"Follow me," he said, as he led Danbury to the back of the house. "This house is symmetrical, front and back, from the outside. But if you go inside, this back corner here isn't," he indicated the side now to their left as they were facing the back of the house. "From the inside, the back side wall isn't as wide. Upstairs in the master suite, there's a bathroom and dressing area that was added at some point. It's not nearly as large as it would be if it were added now, so it was probably added some time ago. But there's a good chunk of the corner there that isn't taken up by either the bath, dressing area, or bedroom."

"On the first floor here, there's a laundry room, but that doesn't extend as far off the kitchen as it should to take up this whole space either. See, there's the window from the laundry room there, and it's near the end of that interior wall, but there's a good six feet between it and the exterior wall out here."

Danbury scratched his chin as he studied the outside of the house.

"And the basement," Matthew continued. "It's not under the entire house, just across this back area that was added later. On the inside, it's all below ground brick foundation until you get to this side, and there's a boiler there with a board slatted wall behind it. Not the exterior brick wall. There are pipes and cables and ducts going into it so it looks like just a conduit area, but it's wider than that. That basement is at least four feet shy of this end wall here."

Both men circled to the end wall in question, but there were rhododendrons and other overgrown shrubs that prevented them from seeing the bottom portion of that end of the wall. There were no windows on that end of the house that Matthew could remember seeing, though they'd be blocked by shrubs if they were there. But he wanted a better look at the inside.

"I wonder what time Malcolm wakes up," he'd muttered aloud when they heard the front door onto the porch creak open and then slam.

Circling to the front of the house, they greeted Malcolm, who looked relieved to see them.

"I thought that was your SUV, Detective. What are you guys doing out here so early?"

"Just testing a theory," said Matthew. "Would you mind if we came in for a few minutes?"

"Come on in," he motioned them to the front door.

As they rounded the corner, Matthew stopped up short. "Wait," he said to Danbury, pointing, "Look!"

Just beyond the front corner of the house, where it wasn't noticeable if you weren't looking for it, there seemed to be a break in the bushes, an opening that you could duck into if you bent at the waist. Ducking, Matthew worked his way in, "It's a small tunnel that goes all the way to the wall," he said. "And then it goes along it!"

It was a narrow passageway, so Danbury ventured in but then backed out when he realized how tight and low it was. "What do you see? Where does it go?" he called after Matthew.

"Hang on, I'm following it down the wall," answered Matthew from somewhere in the midst of the overgrown bushes that stood like sentinels, guarding the end of the house for at least fifteen feet from the wall.

"Hey, there are cellar doors down here!" yelled Matthew from the depths of the bushes. "Two cellar doors that are on rusted metal hinges." He examined the storm doors which were boxed in with slanted walls. The doors were higher as they met the wall and they dropped lower away from the wall to just above the ground in front of him. The whole area was surrounded completely by overgrown shrubbery except for directly above the doors where they would swing open.

Malcolm hobbled around the end of the house and Danbury followed Matthew's voice to just shy of the back corner of the outside wall.

"Can you open it?" asked Danbury.

"I can try," he said, as he tugged on the door on the right side.

The rusted hinges groaned loudly in grinding, screeching protest and Malcolm said, "Hey! I've heard that noise before, from inside the house. That's one of the ghosts' noises, one that made me think that the house is haunted. I've heard it echo throughout the house but I could never figure out where it was coming from. I heard it the night the two guys broke in the house, but they were both IN the house at the time, so it wasn't them."

"I'm no ghost," grunted Matthew with the effort of pulling the second door open, as they all heard the hinges on that side protest just as loudly.

"What do you see?" asked Danbury. "Is there room for me?"

"Not in the overgrown plant tunnel. I see ladder steps going down, but it's dark." He pulled his phone from his pocket and turned on the flashlight feature. "Steps drop down to a floor below, but I can't see anything else from up here."

"I'm coming in," said Danbury as he darted back down the length of the house and bent over to make his way through the tight tunnel of bushes behind Matthew. "Ugh. Bugs!" he said as he arrived at the end of the tunnel beside Matthew. Both men were bent over with no room to maneuver at all.

Matthew rounded the cellar doors as best he could under the overgrown bush cover, still bent over, and allowed Danbury in beside him to shine his phone light down through the opening. Satisfied that he could see enough from above to determine that it wasn't dangerous, Danbury descended the steps quickly and Matthew heard his feet drop heavily to the floor at the bottom. Shining his light around, he called back up to Matthew, "Come on down. There's a whole room down here."

Descending the steps, Matthew realized that the bottom of the ladder was missing so he jumped to the floor from about a foot and a half above it.

"I've heard that sound too," shouted Malcolm from outside the shrubs above. "That loud splatting sound, I've heard it, just like that loud grinding. What do you see down there?"

"It's a long narrow room," answered Matthew. "There's a cot, unmade but not dust covered. It looks recently used. And a little wooden table and chair, with a light above it." He reached up and pulled a chain to turn the light on. It was a single bulb hanging from the ceiling. He remembered the others, identical, that were hanging from the ceiling in the basement on the other side of the wooden slatted wall.

"Hey, Danbury," he said, pointing to a stack of envelopes that was neatly arranged on the table against the back wall of the house.

"Yeah, and check this out," said Danbury, from the other end of the long room, as he shined his phone light on a circular metal staircase that ascended upward.

"Wow! Are you going up?" asked Matthew.

"In a minute. What's that? Mail?"

"Looks like it," said Matthew, reaching for the stack. "Can I do this without gloves?"

"Better not. Can you see a name on there?"

"It's just envelopes, but I'm looking at the back of them," he said, using his cell phone to nudge the stack."

"Let's get gloves," said Danbury.

As they climbed back out and made their way back through the tunnel of overgrown shrubs, Danbury explained that there was a metal grate landing above the circular stairs, with what looked like a door set in a wall, and then the spiral stairs looked to continue up beyond that.

"I couldn't see much," he added. "The shaft goes up. Beyond the first floor. But it's narrow. And dark." Turning to Malcolm, Danbury asked, "When was the last time you heard it? The noise?"

Malcolm pondered for a moment, "I think I heard it last night. Or maybe that was this morning. It might have been both, why?"

"Somebody is still using it," said Danbury.

"Are you going to call in the Peak police?"

"No. Not yet. We need to stake it out. Figure out who's using it. Then we can bring them in. If there's a reason to," Danbury answered softly.

"You think they're still around now?"

"It's possible."

Danbury retrieved two sets of gloves from his black SUV. He and Matthew put them on and, fighting their way back through the overgrown tunnel of bushes, descended the ladder while Malcolm waited outside.

Gloved, Matthew picked up the mail that was neatly stacked in alternating directions. "Oh!" he exclaimed as he flipped it over.

Leaning over, Danbury caught his breath too. "They're addressed to Leonard Lingle. Postmarked three days ago. It's current. And delivered to a street address in Peak."

"Wait a minute, I know that address!" said Matthew. Raising an eyebrow, he continued, "This is the address of the All Posts shop. They provide a physical street address,1300 Sandy Branch Road for their customers. The suite number, in this case 1200, is the box number. It enables packages to be delivered and left at the desk there. Then the employees either put them in the customers' mail boxes, if the boxes are big enough, or hold them behind the counter for the box owners to pick up if they're not."

Danbury flipped through the stack carefully. "I don't see anything personal. These look like financial statements. But this stack doesn't have envelopes. Or, they aren't paired with the envelopes." He peeled an envelope off the bottom of the stack and put it in a small plastic bag and then into his pocket. Then, he carefully replaced the stack on the table making it look undisturbed.

"So now what?" asked Matthew, checking his watch, not wanting to miss anything but knowing that he had patients who would be arriving at his office. "Can we see where the spiral staircase goes? I need to get over to the office soon."

"Sure," said Danbury. "And then I'll check All Posts. And see if they can tell me anything. Anything else about Leo. Or his whereabouts."

"They should be able to," said Matthew. "They had these little informational cards for the box applicants to fill out. I remember thinking that they were so high tech with all of their security and I was amused that they were using handwritten cards to collect and presumably store that information."

"Good to know. I'll check that next. Let's go," Danbury said, leading the way to the other end of the long, narrow room and up the staircase. He had to turn sideways to get his broad-shouldered frame around the narrow winding stairway. He stood on the landing above and tried the door. It was locked, but it easily opened with a few expertly placed yanks. He stepped through as Matthew rounded the last corner and climbed onto the tiny grate platform.

On this floor, the room was long and narrow as it had been on the floor beneath. It wasn't furnished, but there was a panel at the other end around which they could see daylight, so they proceeded carefully along the wall to investigate. After a few false starts, Danbury finally located the right trigger that popped the panel open.

Stepping through it, they found themselves in the laundry room, having just come through the back of the broom closet. Pushing the door nearly closed behind them, they could see that it was the whole back panel of the broom closet that swung out so that it wouldn't be identifiable as an opening at all from the inside. Neither bothered to find the trigger to go the other way but both squeezed back through the opening into the hidden room and, as if in single agreement, they headed back to the circular wrought iron stairs.

Repeating the process on the floor above, they found themselves in the master suite behind the dressing area. The whole panel of wainscoting beside the dressing table swung into the long, unfurnished hidden room this time.

"Wow!" said Matthew.

"The staircase keeps going," Danbury said. "Another floor?"

"It's the attic," replied Matthew. "There are tiny bedrooms along the back wall off to the left, but this end is an attic filled with odds and ends from over the years. I thought that top floor was more symmetrical though. Like it spanned the whole front of the house, just based on the placement of the dormer windows up there."

"Let's go see," said Danbury, leading the way up the tiny spiraling staircase. This time, there was no landing. It ended in the ceiling above.

"Push," said Matthew. "It must open directly into the attic floor, which makes sense for the symmetrical space up there."

After Danbury had been pushing for a few moments without success, he shined his phone light carefully around the ceiling and located a lever. Pulling the lever and pushing the ceiling at the same time, he was able to shift a whole section of the attic floor up from where it was hinged along one side. Clambering up, they found themselves in the attic that Matthew had seen before.

"Did we leave anything open along the way?" asked Matthew, heading for the back staircase on the other end of the top floor.

"Just the opening outside," replied Danbury. "I closed everything else as we came through."

"Good, because I've had enough of that enclosed space for one morning," replied Matthew. "And I need to get to the office now."

Closing the hinged floor panel, Danbury followed Matthew down the stairs.

Pausing in front of Leo's room on the way along the hallway, Matthew stepped inside and motioned Danbury in. "This room is pristine again. I left it as I'd found it, with the closet door slightly ajar, and the shoes here were jumbled," he said as he opened the door to see rows of neatly arranged shoes. "You saw the pictures. The bed was just a bit rumpled, that drawer was open a crack with a sweater pulled slightly out. Huh."

"If I hadn't seen the pictures," started Danbury. "But Malcolm might have straightened up."

"He shouldn't have come up here at all with that knee."

"I'll get the notebooks. Can you do something with them?

"I'm not sure. Penn mentioned that Leo and Allan had a treehouse club, and that they had their own private handshake, secret codes, and everything. She said she wasn't privy to any of that, so I don't know that she'll be of any help. But if we can find Leo, and it looks like we might, then I'm betting he can."

"Wow. Good plan."

"I've got to go, but All Posts should have information on Leo if it's his box. Oh yeah, were you able to get pictures of Leo's bedroom just after Allan's murder? It might be a moot point from everything we know now though. If he's the one using these passages and he's been the 'ghost' in and out of the house, then he's also likely to be the one who left his own childhood room in slight disarray."

"Oh yeah," said Danbury, snapping his fingers. "I forgot to mention. I've got the scribe lined up. The notary public. To get Penn's statement about the financial information. Can we meet at your house? This evening?"

"Yeah, sure. I think I'm finished seeing patients at four, better make it at least 4:30, just to be on the safe side."

"OK. I'll get some surveillance set up here. And let you know what I find at All Posts. I'll contact Libby too. And try to get her to tell me more about Wayne."

"OK, good plan, and it sounds like there's a busy day ahead for you too. I'll catch up with you later."

"Later, Doc."

Matthew went down the main staircase and found Malcolm already back in the house with his leg propped up.

"What did you find? And how did you get up there?"

Matthew quickly told him about the passages, the circular wrought iron staircase, and the panels connecting into the various floors throughout the house. Malcolm just stared back incredulously.

"You haven't been upstairs since you got back from your sister's house, have you?" asked Matthew.

"No, I'd have had to have a really good reason to climb those stairs."

"That's what I thought. And I think we've found your 'ghost.' But I'll let Danbury tell you about that because I've got a patient who should already be in my office. Thanks for all your help, Malcolm!" said Matthew as he pulled his gloves off, stuffing them in his pocket. He let himself out the front door and hurried across the porch and back down the front driveway.

On the short walk back to his office, he called Penn Lingle. "Hey Penn, are you still good for this evening to record your statement and sign the affidavit?"

"Hey, Matthew, yeah, I know I need to do that. At your house?"

"Yeah, if that still works for you."

"It does. What time?"

"How does 5 work? Maybe with a bottle of wine and some hors d'oeuvres to relax with?"

"That works very well. Can I bring anything?"

"Just yourself."

"OK, see you then."

As he was entering the building, he quickly texted Danbury: "It's a go this evening with Penn. My house. 5 PM. Does that work?"

Hearing the ding from his cell as he'd just put on his lab coat and was heading out of his office, he pulled his phone out to see Danbury's texted agreement, "*OK. See you then. Talk later. Thanks, Doc.*"

22. Connections

That afternoon, after seeing the final patient for the day and prescribing a blood thinner for the aging patient with a cholesterol level that had recently shot through the roof, Matthew finished his patient appointments. As he returned to his office to update the charts, he noticed that he'd missed a call from Danbury, so he poked his phone to return the call.

"Hey, Doc. All set for this evening. Got some updates. News on Leo too. You'll love this."

"Oh yeah? What's the update?"

"You know those cards at All Posts. The ones you were telling me about. That all new customers fill out."

"Yeah."

"Guess who Leo's says he's employed by?"

"Thugs Are Us?" Matthew joked. "I don't know. Who?"

Danbury chuckled. "I'm beginning to think you're not far wrong. The Higgins Law Firm."

"Wayne Adams' law firm? Then there's at least a connection, however tenuous, between Leo and Wayne Adams. More than just that Adams manages the Lingle Estate, I mean. Interesting."

"That's what I said. Very interesting. I've pulled the Peak guys in now. It's too much in their back yard. Anderson is checking with Higgins Law

Firm. To see if we can verify employment. Now or ever. They'll stake out the house. For the night. To apprehend Leo if he comes back."

"Did you get to talk to Libby?"

"I did. Met her at Peak Eats at lunch. It doesn't sound like she knows much. She met Wayne at the Higgins Law Firm. When she was getting full legal custody of her boys. He'd just moved to Peak. He came on strong. Flirted a lot. Told her he loved kids. That he'd always wanted sons. Asked her to show him around. 'As if Peak were a huge thriving metropolis,' she said. Or something like that. They started dating. But she said he was very closed. To talking about his work. Any of his business dealings. Or about his past. She chalked it up to client confidentiality. And a very messy divorce. At the time."

"But he still won't talk to her about his past?"

"Nope. He's told her little bits. Just in conversation. But she said he got defensive. Got angry with her. If she pressed him on it. Or asked specific questions. He said he'd escaped a crazy ex-wife. In Lima, Ohio. And that he wanted a fresh start. Before that, she's pieced together little bits of information. He was raised in a strict home. She said it sounded over the top. Rules about everything. And his father ruled the household. What he said went. No questions asked. His mother cowered and followed orders. It sounds like he was bullied a lot. As a child. Both at home and at school."

"That's interesting," said Matthew. "Because when I talked to her Thursday, when the boys finally told us their story, she mentioned that Wayne encouraged Micah's bullying. Or maybe it wasn't encouraged exactly, but he wouldn't help her discourage it."

"Huh. That is interesting. You'd think he'd want to stop that. If he suffered from it himself. As a kid." Danbury was quiet a few seconds and then said, "Wayne has two sisters. But Libby doesn't think he's in touch with them. She says she can see the authoritarian upbringing. Sometimes he's that way with her boys. He loses his temper. Over things she thinks aren't important. And other times he seems not to care. What they do, when, or how. No consistency as a stepfather."

"That's got to be rough on Libby and the boys. Do you think he's abusive when he loses his temper? Or just extremely inconsistent? Or maybe bipolar?"

"I didn't ask directly. But that thought occurred to me too. That he might be abusive. He fits the profile. I told her to call me if she ever needed anything. Anything at all. If he is, I hope she will."

"I wonder why she married him. My neighbor said that she didn't need the money, so if that's true then that wasn't it."

"Yeah, I think that's true. I think she was just lonely. If anything, it was the other way around. Wayne took over her financial portfolio. She told me that he did. She hasn't seen it in years. Or so she said."

"Don't financial planners of some sort usually handle financial portfolios? I mean, he's handling hers and the Lingle Plantation, right? Single-handedly, it sounds like. Don't accountants usually handle at least the tax filings for financial portfolios? Where's the accountability? How did she just hand over her financial portfolio to him?"

"Wayne is very gregarious. Libby said he was charming. When they were dating. He told her he wanted to help her. Take care of that burden for her. And she says he's extremely smart. Exceptionally smart, I think were her words. She says he plans ahead. For everything. Like a chess player. Calculating each possible move. And the probability of it. She says he always makes contingency plans. For every possible obstacle."

"Contingency plans?"

"That's what she said."

"Like what?"

"She didn't say, exactly. Just that he always has a backup plan. A backup story. A way around potential difficulty. And he's always in control. Of every situation. I've made some calls. Asked some favors. Maybe I can get my hands on those tax filings. Might not be that revealing. If he's not letting anyone see the records. He's probably not straight with the IRS either."

"Sounds like he's got lots of issues. But it also sounds like you've got it all under control. Hey, I promised Penn hors d'oeuvres and a bottle of wine for her disposition at my house at five, so I need to get my charts updated and run by the grocery store before then."

"OK, Doc. See you at five."

After finishing the chart updates, Matthew had swung by the nearest grocery store and picked up brie wrapped in a filo pastry, crackers, and raspberry jam. He'd added a small tray of prepared vegetables and some gourmet hummus to his cart, along with two bottles of wine. He purchased it all and then headed for home.

Arriving home, he fed Max, put the brie in a baking dish on parchment paper and popped it into the oven to heat it quickly. Then he changed clothes, pulling on a pair of his favorite jeans and a short-sleeved Henley t-shirt. Quickly opening the solid inner front door, he wanted his visitors to be able to see, through the glass storm door, that he was home and ready for them.

In the kitchen, he opened the bottle of Sauvignon Blanc and pulled down four wine glasses, just in case the notary public and Danbury both wanted one as well. He put those on a tray and then added a plate with the prepared fresh vegetables and hummus, leaving room for a plate of the brie, jam, and crackers. Southern hospitality had been drilled into him, growing up, and he figured it was something that never really left you, particularly if you still lived in the South.

He heard a car pulling into his driveway just as he was finishing the preparations and then heard Penn's voice, "Knock knock."

"Hey Penn, come on in," he called around the corner as she came in the front door. "I was just finishing up the hors d'oeuvre tray."

"Forget the food for a minute. Can I have a glass of wine?" she asked nervously.

"Sure. How's this white?" he asked, holding up the bottle.

"That works," she said, with a grimace. "You know, I'm really not looking forward to this."

"It's OK, Penn," he said, giving her a quick hug. "Danbury already knows the story, and you might be helping to solve your brother's murder. I'm not sure if or how it's relevant, but if nothing else, maybe it'll be freeing to get this off your chest."

"It already was, when I told you," she said, returning his hug aggressively, and then reaching for the bottle of wine. "Where's your corkscrew?"

Handing it and the foil cutter to her, Matthew picked up a pot holder and removed the brie from the oven, sliding it onto the waiting plate. Adding the crackers, a tiny bowl of raspberry jam, and a little matching spoon and cheese knife, he considered his work in the kitchen complete.

"That smells heavenly," she said.

"Good. Here, help yourself," he said, handing her a plate and napkin. After she'd loaded a plate, he took the other three plates, a stack of napkins, and the platter and placed them on the ottoman in front of the sofa. Just then, Danbury and a small woman appeared in the doorway.

Motioning them in, Matthew noticed that the woman was a bit mousey, hiding behind Danbury's giant 6'4" frame. She had medium brown hair, shoulder length, and hazel eyes that were mostly hidden behind huge glasses which had probably been stylish a few decades ago. She was dressed demurely in a long grey skirt and lighter grey short-sleeved mock-turtle neck sweater that tucked just under her chin. She looked like she wanted to crawl into it, turtle-like.

"Hi, I'm Matthew Paine," he said, offering his hand and smiling down at her, "Come on in."

"Andrea Walsh," she said, extending one hand for a surprisingly firm handshake, while juggling an arm full of folders and a notebook computer in the other.

"You can put that down anywhere," said Matthew. "Help yourself to some hors d'oeuvres," he added, motioning to the tray and plates on the ottoman. "I just opened a bottle of white wine if you'd like a glass?"

"No thanks," said Andrea.

Danbury shook his head no but picked up a plate.

"And this," said Matthew, as Penn finally appeared from behind the narrow kitchen wall into the open area, "is Penelope Lingle, for the record, but she goes by Penn."

"Hi," she said ignoring Danbury and tentatively extending a hand to Andrea, who took it and just murmured, "Hello."

"Would you prefer something else to drink?" Matthew heard himself saying, hoping Penn wasn't bothered by his choice of words.

"Yeah, how about a glass of water?" said Danbury.

"Me too, please," said Andrea. "I need to focus, so water would be great."

"Sure. Two waters," said Matthew as he slipped back into the kitchen.

When he returned a few moments later, his guests had settled in,

Andrea and Penn sat on either end of Matthew's leather sofa, and Danbury was perched on the edge of the matching chair across from them. Handing off the drinks, Matthew pulled out the rolling office chair from the computer desk in the corner and sat down.

"Are you ready?" Danbury asked Andrea.

"Actually, could we switch places?" she asked Matthew.

"Sure. Would you like for me to turn the desk around to face the room?"

"That'd be perfect," she said softly.

Having completed that task, Matthew settled into the overstuffed sofa cushions, leaning back to listen and study the dynamics of the room. Penn was addressing Andrea and not looking at Danbury at all, though he was the one asking the questions.

Recounting her movements on her trip home after her mother's death seemed difficult for her, so she was relying heavily on the liquid courage in her hand. Noticing that she was shaking slightly as she explained about her initial involvement with Wayne Adams, Matthew slid her plate over to her without interrupting. She nodded her thanks, took a few bites, and continued her story.

When she got to the part about how she'd gotten angry when she learned that Wayne and Libby were serious, after the night with him, she choked up and got momentarily quiet. Holding her empty wine glass out to Matthew, she asked sweetly, "Would you?"

"Do you want some water first?"

"Not really."

"OK," he said as he refilled her plate, then slipped quietly from the room to refill the wine glass.

He brought it back half full and she grimaced at him as he handed it to her.

"How was the payment made to you?" asked Danbury.

"I picked up a cashier's check from his assistant the next day, right before I flew back out for Denver," she told Andrea, who was busily typing.

"How was it addressed? To you or your company?"

"Um. To me personally, I believe."

"Who was the remitter? Wayne Adams? Or Higgins Law firm?"

"Neither. I had forgotten about that, but there was some company name that I was unfamiliar with."

"What was the name?"

"That's been a while ago now," Penn said, pensively. "At the time I didn't care, as long as the check was good, and now I honestly don't remember what it was."

"You got the cashier's check. And then what? You flew back to Denver? Immediately?"

"Pretty much. I flew out the next morning."

"And was that the last time you saw Allan and Leo?"

"In person, yes, it was," she said sadly. "I haven't been back here since."

"But you've talked to them since?"

"I did talk to Leo a few times but he was all over the place and seemed to be spinning out of control. Then his number was no longer in service and I lost touch. He called me once, about two years ago, from a rehab facility and told me he wanted me to know that he'd be OK. I asked if he needed anything and he said he didn't and that he'd be in touch when he got out. When I didn't hear from him, I tried to find him. All I learned was that he'd been up in Jersey, but I'm not sure if he still is."

Danbury and Matthew exchanged a glance, which Penn seemed not to notice as she continued, "I tried to talk to Allan regularly for a while, but he wasn't much for talking on the phone so eventually I gave up and talked to his caregivers when I called the house. Malcolm was by far the best one he'd ever had. He was on top of everything: medications, doctor's visits, organization of Allan's world. All of it."

"Malcolm had learned to interpret all of Allan's 'I prefer' statements when they weren't completely direct, better than almost anyone except maybe Leo. That's why I'm happy to have him staying at the house now. He can continue to live there until he finishes his degree, as far as I'm concerned. I mean, depending on how the reading of the will turns out, if what I want matters at all." She looked down at her hand, swirling the white wine in the glass.

"You don't know where Leo is?" asked Danbury.

"No, I have less than no idea. He literally could be anywhere right now."

As if on cue, Danbury's phone chirped. He glanced at it and jumped up, setting his plate down quickly. "Be right back," he said as he stepped through the front door and started pacing in front of the house.

"Hey, Penn," said Matthew. "Did Allan write in little notebooks, you know the tiny little ones, when he was growing up?"

"Not that I remember, why?"

"You said he and Leo had a secret code, right?"

"Yeah and a secret handshake. It was all part of their treehouse club."

"You didn't learn the code though?"

"Right. I think I saw it a few times on odds and ends of paper around the house, but I can't really remember where or what the code was."

"But Leo might?"

"Oh, sure. Allan and Leo invented it, but it was probably at least as much Leo's as Allan's. Why?"

"Allan had been keeping little notebooks with scrawling in them. It's hard to describe but it's alpha-numeric-graphic. It's not random. There are patterns. There was a drawer full of them in his room. He had one on him the night he was killed and I was just wondering if it was a code that maybe Leo could decipher. It sounds like Allan didn't talk much to people, but maybe he talked plenty in those notebooks. It might help us if we could get the code deciphered."

"Yeah, Leo would be your best bet, short of an expert of some sort who deciphers codes professionally."

The room grew quiet in anticipation until Danbury returned. For the first time, Penn looked up at him and met his eyes as he walked back into the room. As if she sensed something of importance was about to happen, she tilted her head inquisitively but said nothing.

Perching on the edge of the chair and looking deeply into Penn's eyes, he asked, "What if I told you," he hesitated. "That Leo is here? In Peak."

Penn's eyes flew open wide. "Is he?" she asked, hopefully. "Did you find my brother?"

"I believe so," said Danbury, standing.

She beamed up at him, "Oh thank you!" Standing, she hugged Danbury, who seemed completely taken aback, as she said, "Thank you, Warren! Thank you!"

Sensing Danbury's concern, she drew back and, looking up at him, she asked, "Is he OK? I mean, he's not hurt or, or worse, right? He's OK?"

"He's fine. As far as I know." Stepping back, Danbury looked directly into her face and asked, "Penn, growing up at Lingle Plantation. Did you ever explore odd places? In the house. Rooms behind the walls?"

"What? What rooms behind the walls? What are you talking about? More importantly, when can I see my brother?"

"He's being taken in now. For questioning."

"What? Why? About Allan's murder? He'd never have hurt Allan! They were best friends when they were little. Though he was the younger brother, he looked out for Allan, at least through middle school when you seemed to have taken over that job."

Matthew was dumbfounded to see Danbury blush.

"We believe he's been there. At the Lingle Plantation. Since before Allan was murdered. Several weeks before. We found mail. Addressed to Leo. The postmarks went back more than four weeks."

This seemed to take the wind out of Penn's sails as she sank back onto the sofa.

"So, you're saying that he's in town, he's been here in town, and he's been behind the walls of the house? How is that possible? Any of it? It makes no sense."

"No, it doesn't. Not yet. That's why he's being questioned. We're nearly finished here," he said to Andrea. "Let's just get that last statement. That she didn't know where Leo was. And that she wasn't aware of the rooms behind the walls. At the Lingle Plantation."

"Did you want the one about the code books?" asked Andrea, who had apparently missed none of the conversation while Danbury was away.

"Code books?" asked Danbury.

Matthew quickly explained and Danbury responded to Andrea, "Oh yeah, add that."

To Penn, he said, "We can print this. Make any changes you request. Get you to sign, and Andrea to notarize. Then you can come with me. If you want. To the Peak Precinct. To see Leo."

"OK, I've got it all," said Andrea. "How can I print it?"

Matthew told her how to get on his wi-fi network, the name of the printer to select, and provided the needed passwords. As he straightened back up from leaning over her, Danbury said, "Hey, Doc. Do you have any coffee? It's gonna be a long night."

"Make that two?" asked Penn. "And yes, I want to come with you to see my brother. We've been a fractured family for far too long and he's all I have left. I want to be there for him, whatever that means."

"Sure, coffee coming up," said Matthew. Then to Andrea, he added, "Let me know when it's finished printing and I'll go get it."

She gave him a thumbs up and Penn followed Matthew into the kitchen.

"I'm sorry to be such an imposition," she said. "Can I at least help with the coffee?"

"You're not imposing. I want to get to the bottom of all of this too, both to find out what happened to your brother and to prevent anything else like that from happening again in Peak. You made your brother Allan real to me, as if I knew him, when you told me about growing up with him. And I want to see his murderer caught. But sure, you can help with the coffee. Put about ten cups in here using that side tap, it's filtered water," he said. Handing her the coffee carafe and indicating the smaller tap on the kitchen sink, he put the wire filter into the coffee maker and set the number of cups.

"It's done," called Andrea, so Matthew disappeared down the hallway to retrieve the printed copy from his combination office and guest bedroom. Penn was looking quizzically at him as he returned.

"The top button on the left," he said in answer to her unasked question. "The one on the right is what you use if you're setting it up ahead of time to brew later."

"Got it," she said, poking the button. The house was momentarily filled with the loud noise of coffee grinding as they both returned to the sofa and sat down. "Do you want me to read this aloud?" she asked, taking the pages from Matthew.

"Yeah. Go ahead. And here's a pen. Mark anything you want to change," said Danbury, handing over a fountain pen.

Penn read through her account, decided it sounded just fine as it was, and handed it over to Andrea.

"I'll just copy and paste this into the affidavit form. We can print that and then we'll sign it," said Andrea as her fingers flew over the keyboard again.

When that task was completed, Matthew fixed travel mugs for Danbury and Penn, who thanked him profusely and promised to return them to him. Andrea had declined coffee and packed up, handing Danbury a manilla envelope containing the affidavit.

Over his shoulder to Matthew, Danbury said, "I forgot to ask. You want to come too?"

"Thanks, but I think I'll pass this time. I have a couple of other things I need to do this evening. Keep me posted, though, if you learn anything new and helpful?"

"Will do."

Matthew couldn't help noticing Penn taking Danbury's proffered arm as they walked together down the short walkway to the cars. They seemed to have reconnected nicely, thought Matthew, turning back into the house and checking the time to see if he could manage to get to Cici's that evening and see the odometer reading on her car.

His stomach growled in protest as he realized that he'd only snacked lightly but hadn't actually had dinner. Mrs. Drewer's leftover barbecued chicken, he decided, was calling his name from the refrigerator, so he'd start there and then decide the best use of his time for the rest of the evening.

As he was hauling the tray and glasses back to the kitchen, Max suddenly appeared and brushed up against the back of his legs. "Hey, Big Guy. You were hiding again, huh?" He reached down and scratched the big cat behind the ears before pulling the leftovers from the refrigerator.

As Matthew was heating up the leftovers, he was contemplating having a night off and waiting another day to go to Cici's. After the leftovers though he felt refreshed and decided to go tackle the chore. He went to Cici's house, entered the codes to get in the house, and found the key fob for her car in the desk drawer in her kitchen. Opening the garage door, he fired up the Porsche long enough to get the odometer reading.

Thinking to himself that he should really make an effort to drive it for her once a week or so. Even it if was just around the block and back, that would keep it in better running order, at least until he was able to sell it. He'd jotted the mileage in the notepad app on his phone, closed up the garage, returned the key fob to the drawer, and reset all the security alarms as he left the house.

As he drove back home, Matthew called Danbury to see how things were going with Leo. It was more about his interest in this family now, he realized, than it was about just finding the murderer and conquering that challenge. There was no doubt that he wanted the murderer caught to protect Peak from any further senseless murders. He also knew that he'd regained sight of the person who was Allan Lingle and that drove him harder.

"Hey, Doc," said Danbury, after so many rings that Matthew thought his call was going straight to voice mail.

"Hey. How're things going with Leo?"

"Not great. Leo lawyered up. Immediately."

"What? Let me guess. He called Wayne Adams."

"You'd think so, right? But no. Another law firm entirely. On the other side of Peak. The lawyer is out of town. Won't return until tomorrow afternoon. But Leo's happy. Just sitting in jail 'til then."

"Can you hold Leo in jail until then?"

"He's a person of interest. But we can't hold him long, no. Not enough evidence against him."

"How did Penn respond to seeing Leo again? Did she get a chance to talk to him?"

"Only momentarily. Just in passing. One of the officers put him in a room, pretty quickly. For questioning."

"Would he open up to her, do you think? I mean, I hate to use her as a crowbar, but maybe she could pry something out of him. If he was in the house that night, he might have seen something or heard something that can help you figure out what the two guys were doing in the house and if they murdered Allan or were in some way connected to his murder."

"They surely had means. And opportunity. Maybe there's a motive there. Somewhere. And the All Posts form that said Leo was working for Adams. That's one side, but every story has two. Adams still won't talk to me. Maybe it's easily explained. Maybe there's nothing there. Nothing to do with Allan anyway. But they're both hiding something. And working hard to do it."

"I'll admit, I will rest easier when we have the murderer caught. A brutal murder in this little town seems so random. It makes the town feel less safe. At least that's what the residents are saying."

"I want them to feel safe too. And they don't right now. You're right. Unsolved murders will do that."

"I wonder why Leo is so happy to be there in the jail overnight. I mean, maybe he doesn't feel safe either. And why didn't he call Wayne Adams? Is that who he's afraid of? Maybe he's gotten himself into some trouble. He's mixed up in all of this somehow and he has to decide how to handle it. Hence, lawyering up immediately and asking for a lawyer from across town."

"Those are good questions," said Danbury, pondering a moment. "Those are great questions. That gives me an idea. Where are you? Want to help light a fire under a suspect?"

"I'm just coming into the edge of Peak. But sure. What do you need me to do?"

Danbury explained the plan and Matthew glanced at the time, thinking it could well be a late night as he drove to the Peak Police Station, just down the street from his office.

23. Man and the plan

Meeting Danbury in the lobby of the Peak Police Station, Matthew signed in and Danbury took him back through the offices to the holding cells to meet Leo. Lying on a cot in the corner of the back cell was a slender man that, at first glance, Matthew thought was Allan Lingle. He shook his head to clear the image as the man sat up and then stood, walking toward them.

Danbury unlocked the cell and motioned Leo forward, closing and relocking the cell door behind him. There were no handcuffs or restraints on him and he looked disheveled, like a good shower and shave were in order but he hadn't managed either lately. His sandy blond hair was sticking up at odd angles and he stared at Matthew, questioningly, with hazel eyes. He had a nicely proportioned face which still looked, even on closer inspection, much like Allan's.

"You're free to go, Mr. Lingle. We have no evidence. None to hold you for any crime. You were brought in for questioning. But we can't keep you here. If you won't talk."

"Go?" he asked, looking slightly panicked, "Go where?"

"Anywhere you'd like," said Danbury. "Back to Lingle Plantation. Or maybe with Penn. At that old historic inn. That's where she's staying, right?" he asked Matthew nonchalantly.

"I think so. I think she's staying at the Colonial Inn," confirmed Matthew. The restaurant accompanying the Colonial Inn served the best sweet potato pancakes and made-to-order omelets anywhere around, in Matthew's opinion, and it was his favorite spot for a Saturday brunch.

"It's not too far from here," added Danbury. "You could walk. Get there pretty easily."

"Walk? Out of here?" asked Leo, clearly in a panic now. "Why do I have to leave?"

"Because we can't hold you. You're not under arrest," said Danbury. "We could get in trouble. For keeping you here. If you're not talking to us. Voluntarily."

"But, it's not safe. It's not safe out there," Leo protested. "I prefer to stay right here."

If the guy hadn't looked so terrified, Matthew might have been amused with him sounding so much like Allan. But instead Matthew followed the script that he and Danbury had roughly prepared.

"You think it's not safe out there?" asked Matthew. "I completely agree. It really isn't a safe town anymore, is it? Ever since your brother was brutally murdered for no apparent reason, the whole town is afraid to go out at night. Nobody thinks it's safe out there."

"You seem to know why," prodded Danbury. "Why it isn't safe out there. You do know, don't you?"

"I, I can't say," he stammered.

"OK. Then I'll walk you out," said Danbury.

"No! You can't! They'll kill me too!"

"They WHO?" asked Danbury, pointedly.

"I can't tell you."

"Mr. Lingle, it's your choice," said Danbury. "You can sit down and talk. Tell us what you know. Help us to find your brother's killer. If you didn't kill him. Or, you can . . . ."

"I didn't kill my brother!" Leo quickly and loudly interjected, interrupting Danbury. "I would never have hurt him! You have to believe me! Ask Penn! Ask anyone! I would never have hurt Allan!"

His sincerity felt genuine to Matthew, but, as Danbury had said, Leo needed to fear them more immediately than whoever was out there by using the leverage of whoever was out there. So Matthew said nothing as Danbury stuck to the script.

"I'm not convinced that you didn't," said Danbury, confrontationally.

"If you really didn't kill your brother, don't you want to help find whoever did?" added Matthew.

"You don't seem to want to do that," said Danbury. "Which seems suspicious."

"Why is that?" asked Matthew.

"Who are you, anyway?" Leo finally got around to asking.

"I'm Matthew Paine."

"He's a consultant with the Police Department," added Danbury, purposefully failing to mention which one. "Come on, Mr. Lingle, let's go," he added, taking him by the arm to lead him out.

"No! No! I'll talk. Ask me anything! Just promise that you'll protect me. Maybe I can make a deal."

"What are you offering?"

"Information, I guess. I don't know exactly who killed my brother, but maybe I can point you in the right direction. If you'll help me. Promise me that you'll protect me and Penn too. They could go after her to get to me if they know I'm cooperating."

"They who, Mr. Lingle? Let's get an interview room. And talk."

"OK," said Leo, at last, hanging his head in surrender. He might have known that he'd been manipulated, thought Matthew, but he didn't seem to think he had too many options.

Matthew followed as Danbury led the way down the hallway. The last time he had watched Danbury conduct an interview, they'd been at the downtown police station in Raleigh but he'd never been in the Peak Police Station before this week. Flipping on lights in an interrogation room that was otherwise ready and waiting, Danbury indicated the seat for Leo. He called down the hallway, asking for one of the Peak officers to bring Penn Lingle in quickly, gave them the address, and instructed them what to tell her. Then he closed the door before pulling out his own chair and sitting across the table from Leo.

Matthew had agreed to watch from the room behind the mirror but remain on hand for a softer touch if Danbury hit a wall with the guy. It was their good cop, bad cop routine and it had worked well for them previously, though Matthew had never considered becoming a police officer at all and had jokingly called himself "Notta Cop."

As they settled in, Danbury explained that the conversation was being recorded. He provided the form for Leo to sign agreeing to that and reversing his earlier decision to have a lawyer present. He explained that there would be a transcript of the conversation for him to sign afterward.

"You're protecting Penn too?" Leo asked.

"Yeah. They're bringing her back in now."

"Can I see her? Talk to her?"

"When we're done here. If you cooperate."

"OK," Leo agreed and then signed the initial documents.

"When did you get back to Peak?"

"A little over a month ago, I guess. Something like that."

"Why did you come back? And where have you been? And is it relevant? To your brother's murder?"

Leo took a deep breath and settled back into his chair. "It's a long story," he said. "And some of it might be relevant."

Matthew raised an eyebrow as he heard Danbury respond, "We've got all night." It was already nearly ten, Matthew noticed, checking his watch. He was already very tired. Trying to settle in and get as comfortable as he could, he stifled a yawn while his foot tapped out the rhythms in his head and his knee jumped on the downbeat. At least at the Peak Police Station, the observation room he was in provided a raised platform in front of the two-way mirror so that he was in a chair instead of propped on a stool.

"When I left Peak, it was right after Mom died," Leo began. "I guess you know about how the estate was settled?" Danbury nodded, and Leo continued, "I was really pissed about that. I thought Penn and I should have gotten something more out of it. I guess I understand now that Mom was worried about Allan because he really couldn't take care of himself. Not out in the real world, and she was obviously way too right about that." Leo choked up and it took him a moment to recover and continue.

"Penn and I both got a small amount out of the estate, I think. Mine was meant to cover college, but I had dropped out. And I decided to try to make it grow. I got involved in some start-up business ventures, but they didn't go anywhere. And then came the gambling. I started drinking and then dabbling into drugs," he said miserably.

"I was getting in deep when I was offered what sounded like a pretty sweet deal to carry packages and collect money. I did that for a while, but the pay wasn't covering my gambling debts. I had people after me from two different directions by the time I thought about coming back to Peak. The drug dealers wanted their packages, but I'd sold them to cover the loan shark from the gambling debts. Turns out, loan sharks never really leave you alone. They don't think you're ever done paying, even when you're sure that you are."

Leo took a breath and continued, "I just wanted to get away from it all. I was up in Jersey at the time but I was on the run. I moved around a lot and I was tired. I started searching for information about the estate Mom had left and I got in touch with Wayne Adams. He was managing it. I asked if there had been any changes or provisions for Penn and me long term. He said there were not and the disbursements we'd gotten were supposed to be it."

"Even if Allan were dead?"

Leo's eyes widened with understanding as he replied, "We never discussed that. I didn't even think to ask and he didn't tell me anything about it. So I have no idea what happens now."

"No?"

"No! None."

"OK," said Danbury more calmly. "Back to your initial conversation with Adams. How did that go?"

"Yeah, I think he sensed my desperation and he offered me a deal, a job of sorts."

As Leo looked down, as if ashamed, Danbury prompted, "What job?"

"He asked me how deep in debt I was and I told him my situation. He said he'd get me out of debt and the loan sharks off my back if I'd come to work for him. I should have known it was too good to be true. It had to have strings attached that I would regret later. But I was so tired from running that I jumped at the offer, and I gave him the names of the people who were after me."

"And then what?"

"After about a week and a half, he called me back. I'd been panicking that whole time thinking he'd turn me in to the police or worse, to them. He told me that he'd taken care of it and I could come back to Peak, but that I'd need to stay out of sight for a few months while I took care of some business for him. I knew about the passageways and rooms in the house, so I thought I could sneak in and out and stay there."

"I also figured that Allan would help me stay hidden. I mean, who was he going to tell? It's not like he talked to people much anyway, so it sounded like a pretty good plan. When I got here, Wayne met with me once. Out of town though, up in Raleigh. He gave me a set of instructions and a new phone and told me to call him when I was done."

"What instructions?"

"I had to get a post office box in Peak, but at All Posts, not a US Post Office box. I remembered that business was up north of town near Highway 64 so I hitched a ride there. When I got there, it had moved but somebody in the strip mall there told me where they'd gone. It worked out pretty well because it was close to the house, so I could get to it easier anyway. Wayne told me not to, but I had to put the name of his company on there because I couldn't pay for it all up front. They ask for employer information if you're paying for it monthly."

"OK, and then what?"

"Then I had to text a contact he'd programmed into my phone with a code word and tell them I was ready."

"Ready for what?"

"I didn't know and he wouldn't tell me. He said I didn't need to know yet and the contact would tell me what to do next."

"Did they?"

"Yeah, they asked for the address at the post office box I'd gotten and told me to go check it in three days. Then I was to text them and they'd tell me what to do next."

"You did that?"

"Yeah, there was a package in the box and they told me to take it to

Wayne Adams but to drop it at night in a specific place."

"What was in the package?"

"I didn't know, and they told me not to look. They threatened me with harm if I did. I figured I was right back where I'd been before, carrying packages. I knew where that had gotten me before, so I was scared."

"And nobody knew you were in Peak, no old friends or anyone?"

"Just Allan. He knew I was here. But no, I didn't run into anyone else I knew. I was out at dusk or after dark as much as I could be. So just Allan and the people at All Posts, but nobody there knew me."

"Allan knew you were in the house?"

"Yeah, he knew about the rooms and passageways. We'd found them when we were kids and we'd explored them back then. He'd bring me food sometimes and he knew I was sleeping in my bed upstairs some nights or in one of the attic rooms."

Matthew remembered something that Malcolm had said when he heard one of the ghostly noises and Allan had said it was just Leo. At the time, Malcolm had thought it was strange, but now it made perfect sense, at least to Matthew. It really was just Leo.

"Allan helped you?"

"Yeah, he did. He always would. It was our secret that I was here. Like when we were kids hiding out in the tree house. We talked a little bit and did the secret handshake from childhood and laughed."

"Allan laughed?"

Leo looked as if that was the most stupid question anyone could ask and replied, "Well, yeah."

"Sorry. Just never heard that before. That Allan laughed."

"He had a great sense of humor, of irony really. He just didn't talk all that much and not at all to people he didn't know."

"OK, so go on. You had more work to do for Wayne Adams and you had to stay hidden. What about the night that Allan was murdered? Where were you that night?"

"I was in the house."

"While Allan was out for his dinner and playing Bingo?"

"Yeah, that was his weekly routine."

"When was the last time you saw Allan?"

"Just before he left for dinner at Peak Eats. He came upstairs and brought me a peanut butter and jelly sandwich that he'd made himself, and a glass of milk. He changed his shoes and said, 'See you later.' Then he went downstairs and out the front door."

"He made you a sandwich?"

"Yeah, peanut butter and jelly or honey are, I mean were," Leo said with a slight tremor in his voice. "Those were his favorites," he continued. "He'd still eat them three times a day every day if it were left up to him and be perfectly happy."

"Were you in the house all evening? While he was gone?"

"Yeah, I was up in the attic until Malcolm left. When I heard his Jeep leave, I came down the back stairs into the kitchen to wash my plate and glass, and then I heard the side door open, so I slid back behind the walls. I figured Malcolm had forgotten something and come back, but he usually came and went through the back door so that was weird."

"Was it Malcolm?"

"I didn't look, so I don't know for sure. I just assumed it was. I figured that he had forgotten something and came back to look for it because I heard footsteps all over the house. I heard somebody moving around the other end of the house, first. Then I heard the footsteps go upstairs and eventually they came back down, pretty much wandering all over. Then finally the side door closed and whoever it was had gone. I didn't hear anything for a while, so I came out after that to go take a shower upstairs and then I went back through the wall upstairs."

"Do you know what time it was? When any of this happened?"

Leo screwed up his face, pondering. "I think it was about 4:45 when Allan left. I ate up in one of the little bedrooms in the attic where I could see out to know when Malcolm left. He left about 5:30 or so, I think, and I'd only really had time to go downstairs to wash my dishes and put them away when I heard the side door open. That was maybe 5:45. I probably came back out about 6:30, thinking that I could get a quick shower before Malcolm got back. Allan didn't usually come home until at least 8:30 on Monday nights and Malcolm used that time to run errands, buy groceries, or do whatever personal things he needed to do."

"OK, you were showering at 6:30. Then what happened?"

"I straightened up the bathroom and dried everything down. I had a book I was studying in my old room so I went in and got it and took it downstairs. I sat in the sitting room and read about successful business management for a while. I was just getting up and thinking that it was about time for Malcolm to come home when he did. I heard his Jeep pull in around back and I had to hurry to the laundry room and get through the wall with my book before he came in that back door."

"What time was that?"

"I'm not sure. It was starting to get dark out but I was rushing when I heard his Jeep so I didn't check the time."

"You were in the hidden rooms when Malcolm came in?"

"Yeah, I heard him in the kitchen, opening and closing cabinet doors. Then I heard footsteps going upstairs and moving around at the other end of the house. I assume it was Malcolm."

"And you stayed in the hidden rooms? All night?"

"No. I had gone up to the attic when I heard a commotion downstairs."

"What did you hear?"

"At first it was just a loud bang and then footsteps going down the back stairs below me. And then I heard voices and heavy things being moved and shuffled, like furniture, downstairs."

"What did you do then?"

"I came down a flight of the back stairs and peered around the edge of the railing on the upstairs balcony to see what was going on."

"What did you see?"

"Just shadows in the hallway of people moving around in the sitting room. I could hear things being thrown around and I knew I needed to get out. I went through the wall on the second floor, down to the basement, and out through the cellar doors."

"You went all the way out of the house?"

"Yeah."

"And then what?"

"I ran. I was in the edge of the woods when I heard breaking glass and a lot more yelling, so I just kept going."

"Where did you go?"

"To the treehouse."

"The treehouse?"

"Yeah, Allan and I had a treehouse when we were kids. Our dad and an uncle had built it for us. It was pretty solid and it's still there."

"Can you see the house from the treehouse?"

"Not anymore. There was a clearing there with a play area when we were kids. You know, a jungle gym, sandbox, swing set, see-saw, all of that. But that's gone and it's all overgrown now."

"OK. You went to the treehouse."

"Yeah."

"And then what?"

"It was really windy out that night, so I closed off one side against the wind. It has panels that you can raise and prop up or lower, sort of like having windows that you can prop open, except that they're boards."

"Did you stay there for the night?"

"Yeah, all night."

"When you closed the panels in the treehouse. Did you see anything? Or hear anything else?"

"I heard more yelling and then motors revving and cars leaving out the back way."

"Did you see the vehicles? When you came out of the house?"

"Yeah, they were parked out back, not far from the back corner where I had to come out of the house. I saw them when I came out of the bushes, but I darted into the woods as fast as I could. I was scared that somebody was in them. But I didn't take time to find out and I just hoped that they didn't see or hear me. The cellar doors make a racket."

"What vehicles did you see?"

"There were two. I could see the Jeep that belongs to Malcolm. It was pulled in between the trees where he usually parks. The other was pulled right behind the Jeep. It was a dark sedan but I didn't stop to look at it."

"Had you ever seen it before?"

"Not at the house. I don't know if I'd seen it around town. I didn't get a good look at it."

"Then what?"

"Not too long after that, I heard all of the emergency vehicles and I could see some of the lights, even through the trees. It was completely dark by then and they lit up the sky. I didn't know they were there for Allan. I just didn't know," he said, putting his head in his hands.

The door into the observation room opened and an officer brought Penn in. She said hello to Matthew and then hovered over him, peering into the room where Leo was. They could see Leo's shoulders shaking and she turned to the officer who had walked in with her, earnestly pleading to be with her brother.

When he wasn't budging on allowing that, Matthew stood and approached him, "Officer, the Lingles are cooperating with this investigation. Neither is under arrest for anything. They've just tragically lost their brother and they're requesting to be together for a few minutes. I don't think Danbury would have a problem with that."

"You never interrupt an interrogation unless it's an emergency, or new pertinent information is available. It's protocol," replied the officer.

"If you're worried about Danbury, I'll take the blame if he gets upset. I think they're mostly through the evening in question anyway."

The officer looked Matthew over dubiously, nodded curtly, and motioned for Penn to follow him. Matthew watched as the door was opened into the interrogation room, tentatively at first, and he could hear the officer say something from the hall. Danbury motioned her in and Penn ran to Leo and put her arms around him.

Leo turned and they both spoke at once.

"I'm sorry, Penn, I didn't know," said Leo.

"I'm so sorry, Leo," said Penn, "I've been a horrible sister."

Leo stood and they clung to each other, both in tears, while Danbury looked away and shifted uncomfortably in his chair. He had the first seat to the tragic family reunion. Matthew felt similarly uncomfortable, as if he were intruding on a private moment, and he was happy to be behind the glass waiting to see what happened next.

24. Decoding

After a few minutes, Penn and Leo pulled apart, looking at each other, and Penn asked, "What didn't you know?"

"That Allan would die because of me."

"Because of you? I feel horrible that I moved away and tried not to look back. Why do you think it was because of you?"

"I don't know, exactly. I just think maybe it was. There were people after me and they might have gotten to Allan to get to me."

At this point, Danbury interrupted them, "Leo, do you know who killed Allan?"

"No. But before Wayne Adams stepped in, there were people after me. And I think they might still have been."

"Wayne Adams?!" said Penn.

"Why do you think that?" asked Danbury of Leo before she could say more.

"I don't really know. It's just a feeling," said Leo.

"Here," said Danbury, sliding a piece of paper and a pen across the table. "Write down their names. How to find them. Physical descriptions. What they might want from you. Any helpful information. Anything that you can think of."

"Hey, Leo," interjected Penn. "Remember the secret code you and

Allan had when you were kids?"

"Oh yeah. Allan loved that code," he said distractedly as he was writing.

Just then, Danbury's cell phone went off. "I'll be right back," he said, quickly leaving the room.

"Do you still remember what the code was? It had graphics, letters, and numbers, right?" she asked.

"Basically. It was almost like sentence diagraming."

"Did Allan still use it?"

"I don't know, why?"

"He kept little notebooks full of letters, numbers, and graphics. If it was the code you had as kids, could you decipher them?"

"I guess so. If it's the same code, it's not complicated but there's some guesswork involved."

"What do you mean, guesswork?" asked Penn.

"Well, there were shapes that were nouns and lines between for verbs that connected the nouns. But there'd be initials or something to identify the person, place, or thing in the shapes and different kinds of lines connecting them that meant different actions. It wasn't really specific, so you had to have some understanding of what was going on around you at that time."

"You're saying that without context it might be difficult to decipher?" she asked.

"Yeah, right," he said, and the room grew quiet as he finished writing and then laid the pen down on top of the piece of paper.

"That shouldn't be too difficult though, I wouldn't think? I mean, Allan didn't go far or do much. He was just around town in Peak."

And then things started happening all at once and Matthew was having trouble taking it all in. Penn turned to the police officer, who had allowed her into the interrogation room and had remained in the doorway, to ask if they had the notebooks and if Leo could look at them. Just then, Danbury burst back through the door to Matthew's observation room.

"They found a fingerprint," Danbury told Matthew. "In the Jeep. On the back of the rearview mirror. Just an index finger. So it took a while. But they got a match. There was a partial on the door handle. But the match on the first one narrowed the search. The prints belong to Juan González. He's 26. Last known address was in Miami. The angry eyebrow guy. He's wanted in Florida, Georgia, and Texas. As is his known associate. One Fernando Hernández. We have an APB out on González."

"Well, that's a start. Maybe the Miami police can fill in some blanks for us."

"Yeah. I just put in a call to Miami Dade. They'll call me back."

"Meanwhile, you missed the discussion in there about the code and the little notebooks. Did you get those notebooks? Are they here?"

"All but that last one. The one in the Jeep. But we can get it. Why?"

"Because Penn seems to think that Leo can decode them. It sounds like the code he and Allan created when they were boys. Leo sounded less certain that he could, but it's surely worth a try."

"That's great. I'll ask Steinbach to go get them," he said and then left the room and spoke to the officer in the doorway.

"What about," began Matthew as the door swung closed. "Me?" he said to air. He took a deep breath and blew it out. He knew he should be happy to be a bystander and get to see the events unfold but he wasn't. He wanted to be in the middle of trying to figure it all out and he was frustrated sitting there with nothing to do. He checked his watch, also thinking that he had patients starting at 8:30 in the morning and he hadn't looked at their charts yet.

Danbury appeared briefly in the interrogation room and asked Leo if either of the names Juan González or Fernando Hernández were familiar to him. Leo's face becoming devoid of color as the blood drained from it was answer enough. He slid the piece of paper across the table to Danbury, pointed, and said, "His muscle."

"OK, got it. Did this guy ever threaten your family?" asked Danbury, pointing to the name on the paper. "If you didn't pay up? Or do what he demanded?"

"No," said Leo, barely audibly. "I never told him that I had any."

"OK. Doesn't rule it out though. As motive," said Danbury. "He could get background on you easily enough," he said, as he picked up the paper and left the room.

Leo looked particularly crestfallen over this last thought, and Matthew actually felt sorry for the guy. While Matthew was mulling over all of the cliches he'd ever heard about the company you keep, Danbury stuck his head back in the observation room, "Hey, Doc?"

"Yeah?"

"I need to get on this. The IDs and background checks of the guys from the house. And the guy Leo says they worked for. Officer Steinbach is getting the notebooks. You want to help with the decoding? Leo is willing to try. Maybe you and Penn can help. He says there's context needed."

"I'm not sure how much help I'll be, but I can try."

"Thanks Doc. I'll be back later," said Danbury, holding the door for Matthew. "Y'all can go down the hallway. To a conference room. A more comfortable spot. To work on the decoding," he said to Penn and Leo as he held the door of the interrogation room open for them.

"OK, lead the way."

As Leo, Penn, and Matthew were getting settled around a conference table in a small meeting room, Officer Steinbach came in with a box which he carefully placed on the table in front of them, along with a stack of paper and a handful of pencils.

"I wasn't sure what you'd need," he said. "Danbury told me to get you whatever you needed. Coffee, maybe?"

Matthew raised an eyebrow. "Coffee? How long has it been in the pot?"

Steinbach chuckled, "It's in a machine, but it's not too bad. You want a cup?"

"Sure."

"Anyone else?"

Penn and Leo declined as they started pulling the little notebooks out of the box and restacking them on the table in front of them.

"What do you want in it?" asked Steinbach.

"Cream and lots of sugar."

"Got it. Be right back."

Leo began flipping through some of the notebooks and after a few moments said, "This looks like an upgrade of the code we created as kids but not by too much."

"I wonder if they're in any order at all?" asked Penn.

"What are these codes? On the front page of each notebook?" asked Matthew, pointing over Leo's shoulder to one.

Leo studied them in several of the notebooks that he'd spread out in front of him for a moment and then slowly said, "I think those are dates. Like basic timestamps, except alphanumeric, two numbers for the year, two letters for the month, and two numbers for the day. So 18Ap22 is April the 22nd of 2018.

"Then we do have a way to sort them," said Penn, as she began sorting. "They're mostly in reverse order already. OK, so show us how this code works and we can start working through the most recent ones."

Leo picked up a pencil and, as he flipped through the notebooks, he said, "This is kind of like sentence diagraming. The shapes here are the nouns. I think squares with initials are people. Circles with letters are places. Triangles with letters or numbers are things, objects. And rectangles are the objects of the actions." He drew each of those on the paper he'd labeled "Key" under a heading of "Nouns" and went back to the notebooks.

Matthew's foot tapped out the rhythms in his head and his knee jumped under the table as he pondered the system that Leo was describing. It was both simple and elegant, particularly to have been created by children. The entries were all tiny, but the shapes and lettering were precisely drawn and detailed.

"The lines between the shapes are the verbs, the actions. Dotted lines are always to the squares and they mean that somebody is talking to somebody else. Wavy lines are motions, movement like someone is walking or running, and a solid line could mean anything else. I'm not sure about the zigzags unless it's just a fast action maybe," he added as he jotted each of those on the page under the heading, "Verbs."

"There are symbols in the action lines too. I'm not sure what those are. This one looks like a lightning strike. That one is a smiley face," he said pointing. "It's in the middle of a conversation so maybe that was a happy or friendly conversation."

"The letters and numbers in the shapes are where it gets tricky," he continued. "They're initials for people in the squares and some in the rectangles. I think they're short form for the places and objects in the others. Sometimes there are numbers if there is more than one place or object, I think. It looks like some squares and rectangles have more than one person in them, like a group of people. Others each have their own person, even when the squares or rectangles are grouped together. I'm not sure what that means. But knowing Allan, it had meaning. It wasn't arbitrary."

"You know," added Penn. "It looks like there's just a page or less some days, and some days don't have entries at all. Every so often, days run over to multiple other pages with arrows."

Pulling up a calendar on her phone, Penn began to track the dates to days of the week. "There is a pattern here. The entries seem to be much longer on Mondays and Thursdays. Those go on for several pages. A lot more on Mondays apparently because those are the longest entries I see. That was Bingo night, wasn't it? Mondays and Thursdays start with a circle with PE in it. 'Peak Eats,' I'm betting."

Matthew picked up the notebooks that Penn was looking through and said, "Ah, the hour he spent in Peak Eats twice a week wasn't just about eating. I bet he was listening to the conversations around him from the older crowd. Those were probably considerable, and it looks like he was noting all that was said. There are lots of conversational dotted lines on those entries. The Bingo games on Monday nights were probably also sources of much conversation, gossip, and supposition about what was going on in Peak. I'm betting that between playing his Bingo cards Allan was recording those conversations, too."

"So, they're like a gossip column," summarized Penn.

As he flipped through the notebooks, Matthew added, "This is amazing. Everything that nobody thought he was paying any attention to and it's all in his notebooks. Where are the most recent ones?"

After sorting through them, Penn lined them up and made a log of them on a separate piece of paper. "I don't see any after February," she said. "March, April, and May are missing."

"Hmmm," said Matthew. "How many do you think that is? There wasn't an entry for every day and there are two or three for each month, right? So including the one he was carrying that's in police custody in Joseph County, that's maybe seven or eight of them missing."

"That sounds about right. But why is one in Joseph County?" asked Penn.

"I guess I can tell you this," said Matthew. "Because it was found in McGill's Crossroads. It was found with the baseball bat in Malcolm's Jeep." He wasn't sure how widely known the second murder was so he decided not to mention that but added, "Maybe Danbury can get it sent to us. Or at the very least get them to read the date code in the front so that we know exactly what dates are missing in between."

"Leo, can you decipher the most recent ones? The ones from February at least?" asked Penn.

"I can try," he said as he picked up a piece of paper and a pen and started writing down what he could figure out with some question marks for things he wasn't sure about."

Officer Steinbach returned with Matthew's coffee and motioned him to the door. "Detective Danbury wants to see you a minute."

"I'll be right back," said Matthew as he slipped out with the Peak officer.

As Matthew approached, Danbury said, "I put another APB out. On one Rudy Warrick. He's the guy Leo pointed to on the paper. Where he'd written the names of the people who were after him. Leo isn't safe. He was right about that, if González and Hernández worked for Warrick. This guy's bad news. I'm taking Leo and Penn home with me tonight. And we'll set up a post outside. I want to keep Leo close, anyway. I don't trust him."

Matthew had stopped sipping his coffee, wide-eyed. "And if Leo's in Peak, then Peak isn't safe either," he summarized. "But why don't you trust him?"

"He was a pretty big screw up. Growing up. And I don't buy the whole story. About Wayne Adams clearing his debt. What's in it for Wayne? Something is just off there. With that story."

"I thought he sounded sincere," said Matthew. "And the terror on his face when you asked about González and Hernández was real. There's no faking that."

Neither man spoke for a moment and finally Danbury asked, "How's it going in there?"

"Oh yeah. Leo can decipher some of the coding and he's guessing at the rest. But some of the notebooks are missing. Those were the only ones in the drawer?"

"Yep. The only ones we found. In that top drawer. The other drawers had clothes. What's missing? And how can you tell?"

"The books are dated in the front of each and when the days change with a pretty simple date sequence. The dates go into February, but there's nothing more current than that. You said the one Allan had on him was found in the Jeep, right? Is that still in Joseph County?"

"Yeah, as far as I know."

"Can you get it here? Or at least have them give you the date code from the front of it so that we know exactly what dates are missing. We need to know about how many of these notebooks we're looking for and we're guessing between seven or eight of them."

"Yeah. I can get the date code. At least that much tonight."

"I hate to bail on the party, but there's not much more for me to do here tonight, is there?"

Danbury shook his head as Matthew added, "I have patients first thing in the morning. I don't have any tomorrow afternoon, but I need to get some sleep at least."

"Yeah, go home. Lock up. Set your security system. Call me in the morning. And I'll give you an update."

As Matthew agreed and started to walk away, Danbury called after him, "Hey, Doc." Matthew turned and Danbury said, "Thanks for all your help."

"You're welcome," was all that Matthew's tired brain could come up with and probably, as he reflected leaving the police station and driving home on autopilot, all that he needed to say anyway.

As he drove home, he couldn't help feeling let down. He had thought that Leo with the notebooks would allow Allan to speak through them and explain what he'd been up to and maybe even why someone would want to kill him. Matthew realized that he had been so hopeful that the notebooks were the key and now all he felt was tired and greatly disappointed.

After he got home, Matthew locked the doors and set the alarms as he always did and left a few extra lights on. He set up the coffee maker to go off at 6:30 in the morning. Then he scooped Max up, “C’mon, big guy, let’s go to bed.”

After putting Max gently on the bed, he went through his evening routine. Collapsing into bed, Matthew was wired from the discoveries of the evening and the issues they still had with piecing it all together, as well as the new information about Warrick, the guy who was bad news. As his mind raced, he figured that sleep would come slowly and he was thankful that the next day was Friday, which meant that he had only morning patients scheduled.

Checking to be sure that his alarm was set, Matthew was reviewing the events of what felt like the longest day since his medical school years. That was the last thing he remembered as he fell into a deep sleep much more quickly than he’d have imagined possible. Max left the bottom of the bed, curling up on the pillow around his head, but Matthew didn’t notice.

25. Meetings not of the minds

What is that annoying noise, Matthew wondered, as he slid out from under Max and rolled over to turn off his alarm, but it didn't turn off. Reaching for his phone, he realized that it was Cici FaceTiming him. He clicked to connect.

"Happy Friday!" she said, far too cheerfully. "Wow, you look hung over," she added. "Are you OK?"

"Just a late night working with Danbury on something. Hey, I got your odometer reading yesterday, so I can get a price for your car and see if James is still interested."

"That's great, Matthew, thank you! I did see you at the house last night. On my doorbell camera recording."

"Ah, I forgot you could see me. I need to be careful what I do, huh?" he teased.

"You do. No parading strange women in there, Mr.!"

Matthew just chuckled at her moxie. She'd always been a spitfire. It was one of the things that had drawn him to her.

"Yeah, because I've got such a long parade of them," he answered, sarcastically.

"You could if you wanted to," she said sincerely. "I just hope you don't."

"Have? Or want?"

"Both or either."

Matthew loved their banter and he missed that with her. She could hold her own in any discussion, joking or otherwise. Becoming a lawyer suited someone who always had an answer for everything, he thought, and he told her so.

"When might you be able to get away and catch a flight across the pond for a visit?" she asked, much to his surprise.

"You have time for that?" he asked. "I hadn't really thought about it because I figured you'd be too busy."

"Well, think about it. It has been a really busy week, but I'm settling in and I'd love to show you around and share London with you. There are places I'm hearing about that are out in the countryside and they sound idyllic. I'd love to visit them and share that with you, too."

"That sounds great, Cees. I need to wrap up a few things and then we can plan that."

"You mean, things with Danbury, don't you? It's not cold and flu season and it's not back to school season, so you're not crazy busy right now work-wise, are you?"

"Perceptive as always," he laughed. "It's been busier than usual for this time of year at the practice, but you're right. It's the murder that I'd love to get resolved. I hope we can. It seems like every time I think we're getting close to finding the right answers, something else happens that pushes us farther away from the truth. The whole town will rest easier if we can find the murderer or at least the motive. There had to be one, though it seems really random. That's why everyone in town is scared and on edge right now. They don't know why Allan was murdered, what the murderer was after, or if he's still around."

"Well, let me know when you think you can get away and we'll make some plans."

"That sounds really good, Cees."

"Matthew," she said, and hesitated. "I really miss you. I don't miss home so much, but I do miss you."

Matthew felt like something inside of him melted as he answered honestly, "I miss you too, Cees. I really do miss you too."

They ended the FaceTime session so that Matthew could get ready for work, and she could get on with her day of meetings and whatever else it was that she did over there. Matthew wasn't entirely sure what else that entailed. She had gotten the hang of his schedule and called him at 6:20, he noted, so that his coffee was ready when they finished their conversation at 6:35.

After his usual morning routine, he was ready to go, with his travel mug of coffee and satchel in hand, when his cell phone chirped. He checked it and answered to Danbury's, "Hey, Doc."

"Hi, Danbury. Did you guys get to sleep at all last night?" he asked, stifling a yawn as he locked up behind himself.

"We left shortly after you did. Had an uneventful night. We had a Peak Police escort. From a distance. And then they took shifts. Parked out front. Through the night."

As he shoved his things in the car and got in, Matthew realized that, though Danbury had been to his house on several occasions, he had no idea where Danbury lived. He thought this was probably not the right time to ask so he said instead, "Hang on while my phone switches to car audio." And then he added, "OK, all set. There's no new information or developments to report this morning, then?"

"I didn't say that. Several. The little notebook in Joseph County. The starting date on it was just Monday night. It was a new one. So not much in it. But they're sending it over. It's already been processed."

"Ah, good. If there's anything there, Leo will figure it out."

"And Wayne Adams has called a meeting. Now that Leo's here. To discuss the will."

"But, according to Leo, Wayne knew he was here the entire time. And helped him to get here!"

"Yeah. I need to talk to him. Before the meeting with Penn and Leo. I have some questions for him. About how he cleared the way for Leo. He told Leo he did. But maybe he didn't. Or maybe he got in bed with these people. So to speak."

"I'd like to be a fly on the wall for that conversation. He's slick, isn't he?"

"He seems to be. I've tried before to question him. He's either not in. Or he's in a meeting. He won't return my calls. He said he had nothing to say. The one time I did talk to him, he looked surprised. Like he was amazed that I'd caught him. But I know where he'll be this morning. He'll be getting ready to meet at nine. With Penn and Leo."

"This sounds like it could get rough."

"It could. Penn doesn't know yet. The whole story about Wayne and Leo. She's not going to like it either."

"I don't guess so. OK, so I guess I'm glad I won't be there for that!" Matthew amended. "I don't think I'd want to be on her bad side."

Danbury chuckled, "No, me either."

"When you get the chance, ask Leo if he thinks Allan might have put those missing notebooks someplace else and if he has any idea where that might be."

"I already did. He's thinking about it. Didn't have any ideas last night."

"Yeah, but we were all pretty tired last night. I didn't have any fresh ideas then either. I've got patients all morning. Keep me posted today. Let me know if I can help this afternoon."

"OK, will do."

As Matthew began his morning, he tried to put aside the events of the evening before that were casting a pall over his mood and the conversation with Cici this morning that gave him an inner glow so that he could focus on his patients. Gladys, who knew how to read him well checked on him, mid-morning. As he was coming out of the break room with his refilled coffee mug in hand, she said, "Isn't that at least one more than you usually drink, Shugah? Are you OK?"

"Yeah, I'm fine. It's just been a long week. It was a late-night last night and I'm really tired."

"Uh," she grunted in response. "You're working with that detective again, aren't you? On Allan Lingle's murder investigation." It was more a statement than a question, so Matthew just nodded in response.

"You seem pretty distracted just in general this morning."

"It's nothing that a weekend and some rest won't fix. If I can get any."

"I understand that you're worried. The whole town is uptight right now. But don't let it get under your skin so much. It's not all on your shoulders to figure this thing out."

"You're right, Gladys," he agreed from the doorway as he watched her fix her coffee. "But I know we'll all feel a lot safer if we can figure out exactly what happened and why."

"That's true. I think everyone is looking over their shoulders for bad guys now. And people aren't out walking at night anymore either. At least not alone. If they're out, they're out together and I don't blame them. But fixing it doesn't all fall on you."

"Yes, Ma'am," he said, grinning at her motherly concern. "I'll try to keep that in mind."

He wandered back downstairs to finish with his morning patients, smiling to himself that his nurse was so very protective of him. Just as he was about to step into the next exam room, he heard his phone chirp and pulled it out to see a text from Danbury.

"*Meet us at the Lingle Plantation for lunch? Take out from Peak Eats.*"

Matthew texted back, "*OK. As soon as I'm finished with patients. Shortly after noon.*"

"*Want your usual?*"

Wondering what Danbury thought that was, Matthew knew he needed to get to his patient, so he quickly texted back, "*Sure.*" As soon as he'd opened the door to the exam room, the small child on the other side let out a howl. Diane, the nurse who was rotating with Gladys through the morning patients, gave him a sympathetic nod. Where is Dr. Rob when you need him, wondered Matthew as he closed the door behind him.

*****

As Matthew stepped out onto the sidewalk from beside the huge blooming crepe myrtle tree in front of his office, he was nearly run over by Penn Lingle. She was furious and not paying attention as she stalked down the sidewalk from the other side of the crepe myrtle, also heading for the Lingle Plantation.

"Oh, sorry," she stopped up short when Matthew stepped back, off the sidewalk, and out of her path. The narrow skirt and heels that she was wearing hadn't slowed her down at all, he noticed.

"It's OK, but are you?" he asked.

"No! I'm not OK. Nothing is even remotely OK right now."

“Tell me what happened,” he said calmly as he stepped up onto the sidewalk and she fell into step briskly beside him. Even with his long legs, he was having to work to keep up with her.

“Wayne Adams happened! The man is a snake, a shark, a, a, a, parasite on the underbelly of either one of those!” she finally said.

If she hadn’t been so upset, Matthew thought that was actually funny, but he kept a straight face as he matched her brisk pace and said, “What has he done?”

“You mean this time?”

“Well, yeah. Whatever it is that made you so mad.”

“First of all, he calls a meeting this morning to read a revised will in the wake of Allan’s death. Now that Leo has been found. Oh, and by the way, did you know that he knew that Leo was here the whole time? I really let him hold it for that one! He didn’t tell me that my own brother was here! He postponed reading the will with the excuse that he wanted Leo to be here too. And he was the only one who knew that Leo was already here! Leo says he helped him get here, which of course he denies! He denies all knowledge of the conversations Leo says he had with him. But guess what? This time I fully believe my brother! Why would Leo risk coming back here unless he thought he was safe? He wouldn’t! I’ve only just gotten permission to bury my brother and that, that, that,” she said and finally took a breath. “That ambulance chaser has already claimed and frozen all of the assets!”

“What? How?”

“He says he has a will, one that he says my mother left, with a contingency in it if Allan was survived by Leo or me. In it the estate goes to some ridiculous charity that I’ve never even heard of! My mother never would have done that! It was insult enough that she left everything for Allan’s care, though I do believe she’d do that, and I eventually understood it. But this! This, she would just never do!”

“You can contest it, right?”

“Oh yes! I FULLY intend to contest it! That crook made it clear that he’s not my lawyer nor is he Leo’s nor has he ever been! He’s the lawyer of the ESTATE!” She finally stopped and turned to Matthew, who was beginning to be out of breath as they’d reached the front of the Lingle house in record time. “And that’s as clear as day! Our interests he’s never cared about at all!"

"OK, so let's make some contacts this afternoon and start that process."

"We need to do that fast. The house is part of the estate, so it's to be sold and the funds from the sale get added to the estate. He's told us that we have to be out of it in two weeks to put it on the market! TWO WEEKS! And that's without any of the antiques. He just wants our personal belongings out. As if! That man is certifiably satanically insane! He can't do this! Over my dead body!" Matthew cringed as he was thinking that she needed to be more careful with her words, and he wished she hadn't said that so loudly outside where it could be overheard.

"It'll be OK," he said, trying to calm her. "Let me make a quick call and locate the best lawyer for you. Just give me a minute," he said, as she stormed into the house without him, slamming the storm door behind her so hard that he was surprised the glass didn't shatter. He wondered where she'd just come from if the meeting with Wayne Adams was at nine that morning, but he'd certainly had no chance to ask.

Pulling his phone out, he made the call but it went to her voicemail system. "Hey, Cees, I was hoping I could catch you this evening," he said, deciding to leave her a message. "I need a recommendation on someone from your law firm to contest a will. I need the best you've got, serious firepower, the big guns. Can you make the connection and give me a call with that information? Or text it to me if you're busy. Thanks!"

As he opened the storm door, he took a deep breath knowing that Penn's tirade hadn't completely burned itself out yet and he was likely to hear more on the other side of the door. Reluctantly, he stepped through, only to encounter total peace and quiet. "Hello?" he called, and got no response. Just as he was wondering if he should step back out and knock loudly until someone came to the door, Danbury came from the back of the house from the general direction of the kitchen.

"Hey, Doc. I'm sure you heard all about it. What happened this morning," he said, ruefully.

"I got an earful, yeah. I just put a call in to Cici to get her to connect us with the best lawyer from her firm to contest the will. I don't know what they'll require, but there's only one way to find out. Have you seen a copy of the will?"

"I haven't. I don't think Penn and Leo have either. It got too ugly. And fast."

"What happened? Penn said that Wayne denied having talked to Leo. And he denied having made Leo any promises to straighten things out for him or help him to come back. What's his story?"

"I'm not sure. And I don't know who to believe. I'd like to believe Leo. But he was such a screw up as a teenager. And then his life went totally off track. After he left here. I hope he's getting back on track. And Wayne is," he hesitated. "I'm not sure what Wayne is. Manipulative at least. Conniving most likely. Greedy without a doubt. Dangerous? I'm not sure. But Penn is sure. She exploded on Wayne. About him knowing that Leo was here. He still claimed that he didn't."

"I see," said Matthew. "If he'd admitted to knowing that Leo was here, then he'd have to admit to whatever he was having Leo do, AND he'd have to admit to stalling on the reading of the will – all of which sounds entirely suspect to me. It sounds like the first job for the lawyer they hire will be to get a copy of the will and then go to work on it. I wonder if there's a retainer fee or anything up front or if the attorney just gets a cut when the will is distributed to the rightful inheritors? I'm not sure how these things work."

"Yeah, not my wheelhouse either."

Matthew's phone rang and he could hear Cici's breathless voice on the other end, "Hi, Matthew. Two times in one day! I think it's a record. I'm sorry I didn't pick up. I was in the subway and the signal down there varies from bad to nonexistent. What's up?"

"I need to find the best lawyer from your firm to contest a will. I need the big guns. And I need to know how this process works. Is there a fee up front? Or does the attorney get paid when the will is settled? Or is that contingent on the attorney thinking that the will can be successfully contested?"

"Wow, who died and left you a fortune?" she asked, jokingly, but Matthew could tell that she really wanted to know.

"You know it's not me. They're friends of Danbury," he said looking pointedly at Danbury, who was stifling a laugh at him as he followed Matthew into the kitchen. "They're getting the worst raw deal I've ever heard of and they need help. And we do still owe Danbury a few," he reminded her.

"Oh yeah, I owe him quite a lot. OK, so here's what you do. You call my office number. You still have it, right?"

"I do," said Matthew, picking up a pen and piece of paper from a stack on the kitchen table that looked like Leo's decoding efforts.

"Then when you get my outgoing voicemail message, you don't have to listen to it, just press 1 to skip to the end and then 0 to connect to a receptionist. When you get an answer, tell the receptionist that I told you to ask for Julius Isley or Layne Bennett, whichever of them is more available because you're going to need a lot of their time and quickly. Either of them can handle anything that anyone throws at them. Better than any other attorney I know in or out of my firm. Did you get all of that?"

"Yep," and he repeated it back to her from where he'd jotted it down. "Thanks, Cees. When this problem was called to my attention, I knew who to ask to get help. Danbury says thanks too," he added as Danbury was saying so very quietly. "Are you on your way back to your flat?"

"I wish! No, I'm on my way to meet with the top brass of this client group I'm working with. I think more things are discussed and business deals settled here over a long, drawn-out dinner than on any golf course at home. I guess that's a good thing. You've seen my golf game."

Matthew chuckled, "It's OK, Cees. You have lots of other talents. And you always teased me for moving into a condo on a golf course when I don't golf either, so I have nothing to say about your game."

"Let me know how it goes. Tell them I recommended them to you and either of them will be happy to help. They're amazing at what they do, so your friends are in the best hands I know of with either of them."

"Thanks, Cees. Talk soon!"

"I hope so. Think about when you're flying over, mwah!" she blew him a kiss and, before he could respond, she was gone.

26. Digging in

Danbury produced five bags from the kitchen counter, set them on the table, peered into the tops of them, and handed Matthew one. "Lunch," was all he said.

"Where'd everybody go?" asked Matthew, noticing again how quiet the house was after Penn's earlier tirade.

"Malcolm went to shower. Leo took Penn to show her behind the walls. The rooms and the passageways. Trying to calm her down. Shift her focus, I think."

Matthew had just pulled his chicken salad sandwich out of the bag and was about to unwrap it when he heard a commotion at the front door and he and Danbury put their bags down to investigate. Standing just inside the doorway was Wayne Adams with a slender blonde woman in a mauve shade of matching skirt and jacket.

"Whoa, there," said Danbury. "What are you doing?"

"This is Priscilla Pate. She's a real estate agent out of Raleigh who we'll be working with to sell the house and property," he said, as if it was the most natural thing in the world.

"You'd better turn around and leave before," started Danbury but he was interrupted by Penn, who had come in from the kitchen behind them and launched herself at Wayne Adams.

Danbury had managed to intercept her before she reached Wayne and he'd grabbed her around the waist and held on tight as she yelled, first at Wayne, "How dare you! How dare you just walk into our house like this and think that you can get away with that! You rat! Rodent! Vermin! Snake in the grass! Get out! I said, get out of my house! You are not welcome here and you will never be welcomed here! Out!"

And then she yelled at Danbury, who had picked her up and was carrying her, backward, to the kitchen, "Let me go, put me down! Warren Danbury, you put me down this instant! Put me down right now!"

"He's not worth it," Matthew had heard Danbury say softly to Penn. "Not worth assault and battery charges."

Matthew turned to Priscilla Pate, who stood open mouthed, and said, "I'm sorry, Ma'am, but I think you'd better leave. Their family has been in this house for two hundred years and they were just this morning informed of a will that supposedly gives it all away to an unknown charity. So maybe you can imagine how they feel right about now."

"Oh! I can indeed!" she said, looking Wayne up and down in disgust. "And I will be going now," she said as she turned on her polished pink heel and marched out of the house, across the porch, and was heading down the driveway to her car when Matthew turned to Wayne.

Normally not needing to prove anything to anyone, trying to be intimidating wasn't something he considered doing much. Cici had always said he was "comfortable in his own skin." Naturally a peacemaker, he wasn't fond of confrontation. But sometimes, he decided, there was no point in being 6'3" if you didn't use that height to your advantage.

Those times were rare and reserved primarily for bullies, but he figured that this was one of them, both in the timing and the person. Pulling his shoulders back, taking a step forward, and straightening his tall broad-shouldered frame to tower over the smaller man, Matthew asked, "Have the Lingles even seen a copy of this will that you say removes their property from their possession? Did you provide them with a copy of it?"

In response, Wayne just sneered at him. "I didn't think so," said Matthew. "Please leave and don't come back unless you have that and a court order to take possession of the house in hand."

"You have no idea who you're dealing with or what you just got yourself into, Doctor Paine."

"Then why don't you tell me?" asked Matthew, egging him on and hoping for an outright confession as to who he might be working with.

"I would advise you to stay out of this," Wayne growled. "Or you'll find yourself in a world of hurt indicative of your last name. It's none of your business. And there's your free legal advice for the day. Mind your own damned business!"

"Is that a threat?"

"I don't make threats," replied Wayne, still sneering at him. That sounded a lot like a threat to Matthew but Wayne did turn and leave the house, following the realtor down the drive and out to his car that was parked at the street.

Matthew closed and locked the door behind him, heading down the center hallway and was just about to step into the kitchen when Leo appeared behind him from somewhere, nearly running into him. Matthew stopped suddenly and started to back out of the kitchen doorway.

"What are you doing? My lunch is in there and I'm ready to dig in," protested Leo.

"Let's just give them a minute," said Matthew, thumbing over his shoulder to Penn and Danbury. Danbury still held Penn by the waist, but she was turned to face him, her arms around his neck, and they were locked in the midst of a passionate kiss. That seemed right, at least to Matthew, more right than Penn kissing him. But she seemed to be doing a lot of it, kissing people, he thought as he turned to leave.

"Yeah, I guess she needed that," said Leo, blushing slightly and retreating back the way he'd come. "Let me know when it's safe," he said, plopping down into an overstuffed chair in the sitting room around the corner.

Danbury looked up, as Matthew was retreating and caught his eye. He had a goofy grin on his face that Matthew had never seen or ever thought possible to see from Danbury. Penn turned around, as if nothing at all had just happened, and said, "Thank you, Matthew, for putting the trash out. I'm hungry. Let's dig in."

Malcolm appeared from his room off of the kitchen and they all ate their lunches. Then they cleared the lunch debris and sat around the table discussing the agenda for the afternoon. "I have the contact names for two lawyers who are supposed to be brilliant with wills. One or the other of them can help you contest the one Wayne says he has. If it's OK with you, I'll make the initial contact and then I can hand off the phone when you get down to business."

"Yeah, thanks for that," said Penn. "I don't know anyone in this area much anymore, so I wouldn't know where to start to find someone."

"No problem. This is the most prestigious law firm in the area. They're in downtown Raleigh and they pride themselves on finding and retaining the most brilliant legal minds around, so I trust them." He looked pensively at Penn and Leo, before adding, "Before I make that call, I was thinking about Wayne Adams."

"Yeah? Go on," said Danbury.

"Leo, you said he told you that he'd take care of the loan shark and drug dealer, who were both after you, right?"

Leo nodded and Matthew saw his Adam's apple bob as if he'd just swallowed hard. Penn, meanwhile, looked angry and annoyed at the mere mention of the name.

"Did he say how?"

"No," said Leo, shaking his head.

"And you said it was over a week before he called you back, right?"

"Yeah, I was sweating through that time."

"Did you ask him how he'd gotten them off your back? What he'd done to clear you?"

"No. I guess I should have asked, huh? I just wanted the chance to start over, to get it right this time. I wanted that so badly that I didn't question him and I should have."

"And then when you came back home, you were carrying packages again, right?"

"Yeah, for a little over three weeks."

"How many?"

"One or two a week. One week I think there were three. Maybe eight or nine, total."

"But you don't know what was in them? How big? How were they wrapped? What did they look like?"

"I didn't look in them, no. Some were bigger," Leo said and then held his hands out to indicate what Matthew thought to nearly a foot in diameter by nine inches high and about six inches wide. "A couple of them were smaller," he said, holding his hands about six inches apart and three wide and about as high.

"None of them were huge, then?"

"No, not very big. They had to fit in my post office box coming in or the night drop at All Posts going out."

"When you were couriering the drugs and cash packages up in New Jersey, what did those look like? Were they similar?

"They were close to the same size as the bigger ones, yeah. Those were usually wrapped in brown paper and taped up tight with packaging tape. These were in some sort of plastic packaging, still taped up tight with plastic packaging tape."

"Huh," said Danbury. "I see what you're thinking. Leo was still working for them. Just a few states south. Leo did the dangerous work. The transfers. And Wayne Adams somehow got a cut. Right?"

"Yeah, that's exactly what I'm thinking," answered Matthew. Then, turning to Penn, he said, "I know you really hate the guy now, but what can you tell us about what he was like ten years ago? Back when you got involved with him he had to have had something going for him."

"Oh, yeah. He had a lot going for him. He was charming and gregarious. He remembered people's names in town and called them by name. He would ask specific questions about their families. He seemed like such a nice guy who genuinely cared about people around him," said Penn. "The man oozed charisma. He'd smile and light up the room. It was all very appealing. He would look at you like you were the only person in the room, in the world, when you talked to him. You had his total focus and undivided attention. At the time, I thought that would make him a great lawyer. Now, of course, I see that he used it to be totally manipulative. But I bought the act. It's a very convincing act, very well polished, and he's probably only perfected it more since."

"He's not a nice guy obviously but after having him glare at me and threaten me a few minutes ago, I'm beginning to wonder what else he's capable of. Did you ever see him lose his temper? Threaten anyone back then?"

"No, he was always charming and fun to be around. I didn't see a darker side of him at all until I found out that he and Libby were already together seriously and he'd been with me anyway. I should have told Libby then. I really should have. It was a good indication that he played loose with his moral values, if he even had any. I thought I'd gotten something over on him, when I threatened to tell Libby and basically blackmailed him. But now I think that was just business as usual to him even back then."

"What makes you say that?" asked Danbury.

"Just a feeling. Like it wasn't the huge horrible ordeal to him that I thought it was. Like it was just something else to be handled and made to go away."

Everyone was quiet a moment and then Matthew said, "I'll go call the law office now."

"Leo, how's the decoding coming? Any progress on the old notebooks?" asked Danbury. As Matthew pulled out his cell phone and slipped into the other room to call Cici's office number and follow her directions to connect with the receptionist, he could still hear the conversation in the kitchen.

"Oh, yeah. I can figure out a lot of it. Pretty boring stuff though. It's a lot of who's doing what in Peak and some 'he said, she said' rumors. I need your help, and maybe Dr. Paine's, with figuring out who some of these people are. They're just initials and I'm not sure who did what to who."

"Whom," said Penn from the sink where she was rinsing the plates they'd used.

"Grammar Nazi," replied Leo.

"Sorry, there's just something about this house that does that to me," said Penn over her shoulder. "You know though," she added, turning to face the room. "The first thing we need to do is to figure out what happened to those other little notebooks, the most recent ones."

They were brainstorming the possibilities as Matthew returned to the room, "I left a message to get one of two attorneys to call me back. I name dropped so they should get back to us this afternoon."

"Cici?" asked Danbury.

Matthew nodded as Penn looked at him quizzically. "Cici?" she repeated.

"The woman that I am, but I'm not, involved with," said Matthew, as if that made perfect sense. It did to both Danbury and Penn. Leo looked confused but neither he nor Malcolm chose to ask.

"We were just discussing what could have happened to the missing notebooks," said Leo.

"There are only two options. At least that I see," said Danbury. "Either Allan put them somewhere else. Or somebody removed them. Somebody who has had access to the house. Let's examine both possibilities. Where would he have put them? If Allan moved them. And why? Why would he move just those? And leave the rest? Would there have been a reason?"

"Without a doubt," answered Penn. "He couldn't relate well to other people, particularly strangers, but he was methodical. If he did something like that, there was a reason for it that made complete sense to him."

"Maybe because he'd overheard something or learned something that he was afraid would get him or somebody else in trouble," offered Matthew.

"Yeah, and maybe it did," Danbury grimaced.

"Or maybe he'd logged something in there that he didn't want anyone to see," said Penn.

"Like what?" asked Leo.

"I have no idea," she said. "This is Allan we're talking about."

"OK," said Danbury. "What if it was taken? By whom?" he said, stressing the M and eyeing Penn jovially, "And for what purpose?"

"Back to the theory that there was something incriminating in there that somebody didn't want to be known. Either way it does seem to boil down to a secret, doesn't it?" said Penn.

"It does," agreed Danbury. "We have two possible paths. Two strands to chase. Of the same cord. As the good Doc here says. One is Allan hiding the notebooks. The other is someone taking them. But who? And why? Where'd they put them? Have they been destroyed? The first would seem easier. That Allan moved them himself. But is it? Any ideas at all,

Leo? Malcolm? You two knew him best. And most recently."

Malcolm scratched his chin and shook his head, "I'll defer to Leo on this one. I knew Allan pretty well but that was on a more surface level, everyday activities, stuff like that. I didn't know what made him tick. I didn't even know what those little notebooks were. I just knew that he valued them like a treasure but I didn't know exactly what they were."

"Treasure," repeated Penn, thoughtfully.

Just then, Matthew's cell phone went off and, checking the display, he said, "I'm going to put this on speaker phone in a minute, OK? It's the law firm calling back."

Everyone around the table nodded agreement and got quiet.

"Hello. Matthew Paine," he said.

"Hi, this is Layne Bennett returning your call," said a smooth but businesslike female voice with a midwestern dialect.

"Thank you for returning my call so quickly. Cici Patterson told me to contact you. She said you're the best there is in dealing with wills, specifically contesting one."

"Oh, you're THAT Matthew," she said.

After a momentary pause he laughed and said, "Yes, I guess I am that Matthew. Do you mind if I put you on speaker phone? I have the brother and sister here with me so it'll be easier if they can both talk to you directly."

She agreed and he said, "OK, thanks," as he clicked the speakerphone button and put the phone in the middle of the table. "Can you still hear me?"

"Yes, you're coming through just fine. This is Layne Bennett with Markham, Denton, and Washburn Law Firm. Who am I talking to, other than Dr. Paine?"

Penn, ever the older sister, jumped in and responded, "Hi, I'm Penn Lingle and my brother Leo is with me. Detective Danbury and my deceased brother Allan's caregiver, Malcolm Freeman, are here as well. They've been trying to help us with all of this, but Leo and I, we're the ones who need your help. Is it OK if the others stay?"

"If it's OK with you, it's fine with me. In terms of client-attorney privilege, it's I who can't talk about this with anyone not authorized by you to discuss it."

"OK."

"Your last name is Lingle, you say? I'm going to go ahead and start a case file for you. Is it OK if I record this conversation to transcribe and preserve the background information?"

"Yes, that's fine. And yes, our last name is Lingle, L I N G L E. My first name is actually Penelope and my brother's name is Leonard."

"OK, we're recording. Let's get some background information first. Tell me about the will that you want to contest and why."

After explaining the situation with the estate, Allan's care, and Allan's murder, Penn explained about the addendum to the will that was supposedly left by her mother in the event that Penn or Leo outlived Allan and about the "estate attorney" who told them how the estate was to be dispersed. Penn must not have started yelling immediately at Wayne Adams this morning, Matthew thought, because she seemed to have a pretty good grasp on what he'd told them about the disbursement.

"And you have reason to believe that this will isn't valid?"

"We do."

"On what grounds?"

"First of all, our mother would never have left the estate to anyone other than Leo and me if something happened to Allan. That we're certain of."

"OK, I'm going to play devil's advocate here for a moment. From what you've told me, she left it all for your brother Allan's care initially, correct? Is it such a stretch to assume that there was some reason she didn't want it left to you and Leo and that she'd have donated it to a worthy cause?"

Taking a deep breath, Penn said, a bit through gritted teeth, "Lots of reasons."

"And they are?"

"My mother loved us. Our relationship at her death was not strained or compromised in any way. She left the estate that way initially for several reasons. She wanted to ensure that Allan was cared for because he was autistic, as I explained, and couldn't hold a job because his life had to be predictably ordered for him to function. She left neither Leo nor me in charge of that trust fund because it would have tied one or both of us here."

"Leo was supposed to be away at college at the time and I'd married and made my life in Denver. I was in the middle of a messy divorce and Leo had dropped out of school, but our mother didn't know either of those things. Technically, she left the estate oversight in the hands of Higgins Law Firm, here in Peak, I believe, but it's been handled exclusively by the same lawyer, Wayne Adams. He now claims to be in possession of the addendum of her will that she provided if Allan should predecease Leo and me. It's that will, or that addendum of the first, perhaps? I'm not sure, but that's what we want to contest."

"I see. And do you have a copy of this will?"

"No."

"Have you seen this will?"

"No."

"Do you have a copy of the original will?"

"Probably so, but it's in Denver if I still do."

"OK, first, I need to obtain a copy of this new will or addendum to the old one. An addendum, or codicil, would likely have been created after the primary will. You mother might have chosen to file a copy of the will with the Superior Court for safekeeping, so that's a good place to start. She, as the testator, and any authorized agent she assigned, would have had access to it during her lifetime. If she filed one, and if it has the codicil Wayne Adams described to you, then we will have a fight on our hands. She was living in Peak at the time of her death, correct?"

"Yes, that's correct."

"It will have been filed with the probate court in Wake County when she died, so there will definitely be a record of it there. The Clerk of Court can supply that. I'll just need your mother's full name, her date of birth, and the date of her death to request a copy of it. Then we'll see what we have to work with."

Penn gave her the information and then asked, "So now what?"

"Now, I'll send you an agreement for me to represent you and your brother, if that's what you want me to do. Then, I'll request the documents on your behalf and we'll see what we have to work with."

"Yes, please."

"OK, I can fax it and you can fax it back or I can email you a link to electronically sign an online copy."

"I don't have a fax machine here," said Penn.

"There's one over at my office if you want to use it," volunteered Matthew, whose foot was tapping and knee was jumping under the table in rapt concentration. "Can you sign the electronic copy from your email account on your phone?"

"You can," verified Layne Bennett. "And lots of people do. Will you both be signing? Or just one of you? Penn? Leo?"

Penn looked at Leo and said, "I think we'd better both sign it. Whatever we do, from here on out, we need to do it together. Leo, are you OK with signing with your phone?"

"Ummm. Yeah," he said, digging one out of his pocket. "I can connect to my email account from it."

"Wait," said Danbury. "Is that the phone that Wayne Adams gave you?"

"Yeah."

"Turn it off. Turn it off now. You need a new phone," said Danbury.

"We need to go get you a new phone this afternoon," agreed Penn. "But you can use mine to access your email account by browser, right? Do you know your login information?"

"Yeah," he said, quietly.

"You need to create a new email account," said Danbury. "One that isn't known. By Wayne Adams."

"He's right," said Penn to Leo. "But that's no big deal. Can you do that now?"

"Yeah, if I can use your phone," said Leo, sheepishly. Penn unlocked and handed over her phone.

"OK, yes, Ms. Bennett, please send the documents to our email accounts," answered Penn. She provided hers. After a few minutes of poking around on her phone, Leo proudly announced his new email address too, allanslittlebro@gmail.com. They provided Penn's cell number and their new lawyer agreed to send the documents to them quickly. They discussed fees and agreed on the process and approach.

As they were about to end the call, Danbury said, "Ms. Bennett, this is Detective Danbury. I'm a homicide detective out of Raleigh. I've been working on the murder angle. But I'm calling in some favors on the rest. Can you get the original will? The original signed document. If the copy checks out? I have some forensic favors to call in. I can get the authenticity checked. By some of the best in the business. To see if it's forged. Or manipulated. In whatever way."

"I can certainly try, but I'm hoping it won't have to go that far. I'll let you know what I find. In the meantime, feel free to call me at this number with any questions or concerns, and particularly if you learn of anything else that I should be aware of."

"Thank you so much," said Penn. "We really appreciate your help."

On that note, they ended the call and Danbury said to Penn, "I've already asked a few favors. From a data forensic expert. And you need to know about it. He's digging into the charity. The one the estate is supposed to go to. It's oddly named. So far nobody has ever heard of it. It's a ghost charity. It got 501C3 non-profit status. But under some odd circumstances. That alone provides a starting point. If it's improperly filed. This is attacking the problem from the other direction. Exposing the organization's invalidity. If there's no place for the funds to go. Then it's a much bigger problem."

"You're a genius!" said Penn. "Thank you!" she added as she reached up and threw her arms around his neck.

Setting Penn gently back on her feet, Danbury asked quietly, "Now, where were we?"

"We were digging our heels in about ever having to give up our family home," said Penn.

Danbury chuckled, "In our discussion. About finding the notebooks. Trying to figure out what Allan knew."

"Oh. Yeah, that," said Penn, with a shrug. "I don't think we were anywhere with that, but we've got to figure it out, if there's anything there that would be helpful in finding who murdered him."

27. Treasure trove

Everyone got quiet in their own contemplation and the only sound in the room was Matthew's foot tapping under the table until Leo broke the silence excitedly and made them all jump. "Treasure! Maybe that's it! A treasure trunk!"

"Maybe that's what?" asked Penn.

"Do you remember, when we were kids, Allan and I would play up in the attic a lot? It's why Dad and Uncle John built us the treehouse to begin with."

"Oh yeah. Did you know about the secret passages then?"

"No, we found those later. We just went up the back stairs and played pirates. There are old steamer trunks up there that held our treasure."

"Oh, yeah, I saw those when I walked through the house," said Matthew. "I came to check on Malcolm, but I wandered through the house while I was here," he confessed. "I opened one, choked on the dust I'd stirred up, and closed it pretty quickly."

"So, one is very dusty," observed Penn. "It likely hasn't been opened in a while. But what about the others?

"I have no idea," said Matthew. "I didn't examine the others. I had patients waiting in my office so I had to get back and I really just wanted to see the house."

"I think it's in the last notebook that we have, the most recent one!"

said Leo, excitedly.

Reaching through the myriad of miniature notebooks of varying colors that were stacked on the kitchen counter, he pulled out a green one. "I think this is it." He flipped through to the last page and then said, "Yeah, here it is. Look!"

As they all peered at it, he pointed to the last entry, which was drawn on the inside back cover of the little notebook. The diagram began with a square, in which was written AL. That was attached by a wavy line to a triangle with NB in it that then attached with a zigzagged line upward to a large rectangle. Instead of letters, the rectangle contained what looked like a box with hasps drawn on it.

"This rectangle is bigger," said Leo. "And that box is drawn in a lot more detail than most of the rest of the objects in any of the notebooks. If AL is Allan Lingle, the wavy line is walking, maybe the NB in the triangle means notebook. Then, the zigzag line maybe means he climbed the steps. And the rectangle with the box maybe means that he put the notebooks in a trunk. Like a treasure trunk. He never said anything about any of this to me after I got back here."

"It looks like he added that diagram later," said Penn. "It's in ink. Did you see anything on the inside back covers of any of the other notebooks?"

"Nope," said Leo.

Malcolm, who had been quiet through most of the discussion, spoke up, "I did see Allan going up the back stairs and heard him climb all the way to the attic several times over the past month or so."

"That might have been because I was up there sometimes," said Leo. "But let's go look," he added over his shoulder as he led the way up the back staircase to the attic. They all tromped up behind him. Matthew followed Malcolm, who was still limping and lagging behind, to keep an eye on him. Climbing stairs was one of the things that Malcolm hadn't been able to do with the knee injury, and he really shouldn't be doing it now, thought Matthew.

Positioned between the two front dormer windows was a row of three steamer trunks. Matthew surveyed the four larger ones near the far side wall of the attic space in front of the hidden wall. "I opened that one," he said, pointing to one on the end. "It smelled like moth balls and was covered in dust. It has old clothing in it, but I didn't look to see what exactly because of all the dust."

There was dust all over most of the objects in the attic space, but his eye went to one of the steamer trunks that were lined up between the windows. "That one," said Matthew, pointing to the left of the row of three. "That one isn't covered in dust. All of the others look to have a pretty thick coating."

Leo knelt and waddled under the eaves, grasped the end of the trunk by a handle, and dragged it out into the open passageway. It looked much like the other two that were along the front wall, small with a rounded top. It looked to have once had leather straps across the top. The hinges and clasps were badly tarnished.

As Leo flipped it open, Matthew stepped back, expecting to be confronted by a cloud of dust. When it didn't come, he peered in with the others. Stacks of yellowing paper, neatly tied with faded ribbon occupied the right side of the trunk. A box, that looked to be an ancient hat box which was once colorfully decorated with ribbons and bows but was also quite faded, occupied the other side.

Carefully reaching in, Leo pulled out the sheaves of paper tied in ribbons, which appeared to be letters with envelopes stacked between them, stack by stack, and put them gently on the floor. After the stacks were all out, they could see nothing beneath them except the bottom of the chest. Leo gently removed the hat box, which looked as if it might fall apart at any moment. Beneath it was a wooden box that looked to Matthew to be made of cedar with brass hasps.

Setting the hat box carefully aside, Leo lifted the wooden box out and looked at it with wide-eyed wonder. "This is a box we used to pretend had gold coins in it," said Leo. "When we were playing pirates up here as kids. I haven't seen it in a long time, probably not since we were kids. I didn't know it was still around. I wouldn't even have remembered it, but," and he couldn't finish his sentence as he choked on the words. Finally, he said quietly, "But Allan remembered everything."

As Leo opened the box, Matthew saw four neat stacks of the tiny notebooks, two deep. Almost reverently, Leo closed the box and held it to his chest. Penn returned the rest of the contents to the steamer trunk, closing it softly, and Danbury slid it back into place. Without another word, they tromped back down the stairs and Leo set the box on the kitchen table and began to pull out and sort the eight notebooks that it contained.

Penn checked her email on her phone and announced that the contract from Layne Bennett was there to be signed. She quickly clicked through to sign it.

"Here, Leo," she said and, reluctantly, Leo put the notebooks down to access his new email account so that he too could scroll and click through the online contract to sign it.

Malcolm was seated at the table, but he'd propped his leg up in a nearby chair and Matthew took the opportunity to inquire about it. "How's it looking? Is the swelling down now?"

Pulling his pant leg up to show Matthew the knee, he answered, "It is. It's much better. The bruising looks better too."

"And the pain?" asked Matthew. Is it still tender to the touch around the knee cap?"

"No. Just if I twist or move it the wrong way."

"Good. That sounds like it's healing nicely then. That's great news."

"Always the good doctor, huh?" asked Malcolm, smiling up at Matthew.

"I try," said Matthew with a chuckle.

"There," said Leo, handing the phone back to Penn. "Now, let's check these out." He flipped to the front of each one and lined them along the table in date order, and then began looking through each one in turn. Matthew slid the paper and pens from the kitchen counter and placed them beside Leo, who was already in deep concentration over his brother's diagrams.

"Hmm. This one is late April. It's sometime after the 26th, I guess, because that's the date in the front. Entries after that aren't dated in this book. But here on the last entry in this notebook there are two long strings of numbers written across a dotted line. It's between a square labeled WA and a rectangle labeled XXX. I have no idea what they mean but maybe from the context we can figure that out. Somebody was talking to somebody else and the strings are what they told them, maybe? WA talking to XXX. Weird."

"WA might be Wayne Adams," said Penn helpfully. "But why would

Allan put XXX instead of initials for the person he was talking to?"

"Maybe he didn't want to record that," said Malcolm.

"Or maybe he didn't know," said Matthew, just as Danbury's phone went off and he stepped in the next room to answer it.

"What do you mean?" asked Penn.

"Maybe Allan heard Wayne Adams on the phone with someone or overheard half of a conversation somehow. If he could only hear half of the conversation, maybe he didn't know who was on the other end."

Matthew heard the deep sonorous voice from the next room say, "Detective Danbury." That to Matthew meant that the call was serious police business and not a friend calling to chat. "Hey, thanks for getting back to me." After another pause, Danbury said, "Yeah, whatever you've got."

"If WA really is Wayne Adams," said Penn. "I mean, who else could it be?"

"Not that many first names start with W," Matthew said. Trying for some levity, he added, "Know any Wandas or Wendys in town? How about a William? Walter? Winston? Maybe a Waylon? That's all I've got, I'm out."

"But what are the strings of numbers?" asked Leo, barely breaking a smile. "And why would Allan record them?"

"He could remember long strings of numbers and letters too growing up," said Penn. "I really think it's how he learned to read. I don't think he understood phonics at all. I think he just memorized the strings of letters and maybe the rules for how they should or shouldn't go together. He could spell better than I could though so it worked for him."

"So why revert to the childhood code for these little notebooks?" asked Matthew.

"I think he just thought it was fun," said Leo.

"Allan was a complex person," added Malcolm. "He seemed simple, outwardly, but I knew that there was a lot more to him. A lot that I never got to know," he added sadly.

"What else is there?" asked Penn. "Any other context? Anything else helpful?"

"Dr. Paine's theory might be right," said Leo. "In lots of the other conversations in earlier notebooks the dotted lines go both ways. Like a conversation between two people. In these last diagrams, it's all one way. It's WA talking to someone else and most of them are the XXX on the other end."

"Of the ones that aren't XXX on the other end, what are they?" asked Matthew.

"There are a quite a few here that are MF. Malcolm Freeman? Those have the conversation going both ways though."

"Have you talked to Wayne Adams much lately?" Penn asked Malcolm.

"Back in April? Yeah, several times. He had the windows cleaned and he talked about having the house repainted, though I thought he should have done that in the reverse order. He stopped by a couple of times to look things over while the window cleaners were here. I guess he was checking up on them. And he met a couple of painters here and they walked around outside of the house to look it over."

"But that conversation between WA and XXX is the last thing in the last notebook we have?" asked Penn.

"Yeah," said Leo. "I don't know how many days are in this one because individual days aren't labeled with dates like they are in the earlier notebooks, but that's the last there is. At least until your friend in there can get that final one that Allan was carrying."

Just as Danbury was coming back into the kitchen, his phone sounded again and he shook his head as he stepped back out. Matthew heard the familiar "Detective Danbury" from the next room.

"I guess we can eventually ask him," said Matthew, raising an eyebrow. "He's a popular guy today."

"Apparently," answered Penn, with an odd look on her face.

"Did he say anything more about when we'd be able to see that last notebook?" asked Matthew.

"Not to me," said Penn, as Leo and Malcolm shook their heads.

Matthew heard Danbury from the other room say, "Yeah, that's great. I will. As soon as I can." And then, "You'll have him there when? OK, thanks for letting me know."

All heads turned as Danbury stepped back into the room, and nobody spoke, awaiting a report on whatever he'd just learned. "You're really going to make us ask?" said Penn after a moment.

"No. I was just thinking through the order of operations," said Danbury and before he could say more, Penn's phone went off. She rolled her eyes as she dug the phone out of the small side pocket on her yoga pants and answered it. Her face grew serious and paled slightly as she said, "OK, thank you. I'll call them. Yes, thanks," and put the phone back down.

"They've finished with the autopsy on Allan's body," she said quietly. "The funeral home can pick him up this afternoon or in the morning." As she stood there, looking forlorn, tears started rolling down her cheeks. Leo got out of his chair and went to her. Danbury stepped forward too and they both hugged her.

Matthew's foot tapped under the table as he sifted through the little notebooks, quietly wishing he could be somewhere else at that precise moment. He knew there was nothing he could offer that would help, and he looked up to see Malcolm playing with his hands and looking away too.

Pulling away after a few moments, Penn choked as she mumbled, "I guess I'd better call the funeral home." Then she added, "Maybe we can have the funeral at the church where he played Bingo and the visitation afterward here at the house. Of course he'll be buried out in the family plot on the corner of the property. The casket will have to be closed," she added sadly. "But that's actually fine with me. I don't want to remember him this way."

This was news to Matthew, who didn't know there was a family cemetery on the property. It made sense, he thought, given the age of the house and the family history in it, to have a cemetery on the property. He glanced at Malcolm, who seemed to be taking it all in stride, as did Danbury. Everyone else, he supposed, knew about the cemetery.

"How does that sound?" Penn asked Leo.

"It sounds OK. I think Allan would like that. Will we need to clear a path to the cemetery?" he asked. "It was pretty overgrown the last time I saw it."

"I can probably get that done," volunteered Danbury. "Some of the

Peak officers were asking how they could help. If there was anything they could do. Besides find the murderer obviously. And a couple of the guys at the diner."

"That would be great. If you don't mind asking?" said Penn. "I guess I need to call the funeral home. And the church. I'm not sure where to start," she said, looking a little lost.

"I can help, if you want," said Malcolm. "I can call the church. What time do you want the service?"

"Maybe Sunday at 3?" she said, uncertainly. "I want to give the town time to get to church, have their lunch, and not interrupt dinner either. "If we can get all of the pieces to fit together."

"OK," said Malcolm. "I'll call the church office and see if there's anybody there now."

Penn slipped down the hallway and into the library to make her calls.

Danbury motioned Matthew into the sitting room around the corner. "We have things to do, too," he said. "If you agree to come with me on another road trip."

"Where are you going and what things are there to do?"

"That first call was the Private Investigator. The guy in Ohio. The one who investigated Wayne Adams. A little over eleven years ago now. The guy was hired by Adams' ex-wife. Not his law firm. The PI found nothing about him cheating on her. His findings were all about business deals. Adams left under a cloud of suspicion. Of embezzling funds. And potential money laundering. But nobody could prove it. No wonder the guy thinks he's bullet-proof. Sounds like he's already gotten away with it one time. I don't have the details yet. The PI is sending his files. They're on paper. But he'll scan and send them."

"OK, interesting," said Matthew, thinking that this newest information sounded promising to discredit Wayne Adams in relation to the issues with the will. It had nothing, however, to do with the murder or himself, so he asked, "And I can help, how?"

"The second call," said Danbury. "That was the Savannah police department. The guys we worked with down there last month."

Matthew refrained from pointing out that he personally had not worked with them. Danbury had. But he waited patiently for the relevant information.

"They've picked up Juan González. In a little town off of I-95. Just west of Savannah. He was in a stolen car. That ironically broke down. An officer stopped to help. And he ran. But they caught him. That's some karma, huh?" he smiled broadly. "Anyway they saw my APB. They remembered me and called. They're bringing him in to the Savanah station. Better security. The guy's a felon. Wanted in at least five states. But they said they'd give me a go at him. Just as soon as they process him in. And do the initial questioning. He could be shipped all over for questioning. It could take weeks. But they're going to let me talk to him first. Could be ready by tonight. In the morning at the latest. You up for a trip south, back to Georgia? Oh, there's just one other thing."

"What's that?"

"I'm not officially assigned to this case. I'm on my own dime," he said. "For food. And to stay overnight."

"OK," said Matthew. "No problem. I can pick up my own tab. When were you thinking about driving down? It was about a five-hour trip, right?"

"Yeah, nearly that. I need to go by the station here. Before we drive down. But I can go any time after that. I want to know if this guy killed Allan. And if he did, why. And who put him up to it. Or if he was just in the wrong town. At the wrong time. I need to know that. So do Penn and Leo. For closure. I want to give them that."

"You're talking tonight, then?" he asked, a bit incredulously. He couldn't really believe they were going back to Savannah to begin with. Why Savannah again, of all places, he wondered.

"Yeah, I'm going tonight. Are you in? Road trip?" he asked hopefully.

Matthew stifled a laugh and refrained from shaking his head in wonder that the great Detective Danbury, who barely tolerated him a little over a month ago, now wanted his company on a five-hour road trip and potentially his help. "Yeah, I'm in. If we can come back tomorrow, I can go tonight."

"Oh yeah, tomorrow. I want to be back here, too. And on Sunday. It'll be a hard time for them."

"Maybe you can bring back some answers, some closure as you say. It won't bring Allan back, but maybe it'll give them some satisfaction, some peace, if the murderer has been apprehended."

"Exactly."

"I guess I need to go get my car and get home to feed my cat and throw a few things in a duffle bag then. I'll say goodbye first though." said Matthew. Danbury just nodded as they both returned to the kitchen.

Penn was back in the kitchen but still on the phone, pacing on the other side of the room, one hand running through her hair, and the other holding the phone. "Yes, I suppose that will work," she was saying. "Is that what you normally do?"

Malcolm had gotten off a call and was thumbing through his phone. "I got a message at the church," he said. "They're already gone for the day. I guess they leave earlier on Fridays. But I can get the pastor. His name's White, right?

"It is," said Matthew. "He lives on Goldman Street in what I presume to be the parsonage."

"OK, got him," said Malcolm.

Just then Penn finished her call and said, "The funeral home is all set to pick Allan up this evening. It'll be late for them, but they said they need the whole day tomorrow to have him ready for Sunday. They'll handle transport to the church and from there back here to the cemetery."

"I was just about to call the pastor of the Methodist church," said Malcolm. "There's nobody in the office this time on a Friday afternoon."

"I'll do that," said Penn. "The guy at the funeral home said we should be able to get the church this Sunday. He's a member and an elder. He said there's nothing going on, no weddings or anything that he knows of Sunday afternoon. What's the number?"

"Hey, before you get back on the phone, I'm going to head out," interrupted Matthew. "I apparently have a trip on my evening schedule." As Penn looked quizzically at him, and then at Danbury, Matthew added, "Would you text and let me know the time you decide on, if it isn't three on Sunday? Or even if it is. I can help get the word out, starting with my office right now."

"Sure," said Penn. "I'll do that."

As Matthew headed down the hallway to let himself out, he heard Danbury say, "I guess I should explain. And I need your OK anyway. To share your contact information. With the forensic data expert in Raleigh. In case he has questions while I'm gone. His name is Ed Watson." She must have nodded and Danbury continued, "I'll get you the last of the little notebooks. Before I leave. The one Allan still had. It's at the station here now." And then he'd started to explain the phone calls as Matthew let himself out, closing and locking the door behind him.

Ordinarily he would have enjoyed the lovely spring day that had warmed up considerably during the afternoon hours, as he walked back to his office. But his mind was racing with the events of the afternoon and the trip and preparation for it this evening. How to work in everything and be there for his new friends on Sunday, he mused.

Instead of slipping in the side door of his office, he went to the front door. It was locked. He'd left his keys in his office, so he tapped gently until Maddie, the young receptionist, came to answer it.

"Hi Maddie, I didn't know you were still here."

"Hi Dr. Paine," she said shyly. "I thought you were gone too. I'm helping Trina with some mailings this afternoon but we're nearly finished."

"Oh, well, thanks for letting me in. I'd left my keys in my office earlier. Is everyone else gone already?"

"I think so, yes. I think I saw Gladys leave about a half hour ago and Diane was already gone. Both Dr. Garner and Dr. Rob were out of here right after lunch."

"OK, thanks." As he'd started to go down the main hallway behind the reception desk, he turned back and said, "Hey Maddie, you're on that text distribution group that Dr. Garner used to summon everyone after Allan Lingle was killed, aren't you?"

"Yes, I am."

"Could you send a text out to that group? Allan's body is finally being released and the service is on Sunday. I think at three, and I think at the Methodist church down the street, but I can let you know when I find out for sure."

"Certainly, Dr. Paine. I can do that. Most of our staff will probably want to go," she said. "I will. He was a nice man."

As he was packing his satchel with his computer and a few folders,

Matthew's phone sounded and he saw a text from Penn: "*Funeral is at 3 PM on Sunday, Methodist Church. Interment in the family plot immediately following. Visitation is at our house afterward.*"

Matthew quickly texted back, "*Got it. I'll help spread the word.*"

As he was locking up his office, he heard another ding from his phone and looked down to see that Penn had replied, "*Thanks, Matthew. I'm working on the obituary now. It'll be in the local paper and online tomorrow. That should help.*"

Instead of going straight out the side door that was just down from his office, he went back up to the reception desk and gave the information to Maddie, who promised to text it out to the staff and include all three doctors on the message as well so that they'd all be in the loop for any updated information.

Living in a small town was nice, thought Matthew, as he walked out to his car. People seemed to genuinely care about each other and help out in times of need. Well, all except Wayne Adams, he concluded, with a tension that gripped him suddenly at the thought of the man.

28. On the road again

As Matthew was driving into his neighborhood, he was lost in thought until he saw Cordelia Drewer ahead flagging him down. Some things never changed, he thought, as he tried to squelch the residual feeling of dread that the sight of her waving her arm in the air still seemed to illicit. She'd picked up Oscar and tucked him under her arm as Matthew pulled alongside and lowered his window.

"Hi, Matthew. How are you?"

He couldn't remember her ever asking this question before, so he paused a moment before answering, "I'm well. I hope you are too."

"I am, thanks. We're just out enjoying this lovely spring afternoon. Pretty soon, it'll be too hot out to enjoy it much."

"That's true," and he started to tell her about the funeral arrangements just as she started to say something too.

"Oh, I'm sorry, you first," she said.

Matthew laughed, wondering what polite police had visited his neighbor today. "I was just going to give you an update on the situation with Allan Lingle. His service will be Sunday afternoon at three at the First Methodist Church in town. He'll be buried in the family cemetery on the back corner of the Lingle Plantation after the service and the visitation will follow all of that at the Lingle house. I thought you would want to know."

"Thank you, Matthew, I did want to know," she said sadly and hesitated while Oscar leaned over and Matthew extended his hand, actually able to scratch the little dog on the head without challenge. "And I've decided to take you up on your kind invitation," she said. "To go to church with you this Sunday and to lunch with your family, if that offer is still open."

"That offer is always open. The rest of my family will love to meet you." He hesitated before adding, "And Mrs. Drewer, I'm getting ready to go out of town for the night. I'll be back tomorrow evening sometime, but I just thought I'd let you know so that you can keep an eye on the house, if you don't mind? I'll leave extra food and water for Max, so you don't have to do anything. I just wanted you to know that I'll be away. Just in case. Here, let me give you my cell number," he said as he retrieved a business card and pen from his satchel and jotted his cell number on the back of the card.

"I'll be happy to keep an eye on things," she said, sounding truly delighted. Much to Matthew's surprise, she didn't ask him where he was going or with whom or any of the other questions she previously would have plied him with relentlessly.

"Thanks. I usually leave for church Sunday mornings around 10:15. And we can take the Element, if you'd rather. It's quieter."

"Are you kidding? I've been dying to ride in this one," she said mischievously, waving her hand above the Corvette. "I'll be ready by ten after. Enjoy your trip," she said sweetly. They said goodbye and he drove up to his driveway and into the garage in pleasant astonishment.

"Who was that woman and what did she do with my nosy neighbor?" he muttered as the garage door dropped behind him. He let himself into his house and turned the alarm off.

"Hey, Big Guy," he said to Max as he dropped his satchel on the end of the sofa and scooped up the big grey tabby cat who had come to greet him. "And what have you done all day? Let's go get you some food, with extra, so that you'll be happy for the next day or so. And then I need to get packed," he said, scratching Max under the chin for a few more moments and eliciting a rare purr from the big cat before placing him gently on the arm of the sofa.

After washing his hands, Matthew rinsed and refilled the water bowl and rinsed out, dried, and then filled the food bowl half way while Max rubbed up against his legs and meowed up at him. That was more than twice the amount Max got each morning and night, so that should suffice until the next evening, Matthew thought.

Then from his bedroom closet he retrieved a gym bag and stuffed in a change of clothes for the next day, along with a pair of his favorite sleep pants and a soft t-shirt. Pulling his toiletry kit from under the bathroom counter, he added it to the bag. The kit was always pre-packed with an extra set of everything that he normally used at home – razor, shaving cream, favorite soap, a toothbrush and the like. He dropped the gym bag on the bed, considering it duly packed.

Deciding that he really wanted to make the nearly five-hour trip to Savannah in more comfortable clothes, he changed into jeans and a soft Henley t-shirt. Tossing his khaki pants and button-down collared shirt in the general direction of the clothes hamper in the corner of his closet, he noticed that the hamper was overflowing and he vowed to do something about it when he was home again long enough. Switching to a pair of slip-on deck shoes, he figured that in the meantime he was happy to have plenty of clothes left to choose from in his closet.

He glanced up at the gun safe bolted to the top of his closet shelf. He was thankful that he was just the side-kick on this trip and it was far from dangerous, at least as far as he knew. He hadn't had his guns out in over a month though and he thought he was long overdue at the shooting range. Wondering if Danbury had a particular place that he liked to frequent for target practice, he made a mental note to ask him.

Scooping up the gym bag and throwing the strap over his shoulder, he turned on a few lights as he made his way through the condo. Max looked up at him from in front of his food bowl with huge luminous eyes as Matthew walked through the kitchen but then went back to eating. "Cats!" muttered Matthew. "See you tomorrow, Big Guy." He slipped out, resetting his security alarm and locking up the doors behind himself.

He'd left the garage light on too, a habit now at night since someone had broken into it the month before. He wasn't sure if it said, "Come on in, I'll help you see what you're trying to steal from this end condo unit where nobody can see this outside door anyway." Or maybe, he hoped, it said, "Go somewhere else that's unlit to skulk in the dark of night and steal things." He could always hope.

As he backed his Element out of the driveway and started down the street to join Danbury on this quick overnight journey, he thought about Allan Lingle making his final journey. Across town to the funeral home initially and then back home to the family cemetery for all eternity. A sadness enveloped him. He plugged in his phone and brought up his playlist to blast something happy throughout the boxy car.

As he drove into Peak, he could see people gathered at the Chamber of Commerce, which was housed in the old train depot building. He wondered what the special event of the evening was. An ice cream stand caught his attention. He thought he'd have loved a cone of something chocolate if he'd had the time to stop. He took a left on Winston Avenue and then a right past the soda shop to get to the police station, parked, and texted Danbury that he was there. After a couple of long minutes, during which Matthew was still contemplating the ice cream, Danbury texted back, "*Be right out.*"

Danbury appeared with a small clear plastic bag in his hand and approached the car, "Hey, Doc. I need to run this back by the Lingle Plantation."

"Is that the final notebook?"

"Yeah. I know Leo wants to see it. And he needs to look. But it's got Allan's blood on it. So, I'm not sure about it. About taking it over there."

"Oh. That's a tough call to have to make. You did tell them you were getting it for them."

"Yeah, but I hadn't seen it."

"Why don't you just call Penn and explain? Ask her what she'd like to do about it."

"Good plan," said Danbury, stepping back to look more fully and rather skeptically at Matthew's Honda Element. "You aren't planning to drive that, are you?"

"I can. I mean, I can't off road like your SUV, but long trips and highways are no problem."

"C'mon, Doc. Let's take the SUV."

Matthew sighed. "I thought you'd want to do that. OK, I'll come with you. Under one condition."

"Which is? Not that you get to choose the music," he said, in jest, but probably not entirely so.

"No, but that's important too. We stop for an ice cream cone from over at the Chamber of Commerce on the way out."

Danbury just put his head back and laughed a deep hearty laugh. Matthew joined him though he wasn't sure what he was laughing at. Himself, in some respect, he assumed.

"OK, Doc, you got it. Let's go," he said as Matthew put his window up, grabbed his duffle bag, and climbed down, locking up and double checking the locks. "You know this is the safest parking lot there is, right?"

"Yeah," Matthew chuckled, "I guess it is."

Danbury punched his cell phone while Matthew threw his duffle in the back of the big black SUV and then climbed in. He heard Danbury say, "Yeah, I know. I told you I'd bring it to you. But I hadn't seen it yet. I'm not sure you want to." After a brief hesitation, he said quietly, "It's got dried blood on it. Allan's blood is on it." He listened intently for a moment and then said, "Yeah, OK. I just wanted you to know. See you in a minute."

He put the cell phone down and pulled out of the parking lot, heading for the Lingle house. "They want it anyway," he said, to Matthew's quizzical glance. "And I need Leo's eyes on it. So, I'm glad he'll be OK with it."

"Hey, can you just drop me at the Chamber of Commerce? If you go down Winston to Chapel. Then I can just walk back up and meet you."

Danbury laughed. "Sure, Doc. You're really fixated on that ice cream, aren't you?"

"Yeah, you want one?"

To his amazement, the man who could easily eat him under the table, just said absently, "No thanks."

*****

Ice cream in hand, Matthew walked briskly across Winston Avenue and up Chapel Street toward his office, then turned right when Chapel curved and walked up the long gravel drive to the Lingle house. Danbury was on the front porch locked in an embrace with Penn, so Matthew slowed his approach and enjoyed his ice cream instead. Finally, they pulled apart and Danbury spotted Matthew and said, "OK, let's hit the road."

After maneuvering out of Peak in Friday afternoon traffic, Danbury breathed a sigh of relief, but Matthew knew they had a long trip ahead and they generally disagreed on their music preferences in the car. He decided to strike up a relevant and necessary conversation instead. "What do you hope to get out of this guy? Do you think he's going to outright confess?"

"Yeah, I know. It's a long shot," said Danbury. "But I've got to try. He might cooperate. If they offer him a deal. If the deal is good enough."

"What kind of deal?"

"Remember the guy that Leo said he worked for?"

"Yeah, Rudy somebody."

"Rudy Warrick. He's a much bigger fish. Everybody wants him."

"Everybody who exactly?"

"FBI. DEA. Maybe homeland. The governmental alphabet soup. Name one. They probably want him for something."

"CIA," said Matthew.

"Yeah, maybe them too," said Danbury with a grin. "Anyway, the point is that he's wanted. Much more wanted than González with the angry eyebrows. That guy's just a little fish. Tiny, comparatively. If he gives up Warrick. If he can help find Warrick? Well, then, he'll get a good deal. I want to be part of that. If he gets a good deal. I want him to talk."

"I see," said Matthew. They drove a few more miles in total silence, Matthew contemplating how he'd handle the interrogation if he were the one handling that. "Should we maybe," began Matthew, as he reached for the radio dial.

He turned the radio on and Willie Nelson's scratchy voice filled the SUV, "On the road again, just can't wait to get on the road again."

Both men laughed as Matthew quickly turned the radio off and said, "Yeah, maybe not."

"We can find a playlist to listen to. If you want. But first, tell me something?"

"Yeah, what's that?"

"When we drove up to Walter's Lake. You said you didn't tell me about Savannah. The history lesson. When we were down there last month. I feel cheated. So, tell me about Savannah."

Matthew just laughed and said, "All right, just remember that you asked for it. Savannah is interesting because it's a port town which is laid out in squares as envisioned by General Oglethorpe, who arrived in the 1730s and named the colony Georgia after good old King George back in England."

"Oglethorpe?"

"Yeah."

"What a name. And I had trouble with Danbury. As a kid."

Matthew chuckled, then continued, "Military campaigns were planned and carried out there, both to protect the port city and offer offensive measures by sea. There are forts off shore on the barrier islands for protection, to prevent unfriendly ships from coming up the rivers all the way to Savannah. The most interesting history to most people though is the pirate stories."

"Yeah, Blackbeard and all?"

"There's a tavern, a pub, there that has an entrance to an underground tunnel which leads down to the Savannah River. Legend has it that pirates would hang out in the tavern and when other unsuspecting revelers were inebriated and passed out, the pirates would transport them through the tunnels and they'd wake up aboard pirate ships as captive crew members."

Danbury looked over at Matthew in disbelief. "Really? No way!"

"That's the legend."

"How have I never heard this story?"

"I don't know if it's recorded in history books but the pub, appropriately named The Pirate's House, has a tunnel dropping out of one corner of it that you can see to this day. It supposedly leads down to the river."

"Wow. I need to stay longer. To go to Savannah for pleasure. And not just murder investigations."

"Yeah, they have great food at the tavern too so you'd love it. It's, of course, said to be haunted. There are some other shady places, like Factor's Walk, down near the water front that are also said to be haunted and have similar tunnels leading to the river."

"Lingle Plantation has nothing on Savannah. Apparently." said Danbury.

"Where are we going down there? Where's this police station located?"

"It's the Central Precinct of the Savannah Police Department. On Bull Street. They said it was southwest of Forsyth Park. Which means nothing to me. But the address is in my phone."

"OK, I know where Forsyth Park is. If it's southwest of that but close by, then it's probably just a couple of miles from the Savannah River and the places I was telling you about. Forsyth Park postdates Oglethorpe but it's probably early 1800s, somewhat antebellum, but before the uncivil war."

"What? You don't know the whole history?" Danbury grinned.

"Yeah, yeah," said Matthew, good-naturedly. "I never claimed to know all of history, US or otherwise. It's a pretty big park, though with a nice fountain. It was named after but not donated by a Georgia governor." There was definitely much more to Danbury that he was only beginning to see, Matthew thought – history interest, goofy grins, kissing women, and teasing him included.

As they lapsed into silence, Danbury's cell phone, which was mounted on the dash, sounded and he poked to answer it on speaker phone.

"Detective Danbury," he said, returning to the brusque voice and manner to which Matthew had initially become accustomed.

"Hey Detective, this is Officer Gene Sutherby again. I've just finished processing Juan González in and I have some news, and some of it I think you'll like. We've been given direction from the FBI to offer González a deal. Reduced sentencing to help find and then testify against Rudy Warrick. Thanks for that information by the way. The González and Warrick connection wasn't documented, at least not in the González file, until you called our attention to it. I think it caught the FBI by surprise too."

"That is great news. Maybe I can get some answers." said Danbury.

"Yeah, but there's more. The FBI is flying two agents in from Washington. They'll arrive late tonight. They'll probably hit the ground around ten or shortly after and then drive in. That won't take them long from the airstrip. When they get here, it's all going to get handed over to their agency. How fast can you get here?"

Danbury had sped only slightly above the speed limit on the last trip, Matthew had noticed, but he screwed up his face with this news and said, "We're over three hours out. But I can shorten that. If I need to."

"Yeah, you need to. Shorten it as much as you can. I can hold the FBI guys off a little while when they get here. But they're going to want to take this guy and question him too, and they'll get preference. You know how it goes. They walk in the door and think everyone is suddenly working for them. They run the show."

"Thanks, Sutherby, for the heads up. We'll come straight there." After clicking to disconnect the call, he hit the gas and went around a car moving slightly above the speed limit in the left lane. Then, as he accelerated steadily, he turned to Matthew and said, "Well, Doc, I hope you don't need to stop."

"I'm good to go. We didn't leave until, what, 4:30? We should be there by nine."

"We'll be there before nine," said Danbury. "We have to be. Think you can find a playlist? One we can agree on?"

"Yeah, no rap, blue grass, R&B, hard rock or classic rock. Definitely none of that mournful old country that you like," he added, crinkling his nose at the thought. "Just the pop stuff or newer country, right?"

"Yeah. Right."

"OK," he said as he clicked through his playlists and reached for the cord to plug in. He was happy that moment that he hadn't insisted on driving. Danbury was driving a police vehicle. Granted, it was from another state than the one they'd just crossed into, but Matthew figured there was such a thing as police courtesy. The FBI stance on local police seemed to be an understood phenomenon, he surmised. So, there'd be some sympathy for the cause if a local yokel in any of the smaller towns they'd be blowing through was bored or decided to get cute.

Settling back in his seat, he figured he had time to kill and he could focus on his own thoughts. He grimaced, chagrinned, because the first thought that came to his mind was Cici.

29. Answer the question

Glancing at his watch as they were signing in at the front desk of the police station that he'd helped navigate to find, Matthew realized that Danbury had been right. It was almost 8:30. They'd made record time. Matthew figured that driving a hundred miles an hour through an entire state would do that. They'd gotten bogged in traffic only once and Danbury had smacked the steering wheel with his palm in frustration. Whatever had caused the traffic to slow must have cleared because they were soon cruising at a hundred miles an hour again.

The middle-aged woman behind the desk seemed to be having some difficulty with Matthew's capacity in the visit and Danbury slowed down, as if he were talking to a small and not very bright child. He enunciated, "Doctor Matthew Paine. Consultant. To the Wake County Police Department. Homicide Division."

"Oh," said the older woman behind the counter. "Is that what you said? You've got some strange dialect going there."

Funny, Matthew thought, he was thinking the same of her. Danbury's, he thought, was very clear with only a slight southern twang now and again. He wasn't sure he wanted to know what Danbury was thinking right about then. The guy was clearly frustrated and eager to get to question his murder suspect before the FBI arrived with their agenda, which would supersede all else.

"OK, ID please?"

Matthew handed her his driver's license and she looked from it to him several times, propped it on the keyboard, tapped away on the keys, and then handed it back. "Stand over there," she said. Matthew complied and an old-fashioned flash went off in his face. The woman handed Danbury a plastic card and said, "Hang it behind your picture badge." He complied and a few moments later she handed Matthew a similar card hanging from a clip. "Put this where it can be easily seen and wear it at all times in the building," she said as she reached under the counter to click a button. A buzzer sounded at the door behind her. She motioned them in, "Third door on your left," and turned back to her computer.

Matthew clipped the badge on his shirt and followed Danbury down the hallway. At the third door they hesitated. "This is the interrogation room. By the looks of the door," said Danbury. "If it has an observation room, maybe it's this next one," he added, just as a short, paunchy, middle-aged police officer came around the corner from the other direction. He had been blond once, thought Matthew, but his hair was receding and greying. His face was red, like his blood pressure should perhaps be checked, and his shirt buttons were stretched in the middle, as if the weight gain were either recent or the shirt was just very old.

"Detective Danbury?" he asked, craning his neck to look up as he approached.

"Yeah, I'm Danbury. And this is Doctor Paine," he said, offering a hand.

The smaller man shook his hand and just said, "Sutherby. Good to meet you."

"Thanks for the call," said Danbury. "I really appreciate it. Without it we might have stopped for dinner. Checked into a hotel. Or not pushed it so hard driving down."

"No problem. Your suspect is in there," he said, motioning to the door they were standing in front of. "But the observation room is around the other side. These hallways form squares around the rooms on the interior."

"Could you take Doctor Paine to the observation room? And the perp has been prepped? Completely?"

"Yeah, mirandized on the way over and his personal information gathered and logged here. He hasn't lawyered up. He's agreeing to cooperate for a lessened sentence. He's all yours, at least until the Feds get here," he said as he motioned Matthew to follow him. "This way, Doctor."

Two left turns later and Matthew was being ushered into a room that was dimly lit and already occupied by two other people. Both turned as the door opened and Sutherby did the introductions, "This is Doctor Paine," he said.

"Please, just call me Matthew."

"And this is Josh Marshall and Omar Hakim," he said, indicating the two men on stools in front of computer equipment, an assortment of lit boards and screens on the wall to the left. "Omar will be recording the conversation with your Detective Danbury."

Sutherby disappeared and Matthew was left alone in the cramped and overheated room with the two other men. Greetings were given, all around. As Matthew was wondering what Josh Marshall's role would be, he stepped forward and offered Matthew a seat that was positioned in front of a two-way mirror. Matthew sat down, realizing that he was now very comfortable with this process. He had been in similar rooms in two other police stations, one in downtown Raleigh and the other in Peak.

"Omar, here, records the sound feed and I normally record the video," said Josh. "I'm not sure if we're doing video or only audio for this one?" he asked.

"I'm sure Danbury would appreciate both," responded Matthew, who was amused to be the only non-official one in the room, but the one calling the shots on Danbury's behalf.

"OK, I'll get it set up," said Josh. Just then the door opened, the dim lights came up as if on a theater stage, and Danbury stepped into the room where the angry eyebrowed man was already seated at the table.

Matthew hadn't seen them in the sketch and he hadn't seen the mug shot up close, but there were what appeared to be tattooed tear drops dripping from the corners of the man's eyes. He thought that meant the guy had killed people or had been in prison. Maybe he'd killed people in prison. Matthew wasn't sure. He shivered slightly as he leaned forward anticipating the conversation with Danbury.

"Detective Warren Danbury. Raleigh North Carolina. Wake County Homicide Division," he said, flashing his badge in identification. "I have a few questions for you. And you've agreed to cooperate, correct?"

The man looked up with a dead-pan face completely unreadable, at least to Matthew, and said, "Yah."

"Please state your full name. For the record."

The man rattled off a list of names in which Matthew did hear Juan and González somewhere in the string.

"And you're giving this statement voluntarily? Nobody has coerced or threatened you?"

"Yah," said the guy.

"OK. First, tell me where you were. On Monday evening. May 12th. Around 8:30 PM."

"Some backwoods lil town in Nord Carolina."

"What's the name of the town?"

"It was sumpin' like Pete."

"Was it Peak?"

"Yah, dats it."

"What were you doing in Peak on Monday, May 12th at 8:30 PM?"

"Beatin' on some punk ass guy."

"You were beating up a guy? In Peak?"

"Yah."

"What was the guy's name?"

"It was sumpin' like Leonard. Leonard Somebody or t'other. Pringle. Like da potato chip."

"Leonard Lingle?"

"Yah. Dats da guy."

"Why were you beating Leonard Lingle."

"Got da order."

"Somebody told you to beat him?"

"Yah."

"Who?"

"Da man."

"A man told you to beat him up. What man?"

"Came from some fugazy lawya."

Just as Matthew was wondering what the guy had just said, Danbury translated the street slang, summarizing the guy's statements as he'd been doing all along.

"A fake lawyer told you to beat up Leonard Lingle?"

"Naw. Fugazy lawya tol da man. Da man tol me. See?"

"The man would be Rudy Warrick?"

There was total silence in the interrogation room while Danbury just stared the guy down. When an answer wasn't forthcoming, Danbury grew more insistent. "You've signed the agreement to cooperate. Just answer the question!"

"Yah. He da man," said González quietly.

"Who is the fake lawyer?"

"Don't know. Ain't met him. Don't work like dat."

"Then how do you know there was a fake lawyer involved?"

"We wuz takin' a walk, da man and me, and da phone rung. Da man answer and call him da fugazy lawya."

"But he didn't call the man by name?"

"Naw, he say, 'Yo fugazy lawya ass self want whut'?"

"Could you hear what the lawyer said? Or what he sounded like?"

"Naw. Dint talk long. Den da man say, 'Gotta new yakka fo' ya.' And den he tell me 'bout da punk ass guy who need da beatin' to set him straight."

"He told you he had a job for you. Was it a hit?"

"Naw, jus' a beat down."

"To beat up Leonard Lingle?"

"Dats whut he say, Yah. He say he be jarred and all puro pedo, woffin', ya know?"

Even Danbury was looking a bit confused this time, so the guy clarified, “He was all talkin’ trip.”

“Leonard Lingle was talking too much?”

“Da man say he gon be. He need to be shadd.”

“Rudy Warrick said that Leonard Lingle needed to be shut up?”

“Yah.”

“Did he say why?”

“Naw. I din ask.”

“When was that?”

“Daz Monday.”

“And you went to Peak that same day? And beat up Leonard Lingle? And took a notebook he had?”

“Ya, but deys more ‘a dem. And we ain’t get em all. Ain’t nothin’ in de one we did git but some scribblin’ dat don make no sense.”

“You say ‘we.’ Who went with you?”

“Da man say, ‘Take lil Nando wit ya.’”

“Would little Nando be Fernando Hernández?”

“Yah. Daz him.”

“What happened to Fernando Hernández? Where is he now?”

The guy just pointed to the bottom tear tattooed on his face and said, “You see dis here?”

“You killed Fernando Hernández?”

“Had to. Da man, he say so.”

“After you beat up Leonard Lingle?”

“Yah, daz right.”

“Why?”

“He was cappin’ ‘bout sumpin’ and he ain’t straight wid da man. Don’t know ‘bout wut. Ain’t my place ta ask, Szeen?”

“Yeah, I got it. Tell me about the notebooks.”

"Ain't nuthin' to tell. Ain't find 'em. Somebody else don't like dat Pringle folks. Day trow rocks in da window. We ain't want to get roped. So, we leave."

"And you took a Jeep with you? When you left?"

"Yah. Dope whip. Keys on da counter. Jus askin' to take."

Matthew realized that he was on the edge of his seat through this conversation, trying to follow and understand it. He would swear that the guy wasn't speaking English at all. Though he looked to be of Latino ethnicity, his dialect wasn't discernably Hispanic, just a street slang that Matthew wouldn't have been able to follow but for Danbury's translation.

Given the man's roughened and heavily scared dark skin, dark unkept wild hair, and dead eyes with the tears tattooed from the corners under the thick gnarly eyebrows, Matthew thought it was no wonder that Jacob Wheatley had been terrified of him. This guy wasn't one you'd want to bump into on the street in broad daylight and definitely not at dusk at a house thought to be haunted.

Danbury never corrected the man, Matthew noticed, telling him that it was Allan that he'd beaten or that had been killed in the process. Matthew wondered why the news that he'd beaten up and actually killed the wrong guy hadn't made it back to González.

One thing that did stand out to Matthew though as he was half listening to the continued conversation between Danbury and González, was the "fake lawyer" involved in the directive to "beat down" Leo Lingle. He pondered this, and he checked his watch to see what time it was in England. It was shortly after nine, so he figured it was shortly after two in the morning London time

With eyebrow raised and foot tapping, he contemplated whether to text Cici now or wait until the next morning, which would be part of the way through her Saturday. He knew that she had the Do Not Disturb feature on her phone set from ten at night until eight in the morning when they were dating, but he wasn't sure if she still did. He didn't want to wake her at two in the morning, but he wanted to get an answer as quickly as possible to the question that was burning in his mind.

He decided to take a chance, ask the question, and hope that she didn't see it until her morning. Texting her one long string, he hoped to keep her phone from dinging more than once if it wasn't silenced for the night. "*Hi*

Cees, I hope you're on DND and this doesn't wake you, but if you can answer when you wake up, I'd appreciate it. I need to know if you can tell if a person has NEVER passed the bar exam. North Carolina posted your 'passed' status, right? Do all states do that? Is there a national database somewhere to check? Thanks!"

While he half listened to Danbury grill the guy about when and how he wielded the bat, and where he got it from in the first place, Matthew's knee was jumping as his foot tapped out the fast rhythms running through his head. He was in deep concentration about what it all meant when he heard his phone ding. Looking down, he saw that it was Cici.

"*Hi Matthew. Don't worry, you didn't wake me. I was up anyway. Can't sleep through the night here yet. Bar standards are set by state but lots of them, like NC, administer the Uniform Bar Exam (UBE) that transfers between states. In NC, it's a 2-day exam and day 2 is the standardized test. Pass results are shown in lots of states (NC does) but not all. The scores aren't shown, just pass/fail. You can contact the state bar association to see if an attorney is licensed in NC.*"

"*Thanks, Cees! Sorry you're having trouble sleeping but thanks for the information. What if the attorney is from another state? Like Ohio?*"

"*It's done by state, but if the Ohio state bar association doesn't provide that information, then try calling the Ohio Supreme Court Clerk and ask them to check their list of attorneys licensed to practice law there.*"

"*There's no national database then? I'd have to know the state?*"

"*It's not done at the national level, so yes, you'd have to know the state. Now tell me why, at 2 AM you needed this information?*"

"*That's a long story. I won't keep you up to explain it all, but there's a lawyer in Peak who I think is a crook and I wanted to check him out.*"

"*Tell you what. I'll send a note to some of my colleagues, asking the question about him and include you on it so that they can respond directly with you in the loop. How's that?*"

"*Thanks, Cees, I appreciate your help.*"

"*Sure. What's his name? Where does he practice?*"

"*Wayne Adams. He's at the Higgins Law Firm in Peak but he came from Lima Ohio. There's something off about him.*"

"*OK, give me a few minutes and then check your inbox.*"

"*You don't have to do it right now!*"

"*It's OK. Maybe I'll be able to go back to sleep afterward.*"

"*Thanks Cees. Sleep well and sweet dreams.*"

"*You're welcome. Book your flight already!*" and she sent him a smiley face blowing him a kiss. He texted a kiss back and settled in to listen to Danbury, who had just begun asking more specific questions about "da man." He was having trouble getting answers.

It had been a long day and he was fading when he'd heard Danbury say for about the fourth time, "Just answer the question." Suddenly the door to the interrogation room burst open, slamming loudly against the wall behind it, and two guys in suits stepped through it flashing badges like they owned the place.

"Agent Owens and Special Agent Kent," said one of the men as the badges were flashed. "We'll take over from here. Please step out of the room."

"Damn, they're early," Matthew heard Omar say from behind him as he glanced over his shoulder to see the room behind him.

"Yeah," answered Josh, pulling off his headset. "I guess if you got the funding, you can fly wherever you want whenever you want. This Rudy Warrick guy must be on the top of somebody's most-wanted list."

"Feather in somebody's cap," answered Omar, pulling off his headset.

Matthew asked, "But you got all of that, right? And the Feds can't keep you from giving us a copy?"

"Nah, I'll burn you one right now. Before they get that far," answered Josh, putting his headset back on and going to work on the controls.

"Thanks," said Matthew just as Danbury burst through the door.

"Hey, Danbury, they're burning you a copy of your recorded conversation now."

"Thanks," he said to them. As Omar nodded his acknowledgement, Danbury looked at Matthew, frustrated, and said, "I was so close. If he'd just answered a few more questions. Damned Feds!"

"You got what you needed, though, right? This guy killed Allan, which gives Penn and Leo some closure."

"SOME closure," Danbury said. "But you heard him. There was somebody calling the shots. Somebody other than Rudy Warrick. At least on Allan's murder. And the fake lawyer. Want to place bets on who that is?"

"Yeah, but there'd be nobody to bet against us. You think you could have gotten anything else out of him to figure out who called and told Warrick to have Leo beaten? It didn't sound, to me anyway, like there was anything else he could have told you."

"Maybe not. But I was hoping there was something more there. Something he heard but didn't understand. Something that meant nothing to him. But would to us. The murder isn't solved," he said, his voice raised in frustration, like Matthew hadn't heard before from Danbury. "Not completely. Not until we know who ordered the beating. And why. And put them away!"

"You don't think Rudy Warrick will be of any help if he's found, do you?"

"No, I don't. Because he won't get a deal. He'll have nothing to gain. By giving us the fugazy lawyer."

Matthew just laughed at Danbury's slang, and he tried to lighten the mood a bit as he said, "I'm pretty impressed. I had no idea what that guy was saying half the time. I didn't know you spoke street slang."

"Yeah, not so well. We get regular education though. Seminars and training on talking to these guys. I don't tend to answer them that way. But I usually know what they're saying. Most of the time. Sometimes they'll get one by me. But mostly, I get it."

"Oh, and speaking of the fake lawyer, I texted Cici to get her help checking Wayne out. There's no federal database of licensed attorneys who have passed the bar apparently. It's done by state. I gave her Ohio but that might not be right either. She said she'd include me in an email to some of her colleagues to get their help checking him out."

"Thanks, Doc. That's great. She answered you just now? What is it there now? Like three in the morning?"

"After two in the morning, but yeah, she said she hasn't been able to sleep through the night yet, so she was awake anyway. I'm sure she figures she owes you a few for helping her last month."

"Here, Detective," said Josh, handing over a DVD. "Here's a recording of your conversation with the perp. I hope it helps. I think we'll be here awhile," he added, stifling a yawn. "Long night ahead."

"That was fast. Thanks, Officer Marshall," said Danbury respectfully. And to Matthew, he said, "Let's roll."

They found and thanked Sutherby, who was apologetic for the FBI agents showing up early. "Nah. We'd have missed talking to him at all. If you hadn't called. So, thanks for that," said Danbury, shaking his hand. "Let us know if you need anything. Up in North Carolina," he added as he and Matthew turned to leave.

The outer lobby they'd come though initially was at a constant low buzz with activity when they'd come in, but the noise level had risen considerably already and the room was filling up. Matthew noticed several people milling around a woman with her head in her hands and wondered what fate had befallen her or someone she loved. The noise level wasn't deafening yet, but it was a Friday night, Matthew thought, so it was likely to get that way in a few more hours.

"I don't know about you, Doc. But my stomach is going to eat itself. If I don't get something in it soon," said Danbury.

The ice cream had been long gone hours ago. Matthew had heard his stomach rumble a time or two during the interrogation. "Yeah, mine too."

They turned in their ID badges and Matthew was relieved to step into the relative quiet outside of the station. He could hear a siren going off somewhere in the near distance but it was otherwise much quieter than inside. When they reached the car, Danbury said, "Two choices, Doc. Eat and stay. Or hit the road. And eat on the way."

"You want to drive all the way back to Peak tonight?"

"Hey, I like my own bed."

"Yeah, me too. You sure you're up for it? There's no way that I'm cleared to drive this thing."

"Oh yeah. I drove all night. Lots of times. Over in Afghanistan."

This caught Matthew totally by surprise. Danbury was in Afghanistan? He had so many questions, but he figured he'd start with the obvious answer, "Yeah, let's eat on the way home."

As they climbed into the big SUV, Matthew asked, "When were you in Afghanistan?"

“Right after high school. I joined the Marines. I wasn’t ready for college yet. I knew that. Not right after high school. So I signed up. To get them to pay for college later. I was in for four. Then did school for four. Stayed in the Reserves. Until after I graduated. The stories I could tell. And some I can’t,” he added, mischievously.

Military to cop made sense, Matthew thought, as did Danbury’s haircut and a good deal of his demeanor put in that context. He stood straight and tall always. He was courteous, particularly to women, always. Matthew was curious to hear about Danbury’s life leading up to becoming a detective.

“Where’d you go to school?”

“East Carolina University.”

“Oh. No wonder you were so interested in the pirates in Savannah.”

“Yeah, I’m a pirate,” Danbury grinned. “I wanted a 4-year degree. In Criminal Justice. Had to be at a state school though. Military money won’t cover private. And ECU has one of the best.”

Matthew realized in that moment how very little he actually knew about Danbury or at least about his past. Considering himself a pretty good judge of character and having spent long hours together chasing murderers two months in a row, he thought he knew the guy fairly well. He was driven to do his job well, he cared about people, and he wasn’t jaded enough to think that everyone was motivated by evil intent. What Matthew didn’t know, he realized, was what had made Danbury that way.

“We’ve got four and a half hours for all of the stories you can tell. Let’s find some fast food and then I’m all ears.”

“More like four,” Danbury grinned. “Let’s find one we can go into. Then we only stop this once.”

“Sounds good.”

30. Home smoky home

Transfixed, Matthew listened to Danbury talk about his years in the Marines most of the way home. It was more than Matthew had ever heard Danbury talk at all and particularly about himself. They had driven the last hour or so into Peak with just the stereo playlist for noise and company as they were both engrossed in their own thoughts.

Pondering the outcome if Wayne Adams were determined to be behind Allan's murder, Matthew thought through the process. Obviously it was a case of mistaken identity and Allan was killed when Leo was the true target. They did look a lot alike, though they moved nothing alike. Leo was agile and moved more like a young leopard on the prowl. Allan walked ramrod straight, like he'd break if he tried to bend. But if you didn't know them, he thought, you wouldn't know to look for that difference.

He wondered if Danbury would tell Leo the truth about it. To fully disclose who had killed Allan, he'd have to tell him why. Matthew drew a deep breath and was glad he wasn't in Danbury's shoes. Leo had been grieving the loss of his brother enough without having to learn that he'd died because some hired muscle thought Allan was him.

As they pulled into the parking lot of the Peak Police Station, Matthew glanced at the digital display on the dash. It was nearly two in the morning. Almost the same time he'd texted Cici London time, he mused. He pulled out his phone as Danbury was gathering his things and checked his email account for the note. True to her word, Cici had included him on the note to her colleagues.

"Wow, these people must not have a life," said Matthew, aloud.

"What people?"

"Cici's colleagues," he said, pointing to his phone. "She sent the message like she'd promised to a group of four people with me on copy. Two of them answered her already. Tonight on a Friday night. One said he had contacts in Ohio and he'd check that out. The other said she knows a member of the board of directors for the FBA, that's the Federal Bar Association I think, and she's connecting him in to the discussion to see what he can tell us."

"Let me know what you find out."

"Yeah, will do."

Matthew slid out of the SUV and walked around to retrieve his duffle bag, happy to be able to sleep in his own bed, and to sleep in late. He was thankful that he had nowhere to be in the morning.

"Hey, I texted Penn. When we stopped for food. I'm going to the Lingle Plantation. I'll keep the surveillance in place. Through the night. But I can better protect them. By just being there."

"You're not sleeping in your own bed after all, huh?" teased Matthew.

"Guess not. Have a good night, Doc. What's left of it anyway. And thanks for riding down. If you ever want to change professions, become a cop, I can put in a good word for you."

"You do what you do well, but that's not for me. I'll just stay in my consulting capacity, thanks. Whatever that actually means," he said with a shrug. "Good night," he added as he unlocked his Element, tossed his bag in the passenger seat, climbed in, and started the boxy car.

The drive home was quiet, uneventful, and at that hour without much other traffic short. His favorite kind, he thought. As he pulled into his neighborhood, all was still and, except for a few porch lights here and there, dark. He was glad he'd chosen to drive the Element so that he could drive silently in without disturbing the peace of the night.

He'd hit the button for the garage door, driven in, and dropped the garage door behind him when he heard a noise. It sounded like the roar of an engine firing up loudly. It seemed to be coming from the vicinity of the golf course behind his house. Maybe just some kids out joyriding or making doughnuts on the pristinely manicured grass, he thought. As he stepped through the door and was about to disable the alarm, dropping his bag on the floor to reset the alarm behind him, he heard an earsplitting crash.

Startled, he turned and jumped in one motion. He stared in horror as he realized that the crash was a projectile coming through his back bay window. It was followed, quickly, by a blaze of flame that streaked across his kitchen eating nook, seemed to bounce a few times across the rug in his sitting area, lighting up everything in its path, and crashed at the base of his drapes, which immediately burst into flame. He thought he heard someone howling from outside. It sounded like a rebel yell and then, "Mind your own damned business!"

Feeling like his body was moving through murky mud, his mind raced with two primary thoughts: Max, which sent panic down his spine, and a fire extinguisher. He knew that he had to suppress the rising panic and focus or he'd lose this battle and possibly his cat and house in the process. He couldn't lose Max, but neither could he get to him through the smoke and fire so he fought for focus. In his head he heard the phrase, "please put on your oxygen mask before assisting young children with theirs." He wished he had an oxygen mask but he knew that he had to get the fire out, find Max, and then get him to safety.

He had come in the side door, his small laundry room was just to his right, and there was a full-sized fire extinguisher mounted just inside the door. Grabbing it, he let the security alarm, which he hadn't finished disabling, sound as it joined the wail of the smoke detectors. Quickly thinking through his potential process, he set the fire extinguisher down for a second, grabbed all of his keys from the hook by the door and stuffed them in his pocket, and tossed his duffle back out the door, slamming it closed. Picking up the large red canister, he ran into his sitting area, pulled the pin, and started sweeping the room with the chemicals.

Thick black smoke was rising and his nose and mouth felt like they were already raw from both the smoke and the chemicals that he was spraying, but he didn't let up until he saw no more flame. Pulling his shirt over his mouth and nose, he glanced around. His eyes were burning too but there was no help for them just yet. He hoped and prayed that Max had gone to his favorite hiding spot in the back corner of his closet, as he dashed, bent at the waist, down the smoky hallway to find him. He closed the bedroom door behind him, trying to buy some time from the smoke.

Dropping to his knees to avoid the smoke that had risen to his bedroom ceiling, he crawled into his closet and there, to his great relief, was Max, backed into the farthest reaches of his closet. Scooping up the terrified creature, he got to his knees and scooted on them out of the closet. He clutched Max to his chest, tucked him under his chin, and got to his feet still crouched. He made it to his back door where all of the chaos had begun and out into the fresh night air.

He clung to Max as he got away from his house and tried to breathe deeply, coughing violently and clinging to Max harder with the effort. The last thing he wanted was to lose Max in the pandemonium that he knew would ensue, so he made his way around the end of his garage and dug his keys out of his pocket with his free hand. Letting himself in the end door, he clicked to unlock the Element and then opened the garage door.

The garage had been sealed off from the house with the door he'd closed, so it wasn't smoke-filled and he had a few moments to get situated. Placing Max gently on the back seat, he saw the big cat drop to the floor and immediately slip under his driver's seat. "OK, Big Guy, just stay there. Don't get under my feet," he rasped as he climbed carefully in and backed the Element out down his short driveway and parked it, front end out, in the dead end of the street just beyond his house.

Locking Max in, he tried to jog, coughing as he went, back up his driveway and into the garage. He snatched up the duffle bag from outside the door, threw it in the Corvette, and then backed it out beside the Element. Just then, he thought to call 9-1-1. Before he'd completed the call, he heard sirens coming in the distance and noticed a clump of his older neighbors just down from his house. Several of them were approaching him as the call went through.

"9-1-1, what's your emergency?" he heard.

"I need to report a fire. It's arson, so I'll need the police as well," he rasped.

"Is everyone out safely?"

"Yes," he replied, and then coughed loudly and thought his lungs might explode. "And I think the fire is out but I'm not positive."

"What's your address, Sir?" said the polite professional voice that sounded like the speaker was never rattled by anything that she heard ever.

"8680 Chester Road, Peak," he spluttered. "Beyond King's Country Club on Highway 20."

"We've already received a call and help is on the way," said the voice. "Do you want to stay on the line?"

"No. I'm all right," he coughed violently again as he disconnected and looked up to see Mrs. Drewer standing beside his car offering him a bottle of water.

He opened the door and climbed out, gratefully taking the water from her and gulping most of it down before he tried to answer when she asked if he was OK.

"I think so," he whispered. "I think I got the fire out. And Max is in my Honda," he motioned to the boxy car she had her back to.

"Oh good!" she said, clearly relieved. "I knew you had a cat and I was scared to ask about him yet. The Lewises called the fire in when the alarms started blaring." The Lewises owned the condominium directly attached to Matthew's, between his and Mrs. Drewer's condos.

Just then Matthew's phone sounded from his pocket. He pulled it out and tried to laugh as he saw that it was his security company finally calling him about the alarm that he'd set off without disabling it when he entered the house. But then he went into a fit of coughing. "About time," he'd tried to mutter, as he managed to answer "Matthew Paine" and then spluttered out the security code. He could see the flashing lights coming down the street now, though they'd turned the sirens off. The very last thing they needed were security guards adding to the confusion, he figured, when the Peak Police Officers should be almost there.

"Matthew," she said, looking over her shoulder at the approaching vehicles, "I'm going back to my house and stay there unless we get evacuated tonight. But I'll leave the garage door unlocked for you. You can sleep in my guest room if you need somewhere to go tonight, take a shower, whatever you need, and she told him where she'd hidden the key to get into the house from the garage."

Something about the sweetness of that offer from the previously nosy neighbor that he'd not initially thought too highly of caught in his throat along with all of the awful stuff he'd inhaled already. He choked as he said, "Thank you, Mrs. Drewer. I can't begin to tell you how much I appreciate that." He bent over and hugged his older neighbor and added, "Could you just let the neighbors know that I'm OK and that I got Max out? I'm sure they're very concerned." Having managed that much, he started coughing uncontrollably again.

Mrs. Drewer looked at him, as if very concerned herself, and just said, "They are concerned." Before turning to leave, she asked, innocently, "It wasn't electrical, was it?"

"No," he replied quietly. "It wasn't electrical." He was unwilling yet to admit aloud that somebody had done it on purpose, had gleefully torched his home, his sanctuary from the world. An anger began to burn deep in his gut that exceeded the burning in his eyes, nose, and throat.

Tipping his head back, he splashed the rest of the water bottle over his eyes, wiping them dry with the inside of his shirt and then repeated the process. Just then the convoy of lights reached them and, as Mrs. Drewer turned to go back to her own house, she said, "There are more water bottles in my garage, if you want more. Just help yourself." She padded away in what Matthew now realized was slippered feet and a thick bathrobe back into her house.

"Thanks, Mrs. Drewer. I'm OK, but I might need some for Max," he choked out to her retreating back. He really did need to check on Max, he thought, but two firemen were heading for his house, hose dragging across his front yard with them, and another was coming his way.

"I think the fire is out, but I'd love to be certain," he croaked, coughing.

"Good to hear," said the guy. "We're checking it out now."

"Hey, can you tell them that the side and back doors are open? They don't need to bust down the front door."

"I think it's too late," said the guy looking over his shoulder. Matthew didn't have the heart to look but as he glanced over, he saw something that looked like red spray paint across the front of his house. He clenched and unclenched his fists.

"We need to check you out next," the guy said. "There's an EMS truck right behind the BRFT there."

"The what?"

"The Big Red Fire Truck. C'mon, let's get you checked out."

He'd always heard that healthcare professionals made the worst patients, but he was no expert on smoke and chemical inhalation and he knew that he needed help. He followed the guy to the EMS truck. "Hey, my cat is in that silver Element there. Do you have something I can give him a little water in? He was in there too," Matthew added.

"Yeah, closer to the ground, though. You first, Buddy," said the guy, steering him to the back of the truck and then waddling off, in the plethora of protective clothing, toward Matthew's house.

Two people, dressed in golf shirts with fire department insignias, approached and introduced themselves, one an EMT and the other a Paramedic. Matthew heard their names but he wasn't paying much attention. They sat him down on the back of the vehicle, asked all the usual questions, clipped an oxygen sensor on his finger, and then pulled an oxygen mask down on his face.

Pulling a stretcher from the vehicle, they moved him to sit, propped up on it with his head leaned back, while they administered some sort of eye wash and dabbed at his face, wiping away the liquid. Though it was all a bit of a blur in Matthew's mind, his mind returned again and again to the thought that he and Max were both safe, his house wasn't destroyed and repairs could be made, he hoped. But boiling just beneath the surface were thoughts about who would do something like this and why.

He thought he'd heard the person who he now realized had been on a dirt bike or motorcycle, likely having come across the golf course behind his house, yell something about minding his own business. The last time he'd heard that, it came from . . . . He was having trouble focusing his mind on that thought. The adrenaline that had rushed through him earlier had retreated. Exhausted and probably traumatized, he realized, he relaxed into the stretcher, finally able to breathe with the oxygen mask. The searing pain in his eyes, nose, and chest was lessening.

31. Just breathe

"Hey, Doc," was the next thing Matthew remembered hearing as someone was prodding his arm. Matthew looked up to see Danbury standing over him. The EMT was removing the oxygen probe from his finger, nodding in apparent satisfaction.

"What are you," he tried to ask but there was something on his face. He remembered that he had an oxygen mask on and he slid it up on top of his head as he propped himself up and sat up. "What are you doing here?" asked Matthew.

"The Peak Police were called in. One of them called me. When they realized it was your house. They wanted to question you earlier. But you were out of it. So I told them to collect evidence. And I'd talk to you. The 9-1-1 dispatcher said it was arson. What the hell happened?"

Matthew's head was throbbing and it was all a little murky in his muddled brain. "I'm not completely sure. I came home and I'd just opened the door from the garage to the house when I heard a noise, a motor firing up. I think it was a dirt bike or motorcycle that came from the golf course," he paused, coughing, and then tried to continue. "It was quiet but for that. No noise at all out here. My neighbors are mostly older, retired, and they go to bed early. So it was loud in the still night."

Danbury had pad and pen in hand and he was making notes. "What time was that?"

"I drove straight here from the police station. So it was maybe two by then. Something like that. But I don't even know what time it is now," said Matthew, looking around at the still dark night and noticing fewer flashing lights than he'd remembered earlier.

"Three forty-six," responded Danbury, checking his watch. "OK, then what?"

"I was just about to disable the alarm system when I heard a loud exploding crash. Before I could fully realize that something had just been launched through my back bay window, it was followed by a blaze of flame. A Molotov Cocktail maybe. That's all I can think that it could have been. It wasn't a flame thrower. It didn't last, it was just a streak, but it was setting everything in its path on fire. I'm pretty sure I heard someone yell, like a rebel yell, and then I thought I heard a voice shout something like, 'Mind your own damned business!' " He leaned back, coughing still, though not as deeply. He was exhausted from the effort.

"It's OK, Doc. Take your time," said Danbury as Matthew pulled the oxygen mask back over his face for a few more breaths and leaned heavily onto the raised back of the stretcher as his mind went through the details of the night.

"Max," said Matthew suddenly as he pulled the mask back from his face.

"Who?" asked Danbury.

"My cat. He's in my Element, probably terrified from all of this. I got him out of the house, but he needs water and to be looked at too."

"OK, we can do that next."

"No," said Matthew, sitting back up. "I need to know that he's OK now. And he needs water, at least."

"OK, I'll be right back. Sit tight. Just for a minute."

Matthew leaned back, pulling on the oxygen mask and trying to breathe and relax but knowing that he wouldn't fully relax again until he knew for certain that Max was OK too. After a few minutes, Danbury returned carrying a water bottle and a little plastic cup. Pulling out a pocket knife, he sliced the cup down to about three inches in height, and said, "OK, let's go."

Danbury held onto Matthew as he stood, a bit unsteadily at first. He felt a small breeze of the cool night air on his face and breathed in deeply for the first time without the oxygen mask and for the first time without coughing uncontrollably. The oxygen had done its job, he thought, as he steadied himself and walked slowly toward his Element.

"I need to climb in and quickly close the door behind me," he said. "The last thing I want is for Max to get spooked and run. He's only ever been outside on my back patio with me. Otherwise he's an indoor cat and he has no understanding of the outdoors at all."

"OK, Doc. Whatever you say," said Danbury as he opened the water bottle and poured some into the bottom of the plastic cup.

Matthew pulled the key from his pocket and unlocked the door. Sliding into the passenger's seat without opening the door widely, he took the cup and water bottle from Danbury, and then quickly closed the door behind him. "Max," he said, "Where are you, Big Guy? Max?"

Hearing a meow emanate from under the driver's seat, he slid between the front two seats and crouched on the rubber floor mat on his back floorboard, calling the big cat to him. Max had apparently gotten under the driver's seat and stayed there. Matthew didn't blame him at all. "Come here, Buddy. It's OK. Max, come on out," he coaxed as he saw a bit of grey fur emerge slowly from under the seat. "It's OK. It's just me," he said. "Come get some water."

Max slowly emerged from under the seat and Matthew scooped him up. As relief swept through him, he scratched the big cat behind the ears and under his chin. "Let me have a look at you," he said, reaching up to turn on the dome light. He could see that Max's eyes had been running but he figured, even for a cat, that was a good thing. It was his body's own way of clearing them out. Max hadn't been as exposed to the smoke and chemicals as badly or for as long as he had, which was why he hadn't been frantically insistent that Max be treated alongside him.

Reaching for a tissue package in the seat back, he pulled one out and poured water on it, wiping Max's face and around his eyes with it. "There, Buddy," he said. "Is that a little better? Here, drink some water," he said, setting the cup and the cat both on the rubber mat in front of him. It was cramped between the seats, with Matthew's broad shoulders, but in any other car, it would have been impossible.

Max sniffed the cup as if he wasn't sure what to make of it. He leaned in and touched it briefly with his nose, pulling back like he wasn't sure what it was and sneezed violently several times. "Yeah, I know. It's gonna be OK, Big Guy. Get a sip," coaxed Matthew. Finally, Max poked his nose in and started lapping, slowly at first. Then he picked up the pace until finally he sat back on his haunches and the cup was nearly empty. "Good job," said Matthew, is if he were talking to a child. "I'll get you some place safe as soon as I can," he said, thinking for the first time about where that would be.

He knew that he needed to finish giving his statement to Danbury but, he realized, he'd need to figure out where he was going. His own house wouldn't be habitable for a while he knew. He hoped that he'd gotten the fire out before it had a chance to burn any more than the path across his area rug and his drapes but he wasn't sure even of that.

Giving Max a few more reassuring scratches around his face and ears, he climbed back through the seats and Max crawled back under the seat. Matthew refilled the little cup and set it in place on the back floorboard just behind the driver's seat. After turning the dome light off, he slipped out without opening the door any more than he had to.

"I know I need to finish my statement," he said. "But then can I maybe get Max's things out of the house? I hope it doesn't all reek like smoke but we need his litter box, food, and food bowls at least."

"Yeah, I can get those pulled out. Tell me where they are."

"In my hall bathroom and under the kitchen counter nearest the little desk in my kitchen. The bowls are under that desk."

"OK," said Danbury, poking his phone and talking to someone to make the request.

"Thanks, man," said Matthew, very thankful to have Danbury there with him through all of this.

"They'll bring them out. Put them in the garage. Now let's go sit in my car. And get the rest of this story. If I can stand your stink," he joked, turning his nose up.

"Yeah, yeah, I'm just glad all I do is stink. Do you think they knew I was out?"

"If they did, they didn't expect you back."

"Why do you say that?"

Danbury just pointed to the front of Matthew's house. "I think you interrupted them."

As they walked up into the edge of his driveway, Matthew could see red letters painted across the front of his house that said, "Mind your own da."

"Oh!" he gasped. "But why me? What did I do to make somebody mad enough to threaten me and then try to burn my house down?"

"That's what we need to figure out," said Danbury logically. "Let's go sit in my SUV. With the windows down," he added, with a sideways glance at Matthew.

"I have a change of clothes. Somewhere," said Matthew, trying to remember what he'd done with the duffle bag. "I brought the duffle I took to Savannah out of the house with me, I think. No, I tossed it out before I grabbed the fire extinguisher and then I," he hesitated. "Oh, I put it in the Corvette when I got the cars out of the garage. I do have a change of clothes, but I want a shower first. Sorry, I'm not thinking straight. You need the rest of the story. OK, let's go."

They climbed in Danbury's SUV and Matthew said, "Where were we?"

Danbury consulted his notes, "You heard the crash. Saw the flash come through the window. And heard a rebel yell. Then you heard somebody yell. 'Mind your own damned business,' right?"

"Yeah, I think I was still stunned at that point."

"What can you tell me about the voice? Male? Female? High? Low? Ever heard it before? Anything distinctive about it?"

"Male but not low. It was following the rebel yell, so still kind of screechy but definitely male."

"Did you see the yeller at all?"

"No. It was dark when I drove up. I hadn't left as many lights on as I normally do. I'd only left a few on in the house, but it was too dark to see out through the window anyway. I didn't see anything. I just heard the engine, then the crash, then the yell, and then the firebomb. At least, I think it was in that order. No, firebomb then yell. I see why you have such a hard time getting witness statements straight. At the time, it's like it's all in slow motion, but later it's like it was all a flash or a blur."

"Yeah, I get it. You're doing fine. You didn't notice the paint though? On the front of your house. When you came home?"

"No. It was dark, I hadn't left the porch light on, though I should have, and I was tired. Wait. I think I did leave the porch light on. I'm pretty sure that I did. I just didn't notice that it wasn't on when I got home. I don't think that it was. I pulled into the garage immediately, thinking only to go crawl in bed and sleep late."

"He probably unscrewed the bulb. Or busted it out."

"Do you think he thought I was home asleep in bed and he was going to burn me in? Or do you think he knew that I wasn't home and was planning to give me a little surprise when I got home?" he asked, with a shiver, realizing that in one of those scenarios he and Max could both be dead, and in the other at least Max would have been.

"I really don't know, Doc. We'll do our best to find out. But what he wasn't," said Danbury and then paused. "He wasn't expecting you to come home. You interrupted his message. On the front of your house. You said you heard an engine start, right?"

"Yeah. Just as I was entering the house, I heard the engine start up. I thought maybe it was kids over on the golf course."

"You saw the fire and heard the yell. And then what did you do?"

"I tossed the bag out the door, slammed it closed, grabbed the keys off of the pegs by the door, and grabbed the fire extinguisher from my laundry room."

"Fast thinking. Good thing you had one."

"Yeah and that it still worked. I hadn't tested it since I moved in a couple of years ago. I'm not even sure if you can test those? Anyway I pulled the pin and just kept sweeping across the room until I didn't see flames anymore and then I darted down the hall to find Max. I closed my bedroom door, trying to keep the smoke out and hoping that he was hiding in the back of my closet, where he normally goes if there's something that scares him, like strange people in the house. He was there, and I crawled out with him and got us both out the back door."

"I put Max in the Element and got it out of the garage," continued Matthew. "Then I went back for the Corvette and called 9-1-1 and my neighbor brought me a water bottle. She disappeared into her house when the emergency vehicles were getting here, but you might want a statement from her at some point. Cordelia Drewer. On that end, just there," Matthew pointed.

"Yeah, we'll talk to all of your neighbors. In the morning. My guess is that he was painting. Then you came down the street. So, he gave that up. Went around back. Got on the bike. And then delivered the fire bomb. And the message, verbally. He went back across the golf course. And was long gone. Before you had the fire out."

Danbury's phone went off and he looked at the display before answering, "Danbury." After a moment's pause, he added, "OK, I'm on my way."

"Something else happened?" asked Matthew.

"Yeah. Maybe this starts to make sense now. Maybe this was a diversion. The Peak guys patrolling the Lingle house. They just gave chase over there. I've gotta go, Doc. I'll be back. As soon as I can. Meanwhile, go talk to the arson team. They're in your garage. Where can I find you later?"

"I'm going to Cici's, I guess. My neighbor offered," he said as he climbed out of the car. "But she has a yappy Pomeranian who won't think much of Max. I do have my phone," he added.

"OK. I'm sorry, Doc," said Danbury, as he turned on his lights, made an impressive U-turn, given the size of the SUV, and tore out of the quiet neighborhood that was no longer completely asleep. Matthew looked over and saw that a huddle of neighbors had reconvened across the street. Or maybe they'd never left. He wasn't sure. He thought he owed them something so he walked over to join them.

"Are you OK?" he heard Mrs. Lewis ask as he approached.

"I think so. I'm certainly better than I could have been," he said. "Thank you for calling 9-1-1. I did too eventually, but I was trying to get the fire out and my cat out safely first."

"Cordelia said you'd gotten your cat out. I'm so glad to hear that," she said, and the other neighbors echoed her sentiment. "Do you know what started it?"

Taking a deep breath that he was now thankful to be able to take, he figured that he might as well get it over with. "It wasn't a what, it was a who," he said. "The police will want to ask you all if you heard or saw anything unusual tonight. So do think about that."

He could see the alarm registering on the faces of several of his neighbors under the street lights as what had actually happened sank in.

“Somebody did that on purpose?” exclaimed Mr. Lewis indignantly. “But why?”

“I might not ever know,” said Matthew. “But Warren Danbury, my friend and a homicide detective out of Raleigh, already has a theory. He’s chasing it right now in fact.”

“What happened?” asked another neighbor. “You just woke up and your house was on fire?”

“That could have happened, but no, thankfully I’d just come home.”

“Oh,” she said, looking at him in bewilderment, clearly not understanding why anyone would only be coming home at two in the morning.

“I’d been out of town today but decided to come home tonight instead of in the morning,” he explained. “Though I guess it was morning. Anyway, I’d only just pulled into the garage and gotten in the house when somebody busted my back window and threw a fire bomb through it.”

All of the faces registered the horror they must have felt, he thought, as he calmly told them what had happened. He’d been angry and he was sure he would be again to see his house, his haven, in the daylight. “I won’t tell you more until you’ve talked to the police because I don’t want to taint your testimony, anything you might have seen or heard.”

“I didn’t see or hear anything until your smoke detectors started blaring,” said Mr. Lewis and the others agreed. “And that was enough to wake the dead,” he added, seeming immediately to regret his choice of words. “I mean,” he started to correct himself.

“It’s OK. I know what you mean,” said Matthew. “And it wasn’t just the smoke detectors. It was those along with the security alarm. I was just disabling it when I heard the crash of the window and saw the firebomb come through.”

“Did you see who threw it?” asked one of the women, curiously.

“No. It was too dark out. And at that point, I wasn’t concerned with what was outside of the window though I probably should have been,” he said thoughtfully. “I was just trying to get the fire and my cat both out. And then my cars. And it wasn’t until the EMS folks got here that the adrenaline ran out and I collapsed.”

“Oh, we’re so sorry, Honey,” said one of the women, whose name he wasn't recalling but who looked genuinely concerned for him. "Is there anything we can do?"

"Not at the moment," he answered. "Thanks, but I've got to go talk to the arson squad and police. I was giving my statement when Detective Danbury got called away to chase something that's probably connected. I'll talk to you more about it all later, if you want, but thanks for your concern."

"Of course, Shugah, of course," said the neighbor who he now remembered was Sarah Wright. She'd been some sort of beauty queen from South Carolina, if his memory was correct. He turned and walked back up to his end unit, feeling the weight of every step. His sofa was upended in his front yard, along with most of the furnishings from his great room, but he didn't notice those as he trudged toward the garage that was buzzing with activity, to find the arson expert.

After answering all of their questions, giving them total access to his house, and providing his cell number, he asked them to contact him as soon as they knew anything or as soon as he was allowed to get back in to get things out of it. They told him they'd be there for several hours yet.

Thanking them profusely for pulling Max's things out of the house, he picked up the kitty litter box, carried it to the Element, and set it down behind. It was a heavy box, a self-cleaning unit that raked the box each time Max went in and dumped the clumps into a little bag in the front so that it was easily pulled out and replaced. At the moment, Matthew thought he should try to pull it out, dump it there in the edge of the woods, and put it back in because he hadn't asked them to get the box of replacement bags from the house.

With that chore accomplished, he went back for Max's bowls and food bin, thanked the workers again. He retrieved the duffle bag from the Corvette, locked that up, and tossed everything in the back of the Element. He couldn't remember having been this exhausted recently, though he'd pulled an all-nighter the month before. His whole body felt weighted like he was climbing uphill carrying an extra hundred pounds or so. Checking to be sure that Max had plenty of room where he was still crouched under the driver's seat and that he couldn't get through to get under his own feet, Matthew climbed in and started the car.

He had some phone calls to make. He thoroughly dreaded most of them. He figured it was now mid-morning on Saturday in London, so he started with the obvious one to at least tell Cici that he and Max would be bunking at her place for a while. He was sure she wouldn't mind at all, but it was the right thing to do. Except that he'd have to tell her why. That was the part he was dreading.

"Hey, Matthew," she answered, sounding chipper. "Can't you sleep either? Miss me that much?" she asked, slyly but jokingly.

"I wish I could. Cees, are you OK with Max and me staying at your house for a little while? I have no idea how long. Could be weeks, could be months. I might not even know how long for a little while."

"Sure," she said, hesitating, and then got to it. "Matthew, what's wrong?" she asked, sounding thoroughly alarmed. She knew him better than anyone and she would know just from his voice when he was in trouble, he thought.

He told her what had happened, and she asked, sounding alarmed, "Matthew, are you OK? Really truly, OK?"

"Yeah, I think so. I just need a shower and some sleep. And a place for Max and me to crash for a while."

"You know that you can. My house is there and I'm not. You're more than welcome. Sleep in my bed, the other one's a joke with your height anyway," she said, referencing a day bed that she'd added to her second bedroom to make the office somewhat usable for company, though it never really had been. "I'll turn the air on for you from my app, so hopefully it won't be too stuffy for you when you get there. You'll still need to adjust the appliances. I left the fridge on but just barely. My hot water heats on demand, so you should be OK there. If I think of anything else, I'll text you."

"Thanks, Cees. I need to call my sister. I'm going to be a bad brother and ask her to talk to the parents while I sleep."

"That's not bad. I don't blame you. Your Mom's gonna flip!"

"Oh, you'd be surprised. She worries but she prays about whatever worries her and she's pretty tough. She might not look it but she is."

"OK, please be careful, Matthew, please promise me that you'll be careful. I love you and I want to come home to you. Please promise me that you're OK."

"I promise," he said, refraining from pointing out that he hadn't been uncareful so far. “And I love you too, Cees.”

There, he thought, as they ended the call, they’d said it and it was out in the open between them now. He was too exhausted to know how he felt about that at the moment. Instead of pondering it as he was heading west to Cici’s house, he called his sister just as the sun was coming up behind him in his rear-view mirror.

She sounded sleepy and annoyed until he told her what he needed and then she was immediately alert and concerned. Big sisters could be that way, he thought, as he asked her to call their parents when the hour was decent enough to do so.

“I’m just pulling up to Cici’s now,” he said. “And I don’t think I’ve ever been this thoroughly exhausted. Please just tell them that I’ll call them as soon as I can get Max and me settled in, maybe grab a quick shower, and get a few hours of sleep. The next few days will likely be rough with all of the investigation, the insurance claim, and all of that.”

“OK, Bud. I can do that. You know you’re welcome to come stay with us, if you’d like.”

“Thanks, Sis. Cici’s house is empty and it’s closer to work and my house, but I do appreciate the offer.”

“And Matthew,” she said, choking up. “I’m so glad that you’re OK. And thank you. I knew that you’d always take good care of Max.”

“G’night, Sis,” he said, as he had slipped out of the car and was punching in all of the access codes outside of Cici’s door.

In the end he got Max settled in and collapsed into Cici’s bed, forgoing the shower and any more thought about anything, except the fleeting thought that he’d have plenty of time to wash her sheets and get the smoke smell out long before she came home.

32. By daylight

Matthew awoke slowly with the feeling of weight on him. It was like climbing out of a deep pit. As he began to surface from a deep sleep, odd memories from the night before nudged at the corners of his mind and he panicked, feeling something holding his head down. As he jumped upright, disoriented, he realized that Max had been curled around his head. "I'm sorry, Buddy," he said, as the big cat looked indignantly at him from across the queen-sized bed where he'd landed when Matthew jumped up startled.

"What a way to start a Saturday, huh?" he said, reaching over to scratch the big cat under the chin. "You need breakfast and I need a shower." He remembered having dumped the contents of Max's food and water bowls, along with the contents of the litter box in the woods at the end of his street. He'd managed to fill only the water bowl before crawling into Cici's very comfy bed and gone comatose.

"I'm not looking forward to this day," he said. "But let's get it going." He was stiff and sore as he pulled himself out of the bed, down the staircase, and into the kitchen. Realizing that he smelled horrible, he vowed to tackle that problem next. Rinsing and refilling Max's water and food bowls in the kitchen, he started the coffee maker, relieved to see that Cici had left coffee in a canister that she hadn't thrown out. He set it for a full pot. He figured he'd need it.

Looking around for his duffle bag, he realized that he'd left in in the car. He disabled the alarm and slipped out the front door to retrieve the bag. On the way back in, Cici's next-door-neighbor was openly gawking at him. Well, let her, he thought, as he gave her a big grin, waved, and said, cheerfully, "Good morning!" He didn't realize that it was already after one in the afternoon but neither did he particularly care. He was sure he looked like he'd been in a train wreck and smelled worse, but he didn't care about that either.

Inside he shed his clothes in her laundry room and tossed them all into the wash together, setting an extra rinse cycle and adding some sweet-smelling fabric softener. "That should do it maybe," he muttered to Max, who had stuck his nose around the corner curiously. He fixed a large mug of coffee with extra sugar because there was no cream in the fridge yet. He drank it down and poured a second one. Carrying it and the duffle bag back upstairs, he was determined to get the hot shower that he was truly craving and in dire need of. He wasn't sure how well anyone could see inside Cici's house, but he figured anybody who worked hard enough to stare at him through her windows deserved what they saw. He was in a foul mood, he realized, and he hoped that the shower would improve it.

He had to wait for what felt like an eternity for the hot water to arrive, but he knew that was one of the drawbacks to the gas heat-on-demand concept. While you didn't waste the energy having a big tank full of hot water all of the time, you did waste time and water waiting for it to heat and arrive. When the water was finally running hot, he stepped into her shower and let the hot water sluice all over him for some time before he even bothered to start lathering up. It felt heavenly, he thought, as he stood and enjoyed the sensation.

Sniffing the flowery soaps and shampoo in her shower, he chuckled, thinking that he might smell decidedly feminine for a day or two until he could to something about it. But it would surely be better than the smoke and chemical smell that he'd been sporting since about two that morning. Sometimes getting clean when you felt completely filthy was the best feeling ever, he thought.

When he finally emerged from the shower and was drying off, he heard his phone going off with Cici's ring tone. He dashed out to her bedroom and found his phone amongst the pile of covers that he hadn't bothered to straighten. "Hey, Cees," he said.

"Hi Matthew. You're awake. Do you feel human again yet?"

"I'm getting there. I just got out of a hot shower."

"Oh, enough said. I'd ask if you left any hot water but," and she laughed without finishing the sentence.

He loved her laugh and he hadn't heard nearly enough of it at the end of their relationship, before they'd broken up, he thought. "Yeah, but I could shower all day and not run out. I know, I know," he laughed with her and it felt good. "And it's great once it finally gets there."

"Hey! Don't be knocking my endless supply of hot water! You of all people," she teased.

"I'm not. Thank you, Cici, for giving me a familiar place to stay. My world is going to be a bit up-side-down for a while I think. I wouldn't want to impose on either Monica or my parents, and your place is closer to work and where I can more easily check on my place anyway."

"It's my pleasure. Really. I just wish I were there with you," she added mischievously, with a husky quality to her voice that he knew well.

"Yeah, me too," he said, and truly meant it. Whatever they'd been through over the years and whatever they still didn't see exactly eye-to-eye on, he knew that he loved her and he hoped that somehow they'd work it all out when she got home. But that was too far away to contemplate just now.

"Matthew, the Porsche," she said, and hesitated. "You're going to need my garage space for the Corvette. There's no parking on the streets in my neighborhood." Of course there wasn't, he thought. This was Quarry after all and there was an ordinance for everything. Cici didn't seem to mind but it was one of the reasons that he had no desire to live there. He said none of this and instead waited for her to finish what was on her mind. "I sent you the forms you'll need to sell the car on my behalf. I don't want to pile anything else on you now, but if James will agree to the price and it's a fair one – I've checked – then please sell it to him and put your Corvette in the garage."

"Ahhh," he sighed. "I haven't even checked my mail yet or my voicemail or called my parents. What time is it?" He held the phone out to see and answered his own question, "Wow, it's already after one. Thank you, Cici. I'll see what I can do to make that happen."

"Yeah, you keep this schedule up and you'll be nocturnal. I wanted to check on you and talk to you about the car, but I also wanted to give you the update on the faux lawyer you asked about."

Matthew chuckled at the many worlds between the thug calling Wayne Adams a fugazy lawyer and Cici calling him a faux lawyer. “I haven’t seen anything yet, obviously. What did they find?”

“Mostly that he doesn’t exist.”

“What do you mean, ‘doesn’t exist?’ ”

“I mean, there’s a record of a Wayne Adams, Attorney at Law in Ohio, with a UBE bar result that transferred to North Carolina.”

“OK, so what’s the problem?”

“Nobody can find a trace of the man before that,” she said. “But they’re still looking. You’ll see an updated email sometime later today, I’m guessing. But Clarice called to tell me what she’d found this morning. Or rather what she hadn’t found.”

“Huh, so he’s a ghost. How appropriate.”

“What?”

“Oh, just that he’s haunting the rightful owners of what might actually be a haunted house, if you believe in such things.”

“Not really,” she said.

“Yeah, me either, I don’t think. But the jury’s still out on that one,” he said in her vernacular. “So I’ll have to let you know.”

“OK, you do that,” she said lightly. “I’ll let you get on with your busy day now. I’m so sorry that you’ve been through so much and I’m not there to help you, but I am truly thrilled that you and Max are staying at my place.”

“Thanks, Cees,” he said, and then figured he’d beat her to the punch this time. “I miss you and I love you.”

He could hear the smile in her voice as she replied, “I miss you and I love you too, Matthew. Please be safe!”

They ended the call and he clicked to see what he’d missed on his phone before getting up from her bed and going to find his clothes for the day, which might also be for a few days at this rate. After he’d dressed, he ran his fingers through his hair to comb it, swiped a spare toothbrush from her linen closet to quickly brush his teeth, checked on Max again, and then went out to his car to go find something to eat. She’d cleaned out her pantry, all but a few cans and some sealed canisters of flour, salt, sugar, and the like. There was literally nothing to eat there.

As he opened the door of his Element, the repugnant smell of smoke assaulted his nose. He put the windows down and decided to forgo the air conditioning for a while. He was happy not to actually need it on this lovely spring day. Calling Danbury on the way, he learned that some helpful friends had boarded up his house this morning and Matthew was free to enter when he needed to and to call in an inspector for the initial damage assessment.

"It looks pretty bad," said Danbury. "Just keep in mind though. When you go by there. That there's no structural damage. It could have been a lot worse. You got it out pretty fast. And that's the Public Service Announcement. The PSA for smoke detectors. And fire extinguishers. You should be the poster child. Or spokesperson. Everybody should have them."

"Thanks for the positive spin, Man. And thanks for showing up last night. You must be totally wiped out too."

"I slept a couple of hours. That's all I need."

"I'm off to get some breakfast now. All I've had is coffee. But I swear I feel like I could sleep for a week, even after drinking most of a pot of it!"

He told Danbury what Cici had told him about Wayne Adams and his lack of a paper trail prior to Ohio or about sixteen years previously. "How old is the guy, anyway?"

"Early forties, I think," said Danbury. "Maybe mid-forties. But he's in the wind."

"What do you mean, 'in the wind?'"

"I mean Libby called me this morning. She was frantic. Asked if I meant what I said. When I said she could call if she needed anything. She said Wayne didn't come home last night. She knew there couldn't be a missing person report. Not yet. He hasn't been gone long enough. But she said that she had a bad feeling. She says he's never done that before. Stayed out all night without calling. She said he called when he worked late. Or went out of town. He's not answering his phone. And she can't track it."

"Wow. Oh, and what was that about last night? When you bolted to go chase somebody?"

"Still don't know. I had our guys parked. Right outside the Lingle house. All night. There was a strange car. Circling around on the street. Out in front of your practice. And then they pulled up. To the end of the driveway. One of our Peak boys had an iPad out. The light might have spooked them. They ran. The Peak guys gave chase. And called in backup to the house. I was afraid somebody was luring them away. Away from the front of the house. To come in the back way."

"Did you find anything?"

"Nothing. The Peak guys did a good job though. They circled and came back in. From that back entrance. They thought of it too. That it could be a ploy to lure them away. And they didn't fall for it. Oh, and one more piece of good news. It's a little late. But we got the search warrant. For Wayne's office. Specifically, for the Lingle Estate records. We can enter, search, and seize. Anything related to the Lingle estate. We're putting a team together. To go in later today."

"Wow! I wish that had come through a couple of days ago!"

"Yeah, I'm with you there. I was beginning to think that it wouldn't come through. Not at all."

"OK, I'm going to get some food. And I still need to talk to my parents. Then I'm going by the house, I guess. Ironic, isn't it, that the paperwork I need to call about my homeowner's insurance is IN the house, the house you're calling about when you need the insurance. It's in a fireproof box, at least, but I guess I can see why people get safe deposit boxes at the bank."

"Yeah, it's a process. I'll be around today. Yell if you need anything."

"Thanks, Danbury, I appreciate it."

After placing and picking up his order at a nearby chicken fast food restaurant, Matthew decided that it was time to face the music and he went to his house, eating his chicken biscuit on the way. He was nearing his street when he finished eating and decided to crank up the proverbial music. He had to call his parents. He was thankful to see his Corvette still parked safely at the end of the street as he pulled in his driveway, noting the police line tape that surrounded his house. His mother answered, sounding very concerned.

After telling her what had happened the night before, as best he could anyway, he answered all of her myriad questions and reassured her that he was fine and that he and Max were staying at Cici's. Jackie, of course, invited him to stay with them and she said he could have his old room back. Unlike the Lingle house though where every room looked like the occupant had just stepped out of it, his room had undergone more severe changes in his absence.

"I'd never take your sewing, craft, yoga, and whatever else room, Mom. It's yours now. Besides Cici's is closer to work and to my place. I'll need to be close by as this process unfolds. I'm back at my place now and I need to find the home owners information and get an insurance agent out, pronto. They've cleared me to be in it. There's no structural damage, just a lot of cosmetic and smoke damage apparently."

"Still, Matthew, you know that you're welcome here. We'd love to have you with us. You can have the guest suite with the sitting room and attached bath. It's not the Taj Mahal, but it's quiet and comfortable. You can bring Max. Maybe he and Cleo still remember each other from when he was a kitten." Cleo too had been Monica's cat initially until Stephano's allergies had sent the sweet calico to live with their parents.

"I appreciate it, I really do, but I've got Cici's place all to myself since she's in London and I think she might be offended if I left at this point. She was thrilled that I was going to be staying there for a while."

"And she was OK with Max being there too?"

"She's fine with it, Mom. Really, she is. She wouldn't say so if she weren't. You know Cici."

"Yes," answered his mother with some concern in her voice. "I do."

"I'm still planning to come to church in the morning," he offered. "And I hope to still bring Mrs. Drewer with me. So I will see you tomorrow. And I'm fine, I really am, just fine."

"OK, sweetheart. You'll let us know if you need anything? Anything at all?"

"I promise. I will."

"OK, I love you. Son."

"I love you too, Mom."

Now there loomed ahead the chore that he was dreading at least as much as talking to his parents about what had almost happened to him. He had to go into his house and see the damage by daylight. He wondered if he still had power. He clicked the garage door opener and was momentarily happy when he saw the door open. Then he smelled the putrid odor of indistinguishable charred objects and saw the heaps inside. The area rug that had caught fire first or the wet charred pieces of it were piled in a heap with other indistinguishable items, his drapes probably if anything remained of those.

The firefighters must have sprayed the rug down with water when they arrived. He was hoping that they'd dragged it out first or he'd have severe water damage to deal with. Next to the rug his butter cream leather sofa was upended and similarly charred, sodden, and sagging. He hadn't remembered that being on fire, but then, he had been just sweeping at whatever looked like it was burning until it wasn't anymore. They were smart to flip it over, he thought, to ensure that nothing underneath or within the padding was still smoldering. What he didn't see, and he wasn't sure if it was a good thing or not, was his satchel with his computer in it. He'd left it on the end of this sofa and that had burned.

They were just things, he reminded himself. All things that could be replaced. And then he saw it. His Les Paul guitar was propped against the end of the sofa and it was in shambles. He wasn't sure if it had been stepped on or burned or both. It was a mess. "Ohh," he groaned aloud just as he heard footsteps approaching from behind.

"I guess I didn't do a very good job," said Mrs. Drewer as she walked with Oscar in her arms to stand beside him surveying the garage. Oscar leaned over for a scratch on the head and Matthew reached out and gave him a perfunctory one.

"Hi, Mrs. Drewer. With what?"

"Keeping an eye on your house while you were away."

She was completely serious, he knew, but for some reason this struck him as funny and he started laughing. The more he tried to stop laughing, the more he howled until he was nearly breathless again. She looked at him, incredulously at first, then eventually she joined in, laughing probably just for the sake of laughing with him.

"I'm sorry," he finally said. "I don't know why that struck me as so funny, but I guess maybe I just needed a good laugh."

"I can see why you might. Have you been inside yet?"

"I haven't."

"Do you want to do that alone? Or would you prefer some company while you sift through?"

"I wouldn't subject you to that, but you're welcome to do the walk-through if you want. The garage alone smells pretty rank. I'm hoping that they dragged all of this out of the house before they doused it with the hose. Otherwise, the water damage will be worse than the smoke damage."

"If it helps you to be able to go in, I think that they did. There were people here all night, and this morning all of this was out in your front yard. I guess they pulled it in here for you."

"I guess I should get started," he said, pulling out his phone. "I'm not sure if the insurance company will require it, but I want pictures to document everything."

"Smart thinking," she said and waited patiently for him to photograph the remnants of his belongings in the heap, the sofa, and instruments.

"Just because it isn't out here, doesn't mean it's salvageable," he sighed. "Everything in there will smell like smoke." He pulled the key out and unlocked the door that he'd come through in the middle of the night before, trying to shrug off the feeling of déjà vu that he was experiencing.

As they walked in, the acrid smoke smell hung heavily in the air and Matthew walked through, opening windows as he went. His front door had indeed been busted in. It was the only of the three doors, ironically, that had actually still been locked. It, and the hole where his bay window had been, were both boarded over. That was Danbury's doing, he was sure, as was dragging the sodden remains of his belongings into the garage and out of the front yard. He made a mental note to thank him for it.

He found his satchel tossed against the far corner of the room, with the computer still inside. He guessed that it was not smoldering so they'd moved it when they hauled the sofa out. Other than the bag smelling really foul, the machine inside might still work. He put it by the garage door to take with him.

"You know, Matthew," said Mrs. Drewer, watching his face fall as he walked into each room, "I'll be happy to try to wash some of this for you. Your clothes and bedding might be salvageable. Your bedroom doesn't seem to have been as smoky as the rest, so maybe that'll be OK. How else can I help? You might need someone around when the repairs begin and you're at work. I'd be happy to really keep an eye on things for you this time," she said with a wink.

He couldn't believe the change in this woman who had once been so nosy and asked him all sorts of personal questions and added her supposition to any he wouldn't answer. Since he'd befriended her, she must feel that she had the inside track and she no longer needed to probe. Whatever the reason, he was thankful for her help and readily agreed. He found the spare key in his kitchen drawer, the one Cici had given back when they'd split up the year before.

"Here," he said. "If you're willing to help out, you should have a key. It works on both of the remaining doors. I'd love to just leave these windows all the way open, but there's too much in here that isn't damaged. I guess I'll sift and do what I can, but first I need to find my paperwork for the insurance company and give them a call to get the claim process started."

"OK, I'll leave you to it. Just bring your bedding and clothes over, as you're able, and we'll start the wash."

"Thank you, Mrs. Drewer. I was dreading seeing this by daylight but your company helped. And thank you for your offer of a bed last night. I didn't think that was fair to either Oscar or Max, so I went over to my ex-girlfriend's house."

"Ah, I'm sure that was much more fun than the old lady next door," she teased.

"Oh. I guess I haven't mentioned it, but Cici's in London. She's not there and her house is empty. Or at least it was until last night."

"Is that the tiny little fiery redhead I saw over here a lot when you first moved in? I haven't seen much of her lately, have I?"

A strawberry blond with long, thick hair, Cici was both tiny and fiery so she had it mostly right, he thought.

"Yes, ma'am. That's Cici. And no you haven't seen her lately. We broke up about a year ago. We were just starting to talk to each other again, but she's working with a client in England, probably for about a year. She'd been asking me to book a flight and come see her, but with all of this going on that will have to wait, at least until I can get it all sorted out."

He realized that he'd just shared prime information with the woman that he'd previously considered the biggest gossip in Peak. Something had definitely changed lately and he didn't at all mind telling her what was going on in his personal life. He actually trusted her, he realized.

After finding his paperwork and calling the insurance agency, he hauled armloads of bedding and some of the clean clothes that were hanging in his closet and stuffed in his drawers over to Mrs. Drewer's house. Those could be washed, he figured, while he waited for his call to be returned from his insurance agent. He packed his hamper with as much of the dirty clothes as he could stuff in it and put it in the Element. He threw the overflow into a laundry bag and tossed it in too.

While he was waiting, figuring that a return call could take a while on a Saturday, he unloaded his refrigerator and some of the things in his cabinets, packing some in a cooler from the garage and throwing out the rest. It wouldn't do any good left at his house, he thought, but taking some of the items from his refrigerator to restock Cici's could stave off an immediate trip to the grocery store. He wasn't a fan of grocery shopping. He did it only when he absolutely had to.

On his last trip to Mrs. Drewer's house, he'd insisted on picking her up for church in the morning, and she'd finally relented and agreed. Checking the church's app on his phone, he saw that the next teaching series, which would be starting in the morning, was perfectly titled, "Jesus + Nothing = Everything." That sounded like a good place to start for someone who had been angry with God for over forty years.

Checking his mail, he'd found the note from Cici about her car and a document from his insurance agency. He'd gotten the call back and made an appointment for an adjuster to come by at six to do an initial assessment and begin the paperwork. He figured he had enough time to take a load of his clothes over to Cici's to start washing them. Because smelling like a flower wasn't an option for him indefinitely, he packed his own mountain fresh laundry detergent and pulled his soaps from his shower.

Calling James on the way to talk specifics about the car, they'd agreed to meet back at Cici's. James was apparently very serious about buying the Porsche and about not giving anyone else the opportunity to do so first. Matthew hadn't mentioned the fire yet, thinking that there was time enough to do that in person.

33. Wheeling and dealing

After a white-knuckled drive with James behind the wheel of Cici's Porsche for a test drive, they had come to terms on selling it. James had agreed to Cici's price proposal with a huge grin on his face that Matthew didn't remember seeing much except when there was a woman involved. He agreed to bring a cashier's check to Cici's law office on Tuesday afternoon and meet Matthew there to sign all of the paperwork.

Appearing to be only slightly concerned with Matthew's current fire situation, James just shook his head and said, "Man, how do you get yourself into these things?"

Matthew didn't have a history of getting into much trouble of any kind so he just shrugged in reply and said, "Wrong place, wrong time, I guess."

James left, thrilled with the pending transaction, and Matthew was relieved to have that one thing successfully resolved. Noting that it was after five, he checked on Max, who was happily sunning himself on the end of Cici's sofa under a window. Matthew swapped out another load of laundry, wishing that Cici had opted for the large capacity washer and dryer instead of the stacked units, and climbed back in his Element to go meet the insurance adjuster.

*****

The first order of business apparently was getting industrial air purifiers distributed throughout the house to mitigate the smell and improve the air quality in general to begin the necessary work. Matthew was dubious, but the adjuster said that he'd seen it work with kitchen fires and the like, so there was a chance to salvage some of what was left of Matthew's belongings. He'd have to replace his soft leather sofa that he'd loved, he knew, and the matching chair and ottoman, which were both smoke damaged, but he figured that was relatively small, considering what might have been. His beds might also, said the adjuster, have to be replaced because if the smell of smoke was going to linger, it'd be in thicker fabrics with stuffing, such as these.

After the adjuster left, promising to have the air purifiers and an initial estimate to fix the damage by Monday, Matthew didn't feel like going back to Cici's lonely house quite yet. While he was thankful to be able to stay there, it wasn't home, at least not his. He'd given Max plenty of food and water and he wasn't worried about him needing attention, so he decided to check in with Danbury to see if the raid on Wayne Adams' office had turned up anything and also if the man himself had turned up yet. He climbed into his Element, which was loaded with more clothing packed in trash bags and made the call.

"Hey, Doc," he heard Danbury's gruff voice answer. Something must not be going well, thought Matthew.

"Hey, I was just checking in to see if you'd found anything in the files from the law firm? And if anybody has seen Wayne Adams?"

"We found some records. For the Lingle estate. But they aren't good."

"Oh?"

"I'm in Raleigh now. Just delivered copies of some files. To a data forensic expert. The Lingle accounts are drained. Hoping he can find where it all went."

"What? Penn said her mom came from money and there was plenty of that when she left ten years ago! What do you think happened to it all?"

"I think Wayne Adams happened. I'm guessing it's why he's MIA. That and maybe your fire."

"You think he threw the fire bomb that set my house on fire?"

"He's a person of interest. In that and Allan's murder. Though maybe not directly. He might have orchestrated both. And now embezzlement. Serious embezzlement."

"How's Penn taking this?"

"I haven't told her yet."

"Oh! I was thinking about going by their house to check in before I went back to Cici's tonight. And I'd thought about bringing pizza. Maybe I shouldn't then."

"No, that sounds good. What kind of pizza?"

Matthew just laughed. Trust Danbury to always be focused on the food angle of any situation. "Cici and I have a favorite Italian restaurant just outside of Peak. It's on the way to her house and not much out of the way. I thought maybe I'd call in a take-out order and pick up some large pizzas to bring over."

"That sounds good. I can be there in about a half hour. Maybe one would be pepperoni and Italian sausage?"

Matthew laughed, "You're putting your order in, huh? Sure. Got it. See you there."

Calling in the order for three large pizzas, he figured one veggie, one cheese, and one Italian sausage and pepperoni should do it. As he drove the short distance to pick them up, he wondered how Danbury would break the awful news to Penn and Leo. Once again, he was glad he wasn't on the hook for that job.

When he entered the restaurant, the delightful smell of garlic and herbs greeted him and made him salivate. He was hungry. He realized that he'd had breakfast after lunch time, but that was all he'd eaten so far. The pizzas were ready and waiting for him. He carried them out to the car and vowed that he'd get them all the way to the Lingle house intact though that would be no small feat.

He managed not to open the lids and pull out a slice enroute. He was sincerely hoping that the pizza smell wafting through his car would help to overtake the smoke smell that he was growing used to. Given the smoky clothes in the garbage bags in back and the fact that his seats were cloth upholstery and absorbed odors, he was sure that the smell was still prevalent. As he pulled up to the Lingle house, the front door opened and Penn and Leo stepped out onto the front porch.

"Hi, Dr. Paine," said Leo. "Danbury should be here in just a minute and we thought you were him."

“You can call me Matthew, you know,” he answered, thinking that Leo seemed to be stuck somewhere a decade earlier in his mental assessment of himself. He moved like he was much younger than Matthew, though Matthew guessed they must be close to the same age. Leo was more agile, with a slender wiry build, and not as muscular or as tall as Matthew.

“I brought dinner,” Matthew announced, as he pulled the pizzas across the passenger seat and climbed out with them. “From my favorite Italian restaurant. And yes, Danbury said he was on the way from Raleigh and he should be here shortly.” He carried them to the porch and followed Penn and Leo into the house, down the hallway, and into the kitchen, placing them on the table. Matthew washed his hands while Penn pulled out plates, glasses, and napkins and then he helped her set the table for five.

Leo tapped on Malcolm’s door and he appeared, not limping much that Matthew could tell, and greeted him, “Hi, Dr. Paine.”

Penn took drink orders and had just poured them all when they heard Danbury’s voice from the front door.

“Hello?” he called.

“Back here,” said Penn. “Just follow the lovely aroma of the pizzas that Matthew brought.”

Carrying a box into the kitchen, Danbury appeared unshaven and a bit disheveled, more so than Matthew recalled having seen him, but he himself was certainly no one to talk today, he thought.

“Just put that down over there on the counter and come have some pizza,” she said brightly. “I was going to thaw out some leftovers from the freezer but I’m glad now that I forgot to take them out in time.”

Obeying, Danbury washed his hands and joined the others at the table.

Matthew dipped his head, saying his own blessing and expressing his thanks again for walking away from a fire that could have been far more devastating that it was. The room grew suddenly quiet as they all dug into the pizzas. Matthew thought that he might be hungry enough this evening to keep up with Danbury. He had four huge slices and had to call it quits with half a large pizza, but he watched in amazement as Danbury devoured five before he gave up, finally proclaiming himself satisfied.

With the dinner plates in the dishwasher and the leftover pizza stored in plastic bins in the refrigerator, Penn had made and served coffee when Danbury spoke up. Matthew inwardly cringed because he knew what was coming.

"Penn, Leo, we need to talk. I have some bad news."

Neither of them showed any huge amount of surprise when Danbury explained the monetary situation. "I have statements," said Danbury. "The files that we took out of Wayne's office. That I'd like you both to look through."

"Why?" asked Penn. "If there's nothing there, there's nothing there."

"Yes, but it had to have gone somewhere," said Danbury. "And I was hoping to figure out where. With all of these files. Surely there's a trail in here somewhere."

"OK," she sighed. "Let's have a look."

Leo literally rolled up the sleeves of the jean shirt he was wearing as Danbury placed the box in the center of the table. They started pulling file folders out of it.

"That top stack there. In the accordion folders. Those are printouts. From files on the computer. Some of it looks like gibberish. It doesn't mean anything to me. But maybe you'll spot something. Something that makes sense. Or looks familiar."

Leo pursed his lips and blew air up his face, blowing back the hair that was falling into his eyes. He started glancing at files and making piles of folders.

"This could be awhile, Doc," said Danbury. "You don't have to stay. Unless you just want to help."

"I do," said Matthew. "I don't know if there's anything in here that relates at all to my house being set on fire, but if there is, I want to find it. Besides I'm staying at Cici's now and all I have to do tonight is a ton more laundry that I'm not looking forward to."

"You're welcome to stay here," said Penn. "We have plenty of room as you've seen."

Matthew shook his head, thankful that she was the fourth person in less than twenty-four hours to offer him a place to stay. Everyone except James, who had seen him settled in at Cici's, and the elusively private Danbury had offered, he noted. Malcolm excused himself, looking uncomfortable to be involved in the family finances. He said that he was going to his room to study for an upcoming final exam in his nursing program.

The room grew quiet again, except for the sound of flipping pages and an occasional sigh or throat clearing. Matthew wasn't sure what he was looking for, but he helped sort the folders and started looking through some that contained printouts of ledgers. One set seemed to be a listing of household expenses that Wayne had used funds from the estate to pay for. He skimmed the entries. They looked to be legitimate. Nothing jumped off the page at him, anyway.

Leo, he noticed, was running his finger quickly down rows of intricate number strings and flipping pages quickly. Both of the Lingle brothers must have gotten the knack for strings of numbers, thought Matthew, as he returned to his lists.

After a few minutes, Leo said, "Hey, look at this!"

Danbury, who was sitting next to him on one side, and Penn from the other both leaned over to see what he was pointing excitedly at. "These look like the strings of numbers that Allan had written in his notebooks." He jumped up from the table and ran upstairs, returning after a few minutes with one of Allan's tiny notebooks. "I found it," he said, triumphantly.

Sliding back into his seat, Leo opened the notebook to the page where the strings of numbers were written. He pulled it over the top of the files he was going through, computer print outs that looked to be ledgers. The lines were cryptically coded.

"This one matches!" he said excitedly, as he ran his finger down the columns of number. "Look, this is the same string here as in Allan's notebook. And here's the other one! Maybe they're really the important ones."

"Or they're the only ones that Allan overheard," offered Penn.

"Either way they must mean something," said Leo.

"How many are there?" asked Penn.

Leo ran his fingers back and forth and turned through a few more pages. "I can spot eight of these number strings that are repeated in the pages here. There are more numbers in the columns out beside them and lettered entries too, but they don't spell anything."

Danbury pulled out his phone and poked it a few times to make a call.

"Hey, Ed. Danbury here. Yeah, listen, I've got a question. Any luck with any of the files? We have strings of numbers. A couple of them, specifically. That seem to be important."

After a pause, he said, "Yeah, hang on," and put his hand out to Leo, who handed him the notebooks and the file with the same strings of numbers. "There are two strings. Ready?" He repeated each one twice and provided the timestamp and file name for the ledger sheet that Leo had found them on. "They might be in other places too. But we found them there." After another pause, he answered, "No, I don't know what they are. No idea. I was hoping you could tell us." And then, he added, "Sure. Thanks."

"He's working on it," reported Danbury. "He'll focus on just those strings. Good work, Leo. Putting that together. They were just strings of numbers. Before you recognized them."

"Yeah, but they're still just strings of numbers right now," Leo responded. "I hope your guy can figure out what they are and why Allan thought they were so important."

"If anybody can, he can," Danbury reassured him. "It just might take some time."

"What we do know," said Penn, "is that Leo was carrying packages back and forth for Wayne and associates. Maybe those strings are some sort of access codes for those packages."

"That's a possibility," said Danbury. "They're very likely access codes to something."

Matthew could feel himself fading and decided to call it a night. "I think I'm going to head back to Cici's," he said. "I'm really tired after last night. If I can get in bed at a decent time, hopefully I'll be more useful tomorrow than I feel like I am right now."

"I completely understand," said Penn. "Thanks for all of your help and thanks for the pizza. It was really good. How much was it? I'll go get my wallet."

"My treat," said Matthew. "I'm glad you enjoyed it." Turning to Danbury, he added, "Keep me posted? On whatever your expert digs up on the number strings and anything involving Wayne Adams."

"Yeah, will do."

*****

Matthew changed the sheets and put the ones he'd fallen into early that morning without a shower into the wash. As he was just crawling into the clean sheets in his soft t-shirt and flannel sleep pants, his phone went off. Dreading to have to talk to anybody about anything as tired as he was, he picked it up nonetheless without checking the display first and heard a very excited Danbury on the other end.

"Hey, Doc! We just heard back from Ed Watson."

"I'm sorry, who?" asked Matthew, who was already half asleep propped up in bed.

"The data forensic expert."

"Oh."

"Yeah, he had a computer model running the numbers. Add the right prefix and they're bank numbers. They just didn't have the routing number for the bank. But they match account numbers on accounts in the Cayman Islands. That was the common denominator. All of the eight number strings that Leo found in that ledger. If you add the prefix, they're all account numbers. At the same bank."

"Wow! How could you ever figure that out?"

"I have no idea. But they're pretty sure. And Ed and his team are some of the best. The best of the best. But then it gets dicey."

"How so?"

"Those accounts are owned by a shell corporation. But there are multiple layers of them. Layers of shell corporations. Non-profit agencies. All sorts of offshore accounts."

"I'm guessing if they dig long enough, they'll find the mysterious non-profit agency that was supposed to get the money from the sale of the house? And all the rest of the estate funds too?"

"That's the hope."

"The funds from the Lingle estate have probably already passed through it though, I'm guessing."

"If not that, one of the others. There are a multitude to choose from. They'll unravel it all eventually. But those number strings were the key. Leo was right. Allan knew they were important. He just didn't tell us why."

"Do you think Penn and Leo will be able to recover their estate? All of it?"

"I hope so. It's rightfully theirs. They haven't heard from their lawyer yet. She might turn up good news too. From that end. Meanwhile the news is good from this end. We're chasing where it went. Hopefully, she can determine that it never should have gone there. And then they have a chance. Of getting it all back."

"That's great news! Thanks for giving me the update. I do wonder what else is in those notebooks of Allan's though. It sounds like he was observing and noting everything going on in Peak, some that was important and some that didn't look to be, at least at first glance."

"Good point. Maybe Leo can look again. I'll ask him. Good night, Doc. See you tomorrow."

"G'night," Matthew yawned, sleepily. He remembered afterward only Max jumping up onto the bed with him and muddled dreams of chasing someone elusive that he couldn't catch.

34. Demystified

Sunday morning Matthew awoke thinking that he might be more tired after a decent night's sleep than he had been the day before with a fractured and stressful one. He went through his morning routine, happy to have the supplies from his own refrigerator so that he could fix his coffee the way he liked it, with lots of cream and sugar, and cook some eggs for breakfast.

Mrs. Drewer was ready as she'd promised when he went to pick her up. She looked cool and comfortable, though not exactly stylish, in a seersucker pantsuit. Matthew had told her not to dress up and she'd taken him at his word. After he swapped his Element for the Corvette that she'd admitted to secretly wanting to ride in, they chatted amicably as he drove across town.

"You remembered that I wanted to ride in the fun car!" she said, in childlike delight.

"Of course I did," he replied with a grin.

"I've almost finished with your laundry," she said. "You can pick it up whenever you're ready for it. It's mostly all folded on my spare bed, so it's not in the way if you're not ready for it yet. I had to wash some of it twice, but I think it smells fresh now and not like smoke, at least not that I can tell. It was smart of you to close your bedroom door behind you."

"I don't know how to thank you, Mrs. Drewer. I'm not sure when I'll have a place to put it on my end but I can take it to Cici's and get it out of your house. I'm thinking I might have to use her spare bedroom for storage anyway, so it's a really good thing that she's not here. Now that the insurance adjuster has seen the wrecked mess in my garage, I can get that hauled off this week too."

"It is a mess, isn't it?" she agreed.

"It is. I left all of the windows locked cracked open yesterday, but I really want to just open them all the way up and let the air blow through for a week or two. Or a month," he added, remembering the acrid burnt smell that permeated his house.

"We can open them up during the day if you'd like and then close and lock them overnight," she offered. "I know you have to go back to work in the morning but I can do that much."

"Mrs. Drewer, you're a godsend," he said, with a sideways glance at her. He thought he actually saw her blush. Miracles never did cease, sometimes, he thought. "That'll beat the air purifiers that the insurance adjuster wanted to install any day."

They were greeted in the big open atrium when they arrived at the church by a very excited Angel. She was always happy to see Matthew but doubly so to see him bring in her new Madeline friend. She ran to greet them and then bounced and skipped between them back to where Matthew's family was gathered. After the introductions and greetings, Monica took Angel to the children's area, but only after Matthew promised to pick her up from it after the service as he usually did.

After the service, Mrs. Drewer accompanied Matthew to go find Angel and, instead of their usual personalized version of hide and seek, Angel happily introduced her new friend to the teachers and anyone else who would stand still long enough. Matthew finally managed to get her back to the atrium of the church to join the rest of the family for the weekly discussion about where to go for lunch.

Matthew wondered what Mrs. Drewer thought of the whole process that he found quite comical. Lots of suggestions were thrown out as usual, but he never understood why they bothered to discuss other options because they always wound up at one of two restaurants in north Raleigh. They opted today for a French café and bistro that served both breakfast and lunch all afternoon on Sundays. Angel bounced around delightedly pronouncing and butchering the pronunciation of the word, "croissant" repeatedly as the adults got organized.

The Paine family had been very welcoming, as he had known that they would be. Matthew hoped that his neighbor had felt it. After lunch Matthew and Cordelia Drewer drove back to Peak in the pouring rain to attend Allan Lingle's service and Matthew was happy to find that the whole town of Peak had turned out in force despite the weather.

*****

"That was a beautiful service," said Mrs. Drewer as they were lined up outside of the church in a damp rain-washed courtyard preparing to go to the family cemetery at the Lingle Plantation for the final bit of the service. "I don't know how Penn and Leo both managed to get through talking about their brother. They both seemed to be struggling, but they managed somehow and it was lovely."

"They did do a nice job with the service," Matthew agreed. "And I'm happy to see so much of the town here to support them and to remember Allan."

"I don't know the last time I was in two churches in one day." She added, thoughtfully, "I probably never have been."

As they slid into the Corvette and got in the long line of cars headed to the back entrance of the Lingle Plantation, Matthew wondered if Libby would bring her boys to this next part of the service. He'd seen her with both boys at the church and he wanted a chance to talk to them at the Lingle house, so he hoped they'd venture that far.

A gentle breeze blew, whistling softly through the leaves on the trees, as Matthew parked on the road behind the Lingle property, putting Mrs. Drewer's side of the car on the street so that she didn't have to deal with the ditch or the mud on the side he got out on. As they walked up the back entrance, Matthew noticed that Danbury had indeed gotten somebody to clear a wider swath to the cemetery, and they'd also put down some crush-and-run gravel. That, thought Matthew, was really fast and particularly fortuitous, given the rain that had poured earlier in the afternoon.

Danbury, Matthew noticed, was constantly by Penn's side and she clung to his arm as they walked on the uneven gravel. Whatever tragedy had befallen the family, if the two of them had found each other and Leo was able to come home and start over, then beauty would come from the ashes of a life lost senselessly.

The graveside service was short but poignantly sweet with Leo and Penn both placing white roses from a spray on the ground beside the coffin onto the top of it. Penn kissed the rose she placed on top, said something over the coffin, and stepped back into Danbury's protectively surrounding arm. Tears ran down the faces of many of the onlookers as the pastor spoke of Allan's kind spirit and gentleness.

Everyone was invited back to the house to share memories and have some refreshments. It was a somber group that trooped up the back driveway, which had also been cleared and newly covered in gravel. Some people had returned to cars first to bring casseroles and potted plants. Others slipped quietly away without going to the visitation at the house at all.

"Hey, Doc," said Danbury, as Matthew held his arm for Mrs. Drewer to clutch and make her way up the driveway on the gravel.

"Detective Warren Danbury, I'd like to introduce you to Mrs. Cordelia Drewer, my neighbor from the other end of our condo unit."

"I've seen you in town. And in Peak Eats. But it's nice to actually meet you," Danbury answered cordially as they reached the house. Guests were pouring in the back door, through the kitchen, and into the house.

Matthew didn't see Libby or the boys until after he'd gotten through the house. He finally spotted them on the front porch, which was exactly where he wanted to talk to them anyway, so he excused himself from the group he'd been chatting with and stepped out.

"Hi Libby," he said. She smiled and nodded at the greeting. "Hey, boys. I'm glad I found you out here. There's something I wanted to show you."

"What's that?" asked Marcus, excitedly while Micah looked on suspiciously.

"Remember the night you were up here and you thought the house was haunted?" He purposefully omitted the murder or any of the rest of the traumatic events of the evening. Both boys nodded and he continued, "You said you heard a thumping noise but you didn't see anyone and you were sure it was a ghost, right?" They both nodded again, and Micah was starting to look interested instead of skeptical.

"Why don't you stand where you were standing that night. How close to the house were you?"

"I think about, HERE," said Marcus, jumping down off the porch and taking a stand beside the huge old gnarled maple by the front path.

"Yeah, maybe there," said Micah, looking dubiously at where his brother was standing. "Why? What difference does that make?"

"Go stand with your brother and I'll show you," replied Matthew. Grudgingly, Micah slipped off the porch and went to join his brother.

"OK, now close your eyes," said Matthew, with an eyebrow raised at Micah's jaded expression. "Go on, close them," he said to Micah. Marcus had already complied.

"OK, now. Is this what you heard?" he asked as he tipped two of the rocking chairs back and forth on the porch and the chair rails made loud thump-whump, thump-whump noises on the old wooden porch slats beneath them.

"Yow!" said Marcus, opening his eyes. "Yeah, that's it! What is it?"

Micah opened his eyes, looking dubiously at Matthew and said to Marcus, "It's the rockers on the front porch, Dummy. But ghosts were in them that night."

"Not ghosts," said Matthew as Libby grimaced at Micah. "But the wind. Do you remember that it was a really windy night?"

"Oh yeah," said Libby, joining in the conversation. "It was really windy that night."

"When the wind blows from the right direction around the corner of the house, the rockers rock in the wind and they make that noise across the beams of the porch floor."

"Oooh," said Marcus. "So it wasn't a ghost?"

"Nope," said Matthew. "Not a ghost. Just an old creaky house with rockers blowing in the wind. All of the floor boards inside creak when you walk across them, so I can see why people think that this house is haunted. And there's a spooky attic too. When the light comes in those windows up there," he said pointing up to the dormer windows, "it looks like ghosts dancing on the walls."

"Can we see it?" asked Micah, taking the bait.

"I can ask but it might not be as scary without the sun shining through," said Matthew, returning to the house with the boys in tow.

Libby just looked at him with sad but thankful eyes, he thought. He pondered that as he made his way through the crowd to find Penn. Maybe, he thought, it was that she had wanted a positive male influence in the boys' lives but Wayne hadn't filled that role very well or at all. Whatever it was that Libby was thinking, Matthew thought that the boys, and particularly jaded Micah, needed a positive male role model indeed.

"Hey, Penn," he said, finally reaching her and touching her sleeve to get her attention amidst the chaos that was her childhood home. "Would it be OK if I took the boys upstairs to the attic? I'm debunking the myth that the house is haunted or at least trying to."

Penn nodded her agreement and said softly to him, "If it'll keep them from throwing rocks through the windows, I'm all for it!"

It was too loud in the house to have an actual conversation with people half his height, so Matthew motioned for the boys to follow. He led them up the back staircase. The staircase itself wasn't well lit and Matthew caught a glimpse of fear registering on the boy's faces. When Matthew turned to look, Micah quickly screwed his face into the bored and annoyed expression that was now familiar.

Once upstairs Matthew showed them the rooms that had belonged to the servants. Then they moved on to the more interesting part, the open attic end with the trunks, wardrobes, and detritus from past generations. "When the Lingle brothers were growing up, they played up here all the time. Pirates was their favorite game to play, with all of these old steamer trunks as treasure chests."

"Arrrr, Matey!" said Marcus.

"Walk the plank you scurvy yellow-bellied sap sucker!" joined in Micah, much to Matthew's surprise. He wasn't sure the last bit of that was pirate speak exactly, but he was happy to see Micah joining in the adventure. He waited for a bit allowing the boys to play before telling them that they needed to go find their mom so that she wouldn't be worried about them.

The crowd was thinning as Matthew followed the boys back down the stairs and into the melee of neighbors, mourners, and well-wishers.

35. It's enough

After the last of the friends and neighbors had left, Penn was wandering through the house picking up odds and ends of napkins, plastic plates, and plastic cups and looking lost. Danbury had offered to take Mrs. Drewer home so that Matthew could go back to Cici's house, which was in the other direction, west of Peak. Matthew had stayed a little longer to help clean up. It was just he, Penn, Leo, and Malcolm in the house. Matthew had ordered Malcolm to go sit down and get off of his knee that had started to swell again because he'd been standing and walking on it all day.

Matthew was heading to the front door and saying his goodbyes when suddenly the front door burst open and Wayne Adams exploded into the hallway wielding a gun. His eyes were wild, his hair disheveled. He clearly hadn't shaved in a couple of days and looked to be wearing clothes that he'd slept in, his shirttail hanging halfway out and rumpled all over. "Nobody move!" he yelled as his wild eyes, and the gun he held tightly in his hand, swept the scene. "Stay right where you are!"

Time slowed to a crawl and Matthew could see and hear everything in stark detail. He took stock without looking around. Malcolm was seated on the sofa in the sitting room behind him. He sensed Penn standing immediately behind him and to his right. He wasn't sure where Leo was but he was wishing, in that moment, that Danbury hadn't left quite so soon. Matthew had a concealed carry permit for his guns, but he didn't make a habit of walking around armed with them.

“Why do they always have to have a gun?” he heard somebody say quietly and then realized when he heard Penn’s sharp intake of breath behind him that he’d muttered it out loud himself.

“What do you want, Wayne?” he asked, purposefully aloud and as calmly as he could.

“I want you. And Leo. Front and center.”

Just then they heard the screech of the outside cellar door that opened into the hidden rooms and Matthew felt a tiny wave of relief, knowing then where Leo was. Leo had been back in the kitchen but the back door was in view through the open hallway door into the kitchen, so Leo had apparently slipped through the secret panel in the laundry room and then out through the cellar door.

“What was that?” yelled Wayne.

“It was a ghost,” said Matthew at the same time Penn was saying, “Just a ghost.” They couldn’t have planned that better for having coordinated it, thought Matthew. But now the job was to keep Wayne calm so that the gun didn’t go off, intentionally or otherwise. Matthew remembered his friend Justin telling him that a gun in the hands of a nervous novice was almost worse than in the hands of a seasoned professional hit man because it was more likely to go off without either aim or warning.

Wayne looked around nervously. “Ghosts do not exist! What was that?!”

From the sofa behind them, Malcolm offered, “This house is haunted. I hear noises like that all the time.”

Matthew could see Wayne’s hand, the one holding the gun, shake slightly as he looked from one to the other of them and a bit of drool ran down one corner of his mouth and dripped from the side of his chin. Maybe he’d been drinking, Matthew thought, or he was on some sort of drug or maybe he’d lost all reason and gone completely mad.

“Wayne, why don’t you put the gun down and we can talk about what it is that you want?” said Matthew in an even tone of voice that sounded so calm that it must have come from someone else. It couldn’t have been his own voice, he thought. It sounded surreal to him.

“It’s too late for that! You all know way too much, and you!” he said to Matthew. “You’ve ruined all of my plans. Especially YOU!” he said, waving the gun in Matthew’s direction. “You and Leo!”

He wasn't sure what he'd done to get the blame and apparently Wayne's wrath more than anyone else in the room. He figured his best tactic was just to keep the man talking.

"What did I ruin?" he asked innocently.

"Everything! You ruined everything! I should be on a tropical sunny beach drinking Mai Tais by now! But I'm not. I'm here trying to clean up the shitshow that you and Leo created!" he yelled at Matthew.

Matthew hoped that Leo had used his new cell phone to summon Danbury and it was just a matter of time before he showed up. The job in the interim was just to keep Wayne calm and not get shot. As was the case lately, when his adrenaline was pumping full force, time seemed to slow down and speed up at the same time. Matthew noticed every little nuance of what was happening around him. He heard Malcolm shift on the sofa, he heard Penn breathing rapidly as if she would soon need a paper bag to breath into, and he heard a board creak on the porch behind Wayne, who was still standing in the doorway.

"Now, where's Leo?" asked Wayne again. "I want you both right here right now!" he demanded.

"I'm not really sure where Leo is," said Matthew honestly, though he did have a solid idea.

"Well, we're going to FIND him," yelled Wayne, waving the gun around. "You!" he said to Malcolm. "You're going to find Leo. Where's your cell phone? Pull it out and toss it over here!"

Malcolm stood up and entered the hallway, pulling his phone out of his pocket and sliding it down the boards of the hallway at the edge of the oriental rug runner. It didn't quite make it all the way to Wayne, who then shouted, "Slide it the rest of the way, Paine, but with your foot! Keep your hands where I can see them! And don't do anything stupid."

Matthew looked down and gently slid the phone further along the floorboards toward Wayne with his foot. As he looked back up, he saw Leo emerge in the doorway behind Wayne. Matthew struggled to control his facial expression so as not to give anything away. He wanted to wave Leo away and tell him to wait for Danbury, but he couldn't do that either. Instead, he froze in place and tried to control his expression to make it as bland as possible as he watched Leo sneak up behind Wayne. In conjunction with the ticking of an old grandfather clock that stood under the staircase in the hallway, he could hear Penn's breathing get more rapid and he was afraid she was going to pass out.

"OK, now your phone, Paine," Wayne said just as Leo jumped out from behind him, trying to tackle him. Everything sped up, just then, into a blur of fast motion. Wayne spun halfway around to confront his attacker and a loud blast sounded. Matthew more felt than actually saw a flash go by his right arm. He heard the sound it made as it hit Penn behind him. He spun first her way and saw Malcolm step up and catch her, lowering her to the ground. Then he spun the other, realizing that the recoil had spun Wayne faster than he'd been turning. Wayne and Leo were locked in a struggle for control of the gun, which sailed out of Wayne's hand and skittered across the floor.

Matthew went first for the gun, snatching it up and quickly dropping the magazine out of what appeared to be a tiny Kel-Tec P-3AT automatic pistol. He cleared the chamber and tossed the magazine across the room. He shoved the gun down the back of his waist band. When he turned back, he saw Wayne on top of Leo, arm pulled back, and he launched himself at the man, grabbing the raised fist and coming down hard to one side of him.

Wayne and Matthew both scrambled to their feet. Wayne lunged for Matthew, who remembered a few of the Tae Kwondo moves he'd learned as a kid getting his black belt, and managed to side step and avoid the punch. He used Wayne's momentum against him, grabbing his arm, twisting it behind him, and shoved his chest into the doorframe, pinning him in place.

"Leo, get something to tie him up with!" he said as the smaller man struggled beneath Matthew's weight to free himself.

Leo had gotten to his feet but froze in place as if struck dumb by that request. Wayne managed to turn under Matthew's weight and had raised his other arm to take another swing at Matthew, who decided in that moment that he'd had enough of the struggle. It was enough. Leo was going to be of absolutely no help, and Penn needed his medical attention. Matthew raised his left arm, sending an uppercut punch into Wayne's gut and then caught him square across the jaw with a right hook, knocking him out entirely.

"Now tie him up, Leo, before he comes to!" he said as he rushed to Penn. Malcolm was holding her head in his lap, with his injured leg extended awkwardly out to the side. He had slid the neckline of her blouse down on one side to reveal a gunshot wound to her shoulder. He was pushing down on it with his hands, applying pressure.

Matthew's experience working in the Emergency Department during his clinical rotations kicked in. He assessed the situation, quickly realizing that there was an exit wound on her back and the bullet had gone straight through Penn's right shoulder, just below her collar bone and just inside her arm pit. It had damaged her pectoral muscle. She wouldn't be bench pressing again soon, but it had missed the axillary artery. He breathed a sigh of relief. It wasn't exactly a flesh wound but neither would it be fatal if he could staunch the bleeding. Pulling off his shirt, he wrapped it around her shoulder as Malcolm eased her head to the floor and slid back, making room for Matthew. Stuffing his shirt into both sides of the wound, Matthew pushed down, putting pressure back on it.

"Malcolm, get your phone and call 9-1-1!" he ordered, not willing to let go of the wound long enough to get his own phone out of his pocket. Malcolm's phone was on the floor near where Leo was struggling to tie Wayne up. He scooted over to retrieve it.

Matthew pushed down to hold pressure on the wound with one hand and checked her pulse with the other. She wasn't responsive but he wasn't sure if it was because she had been hyperventilating or because she'd lost more blood than he'd thought possible in a very short amount of time. He was relieved to feel that her pulse was still strong. "Penn," he said, "can you hear me?"

He was rewarded with a thin smile and her eyes flickered momentarily in answer.

"Hang on, Penn, help is on the way." As he said it, Danbury burst through the door and quickly surveyed the scene. He ran first to Penn.

"Penn!" he said, dropping to his knees beside her.

"I've got her," said Matthew. "And Malcolm is calling 9-1-1. Have you got cuffs? Wayne's out for the moment. Leo was supposed to be tying him."

Without answering, Danbury sprung across the hallway, faster and with more agility than Matthew would have thought he possessed. He yanked Wayne's hands away from Leo, cuffing them quickly and not at all gently behind his back. Then he was back by Penn's side, "What can I do, Doc?"

"Find blankets. Roll one and slide it gently under her head. Put the other one over her. I'm trying to slow the bleeding until the ambulance gets here, but she could go into shock."

Danbury pulled a flat pillow and soft, fluffy throw from the back of the overstuffed sofa in the sitting room, sliding the pillow gently under her head and laying the blanket over Penn. Malcolm returned, dropping to the floor on the other side, with one leg extended so as not to bend his knee. He lifted her wrist, monitoring her pulse and checking her breathing. They had held their positions for what seemed to Matthew an eternity when they heard the distant sirens. Matthew heaved a sigh of relief and mentally prepared to transport his patient.

The EMT staff rushed in with a stretcher. Matthew identified himself as a doctor, gave them her status, and started barking out orders to get drips started and check her vitals. He listed all of the things they would need to do to safely transport her to the hospital as they slid Penn onto a stretcher. Matthew climbed into the back of the ambulance and saw Danbury frantically talking to the Peak police, who had arrived on the scene.

"Hey!" he yelled and motioned Danbury over. Pulling the gun from the small of his back, he handed it to Danbury, who pulled a handkerchief from his pocket and gently took it. Matthew said, "The magazine is still in the house. I tossed it back toward the kitchen."

"Thanks, Doc!" said Danbury as the doors to the ambulance closed.

The big detective gestured wildly to the Peak police officers, pointing first at the house and then at Wayne's still prone figure. Matthew couldn't hear what he was saying over the siren of the ambulance. Danbury handed the gun off, then dragged Leo alongside, pushing him into the SUV before jumping in himself to follow the ambulance.

*****

After several hours in the waiting room that felt more like days, they saw the surgeon finally emerge. Looking from one of them to the next, questioningly, he said, "I'm looking for the family of Penelope Lingle."

"Brother," said Danbury abruptly, pointing to Leo.

"Mr. Lingle," said the surgeon as Danbury and Matthew hovered behind Leo, "your sister did well through the surgery. Somebody did a good job staunching the bleeding. She was in pretty good shape when she arrived."

Danbury glanced appreciatively at Matthew as the doctor continued, "She'll be in recovery for at least another hour before they'll move her to a room. Then she'll be on some pretty heavy pain killers throughout the night, but you can see her shortly, if you'd like."

"Yes, please," said Leo, who was still pale from his ordeal that evening, but seemed to exhale the breath they'd all been holding in unison. "I'd like to see her as soon as I can."

"What's the prognosis for her recovery?" asked Matthew, stepping forward. As the surgeon looked down his nose without comment at Matthew, who was still standing in the waiting room in his blood-spattered undershirt, Matthew said, "Oh, my apologies, I'm Dr. Matthew Paine, stauncher of the bleeding," and stuck out his hand, which he had at least washed a few hours earlier.

"And close family friend," added Leo to seal the deal.

"Oh," said the doctor, shaking Matthew's hand. He then explained that the bullet had, indeed, gone through Penn's shoulder and damaged her scapula and pectoral muscle, which they had surgically repaired, so she would have a long and arduous road to recovery. "With proper care and some physical therapy when most of the healing has occurred, she should be able to regain use of her right arm."

"Full function?" asked Matthew.

"I don't see why not, if she follows orders and is patient with her recovery process."

Danbury smirked at this. "She won't be a patient patient," he said. "But we'll be sure she does what she's supposed to. Nothing more. And nothing less."

"That's excellent," the surgeon said. To Leo, he added, "Someone will come and get you when you can see her."

"Thank you, Doctor," said Leo. "Thank you so much." Matthew and Danbury echoed his thanks as the doctor turned and went back through the swinging double doors that were labeled, "Authorized Personnel Only."

Leo dropped into a chair, head in hands. His shoulders sagged and then shuddered. Danbury reached over and put a hand on his back, "She's going to be OK, Leo."

"Yeah, but that was close," said Leo. "What if he'd killed her?"

"But he didn't," said Danbury. "And it's enough."

"What's enough?" asked Leo, raising his head to look up at the two men standing over him.

"It's enough to put Wayne Adams away," said Danbury. "For a good long time. Attempted murder. With three witnesses. It's a sure thing. Much more so than embezzlement. Or conspiracy to commit murder. Or drug dealing. Or money laundering. Or anything else that he's done. It's stronger than any of that. The other charges that couldn't be proven. This time, it's enough."

"Penn will be OK," acknowledged Leo. "And Wayne Adams won't hurt anybody anymore. You're right. It is enough," agreed Leo. "And Allan would have preferred it that way."

Epilogue: A month later

On a sunny Tuesday past the middle of June, late in the afternoon, it was hot and sticky already in the small town of Peak, North Carolina. Matthew had finished work for the day and was heading out of his office over to the Lingle house for dinner. Penn had invited him, though she'd also advised him that she wasn't cooking yet since she was still a "lame duck" as she'd called herself, walking around with her arm in a sling. Therefore, dinner would be take-out. A take-out dinner with good friends was always better than a home-cooked meal alone, Matthew thought. Despite the heat and humidity, he had decided to walk the short distance.

As he was leaving his office and locking up, Matthew bumped into Dr. Rob in the main hallway. They chatted briefly about the town happenings following Allan's death.

"They really did a nice job with that service. I was impressed that both of Allan's siblings managed to speak. Everybody spoke so highly of Allan. I think I treated him only a couple of times," added Dr. Rob, pensively. "When Steven was away at a conference. He seemed like a good guy. I wish I'd really gotten to know him like Steven did."

"I think he really was a good guy. I didn't know him well either but I wish I had. I'm headed over to the Lingle house now for dinner with Penn and Leo. And probably Danbury too, since he and Penn are an item now. He's there a lot trying to help out and keep Penn from doing too much. And Malcolm will be staying, at least until he finishes his nursing degree, which works out well for keeping an eye on Penn's healing process. So, I guess it'll be a full house for dinner tonight."

"Yeah, I guess they owe you a few. You helped catch a killer and probably saved Penn's life from what I hear."

"Well, we'll see," said Matthew modestly. "Hopefully, there's enough evidence to prove that Wayne Adams was behind Allan's murder. There's no doubt that he shot Penn though, so he'll get put away on that charge alone. Even if they can't put enough pieces together to get him for the embezzlement or money laundering and whatever else he was into."

"That's got to feel good to have helped with that. Well, I won't hold you up. I've got a few things to finish up before I head out too. Enjoy your dinner," he added as he went up the back stairwell to his office on the floor above.

The heat and humidity hit Matthew full in the face as he stepped out of the back door and went to put his satchel in the car before taking the short walk to the Lingle house. It was hotter than usual for June, he thought, as he arrived on the front porch and knocked on the door. Leo was standing on the other side, grinning at him as he opened it and welcomed Matthew in.

"Hey Leo. Good news?" asked Matthew.

"The best," said Leo. "Layne Bennett, our lawyer, has been working with Ed Watson, Warren's forensic data guy, and they've proven that the whole codicil, that addendum to the original will, was faked."

"That IS great news!"

"On so many levels," said Penn, joining in the discussion. As Matthew followed Leo into the kitchen, she hugged Leo with one arm. "We always knew that our mom wouldn't do that to us, but it was really hard to think that she actually might have. Like this niggling doubt in the back of your mind that maybe we were wrong. It feels good just to know that she didn't do that to us. You know?"

"Yeah, they're working on getting the money wired back into our family accounts now," added Leo. "Oh, did we tell you that we're staying in Peak?"

"No," answered Matthew, grinning broadly. "That's great news too! I'm sure Danbury is thrilled," he added with a wink at Penn. "What are you going to do with your business back in Denver?"

"Expand it," said Penn, decisively. "I've had my assistant manager in Denver keeping everything on track the whole time I've been here and he's done a great job. I'm going to promote him to manager there and open a second branch here in Peak. It'll be similar, with gym facilities, Physical Therapists on staff to help with rehabilitation, and a full-service spa."

"Starting with your own. Rehabilitation with Physical Therapists," said Danbury, who'd come in the back door with bags and boxes of food labeled with the logo of Matthew's favorite Italian restaurant.

"Yeah, yeah," said Penn as Danbury leaned over and kissed her on top of the head. "I'm behaving and I'll do the whole program. I want my strength and range of motion fully back. In the meantime Leo is going back to school to get a business degree and he'll help with starting up and running the business here."

"Yup," said Leo. "My goal is to get a decent GPA this time around and maybe go for an MBA. There are lots of great programs in this area of North Carolina."

"Wow, it sounds like great news all the way around," said Matthew. "I'm so glad that you're both doing so well after all you've been through."

"How're your house repairs coming?" asked Penn.

"Slowly, they had to rip out more than they'd thought initially, walls and flooring, but it'll be as good as new when they're done."

Danbury had put the bags and boxes on the counter and Matthew started to salivate as Danbury opened them and the aroma of garlic and spices escaped into the room. Malcolm wandered in from his bedroom and greeted Matthew before he started pulling out plates and cutlery and set the table.

"Malcolm," said Danbury, when the table was set and they were sitting down to eat. "I have something for you." He reached around his chair and pulled a large envelope off the counter behind him, handing it to Malcolm, who looked confused but then opened the envelope carefully.

"Oh!" said Malcolm, as he examined the page inside. His mouth hung slightly agape and he was otherwise speechless.

"What have you got there?" asked Penn.

Choked, Malcolm said, "The death certificate of Reginald Duane Wilkins. AKA Reggie. The guy who I thought was after me when those goons broke in the night Allan died."

"I thought you'd want to know," said Danbury. "I tracked him down. He died in prison. Almost a year ago. Probably killed at the order of his replacement. On the outside. One who doesn't know Malcolm. Or care about him," he added to everyone else.

They settled in to eat and the room grew quiet. As they were enjoying their dinner, above them they heard a few squeaks and creaks and then a distinctively loud whump-thump. They all looked up and then at each other.

"What was that?" asked Penn.

"I've been telling you that this house is haunted," said Malcolm. "And not just by Leo. He's sitting right here with the rest of us."

"Yeah, maybe it really is," agreed Leo. "And maybe Allan has joined the friendly spirits protecting us here now." And then he added, "At least, I'd like to think so."

They discussed the strange noises, doors and windows opened or closed that had been left otherwise and lights on or off that hadn't been left that way. Matthew wasn't sure what he thought about any of that. He was just starting to relax and enjoy the company of his new friends when a loud banging made them all jump.

"It's just somebody at the door," said Danbury. They all laughed as he got up to answer it.

The hilarity of the moment didn't last long as Dr. Rob rushed into the kitchen with Danbury, his face ashen. He was clearly panicked. "I need your help!" he said, "My daughter Ariel is missing!"

About the Author

Lee Clark is a North Carolina native, originally from Raleigh, with family roots in Virginia. Clark attended Campbell University, obtained a degree in Journalism from East Carolina University, and then a Master's in Technical Communication from North Carolina State University. After working in the software technology industry for over 20 years, creating and building highly technical user information for software developers, Clark decided it was time to pursue a true passion: fictional writing.

The Matthew Paine character is a fictional character, though inspired by two very important men in the author's life, brother Sean and son Will. Both will see characteristics of themselves in the character and identify with some of Matthew's struggles.

Lee Clark, an admitted coffeeholic, still resides in North Carolina with spouse, two mostly grown children who are in and out, and a small petting zoo of dogs and cats.

Made in the USA
Monee, IL
07 November 2021

c394b8f4-1239-4762-8220-754bab64b1f6R01